To Tom + Michelle
    My greatest ho
Can enjoy this story - You can see
first-hand how it looks when a
plumber gets ahold of a pen. (This
pen in fact wrote the story!)
        all my best -
            Dave Creighton

THAT OTHER TIME ZONE

by

Dave Creighton

ISBN: 978-0-9990822-0-1

TABLE OF CONTENTS:

INTRODUCTION

It has been said that every man should have a son, plant a tree, and write a book. I now have the trifecta.

It has also been said that ancient cities fashioned tiny gates in their walls for after-hours use, to maximize commerce without compromising security. Historical evidence for such a practice is non-existent, though some have claimed that Jesus referred to this when he spoke of the camel going through "the eye of the needle". As I was writing a novel, I chose to use this pseudo-historical allusion, and beg your indulgence.

Most other references to history are as accurate as a novice such as myself can make them. Quotes from God's Word are primarily from the King James Version of the Bible, with the exception of Christ's own words from the later chapters. For those I chose a modern language paraphrase, the Living Bible, for its readability and ease of understanding.

My gratitude must be expressed to all who helped and encouraged me along the way. You know who you are. As I recall, no one told me I couldn't do it. My prayer is that readers will enjoy it.

With gratitude for the opportunity,

Dave

CHAPTER I

Most people fantasize about becoming rich. Some people dream of winning the lottery, or of finding some lost work of art at the local flea market. Ben's story is different.

Ben Parker's ship had come in loaded to the gunwales. Though Ben originally had no goal to be wealthy, and he never really dreamed of it, he did not oppose it. *It's karma,* he thought. *Good things happen to good people.*

To say that Ben (properly Benjamin, but he preferred to be called Ben) met his ship at the dock through some serendipitous happenstance or accident of fate would not be accurate. He knew the value of hard work and trusted the free enterprise system to properly reward him for his efforts. But he would be the first to tell you that he had his grandfather to thank for the basic idea..

Ben's Gramps dealt with life patiently and generously. Ben had plumbed the depths or both of these traits.

He'd spent a lot of time at his grandparents' home because his parents had a need to "share" him with them. And Gramps showed generosity and willingness to share as well. So while his parents pursued a career in corporate consulting, Ben pursued life at the grandparents during nearly half of his adolescent years.

1

As a rule, grandparents issue more grants than parents do. There is not so much that has to be earned, and more is awarded as entitlement. For this reason Ben acquired his driver's license about a year before most of his peers, and used Gramps' old Ford Pinto pretty much any time he wanted. He and his friend Larry had driven on a mountain road in early spring all the way up to the snow line, and had gotten stuck in the mud. They had waited through the night for rescue, and had caused no small amount of worry. Ben expected the worst from the powers that be. But Gramps hugged him and welcomed him home, and never mentioned it again. Ben figured that Gramps would just save it for later.

Then there was the snow blower. It started hard, and Ben had spilled some gas while trying to prime it. When he pulled the starter cord the machine backfired and created a small Briggs and Stratton fireball from which the snow blower never recovered; though many attempted, none could start it. Ben again expected the worst, but Gramps never mentioned it.

Then a young woman entered his picture. She was attractive, but used "salty language" his Grams had said, and a misdemeanor conviction for shoplifting lay in her past. Besides all that, her family situation reminded one of certain celebrities, like Justin Bieber and Paris Hilton. It seemed no mature adults were visible on either side of things. No one had ever learned to take responsibility. Her name was Courtney and she genuinely pained his adolescent heart. Gramps had her pegged as well, but he never brought it up.

Someday he will, Ben thought.

It wouldn't take a psychoanalyst to tell you that Ben owed Gramps a great deal. All Ben's friends knew it. Sometimes they theorized about an upcoming judgment day, and how it would unfold

Ben wondered about that too. He always carried the debt with him and expected that the mortgage would someday be called in.

That was why Ben so eagerly volunteered to help when Gramps said he wanted to learn how to send an email.

How could anyone not know how to send an email? Gramps didn't know, so Ben showed him how to do it. Not only that, he demonstrated cutting and pasting pictures of large game animals onto emails and sending those, and how to make a PDF out of almost any bit of information.

But beyond sending a simple email, Gramps never caught on—not that day, or the next, or the next. It could have been that Gramps had a motivation problem. Nonetheless, Ben felt responsible.

Part of the trouble stemmed from the fact that Gramps, born during World War II, had less electronic acumen than that of a garden variety potato. Ben knew this because under certain conditions potatoes could be used to generate small amounts of direct current, and he was fairly certain Gramps could not do that.

To complicate the situation more, many people (some admittedly quite biased) considered Ben to be brilliant. He didn't excel at team sports, but demonstrated an uncommon ability to grasp factual data and to understand, through mechanical diagram or mathematical formula, obscure practical applications. (His science fair project his senior year in high school demonstrated this; he built a working model of a wind generator which powered an LED display of the first 99 digits of pi. He refused to look these digits up online, but calculated them on his own. He didn't place first, but anyone could see the potential there, despite severe limitations on the practical side. And, he had graduated #2 in his class.)

This obsession with geeky stuff propelled Ben to acceptance at the school of his choice—Texas A&M, of College Station, Texas. It was just far enough from home to fertilize and rototill those feelings of independence, yet close enough to allow for the occasional trip home for the weekend. As another matter of course, the college he'd chosen proved to be very expensive. This served to erect the third tier of Ben's trouble. The corporate consulting

3

business had suffered huge setbacks in the great recession. And he'd chosen an out of state college.

"Need any help?" Gramps had asked. Ben knew Gramps wasn't talking about homework or pulling the Pinto out of the mud, so he gratefully accepted the offer. A guy could have gotten student loans, the presidential election being so recent, and everybody still remembering the promises. But Gramps said, "Don't do that. Use my money. The borrower is the servant of the lender, you know."

Ben thought he knew that. He also thought of his Gramps' help like one would think about a loan, so although the borrower is still the lender's servant, better to be indentured to a loving relative than to a complete bureaucratic stranger. And he knew that the money represented only a small fraction of his total debt.

As Ben prepared to return to college his junior year, Gramps invited him over for a talkabout. Gramps used this phrase as a synonym for a heart-to-heart conversation on the front porch accompanied by Grandma's signature lemonade which the ice cubes did not dilute, as they were frozen from the same lemony mixture. Ben had expected Gramps to employ that particular location for the "Courtney talk" that had never happened.

"How are things at school?" Gramps asked. Ben knew that question, as general as it sounded, required specific information. The borrower is the servant of the lender, you know.

"I think things are okay there, Gramps. I've got two years to go, then I'll have my degree and be able to go to work, maybe even for Texas Instruments."

"What kind of degree?" Gramps wanted to know.

"Computer engineering," Ben answered with just a touch of salutatorian pride. He loved computers and appreciated the predictable relationship between program and response. He'd heard the maxim—garbage in, garbage out—many times, and he knew that this was the pillar and support of the truth where computers were concerned.

4

"The burden is *all* on the programmer," he'd said many times—so many times that one of his friends threatened to spray his lap top with a fire hose. But they got the point. Good stuff in, good stuff out.

When one considers the possibilities, thought Ben, *there's actually very little a computer can't do, especially with the discovery of modified temporal stasis.*

In the computer industry, there are times when it's difficult to know where to lay credit for an idea. In the early part of the twentieth century, automobile manufacturers, such as Ford and Dodge and Chevrolet experienced the same problem. Who first figured out you could mount a mirror on the door to see behind you? Or to put a hinged cover on the front of the glove compartment? Or to keep the spare tire inside the trunk, or even to have a spare tire? Or a trunk? Many of these ideas were in the public domain.

In the same way, modified temporal stasis seemed to appear in a lot of places simultaneously. By this process, computers learned from patterns of usage in order to upgrade programming as needed. Thus a back-set thermostat, when programmed correctly, could learn in a few weeks when to automatically turn the heat down for the night—earlier on some evenings, later on others. Cell phones could be programmed to keep and automatically update lists of most frequently called numbers. Televisions could learn which programs were favorites, almost totally removing the practical part of the necessity of channel surfing. (The impractical part, however, still remains.) The horizon of application remained broad, almost endless.

Ben had a fairly open mind and he had been allowing it to wander. He suddenly realized Gramps awaited an answer, and he couldn't quite put his finger on the question. So he asked Gramps to repeat it.

"Can we keep in closer touch this year? I hate to wait 'til Thanksgiving or some rushed weekend in hunting season to find out how things are going. Can you call me once a week or so?"

5

Ben shuddered. He loved his Gramps, but he knew that with 18 credits and the chess team, it would be a stretch. He had small regrets for his great debt, but he said, "Sure!"

In general, he looked forward to those weekly talks with Gramps, but often he begrudged the time. And sometimes he'd email, which he could send off any time, but Gramps preferred the regular calls.

So in late November, Ben started to talk to his grandfather about 4G, texting and apps, and persuaded him to buy an iPhone.

But Gramps still wanted verbal conversation. No matter how many times Ben demonstrated the basic features, and how easily anyone could tweet or email, little of it lasted in the elder man's mind.

With finals week approaching, a bookish geek with a genetic overdose of moral fiber could see no light at the end of the tunnel. Advanced physics and trigonometry made unyielding demands on his attention, but fickle inspiration chose that moment to strike.

As Ben walked from the library to the dorm, he talked to his roommate, Adam McLeod. Adam possessed that rare mixture of DNA which produced a recessive amount of arrogance with dominant traits of scholarship, athletic ability, and enviable good looks. Adam and Ben had met at a student mixer their freshman year when the two of them had been assigned, seemingly at random, to reproduce some famous Saturday Night Live skit. Lucky for both of them Adam didn't share Ben's ignorance of SNL. So with five minutes of rehearsal, they enacted, somewhat accurately, "Church Lady meets Morton Downey Junior". Adam played Church Lady. Their foray into standup comedy dominated the student mixer, and formed the traceable beginning of that rare kind of friendship that few people experience, the kind that will last 'til one of them dies, then will live on in the other guy's heart.

They discussed Ben's Gramps, and in respite from the focus on upcoming finals, brainstormed about what, if anything, could be done for him. "It's too bad you can't just be around all the time, to teach him," Adam was saying.

"I know I owe him that, but I think he needs even more," murmured Ben. "He needs someone familiar to him that knows computers and that can guide him through these things, step by step. He needs someone like that *in* his computer, or his phone, or more reasonably, both."

"My Mom and Dad have a Garmin road navigator with a female voice in it. They call her Gladys and they think she's a nag," Adam said. "Gladys talks in this annoying voice about left turns they should already have taken. Dad thinks she's useless."

"Does *she* need to learn to give them more of a heads-up since they're older and not used to responding so quickly to new information?"

"Might help," Adam replied, "but Dad's a lost cause."

At that moment Ben saw the solution. Sometimes you stare at random blotches on a paper and suddenly realize it represents someone's face. Sometimes you can see those last few twists on Rubik's Cube before its complete restoration.

"Adam, you need to tell me if this isn't a good idea. Here's what I'm going to do. I'm going to apply modified temporal stasis to Gramps' phone, so it will learn with him. I'm going to give his phone the ability to guide him through any operation the phone can do, and I'm going to use icons that he will understand. I'll need some help from you, and him, and maybe others, but I think it can be done. And I have to start now."

So Ben began his ascent of Mount Everest. He had crossed the Rubicon, had executed the climber's pendulum, and had thrust his entire life and strength toward the solution to that specific challenge. *It's what a good grandson would do,* he thought. In the space of ten days he developed the necessary code to begin the process. He ruined five memory cards along the way. He became a familiar face at the Apple Store, and, to Adam's consternation, ignored completely the meaning of the word

7

"final". He flunked them all. He hoped the sacrifice might balance the Gramps debt maybe a little bit.

But he had a working model, and with the semester break arriving, he eagerly awaited a chance to try it out on Gramps.

People who've lived long enough to be assured of their own ignorance are rather steeped in their skepticism—it is more likely that the USS Enterprise could escape from a black hole than for one of these old dogs to learn a new trick. Gramps lived in that category and cultivated awareness of his limitations. But he accepted the modified phone and the ten minute lecture on how to use it. And with some time on his hands and very limited coaching, he found out what a wonderful thing it is to have a machine that will teach you, using your grandson's voice.

The phone never tired of imparting the same instruction over and over, like an old man needs. It used Ben's voice, so that helped Gramps to trust it, and it just kept patiently saying the same thing. Beyond Ben's expectation, Gramps discovered confidence. With a constant source of help, he could do whatever came up in the menu. Ben began receiving more emails from Gramps than voice messages. Even with emojis.

So that pebble rolled down the hillside gathering companions and gaining momentum until it became an irresistible force, a figurative avalanche.

About a week later, Gramps called Ben and requested one of those talkabouts that required the lemonade with the special ice cubes.

"I met with my antique car club today," Gramps began. (Gramps had a beautiful '49 Dodge, identical to the first family car he could remember as a child.) "We are up to eighty-five members now, and almost all of us showed up. I was taking pictures of cars and posting them to different Facebook pages, when someone overheard your voice telling me how to do it. And pretty soon everybody gathered around, and when they saw what you had done for me, well, one thing led to another."

At this point Gramps pulled out a shoebox full of mobile devices. "These belong to my car club friends, and they're wondering if you could do for them what you did for me. They said they'd pay you a hundred dollars a phone. Can you do it?"

Ben stared at the phones as if they were a bunch of dead weasels. He'd just flunked his finals and had no assurance of any credit for the entire term. The semester break notwithstanding, he had stretched his body to its limits. But he had a desire to repay. *What would a good grandson do?*

"Yes, I can do it," he heard himself saying, "But it'll take some time. And I'm not a hundred percent sure they'll like the results as much as you do."

"Good point," Gramps replied. "Just think about how great it would be for all these old codgers to feel like they were in charge of their phones. What if it *does* work? Wouldn't it be worth a try?"

Ben took the phones home and used the backup data from the "Gramps Project" to make a hundred copies which he then transferred to implantable chips, of which he needed three types. He then carefully placed the proper chips into each phone, and put them all back into the shoebox.

Then he called Adam.

Adam listened to the story all the way through without interrupting except for the audible gasp when Ben mentioned the fact that these people wanted to pay a hundred dollars each to learn how to use their phones. He exclaimed, "That's ten grand! You might want to get some advice from someone who knows the legal side of patents."

"Yeah," Ben agreed, "and maybe someone who does copyrights."

One thing led to another. It took fourteen months to set it all up legally, but in the end, Twenty-first Century Data was born. The company name proved to be overly ponderous, and with Ben so closely associated with his product, it became known as Bendata. And by that time, eleven employees, eight men and three women, all yuppie age and well able to handle their own phones without Bendata, were busily implanting memory upgrades enhanced with Ben's sonorous teaching voice into the products of all the major players at a hundred bucks a pop. The baby boomers didn't even miss the money.

The customer base burgeoned, because any boomer that could take full advantage of social media blabbed it all over, from Facebook to Twitter and everywhere in between. Ten thousand potential new customers retired every day. Paid advertising would have been extraneous. A small percentage of the braver purchasers even took videos of themselves having fun with their phones and uploaded them to You Tube.

And that's when Apple called.

Not Steve Jobs. That would have required the services of a really good medium, because he was deceased. But someone else near the top, near the inner circle, near the center of the conspiracy wanted to talk. They needed the rights to apply his product to Apple's line. At least the call didn't come from Redmond.

The income, the windfall, the profit, the capital. Ben agonized over what to do, how to strike a deal that would protect the integrity of his intellectual property, provide for the security of his employees, fairly reward him for his efforts, and allow him to retain the right to maximum control over events in the company.

The process dragged on. And it presented great difficulty. It costs the GDP of your average third world country to be familiar enough with corporate lawyers to call them by their first names. If you move on to nicknames you're approaching the yearly U.S. deficit. Ben emerged with the agreement he wanted, with Apple happy as well. Uncommon wealth resulted—Ben sat in the top ten percent of those wage earners who bore the burden of half of his nation's taxes.

Life stayed the same, though. Well, mostly the same, with the exception that Ben got a lot more attention from single women his age—at least he assumed most of them were single. And all of them were nicer than Courtney. Partly because of the demanding nature of his job, and partly because of his relative youth (he'd just read that the average male college graduate was twenty-eight when he got married, and he'd been too busy to attend school his senior year) he ignored the sudden influx of discriminate interest, telling himself that they only wanted access to his good fortune. He supposed that he appeared to these young women as a winning lottery ticket.

Then Dell called. They hoped to buy the right to install Ben's voice on lap tops and tablets, and this began a second avalanche of developing code, creating voice prompts, hiring more technicians, and a large influx of what could truly be called extra money. (Gramps used to say that there were no such things as extra money or extra time. It all had its own specific purpose. This bunch of money might have been the exception.)

All of this demanded a toll from Ben's production team, like an extended two minute drill for an NFL squad. The next play had to be in the hopper before the previous one ended. Everyone knew his place, and everyone worked precisely, forcing themselves past challenges and setbacks, until they saw the task through with very few glitches.

So again Ben ascended, so to speak, to wealth's privilege, up in rarefied air. The temptation toward the indulgence of a private jet, maybe a Gulf Stream V like some celebrities had, pulled at the back of his left brain. Somehow he could not make that final separation between himself and standard living. Maybe that influence came from his right brain. But he no longer flew coach.

At that juncture he began to be obsessed with the concept of time. He wanted more of it. He didn't want time to waste on useless pursuits. He knew that the average twenty-five year old male spends three hours a day playing video games. He wanted to spend it judiciously on the front porch with Gramps and a glass of lemonade. If good things happen to good people, can the good people have more time to let them happen?

Could he rely on Gramps, that there were no such things as extras, when speaking of money? Or of time? Did anybody get a second chance at anything? (Ben would have loved to go back and erase some of those difficult moments.) Does someone have command of time? Ultimately, he understood the last question to be the most practical, because it held the answers to the others. He also figured that if extra time were available, few people deserved it more than he. The busy life he'd led the past four or five years had been rewarding, but he had sacrificed a lot of *time* to get it done.

And that's when Adam called. Out of the blue, it seemed.

Adam's life looked flat by comparison. He had married a girl named Laurie, had a daughter named Sherry, and had gotten a typical college-graduate engineering job with DataCo, a software support company in Dallas. Adam flew coach when he traveled and he traveled as little as possible. And he had begun to attend church.

"What? Are you some kind of Jesus guy now?" Ben had gained fame for this type of outburst; they had been dubbed 'Ben blurts'.

The pause at the other end of the phone lasted long enough for Ben to suspect he'd been offensive, but finally Adam said "When can you come down and spend the weekend with us?"

Time again, thought Ben. But he unexpectedly found a rare open weekend just ten days hence. He promised to be at DFW at noon the following Friday.

He returned his phone to his pocket and thought how strange it seemed to have *time* to travel to Dallas exactly when he wanted to go.

CHAPTER II

As soon as Ben had committed himself to the Dallas trip, administrative duties began to attempt to crowd it out. He resisted the temptation to try and reschedule. At this point in his life he could afford to do whatever he desired, even if his lack of flexibility turned out to be costly. He might have been one of the few people around the country who could be totally honest when he said, "It's not about the money."

So there he sat in first class on Friday morning as Delta Air Lines thanked him for flying with them. After a routine flight and landing, and a short taxi to gate E6, he disembarked, happy to claim not only his bag, but a friendly reunion with his former roommate as well.

"So glad you could come!" Those words from Adam were firm, and sincere, not some secret insider frat boy fake greeting. "Now let's head over to Famous Dave's for lunch. Laurie's not expecting us home until around supper; she and Sherry both agreed we'd want some guy time."

Their first hour together was dominated by reminisces of *la vida loca*, the crazy life. They reconstructed the night they hung Watson out a third story window by his heels, the time they set Miller up to get soaked by a bucket of water when he opened his door, and the time they set off the fire alarm in the dorm so they could raid the frig in privacy. Eventually, though, they got a little bit serious

Ben began his cross examination as they sat waiting for their orders. "Are you some kind of Jesus guy now? What happened? You really *are* Church Lady!" Standard Ben blurt.

"Well," Adam replied, "let me tell you my story."

So Ben sat and listened as Adam told him the whole thing. He had been sent to Cincinnati to work on a computer system, and had met Jeff, the CEO of a small Midwestern IT corporation. Jeff seemed to be a really unique guy. He appeared optimistic and unflappable. He didn't expect the impossible like a lot of clients do, and his employees loved him. (They could, because he didn't sign their checks.) Jeff's executive secretary proved to be a wealth of information, and volunteered a full account of the 2003 blackout and Jeff's ability to wade through that without losing his equilibrium. She claimed that Jeff never brought up his employees' past mistakes, and that Jeff and his wife even visited sick employees when they were in the hospital.

Adam thought it was a strange way to run a company

So Adam wanted to know why Jeff handled life so differently, and he asked about it. Jeff gave him a book instead of an answer: a Gideon New Testament.

"I spent most of my spare time over the next month reading it," Adam said. "I overflowed with questions, and fired them all at Jeff. In the end, I agreed with Jeff and a couple billion other people, that Jesus is Lord. My Savior. I agreed with Jeff, and God, that all people, myself included, have what is called a sin problem. At the core of each of us is a natural bent toward doing wrong, and we need to be forgiven and brought back into a right relationship with God. Knowing Jesus is the solution to all of it. So I brought you this."

He held up the worn Gideon New Testament. Ben hesitated to touch it, because danger lurks everywhere. In the end he accepted it and put it in his pocket. But then the objections poured out.

"What if there's no God at all? What if Jesus never even existed? What about the fossil record, and the age of the earth? And where did Cain get his wife?" He inserted that last question unfairly, since it really had no bearing on the others. Ben possessed no knowledge of the Scopes trial, or the origin of the question. He had only heard it used mockingly by a philosophy professor early in their freshman year. It seemed to fit at the time, but in reality he blurted it.

"OK, Ben," Adam answered. "One thing at a time. I asked a lot of these same things and Laurie knew you'd be asking them too. That's why we have the whole afternoon and then some."

Between the salads and the barbecued chicken sandwiches, Adam began his answer. "First things first—the existence of God. I looked into this, and there's a lot to be said about our universe. Do you think the earth has always been here? The sun, the stars, the galaxies? Is it eternal?"

"No."

"Pretty positive, aren't you? Why do you say that?"

"Well, I'll tell you." Ben answered. "It's physics 101. The earth slows its rotation one fifty thousandth of a second per hundred years. Probably due to the friction caused by the tides. If that had been going on interminably, the earth would have stopped by now. Or take the sun. It burns several hundred million tons of hydrogen per second. This can't have been going on forever. Why would it still be in existence, or at least why would it still burn? Or take the moon. People theorized that there would be dust possibly forty feet deep for the Apollo astronauts to land in, but it was only about half an inch thick. Obviously the moon hasn't been out there forever either. And a little at a time, it's getting farther and farther away from the earth. It couldn't have been doing that for all that long. A large percentage of the stars are shining as well. The basic laws of thermodynamics prove that the situation is not eternal."

"Yeah, that's what I thought," Adam agreed. "So if it's not eternal, it's temporal. Or, we could say, it's temporary.

And if it's temporary, it had a beginning. So how did it begin? Where did it come from?"

Ben laughed. "Hey! I'll ask the questions around here! But most people would tell you it was the Big Bang."

"Let's start by supposing that such an event began our universe. There's a great deal of complexity to what we see. The earth revolves at just the right distance from the sun to sustain life. Why? Uranus, Venus and Pluto rotate opposite the other six planets. Why would they, if they all came out of one big explosion? The atmosphere is right, the climate is right, the presence of water seems just right. Bees need flowers and flowers need bees. Whales eat plankton. It's all so interconnected, and seems to have been so from the start. You've heard of the Miller experiments, right?"

"You mean the guy who discovered that proteins begin to line up in a controlled environment the way they'd need to for life to form?"

Adam smiled. "Yes, those are the ones. Do you realize that life needs oxygen to exist, but Miller removed all oxygen from that environment? How could life begin that way if it can develop only under conditions which preclude its existence?"

"So what did he prove?"

"Well, it looks to me that he proved it didn't happen that way. But what if it did happen somehow, and life began. What then?"

"Wouldn't natural selection take over then, and life would go on to develop and prosper?" Ben asked.

"You might think that, but we have several problems there. (Not the least is the mathematically insurmountable unlikelihood of life developing by accident anywhere, but we'll lay that aside for the moment.) Why are there ostriches that can't fly, and hummingbirds that can't walk and mammals that fly but can't see, and mammals that have rejected the land and have gone back to the ocean? Why are there giraffes that can't hiccup and need a special valve in the blood vessels in their head so that they don't get a brain hemorrhage when they get a drink of water? (Sherry loves

16

giraffes.) Why do beavers build dams and why do bees make honey? Why do arctic terns fly all that way every year? I hope you're not going to claim they do what they do because natural selection taught them that."

"Uh, well," Ben spoke slowly now, in the opposite of a blurt. "I've never really thought about that. Now that I give it some thought, natural selection wouldn't really teach or equip. It only weeds if it does anything. Gramps weeds his carrots, and he even thins them out. But I don't think the carrots that make the cut are any different for having made it. I guess I have heard that natural selection cannot add new information. It all must have happened through mutations"

"Well, assuming that, there is the problem of mutations themselves," Adam pressed on. "In the language of today, a mutation is a birth defect. They are nearly always negative, and for any parent a mutation, or birth defect, spells bad news. Generally, for the species at large it would spell bad news as well. But this is the tool Darwinists supply to the natural selection process in order to *improve* life forms. Can you conceive of all the positive mutations that would be necessary to make a land animal into a whale? It boggles the mind when you consider it. Beyond that is the cross-checking nature of DNA. And RNA. These processes are at work day and night to *prevent* any deviation from the parent cell. Does that look to you like it could be the result of a cosmic explosion?"

Ben had difficulty deciding what to say. He could see that Adam truly disagreed with most of his college professors on the origin of the earth and animal and plant life. As he pondered a safe answer, Adam asked him a seemingly unrelated question.

"Ben, how did you get rich?"

I hope he doesn't expect me to admit it was an act of God, Ben thought. But he said, "You know that nearly as well as I do. It wasn't well planned, but it came together. No, I *brought* it together! I had an idea while I was talking to you about five, no six years ago. (Time gets away from me.) And the implementation of it grew into what I have now. I'm not sure how it happened. Karma, I guess."

"But you know, way better than I do, that it could never have come about without someone like you doing it, creating it. Someone had to arrange the data to work in the phones and computers in a designed way. No amount of random guess work or ignorant engineering could have done it. The process needed you, because it's an intelligent process. And not just any intelligence. My plumber could not have done it, though he is not dumb. Someone special had to do it. You had to do it."

"I agree with that," Ben conceded, "But does that actually prove anything?"

"By comparison, our world, our solar system, our universe, *even living cells* are far more complex, far more in need of an intelligent designer than your temporal stasis program. You built it, and it's complicated. It would not have come about without you. The universe seems like Bendata times a billion."

"Well, I did donate the design. And our world is very complex." Ben concurred. And he could tell that his simple admission had forced him over the first hurdle of a long and grueling race. He had agreed that his world, his universe, needed a designer, a caretaker. A maker? It was not its own place. In the back of his mind he realized that for the first time in his life he had consciously conceded that there might possibly be a God.

Adam waited and watched in fascination, attempting to read Ben's thoughts. As the wheels of Ben's mind turned, Adam wished he could control the direction of the spin.

Finally, Ben said, "Well, maybe we should get out of Dave's, and let them use this booth for paying customers." He picked up the check, left the waitress a twenty, and trusted Adam to guide them to a good spot to talk.

Adam did. They wound up in a small park across from the new and improved Cowboys stadium. And Adam let the question of design resurface on its own. Ben reconnected the train of thought.

"You were saying, then, that the nature of the physical world demands a designer. This is new territory for me, so I want to conditionally say, for the sake of argument, yes, okay. Designer. So what?"

"Well, then I think you know that opens the door to God, to faith, to what we call religion. But that brings up a lot more questions."

"Yeah, I expect it does. I guess we'd have to start with who's right, if somebody is."

Adam smiled again. "That may not be confusing at all when you look at things side by side."

"What do you mean by that?"

"Well," Adam began, "could I interest you in a discussion of the uniqueness of the life and teachings of Jesus?"

"What do you mean about uniqueness? Jesus was a good moral teacher, like Buddha or Tao or Krishna. They all had good things to say. Others did too."

"I would agree with some of that. History has given us a lot of wise people who have said some great things. But Jesus did not fit the template of a good moral teacher."

"You cannot be serious!" Ben unwittingly gave his best John McEnroe impersonation. "What I know is sketchy and second-hand, but Jesus did say we should 'do unto others what you want them to do to you.' That's good moral teaching; I run my business like that."

Adam raised one eyebrow, like movie stars can do, but like Ben never could. He said, "Well, that's true. But Jesus also claimed to be God Himself come in the flesh. He claimed to have a relationship of oneness and equality with God. He claimed to have the right to judge every person in the entire history of the world. He claimed that He would die and be raised from the dead. There is no way that someone who was just a 'good teacher' would make these claims. Either the claims were false, and He was merely a very effective charlatan, or they were false and He was nuts, or they were true and He was the Son of God. But there's no way "good moral teacher" can make the list.

Jesus was either far below, or far above that. A merely good man with no special relationship to God would not go around claiming he would rise from the dead and judge all mankind. If Jesus was less than God's son in the flesh, then he was merely a liar and not good or moral. Only perhaps an effective teacher."

Ben had been unaware of the noise of the traffic on the street, the families in the park, the flapping wings of pigeons. He took a deep breath. "Okay, I take it back. He might not have been a good moral teacher. But how can you be so sure that all this 'walk-on-water heal-the-leper give-the-people-free-bread' stuff is not just religious legend developed by some clever monks later on who wanted to secure their own jobs?"

"There are a few thoughts that I have on that." Adam returned. "First, if you made up a religion, would you insert impossible moral imperatives into it?"

"Wait. What do you mean?"

"Jesus calls His followers to deny themselves and take up their crosses and follow Him. He calls us to total subjection to Him, to leave our own desires and dreams behind. He commands us to love our neighbors as ourselves, to 'do unto others' as you said, and to forgive seventy times seven. He even commands us to love our enemies. Is there anything on that list that's even possible, let alone easy?"

"Let's see," Ben replied. "Take up a cross-does that mean you're going to be crucified? Executed?" Adam nodded. "And leave all your desires behind and love your neighbor and forgive up to four hundred ninety times, love your *enemies*—no. None of it sounds possible, or even appealing. None of it looks easy."

"Okay," continued Adam. "If I were going to invent a religion, I'd at least make it something I could actually look good doing. Christianity misses there. And then, add to that the concept that though all of this is impossible, God still expects you to do it. But He knows you can't, so He tells you that if you do the first part (take up your cross—get

20

ready to die to your own life) then He'll make the rest happen. He will give you what you need to live your life for His glory—well, it isn't even your life anymore. You're figuratively dead. But He promises to live His life through you, and to do in you what's impossible for you to do by yourself. In a small way, the original 'Bendata' setup you did for your Gramps is like that. Those people who use it can't do it by themselves. They need you. Likewise, we need God to live His life through us." Ben nodded. Adam pressed forward.

"Now think about this. All other so-called religious systems on this earth have one thing in common. They call on man to make himself better, to pull himself up by his own bootstraps, to find within himself or his own strength (or, in some cases, among his own property) the sacrifice, the payment, the ticket back to God. It seems to me that mankind naturally knows he needs God. The Bible says that He has put eternity in our hearts. The only question is how to achieve it. And this is what I meant by Christianity's uniqueness. Jesus reaches down to man with love and compassion and promises to give us what we could never earn. In all other religious systems, man reaches up to God, working, earning, building little edifices to human pride. You might say that what you can't have by trying is only available by trusting."

Ben took another deep breath and sat back against the park bench. A myriad of thoughts swirled in his head, and he spoke the most obvious one.

"Okay, so the system is cool and unique and all that. But how do you know that it wasn't just a big clever hoax?"

Adam stared at Ben. "There is no way you could have known this, but I asked Jeff that same question, possibly using those exact words. So let's deal with that one. But first, I need a Coke. You want anything?"

"Yeah. Diet Pepsi if you can get it." Then he sat and waited, basking in the mid-afternoon sun as Adam visited a nearby vending machine and returned with drinks.

"Laurie just drinks water. She says it's healthier. But it's no cheaper. And it's boring.

"Anyway, where were we—oh, yeah, about how I know it's not just a clever hoax. Ben, God does a lot of miraculous things inside the human heart, but we are not speaking now of subjectivity. It may be appropriate for later. But for now, consider this. If Jesus died and was buried and not raised from the dead, that would be a hoax, right?"

"Right," admitted Ben.

"So if He stayed dead, the body would have been around somewhere, and all the people who were upset about His followers claiming He was alive would have had to do to stop all that 'nonsense'"(Adam crooked his fingers in air quotes) "was to produce the body. With Jesus' tomb guarded, only authorized personnel were allowed in the area. Pilate sealed it with an official seal, and no ordinary person could mess with it. But somehow the body disappeared. If it were just a dead corpse, it should have been easy to resolve the situation."

Ben began a hesitant reply, but Adam refused to be interrupted. "Some people have thought that maybe Mary went to the wrong tomb. That's a long shot because then a lot of other people were more lost than she was. It would mean that even the soldiers guarded the wrong tomb. But Peter and John knew where they were going, and when they got there they knew where they'd been.

"Some say Jesus wasn't really dead, but had merely 'swooned'" (air quotes again) "on the cross—this, of course, ignores John's account of the piercing of the heart by the Roman soldier, and the problem of the stone covering the entrance of the tomb—it must have weighed a ton. Literally. Hard to move for a healthy guy on steroids, let alone one who's lost most of the blood in his body. So that's very unlikely as well.

"The followers of Jesus have been accused of stealing the body and faking the resurrection story. But that intimidated, disorganized, and terrified bunch was laying lower than a snake's belly in a wagon rut. Not likely to initiate, let alone pull off a sort of terrorist raid on the tomb.

"But nothing explains how all these guys later stuck to their story. They all insisted that what they said happened did happen, even though they were being killed for saying it. You'd think that somebody would have cracked if they were making it all up. But all eleven (you knew Judas committed suicide?) were willing to die rather than change their story.

"But it goes beyond that, too. Maybe this is the wrong way to say it, but there is another link in the chain that's not so objective. It's the love of God that you can feel and know. There's a line from some old song that says 'you were half, now you're whole.' That's probably inadequate, but part of the package in following Jesus is that you get to know the love of Christ 'which passes knowledge,' the Bible says.

"God empties all the mundane and useless things out of your heart and pours Himself in. He takes all of your guilt and shame and loss and fear and hate and replaces it with Himself. He Himself lives right inside of you, Ben! You become the modern version of the temple of God! There is nothing like it anywhere. The joy of knowing God is so rich and beautiful and satisfying, and like nothing else you've ever experienced!"

"So what is he to you?" Ben interrupted. "I mean, is he like a big Boss, or a loving father who lets you do whatever you want? Does he own you?"

"Ben, thank you for asking that. There is so much in that relationship. I am the lost sheep that was found, and the prodigal son that came home. I am at the same time a son and a slave and a servant. He bought me and He owns me, and He has all rights to me, but He would only do what's good for me. No, more accurately, He would only do what's best for me. With Him as Lord of my life, I have nothing to fear about the future. I anticipate it with more optimism than I've ever had in my life-"

Ben again interrupted with a question based on his training as a computer engineer. "Can you prove it's real?" The programmer side of his nature demanded solid data. Adam seemed a bit flustered, but eventually had to admit that for this portion of his spiritual life, he had no proof as such, but hoped that his own experience could count for something. But then he looked at his watch, and what with the drive across town and the traffic, he thought they should be headed home for dinner.

Adam lived in a neighborhood that looked like a safe place to raise a family, with generous lawns and mostly fenced yards, many of them containing children's playground equipment and pets. Adam was master of a modest but comfortable domicile, the fortress that contained the lights of his life—his wife and daughter.

Laurie welcomed them both with a warmth and love that was either very rare, or the product of a great acting job. And when Sherry saw her dad, her face lit up, and she ran to her father and leaped into his arms and hugged him and kissed him. (Laurie had kissed Adam too—one of those gentle yet passionate kisses a woman reserves for that very special man. It crossed Ben's mind again that he sometimes wished, only for a moment, for a more ordinary financial situation, so that he needn't be so suspicious of the way women acted around him.) The table had been set for an evening meal seasoned with generous doses of southern hospitality. Besides all the rest, Laurie proved to be an excellent cook and skilled homemaker, and as a result Ben immediately felt at ease in their home. He quickly became Sherry's newest friend.

After enjoying delicious southern cuisine, Ben sat down with Sherry and got reacquainted with Dr. Seuss, the Berenstain Bears, and Richard Scarry. He found great satisfaction in helping Sherry look for Waldo, and making sure a duck would find its mother. After they found the duck's mother, Sherry invited him to come with her to the zoo the following day. (Of course this had been the plan for the girls from the beginning—except that Laurie had expected the men to want to do other things. But Ben could not resist the charming young lady in question, and his heart had skipped a beat when she raised one eyebrow as she implored him to join her.)

The oldest zoo in Texas is in Marsalis Park, and covers a sprawling 106 acres. It contains an extravagant variety of animals, many of them rare or endangered. True to Adam's forewarning, Sherry insisted that they immediately seek out the giraffe exhibit. She explained to Ben that giraffes would have a serious blood pressure problem were it not for a special valve in their heads that stopped blood flow to their brain when they reached down for a drink. She explained how sea turtles lay their eggs on land and the eggs hatch at night, so the baby turtles can get to the water under the cover of darkness to avoid being eaten by predators. She showed him a bee hive and encouraged him to contemplate the complexity of a bee's knowledge, a bee's need for a queen, a bee's building acumen, a bee's ability, through interpretive dance, to communicate to his comrades where the nectar could be found.

As if all this were not enough, she cajoled Ben into riding a camel. Not alone, of course. She promised to accompany him. And, as is the wont of many small children, she shared everything with her new friend. She talked incessantly.

Ben began to realize just how much Adam loved his wife and daughter. Sherry overflowed with praise for her parents, and for God who created all the things in the zoo. Amidst her chatter, Ben could sense the security that comes from being loved no matter what, and the joy such a feeling of security brought to a child's heart. He figured that no one had to tell Sherry that she was loved. She felt it. She knew it. It flooded out of her.

Ben began to ponder then what the morrow might bring. He realized that his work back home had not crossed his mind since he'd arrived in Dallas, and he began to consider again a private jet. As is the case with many young men, his first real love was a child who respected him. He didn't at that moment consider the impractical nature of all of this, but he knew that when tomorrow came he would have a hard time saying goodbye to Sherry, and he wondered what it would be like to have a daughter of his own.

Sunday dawned bright and clear. Sherry exhibited the inimitable optimism possessed by most children, and remarked on how she loved to see the planes take off at the airport. Ben's mood softened because of the continual love and acceptance he felt from the McLeod family, and he didn't allow himself to cry until after he'd boarded the plane—then it was just a couple of tears and a pretense of problems with congestion while settling into the cushy seat for the long flight home. (And a forward look. Sherry had promised to email him.)

His mind went back then to church. It seemed like such an odd place to him, because it appeared to him that there was a guest of honor, always absent. The pastor stood short and portly in his pulpit, and reminded Ben in some ways of the late Chris Farley—outgoing, somewhat entertaining, but a bit more serious.

Pastor Rick had spoken about Jonah, and how an ultimately loving God had forced the faithless prophet, against his will, to bear a message of mercy to his nation's enemies.

"What do you think of a God like this, who goes to such extremes to allow wicked people to hear a message of grace? What do you think of a people, barbaric and cruel enemies of God's chosen race, ready to repent, but God's man is not willing to share? What do you think of God's problem, not with the heathen on the boat, not with the storm, or the fish, or the heathen in wicked Nineveh? No, God's only problem in his message of generous grace came from His chosen man, His prophet, who fled to Tarshish rather than obey. But God overcame all of his unwillingness. What do you think of a God like this?"

Ben thought again about Adam's insistence on Christianity being so unique. If Pastor Rick was right, God went way over the top for the people of Nineveh. And if Adam was right, a far more crucial thing happened on the cross.

He settled in for a long flight. He couldn't wait for a chance to check his email.

CHAPTER III

Home again, Ben's brain involuntarily evaluated his own life. It didn't have to be this good, he knew. He felt he'd done pretty well so far without God's help. He had learned to drive in Gramps' old Ford Pinto. Even at that time, he had known that was not a cool car, and it never would be. But it did run, and what more could you want at age fifteen? Now he drove a Bentley convertible, and he liked it much better than the Pinto. Who can argue with 567 horsepower? He found himself wondering if Sherry would like it. He perhaps should drive it to Dallas for her approval. He could do that. Any *time.* He had far more freedom and independence than his parents. Or his grandparents.

Yes, he realized, *some things have gone really well.* He could pick anywhere he wanted to live, and if he didn't like the neighbors he could buy them out. (Ben figured the need for this would be unlikely. He made friends with just about everybody, and most people liked him. He enjoyed having that option, though.) And by age twenty five, he knew he'd never have a financial worry in his life. In his case, the bucks did stop with him. He always met expenses. (For most people this presented no problem—expenses lurked

29

everywhere.) He liked the feeling of security his financial successes had given him, and he liked the Bahamas. In fact, he liked most warm and sunny and clean places.

But he wondered about life. If he'd done so well without God, why did he not find more satisfaction?

He heard in biology about the missing link. He wondered why it had never been found. He made a mental note to ask Adam. Now he had begun to wonder if the inner life had its own missing link.

It was then that he remembered the little Bible Adam had given him. He dug it out of his bag and began to read, from the front, just like he would a computer manual. The first few pages were boring and unhelpful, just like a computer manual. Later on, though, the style smoothed out into limited biographical details, and then on into the standard stuff he thought he should read in a place like that. Teaching, miracles, cultural information, fulfillment of prophecy, some of the events of the lives of people who seemed quite real.

Why wouldn't they seem real if they were? Ben mused. He eventually read something that seemed very unreal.

Someone came to Jesus with this question: "Good Master, what must I do to have eternal life?"

"When you call me good, you are calling me God," Jesus replied, *"for God alone is truly good. But to answer your question, you can get to heaven if you keep the commandments."*

"Which ones?" the man asked.

And Jesus replied, "Don't kill, don't commit adultery, don't steal, don't lie, honor your father and your mother, and love your neighbor as yourself."

"I've always obeyed every one of them," the youth replied. *"What else must I do?"*

Jesus told him, "If you want to be perfect, go and sell everything you have and give to the poor. And you will have treasure in heaven. And come follow me." But when the young man heard this he went away sadly, for he was very rich.

30

Ben's difficulty began right there, at the end of that story. He held in his hand a so-called God book. A rich young guy approaches the so-called greatest spiritual teacher in history, and the fish gets away. *Shouldn't everybody find it worthwhile to follow? Did the young man ever change his mind? Why would he not respond to the great master, ditch his possessions and get on board? He sounded like a good guy, a guy who could enhance the makeup of the team. Jesus didn't want him because he was rich? If following Jesus was so great, and if Jesus was so effective, why could he not change the young man's mind? Was he just letting the guy go to hell?* It sounded to Ben like he needed to spend an afternoon with this guy. But of course, that would be impossible.

Ben set the little Bible aside, stood up, stretched, and sauntered to the fridge for a Pepsi. He returned to his chair with the express purpose in mind of staring at the bay, but an outdated issue of 0-1 magazine on the coffee table distracted him. It was open to the classified ads, which Ben purposely ignored as a matter of principle. He figured that anything advertised there was either a lost cause or the ground floor of a new pyramid scheme.

One ad in particular displayed its outline in red ink. Just a gimmick, but it did catch his eye. The ad read:

QUESTIONS ABOUT THE PAST?
CONTACT DR NEVEN RESSER
1221 EVA AVE EKALAKA LAKE MT 406-755-7604.

Who's ever heard of Ekalaka Lake? Anyway, I'm way too busy right now to call. But then he thought, *Busy doing what?* He had just decided to watch waves come in off the bay. Besides, he got unlimited long distance, and he did have a question about the past.

So Ben called.

Some people are hard to talk to. Doctor Resser could be president of that club. The man sounded sincere and convincing, much like a political candidate on the campaign trail, but with far less credibility. Ben worked in an industry heavily weighted toward promise and hope, so he felt accustomed to that. He sometimes found that he had to promise the very difficult. But he now heard a stranger, in confident, level tones, assure him of the impossible.

Evidently, Doctor Resser, or Doc Neven, as he said he preferred, had been researching temporal fixation adjustment, and had recently come to the inglorious end of his government funding. It seemed that his project had been included as a line item in a major research grant, but with greater public scrutiny on the federal budget, no one in Congress had been willing to go on record with a yes vote in favor of time travel, in view of all the unfortunate shortfalls in the food stamp and student loan programs. Besides that, he had located his laboratory in very remote Ekalaka Lake, eastern Montana's least sought after tourist attraction. To say that this was a remote location was akin to Doc offering that water was wet. To say that Neven's claims were credible was like saying that New York City was chock full of polite, outgoing people with lots of spare time to be nice to strangers.

Doc claimed to know how to adjust temporal fixations—that is, how to travel in time. He had not done this successfully with humans, but had succeeded with some smaller organic objects. He insisted that the entire theory checked out, but he needed a few supplies and a small amount of time to make adjustments to his chrono-reversatron. He assured Ben that he could provide a bona fide demonstration on a small scale immediately.

Ben could have told anyone that this was bogus, and anyone would say "What's your first clue? If you fall for this the Nigerian Lottery Winner scam can't be far behind." So, more for laughs than anything else, he brought up Expedia and checked on connections to Billings, Montana. After booking a flight, he called Gramps and shared the joke with him.

Gramps insisted on going along. He claimed he'd always wanted to see Ekalaka Lake, and that he wouldn't be missed around the house at all.

The borrower is servant to the lender. So although Ben had already repaid the financial part with interest, his sense of fairness and respect for his elders motivated him to book a second ticket. After all, the Pinto *had* sustained minor body damage in the mud incident.

Billings sprawled out in the midst of cattle country. He could see that cattle and meat packing figured big into the local economy. Ben expected that some parts of the town would smell like the stockyards of Kansas City. From the window of the plane they could see ranch after ranch, each populated with its share of the brown bovines—even some sheep. Many of the pictures advertising local life hanging around the baggage claim area were of cattle and boots, ropes and spurs.

They rented a car and began the road part of their trip through the monotonous eastern Montana prairie. Their navigation system sent them past the Massey-Ferguson dealership, down past Fuddrucker's onto I-94, then east to the Baker exit and Montana 7. As per Doc Neven's instruction, they stopped in at the Wagon Wheel, a local hamburger joint, and asked for directions to Ekalaka Lake.

"Ha! You must be looking for Doc Neven." came the cheerful reply. The waitress smiled and explained that Ekalaka Lake existed only in theory, not even as certain as relativity. But if they went north twenty-five miles on county road four, then west on Beaver Flats Road, his place would be just across the cattle guard on top of the hill to the west. Then she smiled again and said, "It's pretty dry around here. It's no wonder Ekalaka Lake is so hard to find."

They had some really good burgers, generous patties ground from local beef and grilled to perfection with just the right mix of seasonings. The buns had been baked of whole wheat flour, made with Montana grain, and it all had the taste of good health—tomatoes, lettuce and cheese from a local farm. Ben surmised that those fast food burger places had no concept of how a real sandwich should taste. He and Gramps left a generous tip, thanked the waitress and got back into the rental car. North on 4, west on Beaver Flats, across the cattle guard, and up the hill to the west. It took them about an hour to completely obey their instructions, but they finally arrived in what might be described as the middle of nowhere.

The house did not impress--plain and white, an aging two-story farm place with an old windmill and a water trough in the yard. It stood atop a shallow rise and seemed to rule alone in a solitary domain. The predictable outbuildings stood on the backside—barn, shed, and an outhouse Ben hoped no longer saw daily use. Next to the driveway, an inexplicably placed street sign read "EVA AVE", and next to the sign sat a fairly new Honda Civic. Beside the front door of the house hung the identifying digits, 1221.

Two steps led up onto a spacious porch with an old rocking chair and no dog. (Ben and Gramps thought nothing of this. But the locals knew that because of coyotes, every farmstead needed a good-sized healthy dog with an aggressive nature and big teeth) Ben knocked on the door and waited, like an Ekalaka deputy making his first arrest.

Gramps seemed a bit preoccupied, messing with his cell phone and shoving it into his shirt pocket.

A studious looking man, about sixty years of age, short and slight, opened the door, greeting them with that jovial optimism you rarely see outside of used car lots. He welcomed them to his humble domicile, introduced himself as Doctor Neven Resser and apologized for the lack of a good ranch dog. He thanked them for coming and acknowledged Gramps in a torrent of gracious words that would have been good competition for an eastern Montana blizzard. Then he invited them inside.

The living space of Doc's home provided an assault on their senses, mostly the sense of vision. They seemed to have stepped into another dimension. There were no

34

similarities from outside to inside. Banks of computers lined the walls, and terminal stations, keyboards, monitors and towers of nearly every description waited at the ready. Ben recognized all the major players in the industry, most minor ones, plus a few he had not yet heard of. He could see the kitchen through an open door at the far end of the room. A closed door to his right, Ben guessed, led to sleeping quarters. A Sonos wireless stereo system occupied the corner to his left. Abba softly sang "Dancing Queen" in the background.

"Welcome, friends, to my computation center. Here we track our progress and plot our course. We search for available knowledge that will aid our quest as we serve mankind," he stopped and smiled, "just by showing up."

"Yes, well, okay." The blizzard of words presented a bit of a coping challenge for Ben, but he said, "Very generous of you. But from our phone conversation you're well aware of why we've come. We want to know if you can actually deliver."

"Please, please, accompany me to my office, where we can discuss this in comfort, and perhaps also in the presence of some refreshment." Doc Neven appeared learned, intelligent, and relaxed. "Follow me, please."

He led the way to the closed door, which, when opened, revealed an office space like few Ben had ever seen. His own office showed very nicely—large, dark mahogany desk with red leather trim, somewhat collectible paintings on the walls, view of Lake Michigan, nice appointments. Doc Neven's office seemed quite a bit nicer than that—a place where it would be hard to make oneself at home. Concealed behind what Ben hoped would only be a very good copy of a Picasso lurked the door of a small refrigerator, which the Doctor swung open with a flourish. "What, for my honored guests? Beer from Bavaria? Champagne from Champagne? Glacial milk from Tibet? Perhaps some iced tea brewed by my granddaughter?"

"Do you have a diet Pepsi in there?" The drive had made Ben a bit thirsty.

"If you do, double the order," Gramps added. "And I'd like pictures of your granddaughter on the side."

"No sooner said than done," smiled the good Doctor. "Anyone interested in Katie has got to be a gentleman and a scholar."

"Thanks. How old is she, and does she live around here?" Gramps had that curiosity typical, seemingly, of every grandparent in the known universe.

Ben experienced one of those little spurts of panic. He had not counted on this. Both of these men were grandfathers!

"She's nine, and she lives in Billings. Here in Montana that's close—very close. The state's northern border is nearly seven hundred miles long."

The difficulty in this situation is going to be getting these men to focus, Ben thought. After some seconds of deliberation, he decided to let it go—maybe someday he would have grandchildren, and he knew he'd be the same way. So as the men dug out pictures and began trans-patriarchal sharing, Ben looked around the office. Between two very tall filing cabinets at the far end hung the obligatory collection of diplomas from various institutions of higher learning: Stanford, MIT, and Harvard. Less well-known was MSU—Montana State University in Bozeman. This guy had breathed a lot of university atmosphere.

Beyond the filing cabinets a door stood slightly ajar which led to sleeping quarters, and which, to Ben's relief, displayed fairly modern indoor plumbing. Below the diplomas Ben noticed a collection of news articles in little frames, each touting some positive aspect of this or that scientific project, and all of them referencing Dr. Resser as holding a key position on the research team. All of the projects had to do with the temporal dimension.

By the time Ben had absorbed all of this, the grandparents had swung into the re-entry trajectory, ready to resume actual business. Gramps must have used the iPhone to show some pictures, because he replaced it in his shirt pocket.

The used-car salesman smile returned, with Doc Neven fully behind it. He had pride in his work, he claimed, and wanted to give them the complete tour of his facility. He awarded each Parker man a Diet Pepsi.

Said tour began at the outbuildings, with the outhouse totally ignored. The barn provided shelter for an old worn out horse, a somewhat personable pig and six chickens.

The machine shed told a different story—that is to say, faded delta rib sheet metal covered the exterior in that avocado color so popular in nineteen sixty. Two doors that rolled on cannon track covered the majority of the front wall. They could open to a width Ben estimated to be about twenty feet. These doors stood closed, secured with a chain and padlock, with a man-sized door to the right of them. To that door Doc Neven led them.

The inside of the building revealed post and beam construction with purling strips between for securing the metal siding. Ben estimated it at forty by eighty feet. A mammoth Steiger tractor with center steering and eight wheels dominated the far end. The tires towered taller than Ben. The only equipment of note in the rest of the building stood against the opposite wall, and this seemed to be the focus of Doc Resser's attention. The setup looked to Ben like a pair of large stainless steel propane cylinders, each with a two foot wide by four foot tall opening in the front. Space-age astronaut doors covered the openings, each curved to match the front of its cylinder. From each door protruded a brushed nickel lever handle.

"This," began Doc Resser, "is where it all happens, or rather could happen, if I could get the funding to culminate the project. I need only to verify the Femio-Bosic equivalence. Once that is done, the problems of space and time in relation to physical mass become elementary, controlled completely by temporal fixation adjustment. This is naturally achieved through the generation of subatomic temporal vacuumigration (my own coined word—vacuumigration) which, by careful monitoring, can be effective in moving matter freely through the fourth dimension."

"Do you mean time is the fourth dimension, Doc?" Ben asked. He hoped he sounded nonchalant.

"Yes, Ben, that is exactly what I mean. And not some Rube Goldberg false hype, or some Jules Verne claptrap. This is real, actual, identifiable, provable temporal matter transference. It can be proved in this very room. Today."

"Ha!" muttered Gramps. "I've got to take a leak. Must be the Diet Pepsi."

"Anywhere outside that's out of sight of the farmhouse is fine. Help yourself." Doc waved his hand toward the door they'd entered.

"Is an actual demonstration possible?" Ben again hoped that he didn't sound too eager.

Gramps opened the door and the late afternoon sun momentarily flashed into the shed. As the call of nature drew him out the door, Doc said, "A skeptic at least, if not a true unbeliever. He will soon see it with his own eyes—absolute, incontrovertible evidence that I speak the truth. Come this way, young man. We will discuss the heretofore impossible."

Ben followed Doc Neven to a small booth-like structure—an Island of finished floor in the midst of the machine shed's pea gravel. Between two plywood end walls, a carpeted area contained computers on desks hooked to large flat screen monitors. They apparently stood ready to break the time barrier. Gramps returned from the outside world and rejoined the cadre.

"These monitors," purred Doc, "are trained on these cylinders respectively. I have here a common laboratory test rat. One of my star rats. His name is Bob." Here he paused. What he said next seemed disconnected. "Did you know that at one time research scientists used attorneys instead of rats for their experiments? Do you know why that substitution was so popular?"

38

"No." said a very surprised Ben and an incredulous Gramps in unrehearsed unison.

"Because the attorneys were so readily available, and one did not have a tendency to become emotionally attached to them. Also," he continued, "there are some things you can't get a lab rat to do."

It took Ben and Gramps a full three seconds to recognize this as levity, but once it dawned on them, it did seem humorous.

After the chuckling subsided, the Doctor resumed his researcher's aplomb and continued his explanation of the upcoming demonstration. "As I was saying, I have here a common laboratory research assistant. These monitors are trained by digital camera on these cylinders respectively. Here, I have a record of that left cylinder, on digital video disc, time stamped, of course, from last night—11:59 pm. to 12:01 am. Once we three agree on the nature of this evidence, the actual test may commence."

They stared at the screen as Doc Resser made minor adjustments with the keyboard. Then the trio watched as the left screen filled with the inside of the cylinder, viewed from the top. Nothing happened, and for the full two minutes it continued to happen.

"Now," said Doc Neven with the sense of occasion that can only be earned by graduating from college a considerable number of times, "we will take Bob, the aforementioned rat, and place him in the right cylinder. We will transfer him to the left cylinder at precisely 12:00 am yesterday's date, and you will see him appear on the video record we've just verified. To aid you in seeing for yourselves that no chicanery is involved, Ben, please place your initials on this red tape with this black marker. We will then attach the tape to Bob's left rear leg as positive identification, so that Bob cannot possibly be viewed as an imposter."

Ben dutifully marked BP on the red tape. He drew a small rising sun next to his initials, which he shared with British Petroleum. He had lost some respect for them as a

39

result of the Deepwater Horizon oil spill. Since the tape was only a half an inch wide, the logo was almost invisible. He passed the tape back to Doc Neven, who carefully wrapped it around Bob's left hind leg. He twisted the tape a quarter turn so that the initials could readily be seen from above.

"Now, Mr. Parker, if you will hold this rodent on behalf of mankind's scientific progress."

"Which one?" came the response, unrehearsed, but surprisingly, in unison once again.

"Oh, pardon me. The younger, of course." Doc handed Ben the rat named Bob as if he were a tiny football. Ben, as noted, showed little promise at team sports, and also cradled an irrational fear of rats. He fumbled the exchange. Bob landed on the floor, drawn there by forces of gravity, and began to make his exit.

"Can you gentlemen please apprehend that example of rodentia while I prepare the cylinder?" The Parkers set about to corner Bob and make the capture. With that done, Gramps, who had a less neurotic history with such animals, delivered him to Doc Neven, who placed him in the right cylinder. Before Doc closed the door, Ben and Gramps got a glimpse of a round dais atop which stood a small circular platform with a peg and a chain. The chain culminated in a Bob-sized leg iron. This Doc clamped on the taped leg, and carefully secured the door.

"Now we must resume our monitoring positions," Doc intoned. He held in his left hand a clipboard and pen, and with his right he touched one of the keys. Each monitor revealed an identical background, but the one on the right imprisoned Bob with shackle and tape attached. "We must pass Femio-Bosic enriched Neutrinic gas into Bob's cylinder, and when the concentration reaches a two percent, Bob will have passed from the right cylinder to the left at midnight last night. He will appear on the record we've previewed."

He consulted the clipboard, flipped a large toggle switch on the desk and focused studiously on a digital gauge set above the monitors. In a matter of seconds, the numbers began to climb. As the time stamp of midnight crossed the left monitor, Bob disappeared from the right monitor and appeared in the left, complete with red tape, Ben's initials, the apparent rising sun logo, and the leg iron. This remained the scene for about five seconds, at which time Doc flipped the toggle switch back, and Bob regained his original cylinder orientation.

Doc Neven walked over, opened the right cylinder's door and retrieved Bob, clipped the tape from the star rat's leg and deposited it in the pocket of his lab coat. He placed Bob in a small rectangular cage. "Now, my friends, as you probably know, it's about time for our evening meal. We shall discuss the details of our little experiment over a taste of home cooking."

The western sky blazed with a golden sunset as they reentered the farmhouse through the back door. The aroma of something Ben thought he'd never tasted, but had no doubt he'd like very much permeated the kitchen end of the house. As Doc Neven led them into the kitchen, he called, "Hannah, we've got company for supper!"

Hannah must have known this already, as the table was set for the four of them. This Hannah did not instantly appear, so Doc Neven walked to the stove and tipped the lid of a large simmering kettle. "Ah!" he sniffed. "Beef stew complete with garden onions, carrots and potatoes, the like of which you'll not find in all of Montana's 147,200 square miles. Did you know that Montana is actually larger than the entire nation of reunited Germany?"

At that moment a lady entered from the computerized end of the house, and the Parker men recognized her as the stew cooker, the master of this kitchen. She seemed to be in her mid-fifties, less affected by the years than some women are. She had a ready smile, announcing the warmth of a homesteader's welcome.

"I took the liberty to set the table for you, 'cause it seemed to me like you'd be needing supper before you leave. Can you stay?"

41

Somehow it happened again. "Of course," chorused the Parker men.

"You'd think we'd been practicing that," Gramps chuckled.

With introductions formally made, the four sat down to a hearty ranch meal—real stew made from choice chunks of range fed beef, fresh baked wheat rolls and for dessert ice cream made from fat that had risen to the top of whole milk bought from a neighbor who had squirted it out of a cow. Hannah had topped it off with homemade chocolate sauce.

"I hoped neither of you were lactose intolerant?" Hannah asked. Ben suspected that somehow she knew they weren't.

"Now," she smiled, "You men get out of my way so I can get things back in order here. This kitchen is *my* laboratory."

Ben thought it might be rude in that case to offer to help with the dishes, so he followed Gramps, who followed Doc Neven into the living room. On the couch sat a golden retriever, naturally happy to see them. "This is Otto" Doc explained. "He thinks he owns the place. He's a nice canine, but as I said before, I still don't have a good ranch dog. Otto, kennel up," Doc commanded. Otto seemed glad to do this, promptly resorting to his kennel in the corner. Each man chose a place to sit where he could easily see the other two, like poker players in Las Vegas. *I wish I knew for sure if I could trust this guy,* Ben fretted.

Finally Gramps broke the silence. "Ben says you're looking for funding. My question would be why, since you seem to have it figured out already." He rubbed his chin with his left hand as he gave Doc Neven that gentle grandparent 'something's not quite right here' look. Ben knew that look well.

"You are correct. I do have it 'figured out', as you say. My problem is one of acquisition of materials in order to continue my research, which is classified, by the way. Let me see your phone, please, sir."

Gramps handed over his phone and the Doc whistled. "Far too many pictures of sensitive equipment, my good man. I'll have to delete these. By the way, Ben, your application for teaching old codgers all these new tricks is brilliant. I've become proficient in a host of ways. Hannah especially enjoys my ability to use technology to further our already sizzling relationship."

"Is she a, shall we say, recent acquisition, might I ask?" Ben thought it bold of Gramps to intrude into such private territory.

"Oh, my, no. Heavens, no. We've been married for thirty-four years. And probably much thanks to Ben, here, it appears the best is yet to be."

"Well, I don't think I could take credit for any of that," Ben humbly replied. "You must have cared for each other a lot to have been together this long. But can we go back to this thing about time travel? Can you actually do it, in a practical sense? I mean with a person?" Doc handed Gramps back his phone. Ben thought Gramps looked a little smug.

"Thank you for being so frank and to the point, young man. Yes. I am sure that it can be done. Everything is in place. We need only to position ourselves to take the next step. It reminds me of an old palindrome. 'Are we not drawn onward to new era?' Of course we are, and with a bit more time to research, and a bit more time to experiment, and a bit more funding, we will soon complete the solution to the problem of time travel."

"But why do you need money if you can already do it?" Gramps again, ever the persistent one.

"My good man, Mr. Parker, sir, today's demonstration used my entire supply of Femio-Bosic enriched Neutrinic gas, at a cost to my laboratory of approximately twenty thousand dollars. We have not yet learned of Ben's particular desires, but the greater the distance, both in time and space, and the greater the mass, the more material required. And," he added with a smile and a wink, "it is very hard to acquire it."

"So what other uses does it have?" Gramps, still controlling the interview.

"An excellent question, my good man." At that moment Hannah stepped through the kitchen door with a tray containing a coffee pot and cups.

"Coffee for our guests!" she smiled. "I just brewed it."

The men thanked her, and she returned to the kitchen.

"Great coffee," Gramps announced.

"Now, for the answer to your question," Doc continued. "The gas is used in genomic research. It is useful, as it is made up of such small particles, in studying the Hasidim makeup of DNA, as well as mitochondria research. I am not a molecular biologist, as my diplomas will tell you. But I theorized that such small particles might be applicable to the concept of matter transference. The icing on the cake for me came when I discovered that I could send Bob to yesterday, though I could not send him to Cincinnati, as I had hoped. I could not even send him to Noxon. At least not at first. I can accomplish that now, albeit only in conjunction with a temporal fixation adjustment. But, be that as it may, in transferring him the scant five feet to the next cylinder, I realized (after viewing hours of video and making a plethora of notes) that I had actually crossed the boundary of time. Just as Charles Goodyear discovered the process of the vulcanization of rubber partly, it seemed, by accident, I stumbled upon the blessing of time travel in the midst of my endeavors in the discipline of matter transference. Since my original discovery, that is, of finding Bob in cylinder B the day before I attempted to send him there, I have transported garden vegetables, such as potatoes and onions, only to return them later to the larder and eat them. They suffered no ill effect. And by working with these smaller bits of mass, I have developed a formula by which the amount of gas needed per pound of mass is easily calculable, when the calculation is done by one such as myself. The matter of a rat and a twenty hour period of time is of little consequence. Fifty pounds of potatoes is more difficult. More massive, perhaps I should say. Ben,

44

you originally called me in response to my classified advertisement concerning questions about the past. What, specifically, do you want to know? What is your question about the past?"

Ben had not thought to bring the little New Testament on the trip, so he began to reconstruct from memory the framework of his question. "Well," he began, "there's this story in the life of Jesus, Matthew's version, about a young man, a rich man, who came to Jesus and wanted to know how to get to Heaven, I guess. Jesus said be good, and the man said he'd been good, but there was still something lacking. So Jesus told him to sell all his possessions and give the money to the poor, and to come and follow after him. The man went away sad, because he had a lot of money. That's it. No closure, no resolution. I want to find this guy and ask him if his life was worth it, either way. Did he sell everything and follow? Was it worth it? Did he stand pat? Was that worth it? And if he was so good, why did he still have some kind of lack in his life? I want some closure. Can it be done? Because I think his answer might help me make some sense out of my own life." *Could this man be the Master of time? Should I hope he is, or hope he's not?* Ben's mind was ablaze with question and conflict.

Doc Neven smiled. "I believe it can be. A lot of people by now would be asking about the cost of doing it. You haven't brought that up yet. But I will tell you. The gas, the time, the effort, the use of my laboratory—I think we'll need 1.5 million to bring this about."

"That's a lot of green." Gramps again. "Seems a bit high. Where do you get that floro nervo gas?"

"That's Femio-Bosic enriched Neutrinic gas, and there is none privately owned on our planet—at least none that I am aware of. It's not available down at the Ekalaka Mercantile, or even at Costco in Billings. The Ukraine has probably enough to spare for our project, but it would take three months, minimum, to get it, and they'd want cash up front, 1.2 million dollars."

"Why does it take so long?" demanded Ben, testily.

45

"It is a very volatile mixture, and difficult to ship, even under the best of circumstances. And Ukraine's government is made up mostly of former KGB, all suspicious of the west."

Doc Neven looked at Ben as one man who had seen inside another. "You'd need the three months anyway. You'll need to acquire some local currency, some fluency in the language, you'll need clothing of the period, and probably some martial arts training if you are not yet proficient in that area. You must also grow a beard, and perhaps get some experience handling camels."

Ben's mind flashed back to the Marsalis Zoo. "I have a bit of camel experience, but none of the rest."

Doc Neven gave them a level, calculating stare. Then he clasped his hands together. "Think about it," he said. "I know it's a big decision. It involves a substantial investment, and you shouldn't rush into it. Talk it over between yourselves. You don't have to decide in the next minute. After all, you came to me. I didn't come to you like a Kirby vacuum cleaner salesman. I want to put no pressure on anyone. Just talk about it and let me know. You have my number."

The interview seemed to be at an end, so Ben peeked into the kitchen to thank Hannah, then he and Gramps shook hands with Doc Neven and went out into the eastern Montana darkness.

As they situated themselves in the rental car, Ben said, "Well, what did you think?"

Gramps whispered, "Did you lock this thing?" He quietly conducted a search of the car's interior, above the visors, in the glove compartment, inside the change caddy, in the door side pouches—he even poked around under the back seat.

Ben shook his head. "Negatory—I didn't think we'd need that way out here. Why?"

"They may have planted a bug!" Gramps rasped.

Ben's brain did Olympic style gymnastics at the thought. He could not reconcile in his mind that someone

46

capable of serving homemade ice cream with chocolate sauce mixed on the spot would also be capable of spying.

"Let's talk later," hissed Ben.

They rode on in silence back through Ekalaka, back up 7 to 24, back to the interstate, back to Billings and back to the motel. They passed Fuddrucker's again, but they could see no reason to stop there.

At the Sheraton, Gramps became more relaxed and more willing to speak his mind. He talked as if he had made notes on little yellow squares of paper. And a lot of his sentences began with "Did you notice?"

Sentences like this:

"Did you notice how he dropped the rat and made us chase it? What was he doing during that time?

"Did you notice he took my phone and erased all my pictures, even though I never told anyone I took any pictures?

"Did you notice how he cut the tape off and kept it in his pocket? Why not let us examine it?

"Did you notice how his wife knew, or seemed to know, that we'd have no problem with that ice cream? How did she know that?

"And did you notice she suddenly turned up from the front of the house when we came in from the back? And how did she know I love chocolate on ice cream?"

Ben was not by nature a suspicious guy. His tended to trust straightforward talk and good home cooking. But he had to respect the fact that Gramps had been around the block more than once.

So he took in a deep breath. "I think we should hit the sack," he said. "We can talk more about it on the flight home tomorrow."

CHAPTER IV

The flight home proved uneventful—it included a brief layover in Minneapolis, punctuated by a visit to a gourmet chocolate store and the arrangement for a shipment to be sent to a beautiful girl in Texas. The conversation mirrored the previous evening, with Gramps skeptical and suspicious, and Ben hopeful but cautious. At least on a subconscious level, Ben made the decision to pursue the *possibility* of time travel. Plans that would involve Israel in the first century germinated in the private recesses of his mind. He decided to study customs, currency, culture, cuisine, calendars, and camels. He figured that even if time travel turned out to be impossible, as Gramps insisted, it wouldn't hurt to broaden his horizons a bit.

So things began to slide surreptitiously toward trusting Doc Resser. (Gramps called him Kook Resser, because everyone knows time travel is impossible except kooks, movie producers, and novelists.)

The question of martial arts training reverberated in Ben's mind, and with that decision he used extreme caution. He had no desire to hurt anyone for any reason he could conceive. He knew that such skills would shock his friends, because he lacked that natural aggression most testosterone-loaded young men possess.

Shaving created one of his bigger challenges. Actually the problem turned out to be the cessation of shaving. He should have stopped shaving a couple of years in the past. He wondered for a few seconds if you could go back and convince yourself to get the beard started growing sooner, but it seemed obvious that the logistics were too involved for that to work out.

The martial arts announcement unnerved Adam. "What? Judo? Why judo? Why you?"

Ben patiently replied that he'd chosen judo because translated into English it meant "gentle way". It focused on defense, and he wanted to minimize his chances of hurting anyone.

The classes met Tuesday and Thursday evenings; they lasted a full two hours, and were taught by a man named Ruko. This instructor, or sensei as he liked to be called, had been raised in Japan, and loved the sport and its history. He taught Ben about Jigaro Kano, who initially searched for a way to solve the bullying problem in his neighborhood. Most any father would tell his son to stand up to bullies. Sensei Kano gave young men the tool, the gentle way, to deal with it. Numerous times, Ben heard Sensei Ruko say, "You must not resist the powerful opponent. This will cause your defeat. You must let him attack and cause him to be off-balance, then use his own weight and momentum against him." Yes, numerous times.

Ben enjoyed most of all the kamsetsu waza, the pressure point techniques which allowed for the domination of a larger, stronger man by a more diminutive one. Takheri was the grading system which allowed a person to move through the assigned material step-by-step, mastering one basic skill before advancing to the next. Each advancement awarded the initiate with a nicer colored belt. He imagined communication fraught with difficulty, law enforcement help sparse, isolation likely, and men making their own laws. There would be no American embassy, no Interpol, no system of any kind to keep track of travelers. It might come in handy to know a few tricks.

For the first time in recent memory, though, Ben's biggest problem turned out to be money. Not that he didn't

50

have enough. He did. But market shortages limited the supply of the currency he needed. He'd contacted collectors and numismatic societies, even a guy that claimed to be some sort of centralized worldwide pawn-broker, but Roman money from the time of Christ evaded him, except for one silver denarius from a small private museum in Seattle.

The coin remained in excellent condition, even for being so many centuries old. After some thought Ben decided to have copies made of it. If he actually got back to the first century, he figured he'd need a lot of money, although he knew that after you climbed above a fairly low threshold, things did not change that much. Little practical difference existed between good food and great food, but he could imagine a huge difference between starving and eating. A poor man's camel and a rich man's camel worked essentially the same. Both covered twenty five miles a day at the most. Clothing also had to be considered; there, appearances actually would be a factor.

But the question of how much money became a bit of a problem. A denarius provided a day's minimum wage, something like seventy-five American dollars in one coin. It bought the day's needs in food and transportation. Ben generally possessed a lot of clout financially, but not because he had the money in his pocket in silver coinage. That would be impractical. And whatever he brought had to be portable in a safe and private manner. No use inviting trouble when it finds people so easily on its own.

He planned to spend two weeks in the ancient Mideast. He wanted to beam in to Damascus, and in that context familiarize himself with customs, the society's idiosyncrasies, and the basics of the language. Hopefully by the time he'd made the trip to Jerusalem, he could find this rich guy and make some kind of sense out of the man's decision before beaming back out. If one actually could beam in or out.

So, how much money could he safely carry? He couldn't be too conspicuous. The thought occurred to him that the money problem would be smaller if he just spent the whole two weeks in Jerusalem, but he feared to start down that thought path because as a skeptic, he really wanted as little time near Jesus, if there was a Jesus, as possible.

So how much money was safe? Thirty coins? Each one would be about the size of a dime, so he settled on fifty, which would require roughly four ounces of silver, an amount that would be readily portable, yet allow for significant financial options should any need arise.

Then he commissioned a college buddy who worked in artistic metallurgy to copy the coins. This took some time, because first he had to obtain permission from the International Antiquities Society to manufacture coinage from the Roman Empire without danger of creating counterfeit currency that could later be passed off as genuine. The society finally granted permission after Ben promised to mint the coins with a 95/5 ratio of silver to antimony, a combination that retained all of silver's properties and appearance while leaving an easily traceable link to the fact that they were merely lookalikes. Fifty almost silver coins. Each coin also required a tiny stamp of Ben's initials on the reverse.

The original coin revealed slight wear on the face of the emperor. Should each coin be "doctored" to vary their appearance? They would all naturally show the same pattern of wear. In the end Ben thought that he'd be spending most of them one or two at a time, so he gave the okay to make fifty exact copies of the one available sample.

Conceivably, the fifty shiny coins might attract undue attention, so he asked his copyist (counterfeiter?) what should be done about it. "Overnight in Diet Mountain Dew should give you the reaction you need," he said, "The phosphates in the soft drink will react with the antimony in the coins, and in about eight hours they'll look as if they'd been circulated for ten years. Antique car collectors employ a similar process for some of their parts to make them look old. They call it acid etching."

52

So Ben tried it with one denarius. He bought a bottle of Diet Mountain Dew on his way home from judo practice, poured a little into a small cup and dropped one coin in it for the night. He thought as he looked at it that a miniature wishing well had sprung up in his kitchen. The idea amused him, so he said, "I wish they'd take checks."

The next morning Ben made a bee-line to pull the coin out of the phosphate bath. It looked terrific—that is to say it looked used, circulated. It looked a little bit dirty in that positive way that spendable money is a little bit dirty.

The denarii from that time period had a likeness of Tiberius Caesar on the heads side, and on the reverse was an elephant stepping on a snake. *Interesting political statement,* thought Ben. *What happens when the coins go outdated like when Caesar is bumped off by Brutus?* In any case, he knew the coins represented currency appropriate for the time, so if Doc Neven could hit the spot, what would it matter? And that "hit the spot" reference caused Ben to think about the other side of the world. Would Doc be able to strike a target both geographically and temporally? Doc would insist that he could do it, no matter what. Ben thought he'd require another demonstration, and he began to wonder what it should be.

It amazed Ben how things worked. Judo practice presented no problem—it benefited the cardiovascular system, it only measured his own progress versus himself, and it helped with concentration and discipline. So he easily passed it off to his friends as something he'd wanted to do since college, but had been too busy with Bendata to pursue it. The sudden interest in old money (literal old money) he explained as a hobby, like slot car racing in sixth grade. A more formidable challenge occurred with the study of ancient Aramaic, especially since parts of the language were unpronounceable to any westerner who had already reached puberty.

The most persistent and recurring difficulty turned out to be the beard. He'd ceased shaving for about two months, and had endured reams of surprised questions at the office.

When you are the boss, rank does have its privilege. Fortunately for Ben, his beard grew dark and thick, and seemed to add one extra layer of handsome to his mien. *Yes, brutally handsome,* thought Ben one night as he looked in the mirror.

Sherry identified and confirmed the real problem with trying to look first century. She had invited Ben to her third birthday party; she expressed no enthusiasm for all that scruffy stubble on his face. It interfered with those three-year-old kisses. (Ben also wondered if Laurie's influence was visible in some of this. He noted that Adam sported no facial hair.) She begged Ben to shave it off, and he explained that he couldn't, that he would need it. He promised that he would have his "smooth face", as she called it, by the next time he came to visit.

"So," Adam looked at him like a DA eyes the accused. "What's up with the beard? Does it help you with martial arts? Or maybe marital arts? The chicks?"

Ben knew that anything but the truth would be useless at this point. He swore Adam to secrecy, then he told him about everything from the beginning, how the Gideon New Testament had provided the trigger that got all of this started with his question about the rich young guy, with a slight hint that it all might just be Adam's fault. Adam listened with no comment and very little body language through the whole story of the classified ad, the phone call, the account of the visit to Doc Neven's, the rat, the stew, Hannah, the brief meeting after supper, even all of Gramps' suspicions, plus a rundown on the makings of his life since then. It took some time.

"So," he said again "You could flip me back and forth over your head like the Karate Kid?"

Ben smiled. "Not unless you attack me. Remember, judo is the gentle way. We only use it defensively."

"Okay, but what about time travel itself? Pretty far-fetched. You don't buy this Resser stuff, do you? I mean, you can't possibly believe that he could have found the secret of time travel, and be living in Ekalaka, Montana!"

"First of all, you're underestimating Montana. Famous for the Freemen *and* the Unabomber."

"My point exactly. Home of crackpots and weirdoes." Adam thought this should settle the argument.

"Strange things can happen anywhere." Ben scored himself one for a great comeback.

"Not *that* strange."

"Well, Adam, *you* claim that one guy long ago made all this difference by letting people nail him to a cross and that somehow in that death is my substitution, my way to God. Not only that, but *you* claim he came back from the dead. Pretty strange, I think. And on the other hand, *you* doubt time travel, which seems to me to be the more likely of the two to actually happen."

Adam bit his lip. "Well, when you put it that way, both would be a miracle—going against the laws of nature. What Jesus did was different, though. His life and death made a difference for everybody."

"Well, Okay!" Ben snapped. "And I can make a difference too. There are people like me all over this nation who doubt. I doubt. I think it's all a fraud, because if Jesus were the son of God, he could have helped the rich guy. If there was a God who *loved* this guy, why couldn't he have saved him? If I do get back there, I can find this guy and he's going to tell me what really happened. If there was a Jesus, if he was any help, if his life ever gained meaning, or more likely, that he was okay the way he was. That's what I want to find out." By this time Ben had calmed down. These last words were less belligerent, more like those of a man undertaking a dangerous mission for the good of people he would never meet, and who would never know him.

Adam stared at Ben thoughtfully. If the impossibility of an event disqualified the defense of it, he was totally disarmed. He thought as well of the difference between the stated and the actual, and could not help thinking that Ben might be following one obsession to hide another. He quietly said, "I'll pray that you find what you're looking for."

"I couldn't ask for more than that," Ben replied.

As Ben left the next morning, Sherry reminded him again in that frank manner that only children possess—"Remember, you promised. Next time, no beard!"

CHAPTER V

Ben considered that Ford Pinto stuck in the mud back in that previous decade. You hate to look stupid, but sometimes you can't help it. He must have looked very eccentric at least, to some of his 'enablers'. He had no defense for this, considering his intention. If a guy is worried about what people think, how could he expect to travel backward in time? To maneuver into position to achieve his goal Ben had to encounter a special breed of service providers.

Gloria, his seamstress, was exhibit A. She seemed dangerously humble and almost lethally honest, the sort of person who probably never lied—at least not on purpose. As a result she demonstrated a gift for expecting and receiving the truth from others.

She majored in sewing excellence, and possessed voluminous information as to the history of her craft. So when Ben explained what he wanted, she did not respond as he imagined she might. Usually, someone in her position would begin to explain that the difficulty of finding or producing cloth that could pass for first century livery would be a very, very expensive process. And that to make even one legitimate change of clothing from that period would consume immense amounts of time. And to accomplish it in a span of ten weeks would bend the framework of possibility. Usually by then an estimated

57

price would find its way into the conversation. And that monetary figure would be large.

Instead, she just said, "Why?"

That one word, that single interrogative caught Ben so totally off guard that he stood speechless for several seconds. He knew that the best explanation, as his grandmother would insist, would be the truth, but as he thought of telling her the real story, he flinched inside. He hesitated to admit that he wanted to do the impossible.

He said, "I want to look so totally first-century that no one will be able to tell I'm not the real thing." He expected her to pursue this, but she didn't. Instead, she just looked at him up and down.

"Your beard will help a little. It's pretty short, though. How do the women in your life feel about it?"

"My girlfriend hates it," Ben smiled. "She says it has to come off before I see her again."

"Where does she live?"

Ben's immediate relief over the directional change in the conversation quickly evaporated. But he smiled again and said, "Her name is Sherry and she lives in Dallas, and I can't wait to see her again."

Gloria seemed satisfied with this, and said, "How much do you know about the way people dressed back then? And are you looking for early first-century, or late?"

"Well, okay. Let's say about 30 AD. People wore sandals—I know that's not going to be part of your job, but it's common knowledge. They wore robes—probably something with two layers, like a Presbyterian minister, maybe. And there was some underwear garment. So I'll need the underwear and the robe or whatever we should call it."

"Tunic and kesmut."

"Yeah, that. And, it would have to look like material that people manufactured back then. Do they still make any of this stuff by hand over there that we could get?

Gloria smiled. "Why not fly over and buy the clothes from someone in Israel that still makes them the old way?"

58

The logic side of Ben's brain considered this. Martial arts lessons, language study, tanning booth sessions, besides having to actually spend time in the office all flashed past at lightning speed. *Good idea, but I can't do that,* he thought. "Hadn't really considered it. But I can't swing any time out of the country right now. Maybe I could send someone my size over there, and get it done that way. Would that work?"

Gloria smiled again. "It might. But you would lose personal control over the project, and individual alterations might become a problem."

Ben thought about this. "I would much prefer to have personal input over all of this. Let's just plan for you to take care of it yourself."

"In that case," said Gloria, "we need to answer one major question. Do you want to look rich in the first century?" She glanced out the window of her shop at the Bentley parked at the curb.

"Does it matter?" *It shouldn't matter,* he thought.

"It may. Back then rich people looked rich, and poor people looked poor. And they didn't mix much. Which do you want to be? If you look like a commoner, you'll fit in with the common people. If you look rich, you'll fit in a lot less places. What are you looking for?"

What am I looking for? It took Ben a couple of seconds to realize that she was only asking about the persona he was attempting to portray rather than the total scope of his proposed mission. *What am I looking for?* In that moment he decided that he would roam about Jerusalem looking rich. "I want to look like a wealthy man," he answered. *I'm trying to find a wealthy man,* he thought.

"That may be a bit easier. So then are we dealing with the time of Jesus when you say 30 AD? The ancient Mideast?"

"Yes, good, let's go for that."

"So," Gloria continued, "You will need a robe of imperial indigo, a color made, at the time, from the secretions of the murex snail, an intertidal crustacean native to the eastern Mediterranean. The color was so rare and

59

sought after that the snail snot could be worth its weight in silver. A robe that color will stand out like your Bentley."

Ben considered this with smug satisfaction. *That*, he thought, *would be perfect.*

"Let's get the fabric in the Mideast, and make your tunic and kesmut here. I'll take care of everything, but I'll need five thousand up front to get the ball rolling, and you'll be billed for the balance as the job progresses. I think we can have a lot of fun with this. Stand still while I take some measurements."

Fun, thought Ben. *Like digging potatoes is fun.* But he was thankful for the way it worked out. He didn't have to send anyone to Israel, and he retained control over the process.

As time went on he could see the very professional nature of Gloria's seamy operation. She employed grace and alacrity in every inch of her tall and slender frame. She possessed an economy of motion he had rarely seen. She had kind of a Mideastern look about her—long dark hair and olive complexion, and those dark eyes that almost never look away and don't miss much, and keep young men awake at night. She habitually did things very well, and did them only once. She fitted him with his tunic first, providing it in a color Ben dubbed "off purple".

"Just like a man not to have a name for a color. That is magenta, the perfect complement for a robe of imperial indigo. And I think your sash should be black".

Black belt already, thought Ben, *and I haven't even taken my first martial arts test yet.* "Will it have pockets or pouches or storage compartments?" Ben was a big fan of cargo pants.

"Whatever you wish, sir." Gloria gave that look that said she could make whatever he wanted for a price.

So Gloria manufactured the sash with pouches and pockets, but no Velcro seals, and sewed it by hand, as she did also the tunic and kesmut. She included the occasional imperfection engineered to look like an accident, as one would expect to find in a first-century garment. When finished, all of it would look regal, Gloria promised. It would look expensive, but not as expensive as it was. And Ben spent very little time on the tailoring process, which suited him just fine. He looked forward with great anticipation to the culmination of the tunic and kesmut project.

Area code 406 rang a far-off bell on the far edge of Ben's consciousness as he looked at his phone. An incoming call originated from there. Then he remembered Ekalaka Lake and Doc Neven. After the fourth ring he answered, fearing that Gramps' predictions would be confirmed. (Gramps had said that Resser would contact Ben soon, and would raise his price.)

It *was* Doc Resser.

"Ben," he began, "My sources tell me that you are getting ready for a trip. Does that mean that you've accepted my terms?"

Seldom did Ben become angry, but at that moment he teetered on the verge. He remembered Gramps' suspicion of some sort of bug in the car. He forced calm into his voice. "What sources are you talking about?"

"Your martial arts instructor is an old friend of mine from college days. We spent two semesters in the same dorm while we attended MIT. We still talk once in a while, and naturally your name came up as one of his new students. You probably would not need Mr. Ruko's services were you not planning your ancient Mideast tour, or at least, so I surmise. You couldn't find better man to teach you."

Plausible, thought Ben. He decided to let that pass for the moment.

"What were your terms again?" He thought maybe this could get the ball back in Doc Resser's court.

"That's why I called. There's been a drastic change in the price of Femio Bosic enriched Neutrinic gas, so my original quote is no longer applicable."

Ben sighed. Gramps had become too smart for his own good. He still referred to Doc as "Kook Resser".

"What kind of price change?"

"Concerning what we've been discussing, the price is only half at this point."

"So are you now talking about needing three mill?" Ben could speak of millions that casually.

"No—you misunderstand me. The price change has been a decrease. The government of Ukraine recently signed a treaty that obligates them to liquidate their stock of FBEN gas immediately. They've offered all we need for five hundred thousand, delivered in two weeks. (This doesn't change our timetable, but we will need to pay for the delivery within the next five days.) So those are the new terms. I can now send you back for seven hundred and fifty thousand, but we will need five hundred thousand up front so we can accept delivery of the FBEN gas."

"How do I know you'll actually get the gas and not just skip the country with my money?" Ben knew that Doc knew. No trust yet existed in this equation.

"My good man, I've already thought of that. (No need to apologize. I understand you have to be careful.) If you like, you can deal with the Ukrainians yourself. You pay. You receive the FBEN. You deliver it here as scheduled, and we send you back for the agreed upon two weeks. By the way, when you return, you will re-enter the present less than two seconds after you have left. Negligible time will have passed here, but you receive a bonus two weeks. Do you know how much some people might pay for that privilege?"

Ben felt compelled to ask, "So why don't you sell your service to the highest bidder? A lot of people would want what you claim you've got. Why not offer it on the open market?"

"Many reasons, Ben. Primarily, I must say that I *have* offered it on the open market. I placed the ad, and you answered. Anyone could have, but you did. And you were the only one. Why did I not get a million responses? But I did not.

"Perhaps more important than that is the fabric of the space-time continuum. Time, as you know, is one of the

62

measurable dimensions, and with each little tweak we stretch it just a little. Were you anxious to alter the past in any way, I could not aid you in your quest. But to observe, to inquire, that, my friend, is pure science! Beyond that, Ben, is the reason for everything. I mean, as a third point, there is the reality of divine intervention—that is, I ran the ad, you answered it. These are not random occurrences; these are the warp and woof of the tapestry of time, and of the events of our lives. The hand of God is in this, Ben. There is no escape. Did you know that God is outside of time, Ben? Jesus said "Before Abraham was, I am." (As this was in later pages of the Gideon New Testament, Ben had no knowledge of that statement. It struck him as being an impossible thing, then he remembered his conversation with Adam. *Not impossible,* he thought, *but very, very unlikely.*)

"So God need not obey time's constraints. How often have you heard of the constraints of time, Ben? Yet we have here an opportunity to bypass 'normal'" (Ben could almost see the air quotes, but did not at this point wish he were on Skype.) "to totally bypass it and find out that we can go when we want, and be then. Not the kind of thing you often hear. I am looking forward to, yes, preparing for your trip. And I called to forewarn you—or perhaps remind you—that there can be no positive result from an attempt to change the past. To return to 1939 and assassinate Hitler would not be constructive—perhaps neither effective nor possible. To go to 1941 and attempt to warn the navy of the Pearl Harbor attack could have no measureable worthwhile consequence. To try to stop the Islamic fanatics who did so much harm to our United States on 9/11 would be totally useless. To change any of this would defy possibility.

"Beyond that, you may try to justify a camera, a watch, a recording device of some description to add credential to your journey upon your return. This is not a vacation, Ben. To attempt to transfer actual recordings of anything across time would, I believe, cause serious damage to the fabric. You must endeavor to become an observer only, a seeker after truth. And you must be content with the subjective nature of the results of your research.

"Without your solemn promise that such is your intent, I can, as a student of history, go no further with you in this venture. If I believe that you are out to somehow change the course of history, or alter the past in any way, I will withdraw my offer. Is this acceptable to you?"

Ben had always thought conversation required at least a two-sided arrangement. It had been quite some time since anyone needed his half for input, so it took him a couple of seconds to realize that the ball had returned to his court.

"Yes, Doc, it is," he finally answered.

Doc's apparent frankness and the price decrease presented major problems to his brain. Of course, he could afford it either way—it was just pocket change, and he would have paid the higher price. This would probably have no impact on Gramps' suspicions, though.

"And to reassure you," Ben continued, "I don't want to change anything. I just want to acquire knowledge—as you say, to observe, to discover. So I think I can accept your present terms, but how do I get in touch with these Ukrainians? And how do I store all this gas?" The moment of decision drifted by him unnoticed, but he had passed the point of no return.

"Both problems contain simple solutions. First, call the Ukrainian embassy tomorrow and explain your interest in acquiring the FBEN gas. I will text you their phone number. They will take care of everything from there, but they will also require payment upon delivery of the product. And the amount of gas you require will fit in four twenty pound cylinders. Just keep it in your closet until we need it. But be sure to keep your apartment secured, as F-BEN is very valuable, and there may be some people who know you've got it. Got it?"

"Yes, sir," said Ben, with just a small amount of regret.

"I'll be in touch," Doc promised. He terminated the call.

CHAPTER VI

Ben's final scheduled visit to Gloria's "studio", should have been for fitting purposes only. But Ben had developed some concern about spending two weeks in the ancient Mideast with no wardrobe options—that is, with no alternative but to appear to be wealthy in all social contexts. He knew that though the Emperor in Rome ruled the Mideast, the lack of local law enforcement and the existence of renegade "authorities" could create problems for an obviously wealthy man. People coveted even when they knew they shouldn't.

This train of thought had led him to hope that maybe a second kesmut could be ordered, along with something akin to a day pack—perhaps a goatherd's bag, or something similar, which he hoped could be made large enough to accommodate the change of clothing. He still had his concerns about water supply, but comforted himself with the thought that everyone around him would also be focused on the same problem.

So he now planned to travel incognito, to fly under the radar until he reached Jerusalem, then to assume the stance of wealth and find the young man in question. He thought this would not be difficult, as the city of Jerusalem covered only about one square mile; the nicer part of town being made up of much larger dwellings spread over a very limited area. He could go door to door, he thought, like a

Jehovah's Witness. Or maybe more like that guy with the British accent on "Lifestyles of the Rich and Famous".

He therefore would need a disguise. No, not a disguise. Just more casual dress for that first five days—for the camel trip.

"I just want to be able to try both looks," Ben explained. He knew that Gloria didn't totally buy his story; he could see the unasked question in her eyes. But she did not pursue it. Instead, after receiving the full version of his expanded necessity, she spoke as one who desired not to be sidetracked in any way.

"First things first," she said. "You've got to try these on!"

The tunic, built of supple, thin reddish cloth (magenta, Ben reminded himself) looked almost rectangular in shape. Ben thought it resembled a large gunny sack with a hole for his head and two larger ones for sleeves. It slipped on easily, and he delighted in the freedom of movement he experienced once he had the right appendages in the right openings. Gloria tied a small cord that cinched up just below his naval, and stepped back to check her work, as a carpenter assures himself that the corner is square. Once Ben looked "squared up" and had grown accustomed to this new type of underwear, Gloria said, "Now for the *piece de resistance.*"

She opened a box the size of an orange crate and pulled out the most beautiful purple robe Ben had ever seen. He reminded himself that he didn't get out much, but still, he knew he beheld impressive outerwear.

Gloria unveiled a slightly larger version of the undergarment, with commensurately larger openings for the arms and head. His tunic remained visible at the lower arms, chest, and ankles, and created a stunning two-tone effect. He thought he must be looking as regal as she had promised he would.

He had to admit that Gloria had done a nice job. It was then that he noticed another small package in her hand. "You'll need this to avoid heat stroke," she said as she fitted what looked like headgear for the Shah of Iran around his cranium. A band of dark brown braided cloth circled the top, though the accessory itself had the appearance of a white hotel towel.

This is too much, he thought. He decided, after a second or two, that it might be just enough. He stared at himself in the mirror, contemplating how amply dressed he would be for a different century on a different continent. *It might pass*, he mused. To his embarrassment he realized that Gloria had been speaking to him, and he had been totally preoccupied.

"I'm sorry," Ben repented. "I missed what you just said."

Gloria seemed thrilled about it. "I'm glad you did. How you look at yourself in the mirror shows both of us I've done a good job. I asked about your shoe size."

"Metric or American? Nine and a half American, high forties metric.

"Good, that's what I had guessed. So I took the liberty of adding this to your order."

She held up a pair of sandals—not like his Chacos or Gramps' Birkenstocks. She handed him simple slabs of leather with two thin leather straps strung together at the big toe and separating around his instep, connecting back to the sole just below the ankle. A separate strap stretched from side to side around the Achilles area to secure them. They were obviously new, and they fit very well, but Ben knew he'd need to wear them some before the trip. *Maybe to Aramaic class,* Ben thought.

"Gloria, you've been great. But I really will need a brown robe and tunic in these same dimensions quite soon. And some sort of a day pack. Would you be able to squeeze those things in? Can we rush them through posthaste?" (Gramps always used "posthaste" when something had to be done quickly.)

"Possibly," she said thoughtfully. "I'm not quite done with the indigo one yet. I need to add a couple of pieces of trim. The ancient version backpack you mentioned should be no problem. That's just a leather bag with a strap and a flap. I think it all can be done. Can you give me two weeks?"

"Should work just right," Ben enthused. "Thanks a bunch. I'll await your update with great anticipation." He made a mental note that Gloria deserved a generous tip at final payment.

In his apartment later that evening he sat down to make a list of the things he worried about. His biggest concern related to communication. He figured pronunciation and other aspects of the dialect would change with the passage of almost two thousand years. His linguistics instructor had reassured him that Aramaic had been stagnant for at least fifteen hundred years, and that there really shouldn't be a problem, though he wondered why Ben wanted to communicate with camel drivers who'd been dead for almost two millennia. Ben feared that he'd be unable to communicate with people of any description.

He also fretted about climate extremes. The American upper Midwest differed drastically from the desert of the Mideast. He knew hydration could be crucial, but he took comfort in the fact that the basic needs of the human body had not changed. Everyone else would need water as well, and he theorized that it would be essential to stick with people and go with the flow, so to speak.

Fitting in as a citizen haunted his thoughts, too. What if some mannerism, gesture or subconscious habit turned out to be an insult demanding his death in that ancient culture? What if you coughed without covering your mouth? What if someone sneezed? Should you say Gesundheit? He made a mental note to bone up on Aramaic apologies.

He knew it might be something like the old west—camels instead of horses, but still with an ultimate lack of modern convenience and the propensity for men to live by their own rules.

And then (supposing Doc Neven's legitimacy) what if he were killed back then? What could Doc do about that? Go back in time and convince him not to go? Would he listen? Since that hadn't happened, he had to assume that he had gotten back all right sometime in the near future, or, perhaps even more likely, Doc's legitimacy was on the level with Brian Williams.

And how did you pick the right when? What if he were a month early or late? And how would he know for sure when he'd found the right man? And would he have the right words?

Could he fit in socially? Could there be faux pas that waited for him like mine fields that would detonate in ways that would destroy his mission?

Would he be able to defend himself at need?

What would happen here during his absence? Doc said it would only be seconds. Could he be wrong? What if it took the whole two weeks? Would anybody miss him? He hoped not, because how do you look for someone who's lost in the past? There would be no "where" in which to look.

In respect to all of those haunting questions, Gramps had the best one. "How do you know you're going anywhere to begin with?"

So Ben decided to call Doc Resser and ask him.

The conversation with Doc went well, Ben thought. Doc, with his usual ebullient, positive outlook, set Ben's mind at ease on each point of concern.

He assured Ben of Aramaic's relative sterility, and if Ben worried about communication, he should review his high school Latin as well. (*One more thing to do,* Ben sighed.) He went on to say that probably millions of people had survived the dangers of that culture, and that Ben only had to remain shy and take care. He assured Ben that no time would pass here in the present during his trip—that he would "return" instantly after "leaving", both terms being inadequate to describe what actually would happen, the *doctor* said. The question of physical harm had also already been covered, Doc reminded him. His body, or its remains, would return in whatever state they existed at the end of the two weeks. Any injuries, cuts, or bruises would follow their normal course of healing "before" and "after", both terms being inadequate, the *doctor* said.

Doc became evasive concerning the placement question. As he explained it, the trip would operate like a timed-release medicine. He could pinpoint the two weeks precisely, and could provide geographic accuracy to about a quarter of a mile. (Four hundred meters, the *doctor* said.) They merely had to choose a circle with that radius in a safe place—open country in a deserted area near the location of ancient Damascus.

Ben persisted in asking how this had been tested, and Doc's reply proved too technical for Ben to follow. But Doc assured him that he'd sent a dead pigeon to a small ranch in Texas, where people could use web cams to hunt. So live footage of a dead pigeon landing in view of the camera had been posted on the web, and he gave Ben a link to the site. He assured his young charge that the physical problems would be surmountable, and encouraged Ben to avoid barber shops and to be sure to wear his sandals to the tanning booth. At the end of the conversation he did bring up the topic of money, and asked Ben to bring two hundred fifty thousand dollars in cash, plus the FBEN gas when he reported for his trip.

So. I need 250k in cash. In hundreds? Probably. Not my usual method, but so what? Nothing about this is my usual method. He checked his closet to make sure the canisters were okay.

They were okay.

He wondered if he were really ready. He then regretted having to leave the imperial indigo robe with Gloria. It would have been sort of fun to try it on and see how it felt to wear it for a while. He took out the coins and looked at them, carefully counting them again. He thought of two weeks in the ancient Mideast. Could his body survive it? Could he adapt? Could he communicate?

Could he find his answer?

That would be the hard part, even if *where* and *when* could be worked out. Ben retained nearly unlimited wealth at his disposal. His financial advisor already had his trust fund set up. He had arrived. In a way he dealt with the same affluence guilt that some lottery winners have. He knew he deserved a reward for his work, but to personally earn twenty-eight dollars per iPhone and thirty-five dollars per Dell tablet—let's just say it added up quickly. His parents expressed pride in his achievement. (That omnipresent parental pressure toward marriage sometimes crept in, but he sensed that his failure to make progress so far in that area didn't amount to any demerit. He still had *time*.) All of his employees liked him, and he could not remember insulting anyone on purpose, except maybe Adam. But then, roommates are not real people.

But why would this rich guy in the Bible feel the need to ask the question? He said he'd been good. Kind of like myself, thought Ben. *So why did the guy think he lacked anything?*

Then Ben remembered his observation that life might have a missing link. *Is that what this rich guy wanted?*

Did he do it? Sell all his property and give the money away, and go and follow Jesus?

Was there a Jesus I should choose to follow?

He decided to think about it later. He went to bed.

71

CHAPTER VII

Ben rose earlier than usual the next morning because he
wanted to spend more time on strategies of communication.
The basics of Aramaic defied firm grasp, and he did not
want to rely on the fact that the economic world catered so
shamefully to rich people. On the contrary, it seemed that
the present world in some ways hated wealth, or the
wealthy, or both. He had difficulty in coming to terms with
the fact that wealth triggered anyone's displeasure. National
news and political rhetoric taught him otherwise.

So he began to concentrate on the actual sentences his
brain waited to hear.

"Good master, what must I do to inherit eternal life?"
And the second, "All these things have I kept from my
youth. What do I yet lack?" For Ben, this would be a radical
departure from the standard Pimsleur method, the process
of recognizing vocabulary and absorbing syntax and verb
tense from normal conversation. He thought of
communication as the hill upon which he could physically
die if he ever got back to the first century. And the thought
amused him, because he remembered his skepticism about
Christ, Adam's skepticism about time travel, and Gramps'
doubts about Doc Resser.

Ancient Aramaic had captivated his interest—his
instructor had warned him to focus on the spoken word, but
the written language possessed such a pictorial character. It

fell into a crack between Hieroglyphics and Latin, as some letters appeared as symbols, and some symbols more like pictures. He pursued it for the pure pleasure of it, but without drastic changes in his circumstances, it had no practical use.

He persisted in all of it. Study of the culture, economics, social habits, climate, people. He thought he might tire of it, but he did not. The judo lessons, the language study, the occasional trips to the library, the tanning booth, all of it took on the flavor of preparing for an extended vacation, though Doc had insisted, "This is not a vacation!" And Gramps insisted, "You're not going anywhere."

And then his doubts would assail him as before. *Can Doc Neven actually do it? Has he done it? Is Gramps right to doubt? Is there anything valuable in those canisters in the closet?* But it didn't matter in the end, because Ben knew that he had to be ready in case it did work. All of it added up to innocent fun (very *expensive* fun) if Doc were a charlatan, but considering the small chance that his system worked, Ben's life depended on being able to survive two weeks in a foreign culture. But the odds seemed much greater that Doc could not deliver. Even so, no real harm done.

Eventually Ben did run out of time. His skin accepted an ever deeper tan. He wore the sandals enough to acceptably break them in, though they still looked new. During the final bittersweet trip to Gloria's he realized that he had always looked forward to the next visit. She had provided the capstone to a wonderful job. The 'shepherd's bag' (as she referred to it) provided just enough space for the storage of his "rich man" robe, tunic and belt, with a bit of room left over for other essentials. The brown kesmut made him look much more ordinary, or so he thought. As he was packing his wardrobe into his leather bag, Gloria interrupted him with one last item. "I had some material left over, so I made this for you." She held up a square of purple cloth about sixteen inches on a side. "You never know. It may come in handy. And you should have no trouble looking like a first-century goatherd. Or a rich man!"

She gave him a hug and wished him success in his quest. He chose that moment to pass her the extra five hundred he'd decided on for a tip. She nearly broke down in tears, explaining that her niece needed a laptop computer for school, and her birthday fell in the following week.

"Get her a Dell with me in it." Ben joked. Gloria insisted on a bonus hug, and then he took his leave.

He had been in touch with Doc, and had arranged a launch date for the following Sunday evening, which left him four days for final preparation before his long road trip. He had to drive to Ekalaka because of the FBEN gas, which Doc insisted that he not ship commercially under any circumstances. Since the trunk of his Bentley had not been designed for freight, it would not accommodate the cylinders, so he rented a Chevy Tahoe and loaded the tanks of FBEN into the back, along with his shepherd's bag and his usual traveling necessities. Last, but not least, he loaded the satchel with the twenty-five hundred C notes. He had provided an extreme amount of identification on account of that large cash withdrawal, the final payment on his ticket to the past. With all preparations completed, and final reviews made of the essentials, he had just about enough time to make the drive.

So he left home and spent a few hours on the road that ante-penultimate Friday, stopping for the night at the Hilton in Eau Claire.

Since it didn't seem that late, and with the advantage of the time difference, he took a chance that Sherry would still be up.

She was.

They had talked for only a few minutes when Sherry asked him about the beard, and he had to admit that he still needed it for a few more days. He wanted, for a couple of seconds, to shave it off, and fly to Dallas. *How can anyone so small be such a big part of my life?* He thought. *How helpless would I be if she were my own daughter?*

Then she asked about the reason for the beard. "Why do you need that thing anyway? It's ugly and scratchy."

"Yes it is, but I need it for a sort of costume party. I need to look sort of like a hillbilly, or like someone from the past. Like the man that helped us when we took our camel ride at the zoo."

"Well. Okay. But I hope the party gets over soon, so you can come and see us."

Ben smiled. *Yes, my dear*, he thought. *The party will soon be over.* Then he said, "Good night, sweet princess. And may a thousand angles fly thee to thy rest. Can I talk to your Dad?"

Adam came on the line and the conversation turned philosophical. Ben admitted that he traveled en route to Ekalaka Lake, and that Doc Neven planned to send him to the past that upcoming Sunday night.

"OK, Ben," Adam said. "How about this—what if it works, and you really go back, and you see Jesus in person? I doubt that Doc can actually deliver, but supposing it really works, would you admit that we're right and that you need to follow Jesus?"

"My focus here isn't Jesus. It's to find that rich guy." Ben answered. "But if there really is a Jesus, all that it would prove, assuming all this works, is that he lived. It wouldn't prove he was 'God in the flesh', or that he really came back from the dead. He could still just be that good teacher for all I know. If all this works."

"Yeah, that's what Jesus said too. He said basically that no amount of intellectual proof would be sufficient to persuade an unbelieving heart."

"Look," Ben said, defensively, "I'll give him a fair shot. If he can show me he's Him, or however you'd say that, I'll give him full consideration."

"A fair shot. That's all anyone should expect. I wish you all the best, my friend. But now I have to go and read a story to my daughter."

"Good night, Adam." *He is such a lucky guy*, Ben thought.

76

A day of driving passed with Ben listening to recordings of vocabulary reviews, and nightfall Saturday found him in Bismarck, North Dakota. He did not sleep well that night, and woke early. He took advantage of the motel's continental breakfast, and then continued westward to Wibaux, and took 7 down through Baker to Ekalaka. It bothered him somewhat that his navigation system seemed unable to recognize Eva Ave as a viable destination. But at least Ekalaka found a spot on the map.

He stopped in at the Wagon Wheel for coffee and a donut, where the waitress remembered him as one who had been looking for Doc Resser several months before. The addition of the beard did not derail her memory. Ben remembered her as the one who'd told him where to look for the doctor. She had not expected to see him again, this time in a ride more fitting to the terrain, though with out-of-state plates.

She volunteered information, as waitresses are wont to do. Others had been by lately looking for Doc Resser and some of them looked pretty official, like law enforcement undercover, or like FBI, or like Men in Black looking for space aliens. Some of their vehicles had government-issued plates. Ben discovered all of this without prompting the witness, which, he hoped, marked the gifted investigator. *The secret of finding things out,* he thought, *is in knowing who not to ask.*

The waitress in question suspected that Doc possessed earth citizenship; he liked Montana beef more than extraterrestrials probably would. She asked Ben to say hi to Hannah for her, and Ben promised to do so. He executed the long process of driving north to county road 4, then turned left on Beaver Flats. The farmhouse stood there, on the hill up past the cattle guard. They were all still there too—Doc, Hannah, and Otto.

They had prepared for his arrival, and Doc moved quickly to unload the precious cargo. He explained that ambient temperature must be considered crucial, and that he must begin the acclimatization process immediately. He

77

claimed that failure to match density and viscosity with extreme accuracy could cause a problem. Ben wanted no problems, so he dutifully joined in transporting the canisters to the time shed. He then offered assistance, handing Doc tools and helping position tanks and connecting manifolds.

The final step consisted of purging the impurities, which in this case included atmospheric gases, and securing the lines to the cylinder that originally transported Bob, one of the star rats. The opening to the cylinder had been enlarged to accomplish ease of entry for larger specimens. "Or," as Doc explained, "to more easily accommodate a human subject." They then charged all lines fully with the FBEN gas. The four canisters were deployed on a stainless steel platform, which formed part of a digital scale reading out in milligrams. Doc explained that the accuracy of the temporal fixation adjustment would depend entirely on the accuracy of the scale. "Don't worry about atmospheric dust," Doc reassured him. "One or two particles will only make a difference of seconds. We'll keep air currents to a minimum here as we prepare for your departure."

As Doc finished, Hannah popped into the shed. "Hey, if you guys can take a break from adjusting temporal fixations, supper's about ready. Can you make it into the kitchen At This Time?" She had that rare ability to capitalize letters with her voice.

Doc Neven smiled, and said, "My dear, time is no object."

The Ressers both laughed at this, and after a second or two Ben found that he could join with them. It seemed that the time shed could get along on its own for a bit, so the three of them made their way to the farmhouse and into the kitchen, which smelled something like heaven ought to smell, Ben mused.

"I hope you'll try my bread, Ben," Hannah said. "Neven bought me a wheat grinder since you were here last. Now I can buy bags of wheat, grind it up, knead it—by machine, of course. Neven's claim that time is no object doesn't hold true in the kitchen—bake it and serve it up on a ceramic platter. It's great stuff, and it tastes like its real good for a body. And we've got sweet corn from our garden and potatoes from the root cellar. The fatted steer has provided us with the makings for Swiss steak. The tomatoes are out of the greenhouse."

Ben murmured his appreciation on the basis of the report his olfactory sensors sent to his brain, and sat down to a farmhouse meal that he thought might prepare him for any demand the near future (or the distant past) might hold. He thought it strange that his future could possibly involve the past, though he still allowed for a lot of doubt. He could see also a linguistic challenge developing, even in English. How do you speak of what you *will do* in the past? He decided to treat that line of thought as he did the tax code. It's best not to think about it. He remembered to greet Hannah on behalf of the waitress back in Ekalaka.

After the meal, Hannah insisted on handling the cleanup herself, and in her gentle, persuasive way, drove the men into the living room.

"We need to talk now about your upcoming Temporal Fixation Adjustment." Doc's manner exuded even more than the usual amount of seriousness. Someone must have flipped the 'gravitas' switch inside Doc's head, and it would probably be a bad time to crack a joke.

"First," Doc began, "We need to make the crucial choice of 'when' to send you. Considering your primary goal, I researched the exact latitude of Damascus, which for the purposes of this discussion may be considered to be eleven degrees, thirty-three minutes, eleven seconds south of this point. The longitude can easily be recovered by taking advantage of the earth's rotation, which is accomplished in adjustments to the amount of FBEN gas used.

"The specific target date is crucial to you, as you want to meet a fellow traveler in a distant century in a distant city in relation to a distant man whose existence you quite possibly doubt. With all I've been able to find out, your most likely target date would be March 11, AD 30. I say

79

CREIGHTON / THAT OTHER TIME ZONE

this because you are dealing with the final year of Christ's ministry, quite likely the final month, which occurred in the spring of that year. We believe this is true due to modern research that marks Christ's birth at most likely the year 4 BC. Sissies who have given in to the spirit of the age would refer to this as 4 BCE, but history is what it is, whether a person agrees with it or not. Where was I? Oh, yes. The birth of Christ. 4 BC. This four-year discrepancy has manifested itself due to the fact that early calculations of the date of his birth were made using incomplete information.

"Contrary to the conclusions of many who have studied this, I firmly believe that his ministry in Israel, beginning from the miracle of turning water into wine, his first public expression of power, to the time of the crucifixion, totaled nearly four years. You may check with some other authority if you like. I won't be offended. As nearly as I'm able to determine, the date of 03/11/30 is our most likely successful target. This will install your present body"—here Doc paused and smiled at the thought—"into ancient Syria, outside the eastern gate of Damascus, near the Silk Road, and we will execute your departure at approximately 11 pm, anticipating your arrival outside Damascus at almost precisely 8 am, though that precision is of no consequence, since in most cases minutes are meaningless to those people. They did not even divide hours in half at that juncture of history. For your purposes, though, you must think in terms of minutes.

"You will have *exactly* two weeks for your mission. That is the limit we are able to accomplish with the available Femio-Bosic enriched Neutrinic gas you so effectively acquired from the Ukrainians. At the end of the two weeks, or three hundred thirty-six hours, your involvement in that sphere of time will terminate, and you will return here, so to speak. We refer to time as having measurable dimensions, and we are certain that it is indeed measurable, as matter is, but measured of course differently than matter is measured. Before you ask me how its measurements are taken, let me tell you. We measure time's dimensions with a chronometric caliper, a complex but necessary tool, the workings of which even you cannot trouble yourself with at this point.

"In practical terms, your departure from now, if it can be called a departure, will precede your arrival here, again, if it can be called an arrival, by what I believe most certainly can be called nanoseconds. Have you heard the rancher's expression, 'If we don't leave pretty soon, we'll meet ourselves coming back'? A nonsensical way of saying that we'd best get going or the going is not likely ever to happen. Yet you, Benjamin Parker, will be the first human to accomplish it in truth. You will come as close as humanly possible, I believe, to meeting yourself coming back. It will be a near miss.

"And you will return no matter what. Healthy, injured, dead. Whether you are willing or not, whether anyone in that era attempts to prevent you, there is no escape from your timely return. The Femio-Bosic enriched Neutrinic gas creates the temporal equivalent of a time vacuum, an empty place in the fabric of the space-time continuum. My methods and research have rewarded me with the ability to create the temporal vacuum at any point in known history, being limited at present only by the availability of certain materials.

"We are able to send a subject whenever we want to send him, in the very literal sense of when. As you have surmised, at this moment we are able to sustain the transmission for limited increments, but even to accomplish this must certainly be called a miracle of science."

Doc stopped, inhaled deeply, and fixed his gaze on Ben for a few seconds before continuing. "Young man, we stand on the cusp of what many call making history. But making history is exactly what we must not do under any circumstance, nor must we heed the siren call to *desire* to make history. We must not interfere, must not attempt to redirect, must not attempt to correct what we perceive to be past injustices.

"It may also be that nothing is alterable anyway, and that, my boy, may be part of our research. Are past events malleable or inflexible? We think of ourselves as potential heroes sometimes, assuming that 'if only we had been there' we could have stopped the Titanic from sinking. We could have stayed the hand of Lincoln's assassin, or brought Jack the Ripper to judgment in time's proper course. There are some, my young friend, who may theorize that the crucifixion of Christ represented a miscarriage of justice. We all know he did not deserve it. Yet as I look at these events, I perceive that they are truly unstoppable, that the story as written cannot be altered.

"Still," he went on, more quietly, even more gravely, "you *must not* attempt it. I trust you as a gentleman, as we used to have gentlemen in this country. Will you now give me your solemn promise that you will not attempt to change the past, but will pass your three hundred thirty six hours merely as an observer, no matter how terrible any situation may look to you?"

"I have thought about this," Ben eventually answered. "There is nothing I want to change. The story as written, as you say, is fine with me. I merely seek knowledge—answers for myself. But may I protect myself? May I speak my mind, as I am able? May I live for the two weeks as anyone would?"

"Yes, yes, and no. You may protect yourself, you may speak your mind, but only insofar as you may accomplish that communication using words that represent the time in which you then exist. You must speak like anyone else who lived in that century, not as a visitor from this one. If you have no available word for what you want to say, you must leave it unsaid. We both agree that you have questions about the past. We agree that you want answers, and that you will attempt to uncover them. Feel free to do so.

"But as far as living as anyone would, you must not. You are there to observe, not to participate. You must live the entire two weeks as an observer would. You must take with you nothing that smacks of modern convenience, weaponry, or technology. No watch, no camera, no recording device, not even matches. Nothing must be taken which could accelerate the progress of the rise of modern technology. And you must leave nothing behind. I make the exception here of period-correct currency, although it may be that all such things as you take with you will return when you are drawn back to the present moment. But if not, I find no harm in introducing a few counterfeit denarii into Rome's treasury. The devaluation should be miniscule.

"I must tell you, Ben, I am excited, and you should be as well. Think of Columbus or the Wright brothers, of John Glen or Neal Armstrong. You are like them all—the first to take that small step, that giant leap. And we will take that leap together this very night."

Ben was swept away by what Alan Greenspan might have called "irrational exuberance." Doc transported him (in his own mind, at least) back in time to his junior year in high school, when his school's basketball team had won the state championship. The welcome home rally for the team had been a lesson in psychology. All that enthusiasm had been contagious, and everyone there had caught it. He now had caught Doc's enthusiasm, and for the moment it carried him along. To be an explorer, a trailblazer, an adventurer. To boldly go where no man had gone before. To break through the barrier of time and to stand triumphantly on the other side.

To obtain the answer to his question.

"I'll need to see your entire repertoire of equipment and supplies. Please reconnoiter with me in the time shed," Doc said. Ben immediately stood to go to the Tahoe, where he retrieved his shepherd's bag, his travel robe, his sandals, as well as the satchel containing Doc's final installment. *Not much weight for a quarter million*, he thought. He resisted the urge to calculate in his head what an equivalent value in denarii would scale. He returned resolutely to the time shed with what should qualify, he mused, as a full load. *I'm heavy laden,* he thought, then wondered why those particular words seemed so familiar to him. As he entered the shed, Doc spread a clean drop cloth on a long table.

Ben carefully arranged the clothes he'd brought to wear "on the plane". Or maybe it was "on the plain". He found it difficult to concentrate on the trip and berated himself for not having more mental discipline, especially now. Then he abandoned the thought of now, because it had no meaning if Doc could actually pull it off.

Meanwhile, Doc had separated everything—both robes, the extra square of cloth that resembled a modern day handkerchief of unusual size, the headgear, the black sash, the sandals, the tunics, and last of all, the coins. These Doc held in his hand carefully and thoughtfully. "They look authentic," he said, "but I know they are not because they all seem to have the same wear pattern. Obviously copied from a single parent coin." Then he smiled. "You'll be all right as long as you don't spend it all in one place."

Ben laughed. Gramps immortalized that favorite bit if wisdom. And at that moment, as if on cue, his cell phone chirped with a text message from Gramps. Ben set the phone down on the end of table and decided to check the message later. Either way, whether Doc succeeded or not, it shouldn't be long.

Doc left the coins and began carefully studying the imperial indigo kesmut. He lingered over the pocket sewn discretely into the left pectoral area, where the so-called handkerchief would store. He spent so much time looking intently at each seam that Ben began to feel uncomfortable. Had Gloria cheated and used a machine?

Finally Doc spoke as he began drawing the seams of the more pedestrian brown kesmut slowly through his fingers. "I am attempting to convince myself to my own satisfaction that your seamstress (I assume you did not make these yourself) did not avail herself of a sewing machine. Any observant person from that era would easily recognize stitchery that contained absolutely no human imperfection. Assuming you did not do this, I would also assume that it was done by a woman, not a man. Such work requires abilities which the vast majority of men do not possess. She is excellent at what she does, and it appears to have been done totally by hand, with superb historical accuracy. You should be very comfortable in these garments for the duration of your stay. Now I must ask you, on your honor, whether you have concealed anywhere about you any scintilla of modern convenience—mechanical or otherwise. You did not smuggle any such thing as toilet paper into your belongings, did you? I am prepared to act with scrutiny and intensity *beyond* what is possessed by the TSA if I feel the need."

Ben mentally kicked himself for not thinking of toilet paper, but then he laughed. "No, Doc. I possess no contraband. I merely want to have a look around, as we've already agreed would be appropriate. I just want to talk to one guy."

"My lad," Doc said in a paternal tone, "I am convinced of your utmost sincerity. I trust you to the extent that no further intrusion into your privacy will be necessary. Herein I part company with the TSA. They trust no one. Least of all octogenarian women in wheelchairs.

"However, I feel compelled to remind you that observation must be your only goal, and that contact with people of that century, I mean physical contact, must be minimized, even micro minimized. When you pay for goods or services, drop the coins into the seller's possession without hand touching hand. Do not loan out your clothing. Certainly do not give it away. Be careful in your speech not to make reference to your own time as different from theirs. Do everything you can do to remain as anonymous as possible. Above all, do not become romantically entangled in that era. If it can be done, you must return leaving no trace—physical, verbal, or ideological, of your having been there. It is a difficult stretch in the fabric of time to place you then, and any departure from my injunction is likely to cause even more stress. The continuum has immense compression strength, but very limited tensile strength. At this point, I say again that I trust you, and I trust your

85

judgment. I am willing to take the necessary risks for your temporal adjustment, and in exchange I will require a complete debriefing on your return, assuming you are physically capable of it. And I tell you again that you must be content with the subjective nature of your research. Agreed?"

"Agreed."

Ben then remarked, "By the way, I looked at Damascus on Google Maps, and I wonder if we could discuss the practical aspects of geography."

Doc carefully checked his watch. Then he walked to a nearby computer console and brought up Google Maps. The screen revealed a marker on Damascus, and in seconds they were staring at the east end of the city on a page that displayed an overlay of the estimated perimeter of the wall, AD 30.

"We can be accurate, as you know, to within 400 meters of any temporal target we choose. Since the city has grown, we will want to place you in the modern-day suburbs, probably right about here." He indicated the spot with the cursor.

"It looks like open country, and the road will be near you on the south, with the city lying to the southwest, readily visible from anywhere within the four hundred meter radius of this point. Our target launch time will be 11 pm. More precisely, since we are dealing with time, and since each second does count on the present side of the ledger, our target launch will be 11:00:11. These seconds, of course, are of no consequence to you any more than an arrival schedule is relevant to a passenger on Amtrak. He arrives when he arrives, and so will you. In layman's terms, you will arrive outside Damascus at what you now think of as approximately 8 am, but you must learn to think of that time as the second hour of the day, for such is the local custom.

"You will work your way southward to the Silk Road, and once you strike it you will naturally turn to the west, toward the Gate of the Sun, in ancient Damascus. Because of your reorientation to new surroundings and the possibility of so-called "temporal hangover", or you could call it "time lag", you may find that your mind will be a bit less responsive than it is at this moment. This situation, which you might experience as grogginess, will also slightly impede your thinking and reasoning abilities. Attempt to limit conversation and interaction during this period, as it may be misunderstood by the local populace for overindulgence in the fruit of the vine. Because you will be adapting to new surroundings, and because of the effects of time transfer on the human body, it could well be 9 am or after when you reach the city gate. And because it is incumbent upon us to prepare you as well as possible for your journey, Hannah will be here momentarily with some refreshments. It is my desire that you arrive there neither hungry nor thirsty. And now, as you have probably heard from your parents many times, it is prudent to 'go before you get in the car'."

Ben looked at the cylinder and nodded. He remembered Gramps being able to just step outside, so he headed for the door. The sapphire brilliance of starlight perforated the late evening sky, giving the appearance of tiny pinholes in a purple velvet curtain. Ben wondered if it might someday be practical to relive the beauty of such a night, but found himself discarding the idea, hoping instead that people would learn to value such moments when they were present in them.

Upon re-entering the time shed, he saw that Doc had opened the door to the temporal adjustment cylinder to check something inside. Doc looked around, and when he saw Ben he said, "It seems as if everything is in place. You should probably secure all your belongings and change into your traveling clothes. When you are fully outfitted, we must have an accurate readout of your present total weight, including baggage."

Ben nodded mutely. He opened the shepherd's bag and carefully placed the black sash in the bottom, then the robe of imperial indigo, and last the magenta kesmut. Then he ducked behind a dividing wall in case Hannah should choose that instant to pop in with the predicted refreshments, and stripped quickly out of his modern-day garb and donned his brown tunic and robe. He topped it off with the headgear. He then laid his twenty-first century clothing in meticulous order on Doc's covered table. As he fastened the straps of his sandals, Hannah appeared, announcing "Refreshments for the time-weary travelers."

"We're not time-weary yet. We haven't even left." Doc's face lit up with a broad smile of anticipation. "Nonetheless, this repast will be a blessing to our man-about-time."

Ben snorted with laughter, and joined Doc and Hannah for some of that special bread and homemade raspberry jelly, along with something that looked like chicken nuggets from McDonald's. He tried one, and it also tasted like a chicken nugget.

Many women have mind-reading capability when it comes to their cooking, and Hannah shared that clairvoyance. "They're from Schwann's," Hannah explained. "They're just like chicken nuggets from McDonald's. They're easy to prepare and they taste okay, and hopefully they'll get you through to lunch two thousand years ago. And that's a long time between meals. You may set a record, Ben. Nearly two thousand years between breakfast and lunch, and you're going to do it backwards!" Hannah laughed.

Ben wasn't so sure he liked this levity concerning his journey, so he kept silent, finished his toast and nuggets, and took a moment to do a final wardrobe check. Headgear in place, belt in place, sandals in place. When he looked up from his own visual surveillance, he saw Hannah eying him thoughtfully, making her appraisal. "Ben, you look perfect. Just like Charlton Hesston in the Ten Commandments!" *Approval is written all over her face,* Ben thought. He appreciated the comment, and received it in grateful silence. With a questioning glance at Doc, he shouldered his shepherd's bag and stepped onto the scale which supported the four cylinders of FBEN. Doc looked at the readout, made a note on his clipboard, and turned to face Ben.

"Now, my lad," Doc said, "you must place yourself carefully into the temporal adjustment cylinder. Hannah will secure you in place for your trip. Your hour has come."

My hour has come. For some reason this phrase bounced around in his mind like a racket-ball, but he had no opportunity to consider it. It appeared to him as though his minute had come, his second had come. The training and preparation and provision of the past months all came down to this moment, to this instant. This was his Everest, his Rubicon. *This moment is when we find out,* he thought, *if this is just an expensive hoax, or if Doc can really do it.*

For a very brief few seconds he wondered why neither Gramps nor Adam gave Doc even one iota of a chance of being able to accomplish what he claimed. But then his mind flashed back to the seemingly impossible claims of the resurrection and Jesus being the vehicle through which the true God forgave sins. (*Something else to consider sometime. Does sin exist? No time for that now, of course.*) He figured if the resurrection happened, time travel could happen, because of the impossibility of both. They represented a level impossible playing field.

He regained his temporal footing, positioned his shepherd's bag, and turned toward the cylinder. Since the door had been enlarged, he could readily step in, and did so. He settled easily into the newly installed leather chair, which felt very comfortable, and noticed that the cylinder's updated door had a mechanism for occupants to open it from the inside. He welcomed that news. He expected that should the attempt fail, Doc and Hannah would immediately open the door. Then he remembered that he wasn't going to be actually "gone" long, so in any case the door would be opened in the near future. But he gladly received the news that the worst-case scenario had been covered. He could always get out from the inside.

Hannah approached and began the process of securing him in almost every way possible. Shoulder harness, lap belt, even his wrists were strapped to the chair's arms with what looked like strips of some sort of plasticized fabric. He couldn't remember Bob being strapped in when he made his trip. But then he remembered the little ankle shackle and the chain. Again the mind-reader, Hannah explained. "It will be a temptation to squirm around a bit when the gas begins to circulate. It can be disconcerting because the gas is impregnated with a yellow indicator, and we do not know what effect it will have on your respiratory system. The FDA declared that it is nontoxic, but we haven't used it in this amount before. Besides, breathing some molecules of the gas could hamper you from reaching your destination at exactly the right time. Because of these things, we will provide you with ambient air to breath, and we will be monitoring your heartbeat and respiration as well."

With that, she produced an oxygen mask that reminded Ben of public relations videos for the Air Force, and placed it carefully over his nose and mouth. This she strapped securely into place. She connected one small sensor to the bare skin of his right forearm, and another to his chest. Then she kissed her fingertips and touched them to his forehead and smiled, and said, "Are we not drawn onward to new era?"

Ben nodded. As an afterthought, Hannah added, "You may arrive back here hungry and thirsty. I'll see that you do not lack food and drink upon your return." Her cell phone's announcement of an incoming text message distracted her for a moment.

Nice timing, thought Ben. *Now can we get this show on the road?*

Hannah closed the door and secured the gas proof seal. Because of the cylinder's illumination, Ben could effectively watch as he waited. He could see the digital clock on the opposite wall—10:58. He watched, and waited. 10:59. At that point Doc began to fill the cylinder with FBEN, and Ben watched. Hannah was right. The yellow gas kind of gave a guy the creeps, and he had to fight the urge to fight. He forced himself into composure

90

and waited. Through the gloom, the clock faithfully noted the passing seconds, and he saw it change to the eleventh hour. He could hear a roaring sound, like a yellow jet climbing into a yellow sky.

Then he was conscious of nothing.

CHAPTER VIII

Ben's mind registered a pain in his left foot, and sand and sunlight and heat. The sand seemed to have no limit, and the morning sun ricocheted off the dunes with what you might call enthusiasm if the sunlight were capable of emotion. The brightness and heat oppressed him, and he reached into his shirt pocket for his sunglasses, finding neither pocket nor glasses. It shocked him to suddenly contemplate all of the centuries that would pass before eyes would receive UV protection.

Far away to his right he could see a stone wall which he intensely hoped surrounded ancient Damascus. To follow the plan, Doc had said he must work his way southward to the Silk Road. Attempting to move returned his attention to his left foot, still the source of some small pain.

He seemed to have landed, or resurfaced, or materialized, in the midst of a thorny bush. As he looked around, he could see that he had pretty good chances of doing so. Thorn bushes populated the dunes, more numerous than geeks at a software expo. It took some time to extricate his foot from the internals of the bush, due to the fact that the thorns grew so long, and had also embedded themselves in his clothing.

The source of his small pain drew blood from the wound, and it collected around the thorn's entry point, preparing to make a run for his sandal. He spat on his palm and wiped the excess blood away, hoping that coagulation could begin soon. He wondered when first aid kits found common use. Probably not yet. He took a few moments to observe the perforation, and set his foot on an angle so that a small pool would form atop the piercing. In a few minutes the blood dried enough to allow him to move on, so he began to pick a careful path southward through thorn and scrub.

Things looked good so far. The neighborhood looked right, the city looked right—old and Mideastern, and positioned as predicted.

He proceeded cautiously as he took stock of the situation. His surroundings consisted of low, rolling hills generously populated by ugly, scraggly plant life. Far to the west, beyond the city, mountains jutted up to the sky—lower than the Rockies, but high compared to the dunes around him. The wall of stone completely enclosed the city, as nearly as Ben could tell. If his trip had gone as planned, there would be another range of mountains further west, just out of his view, and beyond that the Mediterranean Sea.

He chose his way carefully, not only because of the rough terrain, but also because Ben was well aware that the animal kingdom contained its own dangers—particularly scorpions and adders. A cautious half-hour brought him onto a packed dirt path about four feet wide, which stretched east and west. He looked east and saw nothing but desert, then turned west. As he stared at the city wall, he could feel the perspiration beneath his robe and tunic begin to evaporate and cool his body. The headgear, he decided, provided much more than just a fashion statement. It afforded practical air conditioning.

The prints of camels' hoofless feet were all over the road, as well as some wheel tracks, plus a few solid waste deposits attributable to beasts of burden. Had he been able to discern them, he could also have recognized sheep and goat tracks among human footprints, but the city distracted him and required his concentration.

It seemed to be about a half a mile away, so he figured he must have materialized on the far side of the 400-meter radius. The road ran across a sandy flat; he spent his time walking and contemplating.

The wall, seen even from that distance, created an imposing barrier. He wondered what it would be like to surround New York City with something like that. *Walls, of course, are no longer effective against intruders,* he thought, *because of helicopters and other such tools of warfare.* But then he corrected himself, as he knew he would many times in this next couple of weeks. *Walls will someday be ineffective. For the present they work very well.*

As he drew nearer the city, features of the wall became clearer. He began to make out some of the details of the *Barb Sharqui,* the Gate of the Sun. It stood open, both doors swung wide to the morning light. The opening revealed by the gate appeared to be a square, about twelve feet on a side. The gate had been constructed of some dark, dense wood. And from that distance, the gate, Ben guessed, would be about a foot thick. As he got nearer he could see the wooden brackets built to receive cross-pieces that would secure closure against all but a very well-equipped and determined enemy.

Above the gate on either side the battlements rose, from which archers could shoot defensive arrows, but at the moment they stood empty. Just inside the framework of the gate, office spaces, so to speak, provided business location for the present bureaucracy. This, Ben thought, must be the ancient version of the receptionist's desk, but these receptionists promised to be uglier for the most part, and more heavily armed than their twenty-first century counterparts.

And he encountered receptionists, the ancient kind. A quaternion of Roman soldiers occupied the reception desk. This added up to five soldiers with all told. Four privates and their commanding officer, all armed in the classic Roman fashion, turned out for review. All had close-fitting bronze helmets, brass breastplates, a sword sheathed at the

left, and a thick leather belt. (This reminded Ben of
Batman, except these belts contained none of those clever
smoke bombs and bat cables) They wore stiff black leather
as protection for their forearms and shins. Their feet sported
the protection of heavy duty sandals. Each man displayed a
crest atop his helmet, but the crest of one towered
noticeably higher than the others.

The man with the taller crest spoke to Ben.

Months of preparation had gone into this moment. Far
from home in both time and space, alone and unaided, Ben
flunked his first test, just like those college finals his junior
year. He failed completely to recognize that this Roman
soldier addressed him, because the man spoke a strange
language. Doc had warned him about time travel's side
effects, but he felt too groggy to recognize his problem.

Precious seconds passed while Ben's mind assessed the
situation. For some reason the words were familiar, but
how? And why?

Ben's thoughts lined themselves up as slowly as an
earthworm exits the dirt on that first warm day in the
spring.

All those hours, he thought. *All that vocabulary. All that
preparation. And for what? To stand here looking
dumbfounded the first time someone speaks to me in
Aramaic.* A casual observer at this point may have thought
he had dropped out of college because of poor study habits.

In time his brain offered a translation for the words his
ears had heard: "Friend, where do you come from?"

The words forced a feeling into the pit of Ben's
stomach, the feeling you get when you and your friends
drive to a secluded spot for a picnic, and you lock your keys
in the car. It's a long way back. Like Robinson Crusoe on
Thursday, he was alone, a stranger in a strange land. No one
would speak his language for many centuries.

He stared at the one who had addressed him. No threat
could be detected in the voice, only curiosity. Ben groped
about in his conscious mind for words that he knew, words

that would be effective, words that would get him past the receptionist.

Slowly and carefully, he answered. "From the desert."

By his accent and articulation, the soldier immediately determined that Ben did not use Aramaic as a matter of daily habit.

"Welcome to Damascus," he said deliberately. "I am called Tullus. We," he then indicated his four charges, "guard this gate and keep it safe." He continued to speak slowly and cordially, but then he said, "From what country do you come?"

What to do, what to do, Ben thought. *How do you explain Leif Ericson, Amerigo Vespucci, Christopher Columbus, the new world, the colonization of the eastern seaboard, the expansion to the west, the eventual addition of Wisconsin to the Union, and the development of the nation that would help to kick butt on the likely descendants of these very soldiers after said descendants chose to back the wrong side in World War II?*

Ben's parched throat offered him no help, His discomfort grew, not only from walking in the heat of the morning, but also from a credible premonition that he may be in some sort of trouble, or at least could be in danger of creating the spark that could light an inferno of curiosity just because (and here his emotion turned a bit toward anger) six or seven college degrees did not suffice to equip Doc to help him foresee this problem. Three quarters of a million dollars also crossed his mind. "It is incumbent upon us to prepare you as well as possible for your journey." Those were Doc's words. His salvation came by instinctively identifying the thing that shoved itself most naturally to the forefront of his sluggish brain.

"Water," Ben rasped, absolutely without pretense. "May I have water?"

"Certainly, mate. Follow the street ahead of you about two stadia. There is a fountain on the left," Tullus recommended patiently.

"After you've been refreshed, please return and tell me about your homeland, where you come from. I need to put it in my report."

Ben nodded his thanks and continued through the shade of the guardhouse into the street called Straight. Most would not suspect that would be its moniker, as it curved from northwest toward the southwest through the city center.

He moved slowly and carefully, avoiding contact with people as much as possible. At the extremity of his vision, he noticed a camel with its face to the ground for so long that Ben thought it must be drinking.

Sometimes a brain has a mind of its own. Ben could not stop his next mental excursion, which brought back to memory a beer commercial from the future in which people were encouraged to visit Mexico, but not to drink the water. Not to worry. Just drink light beer while you're there. More cars inextricably connected themselves to this train of thought. He remembered warnings about roadside taco stands, and assurances that a lot of the local microbes lay embedded in the general populace, which resulted in an immunity to what any tourist could catch perhaps by driving by and waving. He and Sherry had ridden a camel, but no one had asked him to drink out of the same trough the camel used.

He edged closer, like someone preparing to claim first prize in the ugly man contest. Water shimmered there. Did the locals drink it? Did he possess a viable alternative? He waited in a spot of shade afforded by the market tents.

By all he could observe, he had located the livestock pond at the least. He hoped and prayed that humans had some other water source, and then his skepticism got the better of him, and he simply hoped for it.

As if in answer to his hope, a woman brought a clay pot to the water, but filled it in a small pool about twenty feet past where the camel had drunk. In his mind he dubbed the nearer area "Camel Fountain" and the farther area "Human Fountain".

It occurred to him he'd seen no other women in the market since he'd arrived. The street hummed with activity, with men of most descriptions, although noticeably fewer people struggled with obesity than back home. Primarily, men occupied the square, but also a few children, and nearly all of these were boys that appeared to be between the ages of seven and twelve.

Ingesting water had become an intense focus for him by this time, but he preferred now to err on the side of caution. *How do people use this fountain when they have no pitcher or pot? Should I try to buy a pot? What is the first-century equivalent of a water bottle or a canteen?* Having no answer to any of these questions, he decided to edge closer to the Human Fountain. *Does it take courage to kneel and drink? What if I look stupid? What if I get some kind of a disease and carry it back home with me and kill everyone in my century?*

Ben decided then and there that if he couldn't get a drink of water he did not deserve to be then and there. He knew certainly that he deserved to be there by virtue of seven hundred fifty thousand dollars, so he walked over to the edge of the fountain, knelt beside the foot-high stone wall, and reached his cupped hands into the water. It tasted tepid, and it smelled a bit more organic than what he was used to, but he drank his fill anyway. It took a while, but he eventually quenched his thirst. Before he could rise to his feet, a young lad ran up to the edge of the low wall, plunged his face into the water and drank his fill in seconds. *Probably an option worth remembering,* thought Ben. *Quick and effective.*

He stood and looked back the way he had come. The Roman needed an answer for his report. Government bureaucracy had quite a long history. What should he say? Was Gaul believable? Or Samothrace, or Corinth, or Illyricum?

He found a shady place to think, though the second half of that undertaking turned out to be the more difficult of the two. Even as he'd sought out the Human Fountain, the market had become much busier. If he loitered, hawkers would attempt to sell him damask cloth, or silk, or spice, or local produce. For self-preservation, he found he had to focus on the street ahead of him and keep moving. Thus, he could avoid contact with the greatest salesmen in the world, and ignore the brabble that surrounded him.

His clever strategy involved no decision as to direction of travel, so he eventually found himself at the city's center, where Straight Street, the Via Recta, intersected a major street running north and south, the Cardo Maximus. These two were the spine and arms of the commerce in Damascus, and provided a reasonable way to navigate the city, though being lost would not have been a big problem, as each quarter was relatively small.

When he could see the western gate of the city, he turned and began to retrace his steps toward the Gate of the Sun. He grappled with the upcoming conversation with Tullus. He thought it ironic that he'd spent all that time and effort on clothing, money, language study, self-defense, and much more, only to find that his first big challenge arose from the fact that Wisconsin did not yet exist.

As he neared the eastern end of the Straight Street, he settled upon a workable plan. He walked deliberately into the shade of the guard's outpost, and waited while Tullus finished some bureaucratic business with a small caravan just entering from the east. He waited while Tullus made marks on a small leather scroll, probably the precursor to the outmoded day timer.

"So, my friend," Tullus still spoke slowly, "I feared you would not come back. I see you are an honest man. What is your name?"

Ben came prepared for this. "Parker." Tullus made a note of this after he'd pronounced it back to Ben and made certain he had it right.

"And where is your homeland?"

"West."

"How far west? Greece?"

"No, further."

"Not Rome. No, certainly not. Tarshish, then?"

"No," Ben said. He hoped to supply dramatic effect with the studied use of the pause. He remembered from the Jonah sermon he'd heard when Adam had hauled him in to church that Tarshish represented modern-day Spain, the western extreme of the empire. Finally he said, "West of Tarshish."

Despite the fact that Ben's home was so far away, and he had not yet been born, he could still feel the force behind that universal stare from an officer of the law smelling a rat and in no mood for funny business. Tullus used that stare at full power.

Ben stared back. He hoped he looked like Sherry might look immediately after revealing the unverifiable truth.

"We know of nothing west of Tarshish. What is your country's name?"

"It has no name as yet. It is there, far west of Tarshish. That is my home."

Tullus shook his head like a terrier shakes a rat. When he had finished, things looked no better to him. Ben still stood there, and Tullus could see that he probably would not give an answer that appeared presentable in the gatekeepers report.

"Well, my friend, West of Tarshish it is then. Have a pleasant stay in Damascus, and when you're ready to leave, use some other gate. All right?" Tullus looked back to his scroll, and Ben figured this concluded the interview. It had gone as well as one might expect.

So Ben nodded his agreement, thanked Tullus as best he could, and stepped back into the brightness of Straight Street. He wondered if modern-day Portugal would suffice for West of Tarshish, and then reminded himself that now (then) actually is (or was) the most modern day available. No Portugal as yet.

He worked his way back through the markets like a cow grazing through green pastures, taking time to examine everything from architecture to merchandise, high and low. He'd seen pictures of the Aeropagus, the Coliseum, the

Forum. All had been old, decayed, disintegrating. He wondered if anyone else from his time would ever experience anything like this, the thrill of seeing ancient architecture when it qualified as new. He thought of Gramps' antique Dodge looking so great fully restored. What would it have been like the day it rolled off the assembly line?

Pristine stonework decorated the center of Damascus with columns and arches, pillars and porches. Here lay the hub of incessant activity, with caravans bearing products from north, south and east, each laden with treasures from the homeland, each exchanging goods with another to deliver to merchants hailing from some other faraway place. Here at the market merchants bargained, buying and selling. Ben thought how cool it would be to pick up a few beautiful pieces for Sherry. *How great it's going to be when I get back, when I can see her, when I shave off this beard.* He involuntarily touched his face and thought how foreign his own reflection had become to him. He saw a stranger in the mirror. A brutally handsome stranger.

His thoughts snapped back to the first century, which he tried desperately to perceive as the present. *Likely no mirrors here,* he thought. *Polished metal, at best.* Luckily, he had no desire to see his own face in any accurate way, at least not until these two weeks were over.

If only I could have kept a journal or something, some kind of travel log, some record of the trip, he thought. *That ought to make interesting reading someday.* But even as he thought this he knew that the first century had to be like Las Vegas. What happens in the first century stays in the first century.

Among the shops he found a place that sold dried produce from the area—raisins, dates, figs, honeycomb and meat of some unknown description. The meat appeared to be prepared in such a way as to need absolutely no refrigeration. Someone dried, salted, and sliced it, and made it ready to pack. Ben chose a portion of each of these and paid with a denarius. He received a small copper coin in change, and stowed the foodstuffs in the shepherd's bag.

He next located a nearby shop selling cloth, and for another denarius bought enough damask to wrap the fruits and meat so that he could preserve his rich man's garment from stain.

He began to work his way toward the western gate, pausing only to admire the impressive results of stonework erected completely by hand. He both understood and ignored calls from vendors as he passed, and consciously congratulated himself on how right Pimsleur had been. The communication center of his mind continued adjusting to the fact that nothing more was available—that absolutely no one would cross his path who could converse with him in his native tongue. He chose not to listen to the cacophony around him, not even for practice.

The sun had neared its zenith as he reached the long market. This area also teemed with aggressive commerce—the primitive version of a freight terminal. Businesses lined both sides of Straight Street, beginning as near as was practical after the road entered the gate, the Barb al Jabiya, the Gate of Jupiter. Near the gate, camel needs required some space for food, water, and shelter. Both sides of the gate sported stairs leading away from the gate's opening to the top of the wall.

Why not, thought Ben's inner tourist. No one guarded the stairs, and no one seemed to be warding off visitors. He wondered if Doc could possibly disagree with his intention. *Observation only,* he thought. He'd read somewhere that he should proceed until apprehended.

Carefully, he ascended the staircase on the southern side, up the twenty-five feet or so to the top of the wall. The steps could not qualify for OSHA approval, as they were not particularly even, and averaged about twelve inches per riser. And, Ben noticed with a mental smirk, no handrail.

The view from the top of the wall proved educational. The road led west from the Gate of Jupiter across a wide, shallow valley, where it split into a north and a south fork.

The north side connected Asia to Europe, and the south side, which would be his route, led down through the Decapolis area, the Jordan Valley, and finally to Jerusalem.

Camel trains traveled the road, two approaching the city and one departing. *Camels will not be able to compete once the internal combustion engine is invented,* thought Ben—though his preparation had taught him that in many places, due to the difficulty in building reasonable roads, and sometimes a problem acquiring fuel, camels would still be in use almost two thousand years into the future. He resisted an urge to attempt to think in proper verb tenses. *Too complicated,* he decided. *Will contemplate it later.*

On a less grammatical front, we are so far so good, he thought. *The language is coming along all right, and I'm not yet dying of thirst. And I soon will begin my search for a southbound caravan with space for an unspecified traveler.* He carefully descended the stairs.

Since the questions, "Heading to Jerusalem?" and "How much?" were phrases that sprang easily to his non-Aramaic lips, Ben began the task of locating transportation with a reasonable amount of optimism. He spoke with those who looked like Bedouins preparing for departure, and made camel-to-camel inquiry. He found it impossible to care whether he'd asked a stupid question, and kept to his task, hoping to locate a southbound caravan with passenger space available.

Such a train did exist, fresh from the north and having lost two passengers to the city of Damascus. The ramrod of the outfit, a large man called Al-alif, said he wanted ten denarii for passage to Judea. This Ben paid, reassuring himself that his remaining stash should be ample for his stay in Jerusalem, possibly eight or nine days duration. *Also,* he thought, *there's no use saving them. They are practically worthless back home, considering their value is only ninety-five percent of their weight in silver. And, if a guy can spread the wealth around, that can't be bad.*

Al-alif possessed largeness seemingly in all aspects—he stood tall, broad, and thick. He had a hearty laugh and a ready smile, but the smile had lost certain parts. When he showed his teeth a picket fence sprang to Ben's mind. This man looked powerful and capable, and perhaps worthy of trust.

Ben then met the camel-handlers, the Bedouins as he learned to call them. He again submitted his surname as his moniker, and again felt that slight bit of tension when he claimed to be from west of Tarshish. *You'd think I was talking about the palace of Versailles during the French revolution,* he complained to himself. All in all, though, things went well. The Bedouin crew seemed to accept his place of origin as a detail they need not necessarily believe, and each man moved on to his task.

Camel feeding, watering, and loading proceeded. Ben observed various levels of willingness to cooperate, and disconsolately noted that the more cantankerous animals seemed to be reserved for human occupancy. He singled out four of these and felt some satisfaction in that, because he knew some computer programmers that could not count past two.

Before long Al-alif sought him out and introduced him to a man named Sethur who also claimed Jerusalem as his goal. "Your traveling partner, so you may as well be friends! Those women there will also be with us. Perhaps you will meet them at fireside tonight."

Ben's eyes followed Al-alif"s gesture toward two women standing together on the periphery of the caravan's activity. One appeared to be about twenty-five, had long dark hair and beneath her kesmut probably a graceful figure, but how could one tell? She wore a robe of a beautiful (and expensive looking) shade of crimson. The other looked more mature, equally as slender, more plainly attired, and showing slight streaks of gray in her long dark hair. Both women owned that mocha tint to their complexions, and both seemed well adjusted to the process of waiting. They appeared to be both relaxed and ready, traits Ben recognized as rare in his own time, but he supposed them to be much more prevalent at "present".

Al-alif's hearty voice returned Ben's attention to his
immediate surroundings. "What we are doing now we call
shearing a goat. All these preparations are most mundane,
but must be done in order that our caravan might safely
depart. Is it like this west of Tarshish?"

Ben could not immediately reply. Could there be a
centuries-old precursor to the concept of "shaving a yak"?

"Yes, it is like this in my country. I think it is like this in
all places."

After another bit of waiting and observing, the goat
shorn, camels loaded, saddles set in place for the
passengers, links made from camel to camel, the arduous
task of mounting began.

Ben watched as the Bedouins initiated the process of
putting people atop camels. He wished now he'd listened to
Doc and gotten more experience with non-theoretical
camels. Now he could only rely on temporally based
training.

Camels are tall by human standards, and their legs are
extremely long. They are well-adapted to traversing the
desert, but to ensconce a person on the hump can be a
ponderous job.

The Bedouin handling the camel would bellow a
command, and the camel would kneel. This would enable
the putative passenger to slip onto the saddle, thus to be in
place as the camel rose to her feet. (Most people-hauling
camels turned out to be female because of the temperament
problem male camels have with being asked to haul
something that's readily pitched off.) A young man named
Hilkiah, who seemed to be the head Bedouin, brought Ben's
camel to the kneeling position, then nodded to Ben to load.
At his first attempt, the beast rose to her feet before he
could properly place himself, so Hilkiah rebooted the
process, but this time he placed his left forearm directly
behind her head and his right knee at the base of her neck.
Ben mounted and Hilkiah released his hold. The lady camel
sprang up quickly, beginning with her hind quarters, as
camels are wont to do, but Ben was ready because he'd seen

the others go through their mounting processes, and because the same thing had happened to him at the zoo. It struck him during this time that he now took advantage of knowledge that was related to an event which technically had not happened yet, and therefore did not exist, but it seemed to work out all right.

With all passengers and merchandise in place, the camel train plodded through the Gate of Jupiter and out onto the Silk Road. Soldiers protected this gate as well, but these smiled and waved to Al-alif and ignored the remainder of the caravan.

At least I got out by a different gate, Ben thought. He observed that the Bedouins all walked, and marveled the more at the pace they set, a brisk gait, and the ride provided more comfort than he expected.

His mind wandered back to Tullus for a moment, and he wondered whether Roman soldiers, like their twenty-first century American counterparts, struggled with any sort of mental disorders after a stout Mideast deployment.

As they worked their way through the shallow bottom of the valley toward the fork in the road, Ben mused about speed. He knew Jerusalem lay about 130 miles south, and had been given to understand that a camel train could cover about 25 miles in a day. That's a healthy five-day trip, and their first day would be truncated by this seemingly late start. He now surmised that this "road trip" would place him in Jerusalem on his sixth day. He hoped that by then he'd have a reasonable command of the Aramaic language, and ample time to take up his quest.

But he had to wonder about the progress of this method of travel. He could probably walk it himself in that amount of time. But then he thought of food and water and conversation and the relative dangers of the roadway, and realized the wisdom of sitting in that specific saddle. Still, he had imagined everyone mounted and some sort of gentle trot. Nonetheless, here he passed the afternoon, not even going to the trouble of researching whether first-class accommodations could be procured, or if he should have considered a private caravan.

The pace of the trip gave Ben plenty of opportunity to look around. The scenery proved painfully monotonous, and in some strange way reminded him of Ekalaka. Low hills and scrub brush. He imagined that Doc and Hannah's farmhouse might be just over the next rise, although he knew that as desolate as eastern Montana seemed, it was verdant by comparison.

By careful study, Ben made note of local mountain peaks. He did not know their names, but he learned their faces, and could see by them that the land slipped by beneath him at what seemed to be a snail's pace.

Soon the sun worked its way west and late afternoon wore on to early evening. The valley had been crossed and the caravan arrived at its exit. Right to Asia minor and Europe, left to Jerusalem and Africa. They turned left at the intersection and continued south for an unexpectedly short distance, at which time Al-alif called a halt to their journey for that day.

The Bedouins then busied themselves with preparations for the night's bivouac. A nearby spring provided water for cooking and filling of skins. Shelters were erected, and a fire kindled using fuel supplied by that same species of thorn bush that had welcomed Ben to the desert. The thorns burned like the driest brush, hot and fast. A blaze required a lot of thorn branches, but, thankfully, much of it could be had for the taking. All preparations for the evening's comfort came to a quick and efficient completion, with separate shelters erected for men and women. It appeared that the Bedouins would sleep unprotected on the ground. Ben and Sethur checked into the shelter on the north side of the fire, and the women occupied the other. Its location afforded the women some privacy as well as security. At the last of the construction and cooking's completion, the passengers received invitation to the evening meal.

The dining consisted of unleavened bread baked on hot rocks and local produce acquired in the long market of

Damascus, all washed down with tepid water which, Ben thought, had the faint but detectable taste of goat. The travelers partook quietly, speaking to one another only when necessary, so conversation was minimal. When the travelers and crew had finished, and the serving pot had been removed for what any sane person would expect to be a thorough washing, Al-alif announced formally that his passengers and camel tenders should "get better acquainted."

He invited the sojourners and his crew to sit and introduced each in turn, making sure that all knew one another at least by name. The Bedouins, besides Hilkiah, had such cumbersome names that Ben could not immediately place them into memory. Sethur, whom he had met earlier in the afternoon, turned out to be a Levite fresh from helping to establish a synagogue in Damascus. He appeared to be in his early fifties, but Ben knew that in this culture it would be difficult to judge these things.

The younger woman's name was Lydia, and she said she worked in fabric. That is, she supplied franchise for distribution of purple cloth for royalty and military officials of very high rank. At least that's the way Ben understood it. The older woman, Lydia's aunt Patricia, her mother's sister, accompanied her on their business trip. They came from Thyatira and had journeyed to Damascus to acquire damask cloth for their work. They gave no details of their intentions, but merely volunteered that they were on their way to Jerusalem.

Ben entertained briefly the thought of displaying his robe to them and soliciting their opinion on how Gloria had done on the project, but he quickly dismissed the idea. Better, he thought, to remain incognito as long as possible.

Then his turn came to explain his business in Jerusalem. What to say, how much to reveal? No matter what he said, it would be obvious to all of them that he freshly arrived in the area and struggled with the language. So he spoke slowly and distinctly, and he said this:

"I have come from far away to go to Jerusalem in search of truth. My countrymen have heard that much has happened there recently that should be investigated, so I go there to investigate."

Those who sat with him could readily see that he understood Aramaic much better than he spoke it, and it seemed to him a matter of their deference that no one questioned him further.

Shortly after this, as the sun set, each retired to the proper shelter. Ben quickly realized that his pedestrian kesmut not only provided protection by day, but also warmth from the cool desert night. He covered himself with his cloak and used his shepherd's bag for a pillow.

At times like this it is often difficult to lay one's plans and thoughts and imaginations aside. The mind tends to race toward the unknown and unexpected future and to contemplate contingent courses of action. *How long will it take us to reach Jerusalem? What will happen when I find the guy? Will he understand why I need to know? Will he give me an answer? Will my money last me the full two weeks?*

None of these things troubled Ben. Having been awake for thirty-six consecutive hours, he slept without dream.

CHAPTER IX

When Ben awoke the next morning, the chill of the desert dawn clung like a shroud to the sandy earth. Fresh flat bread lay on hot stones next to the fire, and a repeat of the previous night's meal, mostly local fruits, seemed to be in store. The four passengers shared breakfast while the Bedouins broke camp and loaded the camels for the day's journey. The loading presented its own challenge, involving a serious dose of heavy lifting, seasoned with a bit of cantankerous camel. The Bedouins seemed to have no complaints concerning any of it, and Ben felt thankful that his ten denarii allowed him merely to observe and ride.

The sun's position lay mercifully leftward, not directly in their faces. It represented mere circumstance, but Ben felt grateful for that as well. The sun wouldn't be glaring angrily into his soul all morning, and he would be excused from thinking obsessive thoughts about sunglasses. So the day began on a fairly positive note.

Certain aspects of the ride kept Ben from spontaneously breaking into a chorus of *Happy Trails*. Being a city kid, Ben had never heard of saddle sores, and because of the romantic nature of western movies, the process of their formation had never even sidled up to the intersection, let alone actually made its way over the crosswalk of his mind.

The previous day's limited hours aback the camel had laid the foundation for them, though Ben had no knowledge

111

of it. That time of sitting immobile, gently moving back and forth on the saddle, had caused very subtle abrasions on his backside in preparation for the first full day's ride. The promise of building upon that foundation moved inexorably toward fulfillment even as he sat. Little did he know the progression: irritation, abrasion, soreness, healing, calluses. He sat in the midst of a long and painful process, predictable on the rear of the novice rider, and now earnestly at work in Ben's life in a very fundamental way. Having never read the right kind of books, Ben remained uninformed about this. Ignorant, in fact. Maybe Doc had also not anticipated this problem, but it seemed so far not big enough to cause Ben to demand his money back.

But the gentle pain gave him something to think about.

In short order he learned that he could increase his comfort by consciously cooperating with his mount. That is, he found that he could move with the camel to decrease the friction. He also discovered that in only a couple of hours, his body entered into this process automatically with little or no conscious input from his brain. He found it helpful to glance occasionally in Sethur's direction, for there he found an operating model, a visual tutorial.

Beyond the problem of his fundament, he could feel the heat. As the sun rose higher, the previous evening's chill had been deleted from memory. A breeze from the east delivered more than its quota of torrid air from the Arabian Desert. This caused the ubiquitous sweat, which eventually found its way to those small fundamental abrasions, decreasing his sense of well-being. The sweat soon began to evaporate, which had that pleasant effect of a natural swamp cooler, but it also formed very small rivers and pools on his face, which caught airborne particles of dust, and made blinking a scratchy, painful affair. The salt content exacerbated the discomfort caused by the abrasions.

How long can people do this? He wondered. He reminded himself once again that this was no time, so to speak, to start thinking about minutes. It would be centuries before people began using them. Even the concept of half an hour would be foreign. So he attempted to think in terms of hours, then of days. At about noon the caravan stopped for a brief rest. No meal, just water, and a brief respite from riding, which involved standing on hot sand in the shade of a smelly camel. Following this, they continued their journey south.

Occasionally Ben would look back to the north. The first few times he could still see the west and south walls of Damascus, but that view eventually became obliterated by intervening hills. All else changed very slowly, and Ben began to wonder why all the great ideas mankind had spawned had taken so long to develop. With nothing to do all day but wait for night, you should be able to come up with tons of progressive ideas just by thinking about it.

During that afternoon he let his mind wander wherever it would. He thought of Sherry, and her insistence that he shave his beard. He thought of Gramps, and his overt mistrust of Doc and Hannah. *Misplaced, obviously,* Ben decided. He considered what he might do when he arrived back in his own century. His mother was adamant that he should finish college, but at this point he had no idea why he would bother with that. The company hummed along okay with few exceptions. He counted in his mind the people in his corporation that ought to be externally motivated or replaced. He remembered his Bentley, and how comfortable the seats were; he'd have been in Jerusalem in a climate-controlled cockpit in about ninety minutes if he had been driving, but he could not recall which side of the road the Syrians used, and probably would not risk his pride and joy in those circumstances. He added up the denarii he'd spent so far and subtracted the total from fifty—no mean feat without a calculator, or even an abacus. He attempted to anticipate future expenses, allowing for standard contingencies, as any businessman of any time would, and justified the two columns in his mind. He imagined the expressions on the faces of the women in the van when he finally got the opportunity to show them his royal kesmut.

As he pondered this fragment of vanity, he realized that the caravan shifted into low gear. The evening had arrived unannounced, with the previous night's activities repeated with astounding alacrity. In a span of time that could have been measured in minutes, the Bedouins had shelters erected, the meal heated atop the fire, and he had been reunited with Sethur and the women around the desert dining room, the traditional fire-ring. Ben would not have called the repast a festive board, consisting of flat bread, cooked grain, and dried fruit, but neither could he deny his body its required sustenance.

The conversation, however, took a noticeably different turn from that of the previous evening. Ben couldn't follow all of it, but Al-alif seemed to be attempting to draw Sethur into a discussion of politics, centered on the feelings of the Jewish nation toward Roman occupiers. Sethur kept tight-lipped for the most part, but even those who understood none of the spoken words would have been able to see that he had no love for the Romans.

After Sethur had suffered a while, Lydia requested permission to speak, and Al-alif graciously welcomed her to express her opinion.

"The Romans," she began, "have been a stabilizing force in the entire region. In several ways their occupation has been good for many people. Around the empire they've retained Greek as a universal trade language. Anyone speaking Greek can get along anywhere in the entire empire, which involves a lot of places, and a lot of people. Without the influence of some central government, such unity would not exist. It gives us all a reasonable system for records and accounting that will be understandable in many, many places, although I must admit that their number system is a nightmare. Someone should come up with something simpler.

"Then there is the road system. The empire has built and maintained a system of roads that connect everywhere to everywhere, eventually. A Roman citizen can expect workable travel conditions wherever he wants to go. Aunt

Patricia and I have been many places in the empire where we would not have gone except that the empire has built and maintained and patrolled the roads.

"There is also stability. If each nation were a unit unto itself, then we could not feel as safe as we travel. Since Roman law is universal throughout the empire, and since we are Roman citizens, we feel secure as we go about laying a foundation for the expansion of our cloth distribution. It is good for business.

"All in all, it seems like a worthwhile thing. If it were not the Romans, it would be some other empire, and I have heard that there are people far more wicked than they."

As Lydia fell silent, Sethur stirred. He appeared to be struggling to say, or not to say the thoughts of his mind. Finally he overcame his reticence.

"Would you conquer people you do not know in order to force them to serve you, to collect their taxes so that they may pay those who inflict their occupation and defile their borders? And what of the people in these lands? We have just left Damascus of Syria. We go south toward the region of Decapolis, then onward to Samaria and Judea. All of these people should be free instead of slaves, as they are now, paying their masters to keep them. None of these people sought to attack the Romans. The Romans advanced on them. In Jerusalem we look for a Messiah, a deliverer, one that God has promised, who will come and set things right, and rule on the throne of His father David. In such a one we will hope."

He would say no more beyond that statement, though Al-alif attempted again to draw him out.

In the course of this discussion night had silently fallen, revealing the majesty of the heavens. The dark, moonless sky stretched out above, and Ben stared at the tapestry up yonder—that same majestic curtain he remembered from Doc's ranch, thick and totally black, with a multitude of tiny perforations, most notable though they occupied but a small percentage of the available space. *At least the stars are the same,* he thought. He could identify Polaris, Ursa Minor,

Ursa Major, Orion and Cassiopeia. How incredibly bright they looked. He had never seen them in the context of total desert darkness, through air this clean, on a night this clear. The Milky Way, the Horsehead Nebula. Billions and billions of stars, in a galaxy of unimaginable dimensions, in a staggeringly huge universe. He realized that he alone of his companions had any concept of what was out there, and wondered if it could actually be explained to them.

Beneath the rugged beauty of the sky, the night passed as expected. Ben again slept dreamlessly through it, waking as the crew broke camp. He joined his traveling companions for a hearty breakfast comprised of the previous night's leftovers. He began to understand that some of the future can be seen even by a novice. Time travel would not be necessary if a guy just wanted to predict the previous night what would be available to eat the next morning. Fortunately, good and wholesome food made up the board, and since Ben had been forced into eating just twice a day, he shared in it eagerly.

Al-alif bellowed orders at his usual volume, all the while casting furtive glances to the east. Ben thought it odd that he also noticed some of the camels gazing in that direction, for some reason that he could not easily discern.

Mount-up presented more trouble than it had the previous two days, but after a time all four passengers sat atop the humps. The tenders began the trek south, each of them occasionally glancing to the east as they walked. Ben stared in that direction, and noticed a sort of haze beneath the rising sun. He guessed, quite correctly, that a dust storm would intercept their way, and that this caused all that east-glancing, not to mention the skittishness of the camels.

They continued south through a routine morning, with the only departure from the norm caused by the breeze. It became more like a wind that would eventually require some sort of counter-measure on the part of the herdsmen.

Near mid-day, Al-alif called a halt to the van and commanded that the water skin be brought down for a drink. Before his command could be fully implemented,

116

two incidents, apparent chance occurrences, presented themselves in a way that seemed to change the course of history.

The wind's velocity dramatically increased, and a lizard darted across the trail just ahead of Ben's camel. The lizard's crossing might have passed as inconsequential, but buried in the sand, quite literally up to its eyeballs, lurked an adder. It exploded from its temporary concealment in order to obtain the midday meal, and in doing so spooked the two nearest camels. Ben barely remained seated as his mount sprang backward, and the camel ahead lunged forward, stretching the lead rope instantly taut. The air reverberated with the sound of the rope snapping free from the end of its tether, then the last four camels in the train were liberated.

Normally, the top speed of a camel is about 25 miles per hour, much faster than most men could ever run. For short distances, they can reach speeds of about 40 miles per hour, but generally do not sustain this pace for extended periods of time. The four beasts were of one mind, and reached their top speed in a matter of seconds. They tore away from the caravan and into the flying dust before anyone could react. The bellowing voice of Al-alif became lost in the gale as the passengers tried desperately to retain their perches. With no reins and no camel-speak, Ben was basically out to sea on a wildly careening ship of the desert. A quick glance behind him revealed that Sethur and the women had been able to keep position, though the advantage of this remained in doubt.

The storm intensified, and still the camels ran. Thankfully, a camel's gallop is a much smoother ride than its trot. Ben found the simple task of watching to be somewhat difficult. The dust began to fill the atmosphere now, and occasionally the frayed end of the rope appeared in the air near his face. He considered the wisdom of attempting to grasp it, and then to using it to stop the camel.

This seemed like a good idea. If the rope were to become entangled in the camel's feet, no good could come of that. On the other hand, how could he apply brakes to the camels behind him? From what he understood, all were females, as these were more even-tempered and easier to manage in difficult situations. He thought that if he tried to decelerate slowly, the others would probably follow suit.

From where he sat, he could see his rare opportunities come and go. Several times the rope whistled by in front of him, and at each pass he reacted too slowly, like a batter trying to handle an unusually fast pitch. He thought he was in the batter's box for about an hour while he awaited the next pitch. With timing and luck, however, the leather cord slapped into his hand and he managed to secure it.

Though he did not know it, he wrapped the line around his hand in much the same way a Montana bull rider would. In the future such a twist of rope would be called the suicide wrap, because of the difficulty one experiences in attempting to let go of it. But to keep one's mount, the suicide wrap has its advantages.

Rope in hand, so now what? Wait and see what happens? Wait and be pitched off into the storm due to some trick camel maneuver? Pull back very gently? Pull back really hard? Ben thought of those ubiquitous thorn bushes and feared that a camel's sudden evasive action around one of those might land him in their midst, like a seed that fell among thorns..

With such a limited supply of camel knowledge, an informed decision could not be made. He thought the people behind him would know more about what to do, if only he could stop the camel train and ask them. He glanced behind. They were still there, but barely visible. He figured they'd all need shelter very soon.

He decided to attempt a gentle reduction in speed, as that seemed to work so well with his Bentley, and because anything sudden could easily cause a small train wreck. *A camel train wreck*, he thought grimly.

He gently pulled the slack out of the lead rope. He could feel the steady motion of the camel's head as she galloped through the storm.

118

Slowly he began to experiment with pressure, and slowly and ever so gently he brought the rope taut. And to his relief she began to decelerate. "Down one more gear, Baby," he heard himself saying in that gentle, quiet voice reserved for calm in pack animal emergencies.

"Down one more gear," he said again. It seemed to work. She slowed her gallop, and seemed to be flirting with the idea of reduction to a trot.

Behind him all was not well. The camels rearward had not yet gotten the small piece of parchment with the brief message on it. And their passengers had absolutely no control. The camel crew crowded nose to tail in a frantic attempt to keep their feet free of each other. Ben could hear his companions behind him speaking calming words to their beasts. He realized that he had defaulted to English for the emergency.

By slow, careful, and disorganized degrees, the speed of the mini-van was diminished, somewhat through Ben's efforts, and somewhat through the natural tiring process of the camels. The difficult part proved to be the re-entry into the trot phase, because a camel's hump moves precipitously from side to side as the camel moves both front and back legs on a side in unison. The movement is drastic, but fortunately also rhythmic. Each one retained proper throne, though Ben flirted the most with disaster, being also the least experienced. Ungraceful it may have been, but Ben achieved walking speed with the suicide wrap still intact. They had been separated from the main caravan for several hours.

At last the four quadrupeds came to a halt in the wind and dust, and their occupants slid to the dunes, keeping to the lee side of their ships. Sethur approached Ben and shouted something over the wind. After a moment of mental gymnastics, Ben's brain interpreted. Get the camels to lie down.

Ben pulled down gently on the rope, now clutched just a couple of feet below the camel's nose. "I have yet to learn your name, kind lady, but you must kneel down on the sand." Camels naturally want to do just that in a dust storm, so Ben did not expect the obedience he experienced

In turn, each of the others did the same, and Sethur returned from the sandy haze with the women.

"Keep the rope tied to your arm, and let us all take shelter behind this beast. We will await the end of the storm."

So all crowded to the lee side of whatshername. All sat silently, waiting. All listened for the wind's abatement, and looked for the clarity that comes after the storm.

For an hour they waited, then two, then three. Finally, as darkness approached, the wind howled less fiercely, the dust became less dense, and gradually the storm decreased its fervor.

Just as the sun went down it seemed safe to resume normal activity. "Now we must hobble the beasts, lest they leave us in the night," Sethur observed. He carefully untied the lead rope from the first camel, and secured it around her knees. Then he proceeded toward the back of the line, securing each camel as he went, speaking gentle words to them as he imprisoned them. He returned to his fellow passengers.

"It has been many hours since last we ate and drank. Water and food will perhaps become a problem for us."

At this Ben felt he should slap his brow, but thought it may not yet be in vogue to do so. Instead, he said, "I have some food." All day he'd had his shepherd's bag slung over his shoulder like a pack, and it was such a natural fit he'd forgotten it was there.

He untied the thong that secured the flap of his pouch, then unpacked his robe and laid it carefully aside. He removed the victuals he'd bought in Damascus, still in their damask wrappings. He handed the bundle to Sethur, who carefully opened it while Ben repacked his bag.

Sethur divided the food between the four of them, and each had plenty for their evening meal. Some he set aside for breakfast, and after the meal Lydia produced a small skin of water. "There is not much here, but each could have at least a drink." The small community passed the skin from man to man, and woman to woman. Each drank sparingly, leaving as much as they could for the morrow.

"We have fared well in spite of all this," Sethur observed. "We seem to be unhurt, and somewhat fed and watered. We seem also to have, more or less, kept our course. We have covered a significant distance this day. Perhaps too far. We now must wait through the night, but with the sun's rise we must be in search of water for these beasts, for that will be the third day since our departure from the oasis."

None could disagree. Ben covered himself with his robe and rested his head on his shepherd's bag. *What a day,* he thought. *But Sethur is right. We are safe, and not yet out of options.* He wished that Al-alif were there. He wondered about the miles they'd covered, and tried to calculate the time it would take to traverse the same terrain on foot. Eventually, the brightness of the stars distracted his thoughts, and after staring at the depths of space for a while, he fell into an exhausted sleep.

CHAPTER X

Sethur's voice pulled Ben from his slumber. "Friends, we must arise, partake of what food and water we have, and be on our way. I have set out what we have, and partaken myself. While the rest of you eat I will see to the camel's leads."

Lydia, Patricia and Ben shared their meal in silence, sipping water when the food had been depleted. When they had finished, they found Sethur to be as good as his word. The camels had been unhobbled, and tethered together in their caravan formation. Assuming temporary ramrod status, he said, "We must mount carefully, as that has been our most precarious time. My camel is most docile, so I will help all of you mount, then I will mount last."

This turned out to be less of a chore than anticipated, probably because of the beasts' exhaustion from the previous day's extracurricular activities, and possibly because of their separation from their herd and unfamiliar surroundings. The riders all mounted safely, and Sethur claimed that he believed that if allowed freedom to roam a bit, the "girls" as he referred to them, would locate water, hopefully nearby. He assured his traveling companions that the girls needed water badly, and that they had a keen sense of smell. Then he said, "Lead on, Parker."

Ben spoke gently to his ride. "First gear, baby. Let's get going." He gave her the subtlest of nudges with his heels, and she started forward. As the slack went out of the lead ropes, the others followed, stretching out like a line of elephants in a future circus.

Through the first hours of the morning they plodded at a pace that seemed to Ben like compound low, a speed only available in farm trucks these days. Then he reminded himself which days these were. In any case he identified the progress as painfully slow; a person could walk much faster. But he knew none of his companions cared about that. Their desire for the camels to sniff out some water loomed foremost in their minds. If that didn't happen, what else mattered?

Ben wondered about the land. *In an area of a hundred square miles, will there be one place for camels to water? Do camels know these spots, or remember them? Can they smell water over significant distances?* He remembered reading that camels were very blessed in the olfactory department, as Sethur had assured him, but he could only wait and see.

After a significantly long and boring spell, his transport stopped plodding. She lifted her nose toward the southwest and sniffed a gentle camel sniff, as did her trailing sisters.

"Just allow her freedom. It appears she smells water," Sethur said softly.

For the first time that day the little caravan deviated from its due southward course and began to follow what appeared to be a dry creek bed, a wadi, up a gentle slope. At the top of a low rise the slope nearly flattened out, but the creek bed continued westward, gradually up toward what Ben thought would certainly be a box canyon, were this a classic western movie.

Given their heads, the camels worked their way slowly up, slowly in. No prodding seemed necessary, and the riders gave none. The dromedaries were silent and watchful. The homo sapiens also watched, but for different reasons.

Soon canyon walls began closing toward them, and the open flat of the valley floor became narrower. It funneled down to about six feet wide, barely enough space for a camel to turn, let alone for the girls to reverse direction and avoid bumping each other. At the end of the canyon Ben could just make out a small pool, almost invisible in the late morning shadow cast by the nearness of the limestone walls. The lead camel automatically knelt to allow Ben to dismount. *Must be bundled with the software,* he thought, though none of the other camels duplicated the move. So Ben dismounted while the others remained in their saddles. He stood aside and watched his mount drink, while wrapping the lead rope tightly around his right wrist.

In a short time she had accomplished rehydration, so Ben maneuvered her to the far left and squeezed her by Sethur's mount, so that she could then drink as well. "It doesn't smell bitter," Sethur mused. "While this one drinks let us fill our water skin and pass it amongst us."

Lydia retrieved the water-skin and handed it to Ben. He had just enough lead rope to squeeze back through and submerge the skin to fill it, then he squeezed back through and handed it to her. She drank deeply, then passed it back to Ben. He handed it up to Patricia, and she drank the remainder.

The camels moved one more spot, and Ben squeezed between the animals again for a refill. He and Sethur drank, and finally Patricia's camel stood waterside. As the last of the "girls" drank, Ben filled the skin and returned it to Lydia.

At that moment the stranger spoke to them from behind, on the trail.

"Stealing water is offensive to us who live around here." The voice communicated threat, just as a weapon does.

The travelers stared at him. His authoritative figure possessed the middle of the narrow canyon floor. The morning sun revealed a large man, almost as large as Al-alif, but less portly, Ben thought. Had he been a professional athlete, someone watching him would certainly have wondered if steroids figured somewhere into his fitness regimen.

As all of the camels were now watered, Ben pulled the train forward in order to orient them all toward the only way of escape should flight become part of whatever this next step turned out to be.

"No further, you thieves. What gives you the right to steal water from my clan?"

Ben handed the lead rope to Sethur and stepped forward a tentative half pace, hoping body language would help communicate his pacific intent. "We are travelers lost in yesterday's storm. We are separated from our companions and would perhaps have died, had not our beasts somehow located this blessed pool. We will gladly pay fair price for the water, and be on our way."

"Who are you? And who are these companions you speak of?"

"I am Parker. With me are Sethur, Lydia and Patricia, and we seek reunion with the caravan of Al-Alif."

"You will pay ten denarii per camel, and five per person," he snarled. "That will be sixty denarii."

"I am afraid," Ben explained, "that we must negotiate some more reasonable price, because we do not possess the amount you request. Perhaps we could give you ten denarii for the trouble."

"You will pay what I demand or you will die." From the tone of voice, Ben understood that whoever this man was, he truly believed that these were the only two options available.

Ben cast aside any hope that conciliatory body language would be of any use in this situation. He took an assertive step toward the stranger, and positioned himself in front of his camel with the canyon wall to his right. Inside his head, his sensei's voice was speaking. *You must not resist the powerful opponent.* Good. Here stands a powerful opponent, and Ben had no desire to resist him. Behind him, next to the wall, grew one of those nasty thorn bushes. He hoped that he looked calm and sounded nonthreatening. "We wish you no harm. Please allow us to pay this reasonable sum, and let us be on our way."

The adversary did not reply with words. He resorted to his own body language. He pulled a hilted, dagger-like knife from his belt.

Ben considered the knife warily. He could feel fear tightening its grip and wondered if perhaps more were at stake than met his eye at that moment. He knew that men were a law unto themselves in outlying areas, and remembered with some regret his sensei announcing that his next lesson, slated for two days after he was to arrive back at the time shed, would focus on defensive tactics specifically related to armed assailants. *Great timing,* Ben thought.

He must be intending to use the knife on me, or on us. Or why would he bother to draw it? Such clear logic frightened Ben. Just as clearly, he could see in his mind's eye sensei's wall chart of the *kamsetsu waza*, outlining the twenty-three pressure points, those weak spots in the human body. He knew about other vulnerabilities as well, and for a brief moment he wished he were wearing those sharp-toed cowboy boots he'd purchased his sophomore year at College Station.

The man moved forward with the smoothness of a viper. He wore a dark brown robe, and Ben thought his belt was leather. He held the knife in his right hand, and appeared to be very familiar with the tool. Ben concentrated on the knife hand, and on the man's midsection, which enveloped, his high school wrestling coach had assured him, the center of all bodily movement. Sensei had reinforced this thought, insisting that people fake with their head, with their limbs. Hip fakes were unheard of. So he prepared himself and watched and waited. *You must let him attack and cause him to be off balance.* Great! It looked as if the man would be attacking any second now. What could be better? Neither Ben nor the assailant spoke.

Waiting for him to attack would be the hard part.

The extortionist stood about Ben's height, and carried a well-muscled frame, honed by the hardness of desert life. *Gentle way,* thought Ben, but he wished for a five iron or a

127

baseball bat. While he wished for weapons, his adversary lunged, knife hand first. *Use his own weight and momentum against him.*

Ben sprang to his left, failing to notice that he'd startled the girls just a bit. But he avoided the thrust, and as the knife went past he grasped the right wrist in his left hand, and the knuckles with his right. Then he bent the two together with all of his might.

This was a great surprise to a desert bully who had never seen a Jackie Chan movie. In less than a second he had dropped the knife, and his momentum *(Use his own momentum against him.)* had carried him past Ben, who slid around behind the man, still fully in touch with the right wrist. "Resist me and I will break your arm." Ben confided to his charge. Good posture became impossible at this point. Ben kept the man bent forward a good bit, and kept up a good defense from behind.

Now what? thought Ben. *Do I have Sethur find some way to tie this guy up? If we do that, how do we make sure he doesn't die out here?* Momentarily, he knew the answer. He shoved the desert thug squarely into the thorn bush and stepped firmly in the middle of his back for good measure. The man howled in pain, and due to the ubiquity and sharpness of the thorns, he became, for the moment, immobilized.

Ben picked up the knife and tossed it into the pond. He seized the lead rope and started the train back toward the open desert. The girls naturally shied away from the struggling mass in the bush. He attempted to kick at the camels as they passed. All were able to slip by, and none were harmed.

Ben led the train briskly for about a hundred paces, then stopped. He again handed Sethur the lead rope and set his shepherd's bag on the ground. He found his stash of denarii and counted out ten. Then he changed his mind and made it eleven. He walked to the back of the caravan and saw the man still struggling to free himself. He shouted. "We leave the price of the water here in the path!" With that he dropped the coins in the sand, and returned toward the front of the line.

As he passed Lydia, she gasped, "Parker, you are wounded!"

Ben looked at her, then at his left foot. Somehow in the skirmish he had suffered some bodily harm, though it amounted to nothing more, he thought, than the reopening and enlargement of his former thorn-wound. *It must have happened when I pushed him down into the thorns,* he thought. As he examined the laceration, he could see the blood already beginning to coagulate, and that the bleeding would soon stop, though the cut was ugly. The reopening of the wound had narrowly missed the strap of his sandal, and the look of it was not a cut as much as it was a rip, The nature of the wound reassured him that he'd not accidentally run the knife into his foot while it lay on the ground.

"We'll see to it later," he said. He reclaimed the rope and continued down the trail, anxious to be out of the constriction of the canyon and into the open.

They'd come farther in than he'd thought. It took him about twenty minutes of solid walking before the feeling of vulnerability to attack gave way to the open freedom of the dunes. As they left the canyon, Sethur addressed Ben.

"We will speak later of your heroic deed and what you have accomplished for us this day. For this moment we must choose a course. It is likely Al-alif will be in pursuit of us, most especially of his camels. We have no food and little water, so we cannot survive long in the desert without help. It is my advice that we attempt to retrace our path back to the north. Likely in this open country we shall see Al-alif, or even more likely that he will see us. Thus the problems of food and water would both be solved, and we would be restored to our guide. But over these hills to the west is the Jordan Valley. Across the Jordan is Israel, and south of Israel is Judea, wherein lies Jerusalem, our destination. We could attempt the crossing and hope to find water and food along the way. If we happen upon any of my own people, they would certainly give us aid. Both choices seem equally dangerous. What do you say?"

Sethur looked at Ben as he spoke. Both of them understood that the camels had come to water of their own volition, but it would now be necessary to lead them, as the Bedouins had done until the incident with the storm, the lizard, the snake, and the broken lead rope. These varied and numerous factors presented them with the danger of their plight. One of the two men would have to walk before the train at all times regardless of which direction they chose. In Ben's mind, he considered the camels "borrowed" and thought they should try to get them back to their proper owners, but he also realized that Al-alif might eventually abandon the search and head for Jerusalem without them.

The women sat quietly on their beasts, so Ben asked them, "What do you think? Whichever way we go seems to involve great risk."

Neither Lydia nor Patricia spoke. After a few seconds, Sethur broke the silence by saying, "The women expect us to lead them and protect them. What do you say? North or west seem to be our only choices. To the east and south lie wilderness. But one of us must be on the sand now, whichever way we choose. We must become Bedouins."

This, thought Ben, *is not politically correct. It's not even right. Why should the women not have a part in making this decision? Why should they not speak their minds? How backward can we be?*

"I think we should try to find Al-alif," Ben answered. "I will walk as far as I can, and then you can take your turn."

Sethur nodded, the women exchanged a glance that said "I told you so." And Ben started out. To say that the midday desert sun is extremely hot is an understatement. Ben had been told that one hundred thirty degrees Fahrenheit is the threshold for first-degree burns. The sand scorched his feet, and the heat just kept coming. Throughout the middle hours of the day, every step brought literal pain. As his brain had no reasonable way to process the data, it ignored the messages, so after a while the nerve endings stopped sending them in.

The sun, apart from shedding light on their way, helped them very little. The thought of sunglasses crept through Ben's head again, but he pushed it aside and plodded north. He let his mind think what it would.

He thought about Doc Resser and his assertion that Ben would return to the time shed in whatever state of physical health (or abuse?) he had achieved in the past—that even if his body were dead it would return to the future in its static condition. He thought of the coroner's report—sunburn on the hands, wrists, cheeks and ankles. What seem to be saddle sores on the buttocks. A flesh wound on the left foot. Extreme dehydration.

Then he laughed to himself. *Everyone knows that time travel is impossible. Michael J. Fox could do it, but that was only in the movies. Then you need a DeLorean traveling 88 miles per hour and a jiggawatt of electrical power, besides the development of the flux capacitor and a highly-paid Hollywood director to make it all happen.*

Then he thought of Sherry. Wouldn't she be surprised to hear about what he'd just done—not so much as an act of courage, but of necessity? She'd be pleased that he'd paid for the water and even left a generous tip. He thought of her face and her voice, and her father. He remembered in great detail every aspect of her life. He thought about how strange it was that a child of three should be among his best friends. Then he thought that everyone should have a friend like that. His mind then drifted to some lines from Lord Byron—"She walks in beauty like the night of cloudless climes and starry skies, and all that's best of dark and bright meet in her aspect and her eyes, thus mellow'd from that tender light which heaven to gaudy day denies."

Lydia fits that too, he thought. He found himself wondering about her. Deep in his subconscious he knew that he only played a game to keep his mind off the heat and the brightness and the breeze out of the east that brought more of the same, and the waves rising from the sand like he'd seen on hot days above the hood of his Bentley. But he had to admit he enjoyed the game. It broke the boredom of that unmitigated noon.

After this, and after many more meanderings of the mind, the voice of Sethur recalled him from those mental excursions.

"Parker, you must take water and rest. I will take a turn at walking now." He slid from his mount without attempting to have her kneel. Lydia passed the water skin around and all urged Ben to drink deeply, though the others contented themselves with a sip.

"It is the ninth hour. If we must spend the night in the desert, unprotected, we should walk perhaps three more hours. Parker, you must find a way to the top of the camel."

Sethur took the lead rope from Ben's hand and gently pulled until her nose nearly touched the sand. Then he softly said "kneel." She moved slowly, like an old door on rusty hinges, but eventually she bellied down. Ben seated himself as quickly as he could and leaned back as she returned to the standing position.

They began to move again, with the second camel bearing no one and Sethur striding through the dunes, leading them confidently north.

The camel's saddle became to Ben a rocking cradle. For some days he'd been writing checks on his body which caused an overdraft on his sleep account. The relatively sleepless night in Bismarck, and the thirty-six hours without rest from the first day of his trip were an IOU demanding satisfaction. So it made perfect sense to him when he realized that he'd been asleep. His first thought when he awoke was that he was grateful to still be mounted.

The sun burned slowly toward the horizon. They had no particular destination in mind, but could stop as they saw fit.

He looked carefully at Sethur, seeking signs of fatigue or listlessness. He could see none. The Levite walked before them, capable and resolute, and determinedly led his small charge of "ships of the desert" on their northward course.

The topography changed subtly, if at all, and made little difference to Ben. But Sethur considered the dunes they passed. He eyed the sand hills as they crossed them, and even to the casual observer it would have been clear that he was deliberating.

Ninth hour, Ben thought. *Six p.m.* Sethur stopped. He approached Ben and asked, "Do you think it proper to conceal ourselves from possible enemies, or to remain in a place where a fire would be a beacon for Al-alif?"

Ben considered this. He thought that most miscreants would probably not investigate a fire in the open, supposing that only those who lack protection would camouflage their campsite. Any who would build a fire in the open would most likely have some sort of weaponry and man-power. To be unnoticed, on the other hand, might cause Al-alif to pass nearby in darkness, were he still searching.

As he analyzed this, he realized that he wanted Lydia and Patricia to have input. He let that pass, and relayed his thought to Sethur, with the conclusion that he would like to be visible if such could be accomplished safely.

"Nothing is truly 'safe' anywhere out here," Sethur replied, his tone of voice supplying the not yet discovered air quotes. "We must do our best to reunite with our caravan, and greater visibility gives us greater chance of that. Yonder dune's top should be as good as any spot."

They worked their way to the top of the dune, and Ben dismounted as Sethur had, without kneel. He immediately turned his attention to Lydia and Patricia. By gentle persuasion, he achieved kneelage and offloaded the women without serious incident. As he did so, Sethur hobbled the camels. Suddenly, Sethur asked, "Lady Patricia, is this your parcel?"

Patricia shook her head, and Sethur removed a small bundle tied to the back of her saddle. "Praise be to Adonai!" Sethur cried. "We have a bit of food! And oil! And flint! Our deliverance cannot be far off, for so I have prayed."

There were strips of meat wrapped in the bundle—primitive jerky, Ben surmised. He remembered high school world history, when his teacher had told (would tell?) the class that some tribes cured jerky beneath saddles of pack animals. Salt in the animal's sweat accomplished the preservation. He decided this would be a good fact to keep to himself. But it would have made no difference to any of them. It would be eaten no matter how it was cured.

"The flint is a great treasure! I wondered how we would build a fire, and prayed to God to help me find a way. Parker, can you gather some dry thorn bushes?"

Thorn bushes seem to be everywhere in these parts, thought Ben. *It is no wonder that I landed in one.* He counted twelve different bushes within thirty yards of the campsite.

After a careful gathering of the dead branches, and a careful piling of them near where Sethur intended to build the fire, Ben began to survey the place of their bivouac. They had chosen the highest dune around, and nothing moved that he could see. He remembered how all this got started, so he searched for those small pairs of indentations in the sand that would indicate an adder buried, waiting for the unsuspecting lizard. He found none of those telltale signs, in spite of a careful inspection.

Eventually, Sethur kindled a very small fire. "We have no cooking to do, we must seek only to be noticed, and only by Al-alif. I would not expect him to be searching in the night after the first watch. We will share a meal now, such as God has provided. Then we must keep the fire burning and await our rescue."

Sethur seems confident, thought Ben. *I think the odds are slim, but then, I'm not from around here....*

A slight gasp disconnected the last few cars from Ben's train of thought. He turned to see Patricia staring at the sand, and at first could not discern the source of her fear.

Then he saw it, a sandy shape on a sandy surface. A scorpion.

"The camels will not like this," Sethur warned, and brought a long forked stick from the burn pile which he used to flip the offensive invader about fifty yards down the dune's raspy surface. All eyes were then trained on the surrounding sand, and eventually more were discovered—one very near the camels.

"We cannot sleep with these about, and the sun is going down. Darkness is their time to move, and it seems too late to choose another place. Under starlight they are nearly impossible to see." Sethur flipped another intruder far into the night.

Ben attempted to recall what he could about scorpions. *Eleven hundred species, all with the ability to sting. Thirty species possibly fatal to humans, very intricate mating habits, visible under black light. Is this the dune I want to die on?*

He wondered if it could work. Then he thought he might as well try. So as twilight engulfed the camp he stretched the bonus piece of purple cloth in a large square on a branch of thorn-bush. He ripped a small amount of gray-brown cloth from the damask he'd bought to protect his food purchase, and wrapped it around the end of a stick, then saturated it with some of the oil Sethur had found.

Then, as darkness was closing in completely, he ignited the torch in their watch-fire. He asked Patricia to move next to the camels and called on Sethur and Lydia to bring 'flipping sticks'.

He led them in concentric circles around the dune, and they relocated scorpions as they encountered them, as the torchlight through the purple cloth provided enough black light to identify the enemies. They swept the dune slope clean in the space of about two hours, with a few returns to the fireside for more torch sticks and replenishment of oil and cloth.

After the first sweep, Sethur sent Lydia to keep Patricia company by the camels, and the men spiraled their way again to the dune's bottom, locating very few scorpions. Ben felt like the primitive version of the Orkin man. After a recheck of the area immediately around the camels, they extinguished their torch and put their sticks back on the wood pile. They had exhausted Ben's store of damask cloth. Finally, they sat down near the fire, each leaning back against a camel.

"Now God has provided us with a safe campsite as well. Deliverance must be near at hand," As Sethur said this, he closed his eyes. He seemed ready to sleep, Ben remembered his own afternoon of slumber aboard the camel, and thought he might try to stay awake for a while. But then Sethur spoke again.

"Parker, we must soon take note of our camels' need to eat. Perhaps we can let them graze a bit before we begin our trip tomorrow."

Ben wondered why he hadn't thought of this himself. "I'm sure you know that much better than I. Please get some rest, Sethur. I can keep watch for a little while now."

Sethur drifted off to sleep, and Ben stood up. The chill of the night air seemed to reach out and touch his skin as the sky's darkness became complete. The fire had nearly burned itself out. The flat blackness of the sky, the bright points of light, thousands, millions, billions, trillions, instilled in Ben the feeling of irrelevance, of insignificance, of isolation.

What if we all die out here? Who would know? Who would care? He thought of Sethur's insistence that God had given them meat and oil and flint. *Would he also put purple cloth on his list? Pure coincidence.* Then he looked again at the obsidian sky. *Are the three hundred sextillion stars also pure coincidence?* He moved to the woodpile to get fuel for the watch-fire

Eventually, he detected a quiet noise, a susurration, the sound of a man walking on sand. He listened until he was absolutely certain, then he woke Sethur. He whispered, "I think someone approaches. Listen."

As he spoke, the edge of the dying firelight revealed a robed figure who stopped as they saw him.

136

"If you are a friend, you are welcome at our fire." Sethur spoke a standard desert greeting.

"I have seldom been so glad to hear a voice. Sethur, that must be you. Are the ladies and the young man with you? And the camels?" They heard the voice of Hilkiah, Al-alif's head Bedouin.

"Yes, Hilkiah, we are all here, all safe, thanks to the providence of the God of Abraham and the interventions of our friend Parker. Is Al-alif nearby? We are wanting both food and water, and fodder for the beasts. We fare much better than we might."

"Al-alif will soon be here with whatever you need. I will signal that what we had hoped is true."

Having said that, Hilkiah drew a branch from the dying fire, added oil by drops to increase the flame's intensity, and waved it slowly back and forth five times, Ben thought. After about two minutes he repeated the signaling, then replaced the brand in the blaze.

"I will gather more fuel. Al-alif will soon come." He disappeared into the surrounding darkness, but they could hear him nearby, breaking the dead twigs from their thorny nests.

When the fire had been restoked, they heard from across the desert, far to the north, "Hilkiah, have you found them?"

"All is well, master. We await your arrival, and we require food and water."

They stood in silence, all awake by now, circling the fire, and gathering closer as the radiance subsided. Presently they heard the sound of camel footfalls on the sand, and the grunts of their hobbled beasts in recognition of camel herd companions. "Greetings, my friends. With great pleasure I see your faces. We had despaired of locating you, and Al-alif has never failed to deliver passengers safely. (One man did break his leg when his camel got into a fight and threw him off, but since then we've enlisted only she-camels for passengers.) So we will share a meal here and tell of our fortunes since we've last seen each other. Hilkiah, I've water, some goat meat, lentils,

137

and wheat flour enough for us here. The cooking pot is in my camel's baggage."

As Hilkiah went to work, Al-alif began to question the four on how they fared. Suddenly, Lydia interrupted and said, "Have you ointments? Parker is wounded!"

Ben had completely forgotten about that. He had not noticed when it happened and it had not bothered him since. But when Al-alif saw the wound, he brought some sort of balm or salve from his camel's pack, and asked Hilkiah for water and clean cloth.

Lydia spoke again. "May I dress the wound? Parker received it in our defense."

Al-alif bowed and backed away, knowing that this amounted to a demand, not a request.

Ben sat where he could modestly allow Lydia to touch his foot. She asked also for a cleansing agent, and gently removed Ben's sandal.

This entire process provided a new sensation for Ben. He had heard about reflexology, and how the feet contained nerve endings connected to most everywhere else in the body. All of this, he reasoned, could only be theory. But gentle hands on his fatigued foot, massaging away the day's dirt and grime, and in this case, a bit of dried blood fit into Ben's definition of a singularity. Nothing in his life could be compared to it. He very nearly fell asleep as Lydia performed this act of reverent service. It seemed almost magical. But Al-alif broke the spell when he announced that the meal was prepared—roast goat and lentils and flat bread, all lightly salted. The taste of that meal ranked, in Ben's mind, among the top ten at least, even though it was goat meat.

After the meal had been eaten and the leftovers set aside for the breaking of fast, Al-alif requested that they remain seated around the fire in order to discuss the events of the last two days.

"Let me begin, please, by telling the four of you that when Parker's camel was spooked by the serpent, and broke free of her lead, we immediately unlade our fastest camel and I sent Hilkiah after you. You were only three or four stadia distant when he mounted to pursue you, but lost sight of you soon because of the storm. We knew that camels in such straits might run for miles, and Hilkiah's mount was in no such straits. When the storm struck, she closed her eyes and her nostrils and lay in the sand. So he waited for the storm to abate.

"When the wind subsided, though he could see for miles to the south, you were not in view. He then returned to us, and we mounted a more organized effort to attempt to locate you. We searched in vain through yesterday evening, and continued south through today. We reasoned that if you were still alive and able to travel, you would either attempt to reunite with us or continue west into the Jordan Valley, (That is, assuming you knew the lay of the land).

"So today we pushed further southward, hoping to see you or to find trace of your passing. We saw no sign through the day, as the storm had obliterated all evidence of your flight, and as night pressed in we thought to make camp and return north in the morning, committing your fate to the gods.

"As darkness came upon us, from some miles away we saw the light of a campfire, this very fire. We thought little of it at first, supposing it could be a goatherd, or another caravan. But soon after dark we observed a light, a lesser light, passing across the face of the hill, curiously moving lower each time it passed. We thought then that perhaps someone attempted to signal us, so I sent Hilkiah this way, with instructions to alert us to come if he found you, or needed us for other reasons. So we have come, and, against all odds, you are here and safe. What has befallen you, and how has Parker suffered this wound?"

Sethur began by telling of the ride into the storm, and of the wind and sand, and of the eventual capture of the lead rope he'd observed Ben accomplish. He went on to speak of the first night in the open, the shared meal after the storm—the dried fruit and honeycomb from the Damascus market, and of the water from Lydia's limited supply. He

139

told of the morning, of allowing the camels to seek water, and of the wondrous finding that the girls had accomplished.

He then spoke of the attacker—not in glorious terms of exaggeration, but soberly and factually—how he looked very strong yet Ben had gently but firmly disarmed the man, and parked his body in a thorn bush, and had thrown the knife into the pool. He described Ben's payment for the water and their trek through that day. He then covered the discovery of food and oil and flint behind Patricia's saddle.

The verbal record of the evening turned somewhat sketchy, as he explained how Ben had made a shade out of purple cloth which rendered the scorpions visible after dark. At the end of the story he made the point that the reunion they experienced may never have happened without the scorpions, for Al-alif had misinterpreted their anti-arthropod sweep as a desperate signal.

He finally fell silent, and Ben felt that everyone was staring in his direction.

They were.

"Parker, may we question you about these things?" This came from Al-alif.

"What would you like to know?"

Al-alif began. "Do you not know that two denarii, or at most three, would have paid handsomely for the water?" Ben sensed that this question carried serious import. He replied carefully.

"No. I did not know. But I had offered him ten, and also some damage will come to his cloak, and to his body, from the thorns. I do not know whether he can recover his knife. Did I do wrong?"

"No. And it will be a good thing if he never gets his knife back. Somehow we must find a way to keep such tools out of unworthy hands. Our problem is, if knives are outlawed, only outlaws will have knives. But can you tell me how you disarmed him? From Sethur's account, it must have been some sort of a trick. Could you also do this to me?"

"Yes, sir. I bent his wrist until he dropped the knife, and then, not knowing how else to disable him, I put him in a thorn bush, which must have kept him busy for some time. I have been trained, somewhat, in my homeland to disarm certain attackers without harming them. It is unlikely to work on you, or anyone who is expecting it."

"We must allow that to stand for now. My greatest curiosity concerns the scorpions. How did you know that light shined through the purple cloth would make them visible in the dark?"

Ben had no immediate reply. How could he explain ultraviolet light and the spectrum and wavelengths and the properties of a scorpion's outer shell and Wikipedia and a natural interest in arachnids? At length he answered. "I did not know that the cloth and torch would work as it did before I tried it. I hoped it would, because similar things are done in my homeland."

Al-alif gently shook his head and smiled. "Parker," he laughed, "That is what we call thinking outside the tent."

Sethur then asked, "Twice, perhaps thrice during the storm, I heard you speak in some strange language. What were you saying?"

"That is my mother tongue. I have spoken this language very little, as all of you must know. I only began to learn it three months ago." Here he paused, thinking briefly of the Pimsleur method and the importance of vocabulary. "I still do not understand all of what you say. I speak not as well as a child. But the tone of my voice perhaps calmed the camel. It was desperate, but it seemed to work."

No one spoke for some time, after which Lydia asked permission to "question Parker". When Al-alif nodded, she began.

"In your homeland, do people wear shoes?"

What? What is going on here? What kind of a question is this? Ben finally regained his composure. "Why do you ask me this?" he said.

"When I dressed your wound I had to remove your sandal. There were not the regular pale lines beneath the

141

straps of your sandals—only uniform brown skin. I thought you must usually be without shoes for this to be the case."

Doc's voice echoed in Ben's head. *Be sure to wear your sandals to the tanning booth.* Doc. Such a know-it-all.

"And also," Lydia continued, "the shoes you wear look quite new. You could not have worn them from west of Tarshish to this place and still have them looking so new."

What is it with women and shoes? he thought. He contemplated his answer. "Yes, the shoes are new. I purchased them for this trip. Most of my countrymen wear shoes. My own case is unique, but normally you would see the pale skin beneath the places guarded by sandal straps."

Lydia seemed to accept this, then she said, "You must be a man of great wealth in your own land. Are you?"

Is this Miss Marple, first century edition?

"And why do you ask me this?"

"When you unpacked your shepherd's bag (a very nice bag, and again, quite new) you removed a robe that is the sort that only the very rich would wear. You wrapped your foodstuffs in damask cloth, which is an expensive way to wrap food. Clean rags would have been very effective. You also seemed to be content to burn such expensive cloth as you rendered the scorpions visible. And you paid so generously for the water. And you seem to me to be a man of royal breeding."

"In my homeland," Ben began patiently, "I am considered to be very wealthy. The robe is for me to wear when I get to Jerusalem, but I thought it best to travel more as a commoner would. The damask I purchased as a matter of convenience as I passed through the market in Damascus, and as for the water, I thought it only fair, though I admit I do not really know how much a denarius should buy, being from far away. Our money is very different from what you have here. So I did not know I burned such expensive cloth."

"And why are your toenails so uniform and well-kept? Your fingernails as well—they appear to be shaped by an artist."

142

"In my homeland, tools to cut fingernails and toenails are common. I take care of that job myself, and it is very easy to do. These tools are not available here, so soon I will look no different in that regard."

Lydia contemplated his answer. To her, Ben thought, this could have been the most important question. Then she said, "Men do not have beards in your homeland. Is that right?"

"Some men have them. Most of us do not. I did not have a beard until I decided to visit here. I let it grow in order that I might better fit in with the men of this land. Tools are available for cutting beards off, and many men do this each day, and their faces appear smooth and hairless. Some of our women like that."

Lydia smiled. "I am glad that you finally spoke of women, because I think you have no wife at home. That is true, is it not?"

"All too true," sighed Ben. "There is a special woman that I care deeply about, but alas, she is only three years old."

"And can you wait the ten years?" Lydia asked.

Ben could barely conceal his shock. *Ten years. Thirteen.* The thought turned his stomach. "Women wait much longer to marry there. It will probably be at least twenty years before she is ready. And no, we are not meant for each other. But she is one of my truest friends." Ben wondered for a brief few seconds if time travel could have a practical use in this regard. The thought did not seem right.

"And," Lydia began again, "I wonder about your women. Do they help you decide what to do as you showed when you asked us which way to go this morning?"

"They help with many decisions, and I am accustomed to seeking their opinions when the outcome matters to them. But now, let me ask you. Did you not expect exactly that response when Sethur asked me about the choice?"

Lydia seemed taken aback. "How did you know this? We said nothing to you."

Ben smiled. His turn now. But this was not the time to bring up the basics of body language. He said, "I just knew."

"And what of that square of fabric? Is it from your homeland, and may I examine it more closely?" Ben retrieved the cloth from its thorny frame and handed it to her. She left off asking questions, and began a careful examination of the cloth.

The interrogation seemed to have stalled out, so after a brief pause, Ben turned to Al-alif. "May I ask some questions now?"

Al-alif nodded again, and Ben turned back to Lydia. "What are you and Patricia expecting to accomplish in Jerusalem?"

Lydia looked up from the square of cloth. "Parker, my deliverer, this must be a long answer, and I will try to give it fully and honestly, as you deserve.

"We live near the great water far north and west of here. Our family owns property at the shore of the sea. Some years ago, my father discovered that when the tide ebbed, mellux snails could be seen. Because he is a man of wisdom, he knew that these animals provide the base component in the dye used in garments for the very wealthy, royalty, and certain retired military officers. Immediately, he began to harvest the snails in hopes of marketing the dye. He soon found that the snails reproduce at a snail's pace, just as they do all things, thus limiting his ability to earn generously from his snail farm. Our operation fared meagerly until about ten years ago when I, as a young girl, began to spend much time helping my father. I studied the snails for hours at a time. Some days I would get nothing done except watching the snails to see what they do. They do not do much. And what they do is not exciting to watch.

"But as I observed them, I noticed things about them that others had not seen. I devised a way of milking the dye color from them without harming them. Along that shore where we live, which is among very few places where these

144

snails breed, no one else can do this as yet. My father's operation is more profitable than any other because we do not harvest the snails. We milk them and set them free. We have more dye per foot of shoreline than anyone else in the world.

"Father sent us then, Patricia and me, to Damascus to purchase their uniquely designed damask cloth, on which to experiment with our dye. He instructed us also to visit Jerusalem and speak with an acquaintance of his, one Pontius Pilate, concerning the possibility of supplying our cloth to those who have retired from military service and other government officials, and possibly royalty. That is how we have come to be here. But I believe our trip would have ended in tragedy had it not been for you. When my father hears of this, he will want to reward you handsomely."

As she was speaking she had smoothed and refolded the cloth into a pocket sized bundle. She seemed to be finished with her answer. She handed the folded cloth back to Ben.

"Thank you," he said. "Perhaps our paths will cross as we do our business in Jerusalem."

Ben turned to Sethur. "You seemed to credit God for our discovery of food and for our ultimate rescue. Do you believe that God is there? Who is he, and how do you know him? What is he doing?"

CHAPTER XI

Sethur's face revealed an expression of joy. His voice was level and controlled despite his enthusiasm.

"This, friend Parker, will be another very long answer. But let me say first that you may not yet realize, because you do not understand the ways of this land, what happened today. It seems so long ago, but it was just this morning your attacker accosted you. He planned to kill you, and me as well. He would have wished to do so even if you had been willing to pay the villainous price for water that he demanded. Even more so then, because a man with that sort of money would be bound to have more for the taking.

"The women would have been saved alive and either taken to his home to be his slaves in all ways, or sold to another for the same purpose. You and I would have had the easier fate, and so the gratitude of the women will far exceed even my deepest thanks. That man would have taken all our worldly goods and the camels for himself. All of us, myself, the women, and Al-alif are deeply in your debt. On behalf of us all, I say 'Thank you!'"

Ben smiled, and inclined his head slightly. He thought this was a bit much, but said nothing.

"As to your questions of spiritual things, though I shall attempt brevity, I must also speak with clarity.

"Our sacred writings tell us that long ago the invisible God created the heavens and the earth. Into this earth He put all sorts of life, meant to reproduce after its kind. Birds of the sky, camels and dogs, snakes and scorpions and snails. Were this not enough, the scriptures tell us that he made the stars also. This is among the Lord God's most amazing accomplishments, as there are so many of them. Hundreds, thousands. All lighting the night. But I promised brevity.

"Into this world of perfection He brought the man and the woman, whose lives were torn apart, so to speak, by the entrance of sin into the world, which came about when the man and the woman disobeyed the Lord God.

"Following this unfortunate turn of events, the ensuing tragedy of human history began in earnest. People multiplied on the earth, but they grew more and more intent on disobedience, and the fulfillment of their own desires.

"In response to their disobedience, God called Noah to build an ark in which to house the land dwelling animals during the judgment God sent through the great flood. Noah built a large barge, and preserved life on land through it. He and his wife had three sons, and from these three families all human life on earth is descended, for all beside them were destroyed in the flood.

"From the line of Shem, one of Noah's three sons, God chose a man called Abram through whom He intended to bless the world.

"Abram heard God's call in Ur of the Chaldees that he should leave his own country to live in Canaan, just across those mountains to the west. God promised him ownership of the land, but he did not actually possess it. However, God had said to him, 'In thee shall all nations of the earth be blessed'. And God changed his name to Abraham.

"Abraham's son Isaac fathered Jacob, who had twelve sons. These, by the sovereign hand of God, were brought to Egypt. There they spent four hundred thirty years, becoming a large company, one that would be difficult to account for using the numerals these benighted Romans use. The people of Egypt mistreated and enslaved them, and they cried out to the Lord God. He heard them and delivered them, sending them from Egypt with great wealth, and destroying Egypt's military power in the process.

"Jacob's children wandered in this wilderness where we now camp for forty years, led by a man called Moses. God chose him to be their leader, their deliverer, and their lawgiver. He became as a father to the entire nation, guiding them from Egypt to the land promised by God, and establishing them as a nation.

"Moses told them not to worship graven images, as the people of the land were doing. He told them that the invisible, all-powerful God could not be represented by an image of any kind, no matter how intricate or beautiful. He gave them Ten Words to live by, and established the Jewish religion, of which I am a part.

"That was over forty generations ago. Since then, the Lord God has spoken to us through many prophets and holy men, promising to give to us a new King in the future who will sit on the throne of our greatest king of the past, David. He won total victory over the people of the land. He united the twelve tribes in triumph, and led the nation to wealth and prosperity.

"Following David's long and benevolent reign, his son Solomon ruled for forty years. The prosperity Solomon brought to Judea doubled what it had been under David, or perhaps even trebled it. The silver that makes up our denarii possessed no more value than common stones in the time of Solomon.

"Solomon met with the Lord God twice—once early in his reign, and once later. The Lord God commanded him to remain true to His statutes, and promised blessing if Solomon would obey.

"And though David's son was excellent at planning and finance and building and politics, he disobeyed the Lord God by marrying many foreign wives. Most of these women brought to Jerusalem their own customs of worship, and we know that these women turned Solomon's heart away from the Lord God. He followed those idols instead of the Lord his God, and as such led the people away from their refuge and protection.

"This began, as far as I can tell, God's judgment on my nation.

"First, God brought a war over taxes. Solomon's son, who reigned in his stead, refused to listen to the people, and this ultimately resulted in a civil war and a divided kingdom. Israel in the north with ten of the tribes, and Judah in the south with but two tribes. The north chose their own king, and the south chose their own king. The twelve tribes were never united again. They helped to bring about their demise more quickly by fighting each other.

"This war raged, on and off, for centuries. Step by step, both half-kingdoms forsook the Lord God. After many kings and hundreds of years, my ancestors completely exhausted the mercy of our God. He had need of a method to perform His judgment, and He used the Assyrians from Ninevah to chastise and defeat and deport the northern kingdom." *From Ninevah,* Ben observed silently. "The Assyrians conquered and dispersed them abroad, then intermingled them with heathens and later reinstated them on the land of their forefathers. They dwell there now, the half-breed Samaritans.

"Judah in the south fared somewhat longer, but little better. More good kings reigned over her than Israel, but over time she matched her northern brothers in disobedience to the Lord God. At last He also poured judgment on them, calling Babylon from the east to come and destroy Jerusalem and carry her inhabitants into captivity. The Lord God had commanded Israel's children to let their land rest every seventh year. In four hundred twenty years, the land had never received her Sabbath. The Lord God did not accept this shoddy stewardship, this disobedience. The avarice of our fathers led them to lust for silver, and they planted each year, never leaving the ground fallow as He commanded. The Lord God did not forget His edict, nor His land. He took Judah to Babylon for seventy years, thus giving the land its promised rest.

"During all this time—the rebellions, the judgments, the captivity, God sent messengers to his chosen people. He assured them that He still loved them, and insisted on their return to obedience to Him. Sometimes they listened, and even experienced small revivals of passion for Him, but most of these holy men were ignored, though they spoke for God Himself. Some they tortured, some they killed, some they hounded into misery, and some few were heeded. Even in Judah's seventy-year captivity, our God sent His messengers to us, and assured us that though we experienced His correction, we remained His people still.

"Our last verbal message from our God came four hundred years ago. He indicted us for our apathy and called us to a passionate life for Him, and left us with a promise of a deliverer. Many of our holy prophets have spoken of a king from David's line, a righteous and pious king. Moses also promised a leader like himself, to whom the people would listen.

"Since that last message, our people have suffered much. We have been subjects of Persia, who demanded tribute, but left us alone to serve our God. Cyrus supported our way of life, and helped us to rebuild our temple. Eventually the Greeks, who were far worse, displaced the Persians. They attempted to contaminate our faith with Greek ideas, but we resisted them. After Alexander, their emperor, died, a series of rulers of lesser power than he each had their turn. Most were very wicked. The worst of these, Antiochus Epiphanes of Syria, attempted to destroy our priesthood by planning to force us to offer a filthy pig as a sacrifice to our God.

"At that time the Lord God raised up men to stand in the gap for His people. These men were the Hasmoneans, though my people call them the Maccabees. This word "Maccabees" has many meanings, like hammer, or extinguisher, or general, or hero. All meanings are tied to

151

the idea of a person or tool of conquest. It matters not which name you settle on. Mattathaias and his sons brought deliverance to our land, a freedom that lasted over a hundred years. When they finally liberated Jerusalem and cleansed the temple, they set up a menorah. It is a lamp that requires a special oil, the ingredients of which are ordained by God Himself. We could obtain enough ingredients for a single day's allotment, yet the menorah gave light from that single measure of oil for eight days. Eight days! Thus we celebrate yearly that liberation with a festival lasting eight days.

"Following that deliverance, great powers bartered over us—Rome, the Mithradites, Carthage, then factions within the Roman empire. None of these remained content to collect tribute and let us be. All meddled, all attempted to stop us from worship of the true God.

"Almost seventy years ago, a man named Herod received appointment to be our king." He spat the name Herod with a contempt that surprised everyone around the fire. "This Herod hailed from Idumea. That is, he descended from Abraham through his oldest son, Esau, who had then, as his descendants have now, no claim to the promises of the true God. He pretended to our faith just as he was a pretender to the throne upon which his ugly carcass sat. He forced his will upon us in some ways that were even more vicious than any we'd seen up until then. He murdered many of his own family, not to mention many of my tribe as well—peaceful godly men.

"Near the end of his reign, some very strange events occurred, both tragic and puzzling. As I have told you, our Holy Book promises a deliverer, a king, one who will lead us to victory, to dominance over our enemies, just as David did for us so many centuries ago This one is a promised descendant of David, and those devout in our faith look for him to come to rid us of the likes of the Romans. Around here it seems someone always wants to rule over us.

"But back to these events—an old man, a priest named Zacharias served God in the temple in Jerusalem, and it was during the time allotted, that is, chosen by lot, for him to perform his tasks in the temple. It would have been late spring about thirty years ago. During his service in the temple, he came out of the holy place after the sacrifice, and he could not speak. He could only sign to us, and it seemed to us that he had been given some sort of vision. I had just begun my Levite's duties, but I remember it well. He fulfilled his temple service as a mute, then went home to his wife in the hill country. They must have had some interesting conversations during those days. She had reached fifty years, still barren, but just as Sarah bore Isaac in Abraham's old age, Elizabeth conceived, with child by her mute husband.

"After a period of three months, her young cousin, a girl named Mary, came to visit. Following Mary's time there, after her return to her home in Nazareth, she also was found to be pregnant. The hill country must have an amorous effect on women. It is good, perhaps, that something does that. Anyway, the challenge, of course, with Mary was her claim still to be a virgin. You see the problem. How can a virgin be pregnant? She insisted that nothing untoward had happened to her in the hill country. She claimed to be expecting before she even left Nazareth.

"This opened the door to all sorts of suspicions, considering that Nazareth is a crossroads town and a Roman garrison. Sin is rampant there.

"We suspected a soldier. We suspected, perhaps, her intended, for she was betrothed. And our countrymen have no end of lewd jokes involving traveling merchants and the daughters of the land.

"But she and her man both insisted that all of this represented God's plan. They said angels had told them this.

"When the time arrived for the child to be born, perhaps the middle of autumn, the young man (who stood by his bride—I must respect that) compelled by a tax edict from Caesar to return to his ancestral home, traveled to Bethlehem to participate in the census. That is, to be placed on the tax rolls so that the Romans could have accurate

153

record for their extortion. They had no care for the numbers of people. What are a few thousand Jews to them anyway? All of that aside, they went to Bethlehem, to David's city to be counted.

"It turned out that the Romans could add one more to their census, for Mary gave birth to a son when they came to Bethlehem to be counted.

"Things stranger still began to happen to them—it is strange enough that both parents insisted this child came from God, or from some intervention of spiritual source, but upon the child's birth shepherds came, and also claimed to have been told by angels that God had provided in this child a Savior.

"Maybe he was meant to be the promised one from David's line.

"But you all know shepherds. Out, away from their families, night after night for months. What do they do to break the monotony, to fight the boredom?

"They make up stories about what they have seen. For this reason the testimony of a shepherd is not accepted in our courts. Shepherds cannot be trusted.

"One of our retired priests, an old man named Simeon, worshiped in the temple the day Mary and her husband brought the boy to be dedicated. When he saw the child, Simeon prophesied that this one displayed the glory of Israel, and would be a light to the Gentiles.

"Most Jews hate most Gentiles. Not all of us hate all of you." (He said this with an encompassing smile and a bow.) "But Simeon said that this child would be a light for you, and the glory of my people.

"And about two years later, a caravan came to Jerusalem full of magi, wise astronomers from the east, looking for a king of the Jews recently born. This put all Jerusalem in a stir, and most notably the wicked Herod. He inquired of the priests where this child should be born, and they quoted our prophet Micah, who said he should be born in Bethlehem, in Judea.

"So Herod sent these magi ahead to Bethlehem, and asked them to return with a report of the child's whereabouts, that he could also pay homage.

"Strangest of these many strange events happened as the magi left Jerusalem. All of us could see a light above them that led them forward, in the direction of Bethlehem. All who lived in the city at that time saw it, for those who noticed it first woke their loved ones, so that they too could witness this sight. We thought it might signify the end of all things.

"The magi did not return to Jerusalem, and Herod could not tolerate the possibility of any king besides himself. He ordered his soldiers to the Bethlehem neighborhood, and gave them the unthinkably cruel mission of killing every male child two years and younger. Do you understand me? He killed them all! There were over twenty of them, helpless sons. That act of wickedness measured this so-called *king*. The best for us that Rome had to offer!

"Nothing of note came of all of this until about ten years later. A young boy showed up at the temple following one of the feasts. He seemed brilliant by any standard, both asking questions and answering them. How could one so young have so much wisdom? When his parents finally missed him in the caravan, for they had come for the feast, and as they left they thought he had booked passage among their relatives, they returned for him. We saw then that his parents were this same couple from the Bethlehem census—the same young woman called Mary, and her husband Joseph. They had left the Bethlehem area, evidently before Herod's soldiers had arrived, and had since moved to Nazareth. That shocked us all."

At this point Al-alif interrupted. "Sethur, does this tale have many more chapters? Our journey requires that we soon get to shelter and to sleep." Ben's glance around the fire detected no fatigue. All wanted to hear whatever more chapters the story contained.

"There is little left to tell. At least compared to what has been told. Several years ago, a man wearing a leather girdle and making a diet of locusts and honey appeared out of the wilderness. People called him John, and he proclaimed that we ought to get ready for the Messiah. He told us to 'Prepare for the way of the Lord'. When we investigated this man, we found him to be the son of Zacharias and Elizabeth, whose birth caused such a stir among the priests.

"He baptized people in the Jordan River, and told them to repent, and live better lives, and to share their belongings with those in need and to give place to God in their ways.

"One day that same man, John, saw someone coming to him for baptism and said that this one was 'the lamb of God that takes away the sin of the world.'

"He identified this same child, grown now, a man of about thirty years. The one from the temple, the wise child. The one born in Bethlehem. John said that this one is our Messiah.

"That happened nearly four years ago. Were the story to end there, it would be simpler and easier. But it does not end. That man, Jesus, he is called, has gone about our nation doing all manner of annoying tricks or signs or whatever you want to call them, and calling our religious leaders hypocrites, and whitewashed graves.

"Parker, you ask me what God is doing. I wish I could be more certain of His methods. Many of my brothers see both political and religious ruin ahead, especially as it relates to this Jesus. As for my nation, and as for this time, I have told you what I know and what I have seen. God is faithful to my nation, and no doubt is in control of even this. I still seek, as I said to you two nights previous, for a deliverer sent from God to our people. We wait for Him."

Sethur chose this place to end his narrative, but Ben felt sure much more could be said. The words awaited the opportune time.

Al-alif stiffly rose from his seated position and said, "As a boy I remember seeing those magi when their caravan came through my village. They appeared to be very rich, and very well attended. I had no idea there was that much more to their tale. But now Hilkiah has seen to the shelters as best he could in this darkness. Sleep well, my friends."

As the companions parted for the evening, Al-alif moved quietly to the north side of the encampment. Ben watched him as he pulled from a pouch a small brass square with a string on it. He captured the string between his teeth and held the metal square up to the sky. He seemed to be peering through it.

Ben approached him, drawn by his curiosity. Though Ben did not speak, Al-alif sensed his presence, and explained. "What you see here, Parker, is a K'mal. By holding this small lash in my teeth, and peering through this hole at Dhruva Tara, and counting the knots used to make the visual connection, I may calculate with some certainty how far to the south of our way we have come. It appears to be nearly a full day's journey until we can find our way west. This will cause our trip to Jerusalem to be extended by three days. But do not worry. I will not charge you for the additional time." He looked at Ben and laughed, as a man relieved of a burden. Ben realized, too late, that a comrade joked with him.

Time. Three days lost and an inflexible deadline looming. Perhaps achieving his goal would be easier than he had hoped, and then perhaps it would be impossible. He cradled hope because evidently Jesus still occupied the landscape, stirring things up. And his optimism received buttress by the four years Sethur had mentioned. Doc said that he thought Jesus spent four years in ministry, rather than the traditionally held view of three. Still time to search. Time. Time would tell. He retired to the shelter and fell asleep.

CHAPTER XII

The morning dawned clear and calm, with the fast broken by sharing the previous evening's leftovers, which provided nothing less than a feast to the travelers. The train began to move at that standard pedestrian pace that lulled one's thoughts into neutral. Ben began to muse on the unbidden, whatever came to his mind.

He thought of the stars. They were traveling in the dark of the moon, so the thousand points of light would be visible this night, if the weather remained clear, through that horizon-wide curtain of ebony. He decided he'd never actually seen black like the night sky of the desert until *now,* whatever *now* was. And he thought he'd never seen stars so brilliant, and thought perhaps if he ever got back home he'd try to spend more time looking at them. Maybe he'd need a place in some isolated corner of the desert, somewhere near area fifty-one.

The modern GPS system crossed his mind, perhaps a little improvement over the K'mal. But the ramrod's method sufficed for the present. Al-alif seemed sure of it. What had he called that reference star? Dhruva Tara? No matter. He had been staring at Polaris.

He meandered into thinking about cell phones and how great it would be to be able to call 911 in an emergency and expect that someone would send help. This led to his minor regret concerning the desert mugger he'd dumped into the

thorn bush. *That will have to leave a mark,* Ben decided.
Then he laughed to himself. *Hopefully many marks.* But the
GPS thing, the cell phone thing, the communication thing
all seemed to him to eclipse the problem of transportation.
It seemed to be more crucial to be able to talk to someone,
and to know exactly where he was. But the challenge of
getting satellites into the sky would not begin to be solved
until AD 1957, with Sputnik's launch by the USSR.

But as yet no Soviet Union, no cold war, no Auschwitz,
no Ravensbruck existed. No World War I or American
Civil War. Life was simple and could be handled with a
minimum of convenience. If he could develop a method for
making pipes and valves, he could bring running water to
homes.

Running water. Showers. He'd forgotten what a shower
felt like on his skin. He thought about that. A cool shower.
Maybe he could set up a booth along the Silk Road and let
weary travelers shower for ten minutes for a denarii. Would
it work? And what about a toilet? No use. He knew that Sir
Thomas Crapper would not be along for almost two
thousand years. A lot of time to wait to use the john. He
didn't think he could hold it until then.

Add to that this whole problem of government. The
Nobel Prize for peace could not be passed around to anyone
he'd heard about lately. And Sethur knew what had
happened around here for centuries. He did not forgive, nor
did he forget.

He thought also of the other matter, or the other two.
Evidently he had found the right time. Jesus still roamed
loose, but with many more credibility problems than even
Adam seemed to know about. The majority of the big
religious guys played things pretty close to the vest, but that
rank and file folk were being taken in.

Maybe that's always the way it is, he thought. *The poor,
the disenfranchised, the uninformed are always ready to
jump on the band chariot in hope of something new and
better.* And then he thought again of Adam. *Not poor. Not*

ignorant. Not disenfranchised. Yet there was one who followed Jesus. Or, there will be one.
Will a person of another century be free to wander about Jerusalem in search of the outer circle of friends? Will this rich young guy be spottable? If he is identified, will it be possible to engage him in meaningful conversation? Immersion in the language provided the predicted improvements, but Ben still felt a bit out to sea, especially when speaking of intangibles.

And he still faced this question of money. He thought he'd prepared well, but already he'd used up nearly half of his supply. He thought expenses might level out once he got his bearings in Jerusalem. And he smiled to himself when he thought of Al-alif's joke of the previous evening. *No extra charge for those three days, eh? Whose rope had broken? And who had persevered against some pretty long odds to bring everything back safely? Maybe I should be charging him for returning his camels.* Ben again laughed to himself.

He immediately abandoned this line of thinking. He had only done what should be done, and knew that no one owed him anything. But good things do happen to good people

As usual in these streams of consciousness, that three-year-old brown eyed girl popped in. She smiled and reassured him of her undying love and her anticipation of seeing him very soon, without the beard.

But the word "soon" presented difficult implications. *What is soon?* By the end of his trip, his reunion with Sherry would be very soon indeed. But it would not happen, in real terms, until many generations of the globe's population entered and exited the world's stage. The industrialization of western civilization would grow apace and *things,* like the sewing machine, the automobile, and the computer would all be developed. He decided that the problem with making a foray into the past stemmed from knowing so much about what had to happen. But the problem with the future is knowing whether there will be any. He thought that if he ever made it home, he should perhaps stay there.

The operation of his camel required no thought.

The troop stopped for water and a brief rest near mid-day and resumed their pedestrian-speed travels to the north, as the sun made its relentless trip from east to west. The sand radiated the sun's warmth upwards, and the heat waves rose from the dunes like slow, invisible volcanic eruptions, but a bit cooler. *Slightly cooler,* Ben thought, *yes, slightly.*

The afternoon brought other thoughts—he wondered, for example, why central air conditioning took so long to develop. He wondered about the architecture of Damascus, and his wonder became kindled the more because of his memory of the temple of Jupiter in such pristine condition.

Then he considered the Roman officer at the eastern gate, so baffled by Ben's claim to have come from west of Tarshish. He thought of never-never land, and Middle-earth and Alice's looking glass, and wondered how he'd respond should someone claim to be from any of those places. Everyone knows, or will know, they're nonexistent.

In the same way, these people knew of nothing that lay west of Tarshish. So how could anyone originate there? The idea would seem to these natives rather ridiculous; it would require the willing suspension of disbelief.

His mind wandered back to Doctor Resser and Hannah. Soon, if such a thing as soon exists, he could report to them that the plan had worked.

This naturally led the stream of consciousness to a place whose shores Ben had not yet explored. For months he'd been obsessed with arriving at this point in history. He had not, until now, (whatever *now* was) considered the possibility of being unable to return home.

After all, he thought, *none of this is actually in my power. I flip no switch, I make no connection. I will nothing to happen. What if only the first half of the theory is workable, and I am left here?*

162

This avenue of thought created in his mind a picture of a freeway interchange he'd seen near L. A. International Airport a few years previous. A lot of merging took place there, a lot of people getting on and off. His thoughts accessed the cloverleaf at a pretty unhealthy rate. What would he do for a living? Could he cope with this kind of a life indefinitely? This place took the cake for primitive. It was almost infinitely more primitive than Gilligan's Island. (He'd always wondered why Ginger had such a voluminous wardrobe along for a three-hour tour. It made no sense. But so did the rest of it.) He recognized that his present situation offered little practical difference between the comforts available to the very rich and those available to the poor. All of them shared alike in many great lacks. No one could cure malaria, and no one could filter his own water supply. No one could possess a flat screen TV, or a Bentley. As far as he could tell a camel was a camel. Some of them probably had more miles on them than others. But still, with few exceptions, the life of a rich man looked as if it would be nearly as uncomfortable as that of a poor man.

A lot of people could have servants. But no one could have a refrigerator or a stereo or a microwave oven. Living in the twenty-first century made it easy to take for granted the ideas that had put a man on the moon and a phone in his pocket. Money could buy service, or perhaps servants, whose job it would be to make the master more comfortable. But in the end all shared equally in what the first century lacked.

But he knew he thought of life in terms of his twenty-first century framework. Of course there was a difference between rich and poor here. And the difference was money. Material wealth. Lydia had accused him of being rich. Was he? Twenty-seven days' wages in his pocket. A month's salary. So what? What about next month?

The brakes were applied to Ben's train of thought by that single startling realization.

What about next month? He'd never thought about next month in that particular way. *Will I have enough? Will I get by? Will I be comfortable? Well off? Or not?*

He began to hope more intensely than ever that Doc had correctly calculated the return trip. But Bob had come back. Hadn't he?

When the western sun had declined to about a camel's head above the horizon, Al-alif stopped the caravan for the night. Ben's body welcomed the stop. He thought that Sethur and the women would be as relieved as he, because their ordeal had taken so much energy, and the previous night's rest had been somewhat truncated.

"We will make camp here tonight," the ramrod began. "In the morning we will make our way through the Yarmuk Valley. We must travel west now, until after we ford the Jordan. For the moment, take your ease. Our evening meal will be served soon."

Ben could not resist the thought of airline flight attendants and messages from the captain. *"Sit back. Relax. Enjoy the flight."* His camel knelt, so he dismounted, glad to stretch his legs. The sand still radiated heat from the afternoon sun, but the ambient air brought a promise of cooler temperatures. A slight breeze flowed from the saddle above them, bringing the mountain air from the higher ground.

Sethur, Lydia, and Patricia soon dismounted as well, and the four of them naturally clustered together as they waited for the word that the evening meal had been made ready.

"If there is talk around the fire tonight, may I ask you more questions?" Lydia had spoken, and Ben assumed she had addressed him. He had been looking away toward the setting sun. But then he heard Sethur's voice in answer. "Certainly, Mistress Lydia. I would look forward to sharing with you anything that brings clarity to your life."

This, Ben thought, *is a first. Someone wants to interrogate somebody other than myself. This should be relaxing.*

The flat bread, goat meat, and dried fruits were served about dusk, and as the meal drew to its perfunctory close, the campfire talk seemed also to have its natural beginning.

"Mistress Lydia asks permission to question me. I assume that her inquiries would relate to some of our conversations of last night, and perhaps would be spiritual in nature. Is this true, Lydia?"

"Yes, sir. You are correct."

"Under normal circumstances," Sethur continued, "I would direct you to your husband, your father, or your Rabbi. Since you seem not to be a Jewess, it is likely you have no Rabbi. Since you travel on business unaccompanied, I assume also you have no husband. Is that so?"

"Yes sir, these things are so."

"And would your father be available to answer questions of a spiritual nature?"

"It appears you have knowledge not available to him. He knows only the Greek myths. And he entrusts my care, mine and Patricia's, to Al-alif. He may grant permission for this conversation."

Sethur directed a questioning glance to the Ramrod, who nodded his assent.

"Then with the permission of your guardian, let me stand in the stead of those who are not here, dear lady. Please ask me whatever you will. I will provide answers as I am able."

"May I, sir, speak first of my situation and my perspective, that you may better understand my inquiries?" She waited for his reply.

"Certainly, Lydia. Please bring us all to the same place on the parchment roll, so to speak."

She began as if she had memorized her speech. "Gentlemen, I have considered in my mind some of the things of which we spoke last night, and other questions as well." Here she paused, aligning her thoughts. "It seems to me that there must be one true God, who made all that is. Al-alif can scan the stars above, and they tell him of our

165

path here in the desert. Parker can find a way to clear a campsite of venomous scorpions at night. The camels, left to themselves, could find the hidden water. Even the snails in the tide pools seem to shout out to me that One made them, One designed them. All has design, it seems to me. All has purpose."

She paused again, but no one spoke, as she obviously had more to say. She continued.

"I have been many places, and wherever I go, men and women worship some sort of god. The peoples of every land have their deities. Near Jerusalem the ancients worshiped a god named Moloch, and a goddess named Ashteroth. Each village had a Baal, or a Master. Did not the people of Ammon worship Chemosh, and were there not local deities for every small nation?"

She looked at Sethur, He nodded mutely, and she went on.

"And did not these so-called gods exact from the people, in darkness and shame, the very lives of their little ones, their new-born sons?"

Sethur nodded again.

"Moloch demanded—" her voice caught in her throat. She began again. "Moloch demanded that parents sometimes offer their newborn sons in bloody fire." Tears streamed down her face, but she composed herself and pressed on. "And I have been to Rome. I have seen the Pantheon, and I have been to Athens, to Mars Hill. There! There stand idols of every description, deities of many types, most of them seeming to be gods made in the image of man. Their lore is that of deceit, anger, rape, incest, and murder, the ugly deeds that men commit, but on a grander scale. They require little or nothing of their followers, and they seem to resemble only morally bankrupt but powerful people."

She spoke more quietly now, almost a whisper in the silence of the desert. "Sethur, I know there must be a true God. I have seen many of these lesser ones. You must know. You must see, as I do. They are not only inadequate. They are evil.

"Last night as you were speaking, it seemed to me that I heard of a God both good and powerful, one that would nurture children, and not require their charred flesh as sacrifice. Can you give me hope that such a God exists? Can those of us who are not Jews worship Him? Can He see us now?" Her voice was rising like wind that precedes a storm. "Is He here in the desert tonight?"

Her question hung in the night air, reverberating in the darkness. It echoed from heart to heart with unmeasured resonance. *Is He here in the desert tonight?*

Sethur waited to be certain that she had finished. Then he got to his feet.

"Kind and gentle lady, all of your mind's musings are reflected, I believe, in each of us. We see for ourselves what must be, what *has* to be, and we see how God and His work have been distorted and destroyed.

"I would like to remove all of your doubt. I cannot do that. But you do see the truth. Two days ago we were lost in a sandstorm, beyond hope. Only through either the slightest of chances or the providence of God we survived the storm and arrived at water.

"We survived also the acquisition of the water through God's providence, and through Parker's resourcefulness. We discovered food, and flint and oil at need, and were shown a way to easily clear a campsite of scorpions. Had it not been for the scorpions, Al-alif may not have found us. These circumstances show me that He is here in the desert tonight. Does all of this mean anything to you?"

Lydia stared at the campfire. She seemed deep in thought. At length she spoke.

"Yes. Yes, it means He must be here tonight. Now. But what of the other situation you mentioned last night?"

"And what situation do you mean?"

"I mean that whole business of the young maiden and the shepherds and the magi and the star in the sky—the young boy in the temple, the mad prophet out baptizing

167

people, and all the accounts of amazing miracles and strange teachings? You seem to be sure this man is not sent from your God."

Sethur waited again to be sure she had run out of question.

"Some among the elders of my people believe that this new teacher has come from God. They are a very small minority, and some of them listen to his teaching and fall prey to his hypnotic spell. He speaks of the poor as if they were the blessed ones, when everyone knows that our God led all of our patriarchs to great wealth. Abraham and Lot chose to separate because of their great herds of livestock—of sheep, and goats, and camels and donkeys. Our fathers plundered the wealth of the Egyptians as they were leaving that land. We occupied walled cities built for us by those from whom we confiscated them. Their erstwhile gods could not protect them from us.

"This man says that if we are compelled to go a mile with a man, we should go two miles. Do you know who compels us to go a mile with them? The stench-laden Romans! They can conscript us to carry their packs for a mile, then we may throw the burden on the ground. This man calls Israel to grovel, whimper, and cower. Do any of you know how many Romans it takes to change one soldier's tunic?" He smiled a villainous smile. "No one knows, because they never do it. That is why they are so laden with stench. But back to the present consideration.

"This Jesus comes to God's holy temple and overturns the tables of those who exchange foreign currency for the shekels necessary for temple use. He releases the animals being held there for purchase, for the use of those who cannot bring a live animal so far—those intended for sacrifice to our God. He disrupts our worship, and teaches the people as if he himself were God.

"Possibly worst of all, he breaks the Sabbath, and allows his followers also to do the same."

Here Sethur paused, then realized as he looked at his companions that he had made a statement that none of them understood.

"Let me explain further," he added. "When my people left Egypt, they were led by Moses, our lawgiver. (To add more insult, this man claims to be greater than Moses! Even greater than Solomon, David's son, our wisest and richest king!) When we left Egypt and arrived after a time at Mount Sinai, our God gave us our law. No, that is not entirely correct. God gave us *His* law. He entrusted it to us.

"One part of the law was the Sabbath, the seventh day. He said it should be a Holy day, and no servile work should be done that day. Not even gathering sticks of wood for a fire like this one. People received capital punishment for any minor departure from this rule. This is our God's way, brought to us by Moses, our lawgiver, and written in stone by the finger of God. "Remember the Sabbath day to keep it holy".

"This teacher allows work on the Sabbath."

In the silence that followed, all eyes were fixed on Sethur. He seemed to have come to a pause in his presentation, perhaps to allow for questions.

After some drawn-out moments, Ben spoke, and later wished he hadn't.

"I have read of some of these things. Are they not harmless, such as healing people of diseases and doing good?"

Lydia stared at him. Sethur wore a look of shock and disbelief.

After another awkward pause, Lydia asked, "Has word of this man bypassed Thyatira, but found the west of Tarshish? How have you heard of this, being from so far away?"

He then could see a clear picture of why Ben blurts formed such an extensive part of his life. They come from disobeying that simple rule; first think, then speak. His grandmother had told him that the complete and simple

169

truth always provided the quickest and safest way out of a tight spot. He ventured to employ her maxim.

He took a deep breath. "There is no secret here. News of this man has come to my land, brought there by people who have heard and seen this man. I go now to Jerusalem, not to seek him, but to find answers about him from one who has spoken with him."

"Do you know this one you seek, then?" Lydia's question penetrated Ben. Her intensity eclipsed the levels he had so far witnessed in her.

Ben hated it when all the gears of his mind attempted to engage simultaneously, and he knew now that refusal to answer would not suffice. He simply said, "No."

She looked at him thoughtfully. "How will you find him?"

And I thought this was going to be relaxing. "Odd things seem to be the order of the day for me," he replied. "A lot of strange circumstances have befallen me on my journey. Many of them you have seen. I believe that somehow I will find him. I will be given an answer." *And good things happen to good people.*

He spoke with the force of conviction, and as he looked at the faces of his companions, it appeared that no one would challenge him.

Lydia said, "I seek none of his friends, but while we visit Jerusalem, I would hope to speak to him. But as I am a woman, it is not likely to happen."

"Why would that be?" Ben injected this gladly. It turned the conversation away from the fact that he seemed to possess some sort of inside knowledge of events and circumstances in Jerusalem.

Sethur provided the answer Ben sought. "In the Holy City of Jerusalem, and indeed, in all Judea, women may not address men in public places. Were there nine more Jewish men here now, I could not allow Lydia to speak to us. She shows much thought and consideration in asking permission, but in Israel she must keep silent, as all women must, when men are present in public."

Ben let this concept dance through his head for a few moments—women not allowed to speak in public if men are present. *Would that solve any problems?* He shook his head, like one trying to assemble a jigsaw puzzle by shaking the box. Something told him that madness lay down that path. Sethur whip-lashed Ben back to reality.

"This man speaks to *women* in public. To *women* with unclean issues of blood, to *women* with unclean issues of morality, to Samaritan *women,* to Gentile *women.* This man touches *lepers.* This man touches *the dead.*"

Ben heard the indictments pour out, verbally stacked, one atop the other, each accusation sounding more horrible than the preceding one. The last indictment was the most severe. *Surely,* he thought, *there must be nothing worse, nothing beyond this.*

Again a silence followed. The stars pierced the black velvet sky and illuminated the desert with the palest gray. The camels could be heard softly breathing nearby. Nothing of the fire remained but amber coals.

"Perhaps it's best to leave some questions over for the morning," Al-alif said. "Hilkiah has prepared the shelters. Let us take our rest, for tomorrow will have its demands upon us all."

Thus dismissed, the caravan of Al-alif retired until the break of day.

CHAPTER XIII

The chill of the desert in early morning is an
invigorating thing. This thought occupied of roughly two
thirds of Ben's conscious mind. The other third, the third
third, hovered around the nature of reality. In that third, a
memory of a movie called Lawrence of Arabia cavorted in
the coolness of the morning. His grandmother had imposed
upon him the task of watching it with her some years back.
(Back?) In part the experience stuck in his mind because the
VCR broke that day. This, of course, did not constitute big
news except that Grandma had owned that particular unit
for years—long enough to know the basics of how to use it,
even to the extent of being able to set the timer to record
The Price Is Right if it came on while she was out.

This is where Lawrence of Arabia had come in.

The day they wanted to see it was the very day the VCR
had met its demise. Since Ben had problem-solving built in
as part of his DNA, he had volunteered to help her buy a
new one.

Most anyone else would have seen the flaw in this plan.
The advent of DVD eradicated nearly all choices involving
VCR, so Ben had bought a DVD of Lawrence of Arabia,
and a DVD player. This put the learning curve back to
square one, and Grams, through solid training and
determination, regained her footing as far as turning the
thing on.

He did wind up watching Lawrence of Arabia with her that afternoon.

The movie told the story of a sort of Bedouin takeover of Damascus during World War I, and it featured the late Peter O'Toole in the starring role. But as Ben thought about it, the scenery did not look like what he'd seen around Damascus. He wondered if the filming took place in California, but then he remembered that the British had produced the film, so probably not. The phrase "willing suspension of disbelief" still stuck in his mind.

But now, surrounded by endless sand and endless sky, oppressive heat and the ubiquitous lack of water, these tents and these camels looked real, and his memory of his Grandma's house reminded him of the set of Lawrence of Arabia. Thus the struggle with the nature of reality. *Reality,* he decided, *is whatever you're presently doing.*

After a predictable breakfast and minimal conversation, the caravan set out. Ben began to think of them as pilgrims, as seekers after truth, but as far as he could tell that moniker applied only to Sethur, Lydia, and himself. Al-alif maybe. But he could not remember Patricia ever saying a word about anything. She had not spoken to Ben at all. And Bedouins were just Bedouins, were they not? But the train carried the passengers. The purpose presented itself, for each of them to find what each sought. The camels were only tools, like his Bentley.

That was a shock to him—to think of his Bentley. And to equate it with a camel.

The day passed uneventfully. That is to say, from Ben's perspective, no one tried to kill him, and he perceived no danger of dying of hunger or thirst or of being lost in the desert. That does not imply boredom, though time did seem to pass slowly. Mountains loomed to the northwest and southwest, with a gentle slope upward between them. Upon this slope they traveled for most of the day, and in late afternoon they arrived at a summit of sorts, or more of a saddle. That summit divided the land between the Syrian plains to the east and the Jordan Valley to the west. The land sloped just as gradually down, offering occasional views of the Jordan River and its environs. They seemed to have found a camel path, with the possibility of caravan traffic, though they saw no one.

As afternoon waned into evening desert heat gave way to desert cool. Daylight gave way to darkness. Evening meal, campfire. No more challenging or unusual topics. No embarrassing blurts. Rest under the stars.

Al-alif roused them at dawn. The air felt cooler than the morning air of the desert floor. Hilkiah tended a cooking fire, and the remnants of the previous evening's meal provided the aroma of breakfast. The Bedouins lade the camels as the travelers ate, and they made their start with punctuality.

The train proceeded along the Yarmuk River, following near the watercourse. Little of note happened that morning, and by mid-day the valley widened before them, enabling more regular glimpses of the Jordan. Al-alif appeared relaxed as he traversed new territory. He had no first-hand knowledge of the area, so he did not trust himself to choose a ford at random, and none of the company, with the exception of Ben, knew how to swim, though Lydia stressed to the entire entourage that she had no fear of water.

Here we go again, thought Ben. *Some common practice of my own time will probably prove to be legendary. But maybe not this time. After all, a lot of people can swim.*

Al-alif had heard by word of mouth from other guides that they could access a ford about an hour's walk upstream. He looked toward the sun and noted its position, then led the troop north.

In the specified time they reached a place where a shallow riffle extended from bank to bank. Ben offered to wade the ford and return, playing the role of military scout.

The river had little water, as the spring thaw from Mount Tabor and the hills ranging to the north around the Sea of Galilee had already surrendered their snow cover. The trip across and back proved uneventful, and Ben feared no danger of being swept away. They executed the crossing, wetting the camels only up to their knees, and took a rest stop on the west bank. They filled water skins, rehydrated camels, and reloaded people for what remained of the day.

Al-alif claimed that rumors spoke of a small Roman outpost, called Alexandrium that should provide a reasonable place to camp that evening, though he was still in unfamiliar territory.

Early in the evening Hilkiah gave a shout. He pointed to the northwest where a village sat perched on a low ridge. It possessed wall and fortification, though it appeared very small. Al-alif chose for their night's camping spot a sandy flat just below the northern wall, just more than a bow-shot from the fortress. As twilight asserted itself a bit earlier in the valley, the company settled in quickly to avoid having to work in the darkness. Occasionally, the glint of steel from some implement of war would reflect the sun's last rays their way while indicating life and movement in the fortress. The companions hoped for no contact, and it seemed the Romans might be willing to comply.

With the camp's setup finished early, the passengers volunteered to assist in preparation for the evening meal. As Ben and Sethur gathered wood for the fire, Ben noticed five men walking toward them from the direction of the Garrison.

Since he worked nearest to the fortress, the men approached him and stopped about ten feet away. They grounded their spears in the sand. Four of them appeared to be common soldiers, privates, so to speak, with standard caparison. But the fifth and foremost of them showed more gilding around the edges of things, and a taller crest on his helmet. He approached two more strides, then stopped and spoke.

"Strangers," he said, "We are Romans, as you can see, stationed in yonder garrison, which is called Alexandrium. You are welcome to camp here, or, if you wish, you may move inside the protection of our walls. News from southeast of here has come to us of a marauding band—four people, two men and two women. One of the men has the mark of a *Sciarii,* one who may silently kill and silently slip away. It may be that for your own protection you should join us within the wall."

Ben at first said nothing. He processed the information, translating it in his brain. The company had already decided not to enter the Roman fortress, and already had set up camp in sight of the wall. This probably offered enough proximity to receive aid should any emergency arise which required military assistance.

He thought initially that Al-alif should speak to them. On the other hand, he naturally took charge in such situations, at least in some time periods. So he took it upon himself to address them.

"We are journeying to Jerusalem. Our caravan has a leader who is capable of bringing us there safely. Our way is peaceable, and we mean harm to no one. We have decided to camp here in the open, and trust that if aid were needed you would send it. We plan to move on tomorrow as soon as light enables travel. You five men are welcome to share our evening meal with us."

The Roman officer stared at Ben, then cast a glance back at the four with him. Ben could see that the four suppressed laughter. Eventually, like a dam cracking, one of them began to chuckle. Then the dam broke, and all five men laughed heartily. When the levity passed, the officer nodded to Ben, and the five turned and marched back toward Alexandrium. When they had covered about fifty feet, they burst into laughter again, this outbreak lasting most of the way to the gate, which had been left ajar for them.

Ben turned back toward the camp, baffled by what had occurred. Sethur, Lydia, and Al-alif stood about fifteen feet behind him, each with a look of incredulous shock on his (or her) face.

"What just happened?" Ben demanded.

177

Sethur smiled. "Our occupiers came calling, and you entertained them and sent them away."

"How did I do that?" Ben demanded again.

Al-alif responded this time. "Parker, we here know that you are but a child as far as our language is concerned. We speak to you, and before you, in limited terms you can understand, though you do not realize we do it. Yonder Romans had no forewarning.

"I will take liberty now to help you understand what those soldiers heard you say." He assumed a mocking Ben-like position, arms stretched out as if carrying sticks, feet apart like Ben's were when the soldiers approached. He even managed to mimic the voice inflection and Ben's difficulty with the guttural consonants in his own crude style. Then he gave Ben the amplified version.

"Hey there, you peasants. Get out of our way, because we are going to Jerusalem, led by our tent pole. Our tent pole will lead us on a sure path, and when we get to the city we will conquer it without even shooting an arrow! We will in no way come near your puny garrison, nor would you be able to compel us by force to do so. By morning, nothing would be left of you. We would like to eat the five of you for supper."

At that point, the same phenomenon that had afflicted the soldiers worked its way through the three of them as they looked at Ben. They tried unsuccessfully not to laugh.

After about a minute of this torturous joviality Sethur said, "Parker, (Ha ha) you (Ha ha) are out there on the sharp edge of the sword. (Ha ha) You have taught me a new method in dealing with our oppressors. Ever you are a surprise to me! Did you know that the marauders, the two men and the two women he mentioned were us? Us four! This rumor has preceded us here from the watering hole. And the *Sciarii* they warned you about was you!" Here he stopped his speech to laugh again, and after a few seconds he controlled himself and resumed. "Thank you, friend. I would much rather spend tonight out here under the stars, protected by my companions, than be locked inside those walls, imprisoned by those Romans."

Wood gathered, fire tended, supper cooked and eaten, Al-alif and his passengers sat for a few minutes around the glowing embers.

"Need we set a watch tonight?" Ben spoke his question very carefully. He had completely lost his early Pimsleur confidence in the ability to understand and to speak clearly.

Al-alif answered. "If the Romans choose to eat us for supper, we cannot stop them. If others attack, I have a military trumpet. I will blow the signal of distress, and they will come from yonder Alexandrium. On any night, one of my men is ever on watch, and tonight is like any other night. We will show standard vigilance."

"May I speak?" This was Lydia. Men didn't need permission, and Patricia spoke to no one publicly.

Sethur and Al-alif nodded. When she cast a questioning gaze at Ben, he also nodded.

"Parker, it seems to me that you desire to know more specifically how to speak. If you do not want this, you should. But you seek one thing, one person, and I believe you want to know how to find this one without mistake. You say that you believe it will happen. But you must know the difference between a guide and tent pole, and the difference between an invitation to a meal and a warning that someone is about to be eaten." Then she smiled. She evidently still found humor in the situation. She continued. "May we help you?"

Thoughts travel at something near the speed of light, and Ben's brain acted at that moment like a super collider. *How has it happened that over the space of these past few days these people have actually become my friends? How has Lydia guessed the present occupation of my mind? How have I been so available to make such a complete fool out of myself, but now find these companions willing to struggle on my behalf to help me regain my self-respect? How have I so over-rated my communication skills? How am I going to learn?*

He knew the answer to that last question—his friends would help him. Lydia in particular had offered help. And he knew that Sethur and Al-alif would do what they could. He surmised that this would suffice, and also that he could hope for no more than that.

"Yes," he finally said. "I will need your help with some things."

So how do I explain what I need? How do I tell them that I know what someone is going to say, and to whom it will be said? How do I explain that I know what the answer will be? I know who says it—just not where and when.

In the end, Ben forced his thoughts to do their colliding in his subconscious so that he could function somewhat "normally". On the surface, where he worked and lived, he concentrated on the hard facts and real answers while those subterranean issues worked themselves out on that other level.

"The phrase I must be able to recognize is this," he began." 'Good Master, what must I do to inherit eternal life?' And beyond that I must be able to recognize 'All these have I kept from my youth. What do I still lack?' Can you teach me these words?"

Lydia stared. In his direction she stared. Not at him, but through him, it seemed. And like so many of the exchanges he had with his companions, it had at its practical terminus a very awkward silence. This silence, however, blasted through the level of awkward like Chuck Yeager blasted through the sound barrier. It rose like a Jack Nicklaus nine iron shot past awkward into very uncomfortable, and had for its zenith totally embarrassing.

Lydia inhaled deeply. How had she survived that entire silence without breathing? "Parker," she said plaintively, "what is eternal life?"

This was *unfair.* It bypassed all those technicalities of time anomaly, of knowledge that should not be available, of someone knowing things which could not possibly be known. It blindsided him like little else could have. The

180

present context of space and time diminished to nothing in comparison.

The question was sharper, deeper, more crucial than anything he'd considered up to now. It cut to the quick of his mission, though he'd never contemplated it apart from the fact that someone had asked the question of someone who should know the answer to it.

And Ben's problem was that he did not know. Part of his brain was screaming to the other parts, *HOW COULD YOU NOT KNOW?*

He resorted to his grandmother's technique. "I don't know. But I think that these are the words I need to recognize. I will need your help."

That no one immediately replied relieved Ben. It probably meant that no chasms of misunderstanding would now have to be bridged, no epistemological hurdles overcome. So he waited.

"I would like to teach you these words, as they most likely would be spoken by one such as yourself—someone your age, perhaps, and wealthy, as you obviously are. I will need some time to consider this, but by the morning I will know how it should be done.

"Parker, you startle us all again and again. Most puzzling to me now—beyond your ability to master a thug with a knife, or the proven character you demonstrated in seeking to reunite Al-alif with his camels, or the strange wisdom you showed in ridding our campsite of those horrid scorpions," here she shuddered, revealing a fear or revulsion she had concealed through that ordeal. "Beyond all that, and your obvious skill in matters of state," now she smiled a smile of mirth. "But no—I will not ask. I see that there is much you cannot reveal as yet, or perhaps ever. I think I speak for us all when I say I trust you, Parker. I will teach you these words tomorrow."

Al-alif stirred, and wanted to know if any further pressing business need be addressed that night. When the three were silent, he directed them to their shelters.

CHAPTER XIV

Ben lay on the sand for what felt like hours. He could not achieve sleep. He told himself to try and relax. But then he wondered if you actually could try and relax, because if it required effort, could you be relaxing? Wasn't it a contradiction in terms? He knew that this train of thought only provided a distraction, and had nothing to do with the real reason for his insomnia. Dealing with this paradox resembled rearranging the deck chairs on the Titanic. His real problem lay in his readiness, or his lack of it.

And he'd put so much thought and effort into preparing for this time. Circumstances threatened to sweep him far afield of his goal.

So he began to crystallize it in his mind. *What is my goal? I want to find this guy and ask him if it made any difference. If Jesus is so great, why would you not follow him? Is that eternal life?* Lydia's question posed a problem, but solving that problem created a detour he could not take. And how could he know if it really was a detour?

But the question remained, undeniable, like a tsunami, and it pushed him where he did not want to go.

"What is eternal life?" Why did she have to ask that? Is that what the rich guy really wanted? Is that what I want? Why isn't Adam here to give an answer, or portly Pastor Rick from church who talked about Jonah?

An unwilling prophet. God had no problem with anything in the whole story except his own guy. What do I think of a God like that?

What is eternal life?

At some point the sheep must have come to be counted, because Sethur roused Ben with a nudge of his foot. "The morning meal is nearly ready. You are lucky that those Romans did not eat with us last night, lest there be nothing for us to start our day."

As the passengers ate, Al-alif and his crew disassembled the shelters and soon had the camels loaded. They could see no sign of activity on the wall, and no smoke rose from any fire within the fortress. The company knew that the Romans had them under surveillance, and that they most likely were the butt of many jokes told in Latin inside the citadel.

The terrain south of Alexandrium presented more challenges than any they had seen thus far. The ridges rose more sharply; the way involved more turnings. These circumstances did not impede their progress, but they could no longer choose the direct route. Ben remembered a story he had read about settlers in America moving west, following the Missouri River. They worked their way fifteen miles upstream in a single day, but made only three miles of westward progress by sunset. *At least that's how it will be later on*, Ben thought.

Al-alif's train fared better than those future settlers, but all could see that their hope of reaching Sychar in time to set up camp by nightfall hung by a camel's hair.

From time to time Ben stole a glance at Lydia. She appeared to be concentrating, sometimes forming words with her lips but making no sound, occasionally shaking her head as if hitting the clear key on a pocket calculator and starting over.

This should be good, thought Ben. *She has had nearly twenty-four hours to think about it. It should fall right into place in that analytical mind.*

What a great employee she would make, he observed.

184

He looked at the sky. The mostly empty sky. Only a few birds. No planes, no superman. He reminded himself that chem-trails would not become visible for over nineteen centuries. The sky didn't look normal, though, without a few white lines drawn across it like crayon lines on Sherry's wall at her home in Dallas.

He contemplated his camel trip, these last seven days, and wondered at how simple life could be. *Here we are. There is where we want to be. We ride these camels, and they deliver us there. No jets up there, no satellites in their geosynchronous orbits high above, out of sight. No GPS. No Skype. No interruptions.*

He no longer wondered what life without a cell phone would be like. It seemed okay not to have one if no one else had one. *Who would I call anyway?*

One thing is obvious, he thought. *It appears that more goes into the cogitating part of life when you get rid of all those interruptions. Lydia has been able to think all day, with little to distract her. No email, no voice mail, no phone calls, no text messages. Fifteen years ago maybe faxes provided the interruptions. Forty years ago it might have been land-line phone calls. But now,* (he relished the word now—it was pregnant with meaning) *the only interruptions are the occasional windstorm, some runaway camels, a hooligan threatening to kill us and the danger of an arachnid with poison in its telson. It doesn't sound at all attractive when you list it out, but all in all,* Ben mused, *it's not too bad. At least not if you get instructions on the "gentle way" before your trip.*

The day meandered past in twists and turns, with the occasional straighter road when the trail cut through some valley floor. Al-alif kept his men marching apace when the land lay flat and the road ran south like an arrow; they met no others on their way. Sometimes they saw herds of sheep and goats on the hillsides with their attendants, and Ben thought again of the irony that Christ's birth announcement came to, and then through, these people with no credibility.

If it was all that important, why wouldn't God give it a more credible foundation?
Now the credibility problem. You can't believe shepherds any more, he thought, *than you can believe a man who claims he is from west of Tarshish.* But his own lack of credibility in Israel at this time could not be compared with what he knew he would experience when he returned home. *Will Adam believe me? Will I be able to tell sensei about the incident at the water hole?* He could not get his face on the six o'clock news, or write some article for a local paper. He knew that he would have none of that precious commodity. *No credibility. Worse off than a shepherd.*

Just as Adam will someday have no actual "proof" for what he will believe. Was the testimony of the apostles enough? Was the historical claim of the empty tomb enough? Was Adam's insistence on a changed life enough?

No! No, he thought. *If Jesus is real, he has to be real enough to save a guy like me from his own time. It seems sort of phony that the guy left the question on the table. No loose ends tied up. No closure.*

As the afternoon waned, (the day was a bit more pleasant in that area—occasional shade, a bit cooler temperature, water nearby) Hilkiah claimed he could see a village about an hour's walk from their location. After he pointed it out, the travelers also recognized it, obscure in the dust, and an appreciable distance to the south; an unwalled village, but clearly a group of huts for humans.

Al-alif's spirits rose as he realized that their hard work through the day had rewarded them with Sychar as their resting place, and in good time. The Bedouins had camp set up before the sun set, and one of the men procured a few grapes and figs from a vendor in the village to complement their meal. No one from Sychar (about four hundred yards to the west) came to greet them or to sell anything to them. *Or, to threaten us,* Ben thought. So he did not have to display his ignorance of Aramaic, or try any judo moves on anybody.

The supplemental fruit greatly enhanced their board for the evening meal. The conversation quickly turned to Ben's desire. Both Sethur and Al-alif listened with great interest as Lydia explained her choice of words, and intermittently one or the other would comment on a particular option. In the end, the phrase committee, as Ben began to think of them, told him to look, no, to *listen* for these sounds.

"Good master, what must I do to inherit eternal life? All these have I kept from my youth. What do I still lack?" He pounded every nuance of these Aramaic phonemes into his brain with tenacity—mood, tense, voice, case, gender, number, overtones, syntax, until he had no doubt. He received a total refinement of the crude sentences he had memorized in some time future.

Al-alif and the other passengers agreed that phonetically, if Ben listened for these things, his opportunity would not slip by. Unspoken questions hung in the air like clichés at a business meeting, but no one intruded on Ben's privacy. They had given him the requested aid, and the evening's activities were drawing to a close when Lydia asked, "Parker, may I check the dressing on your wound?"

Al-alif volunteered, "We have water in plenty, and clean rags for bandages."

Ben nodded, and sat down on a camel's saddle. Al-alif sent one of his men after fresh water, and Lydia began to remove the bandage she had set in place three evenings previous.

At first Ben thought it must have healed completely, but as Lydia removed the last of the wrappings, he could see by the dim firelight that his foot needed some attention.

The water delivered, Lydia began that gentle washing process that seemed so therapeutic in itself. When she had finished with his left foot, she asked permission to wash the right as well. Ben nodded, so the experience continued. He could sense her gratitude in the gentleness of her touch. This should be their last day on the trail. They should be in the city by tomorrow night. She took advantage of her last chance to touch him in public with no repercussion.

When she had completed the washing, Lydia applied healing ointment to the wound, and claimed that the bandage could be removed in another two days. Following that it would need no further medical care.

The party retired, each to rest, to dream, or not to dream.

At sunrise Sethur again prodded Ben awake in time for the breaking of the fast. He found that grapes and figs also went well with a morning meal, and looked forward to a greater variety of diet afforded, he hoped, by city life.

Thankfully, the day unfolded much as one would expect. Hilkiah pointed out a well supposedly dug by Jacob, one of Israel's patriarchs, as they set off on the road to the south. The land continued its ups and downs, requiring careful camel work.

This path led them slightly southeast, down toward the Jordan valley, and along the river to Jericho. The declension progressed steadily down to the plain, but still the going was slow. The road had been built as a camel-wide track, with no possibility of meeting oncoming traffic without delay. More herdsmen populated that area, and at times sheep and goats demanded right of way. On several occasions, smaller caravans, would displace them, and each delay intensified the look of consternation on the face of Al-alif.

By mid-day Jericho came into view, an imposing structure with a hefty wall, though the city proper was small. If Ben had been the product of Sunday School, he would have been disappointed that the wall of Jericho surrounded little more than a city block.

They did not enter the fortress, but availed themselves of the first century equivalent of a truck bypass. As they skirted the town they took a brief rest in the shade of the eastern wall. Romans occupied there as well, but the travelers kept to themselves; they could ignore the foreigners at no cost.

After Jericho the trail began to ascend. The road from Jericho to Jerusalem gained about three thousand feet of elevation in fifteen miles. Had Ben known this, he could have been impressed by the fact that the Bedouins and their beasts would be forced to climb the equivalent of over half a vertical mile of stairs. He did not realize that he was below sea level for the first time in his life, not counting a brief snorkeling trip in the Bahamas two summers ago, speaking in terms of his own temporal adjustment.

To the south, the Dead Sea stunk things up. The wind behaved favorably, so they had no encounter with that pungent bouquet. But as they climbed the rugged path, always rising, they met more and more traffic—larger herds of sheep and goats, local travelers on donkeys, one Roman soldier mounted on a horse, and a handful of caravans such as their own, each exacting its own delay. The trail constricted them so much that at times it felt dangerous.

Before they had covered half the distance to Jerusalem, Al-alif had become much calmer and more sedate. Ben observed that the delays no longer seemed to bother him.

They continued their ascent as the sun neared the place of its setting, and all of them understood that they would not reach the city gate before dark. They might be close—within sight of the city before the gate-closing, but rules, as everyone knows, are rules. At dusk the gates are closed. At dawn, they are opened.

They preserved enough daylight to see the basic outline of the city as they approached it from the north. Ben had prepared himself for the size of Jerusalem. He had seen the maps, and knew that its footprint compared to that of Ekalaka. He knew he would encounter much less than a square mile, though its shape was nothing like a square. The city wall reminded him of an old farm house he had spent some time in as a young boy. Gramps' brother had gotten the house from their family patriarch, and had added space as the need arose—five additions in all. Neighbors referred to him as the guy who never knew when to quit. As a result of this behavior, Ben had many cousins.

189

Jerusalem's wall could have been masterminded by Gramps' brother. It had been extended and built and rebuilt and reinforced on many occasions, and one could discern the old from the new. Some changes appeared to be required by growth, and some by security. A lot of alterations and additions had been necessary.

Three towers dominated the east side of the city, and what he would later discover to be Herod's temple marked the west side. Lower down, north of these areas, the buildings were much more crowded, indicating perhaps the poorer portion of town.

Two deep valleys defined the near boundaries of the city. One sliced down from the southwest, the other coming in from the southeast. They met like a spear's point at the northernmost and lowest part of the city. The way in seemed to be through the steep ravine on the west side.

A small footbridge, which Al-alif ignored, spanned the ravine. He led the caravan past the bridge and into the bottom of the Kidron valley. The road corkscrewed in and out of the dark valley with a series of switchbacks, and in the bottom the air smelled foul. *Local dump*, thought Ben. Eventually they arrived at a gate that stood quiet and unattended. Al-alif turned to his right then, skirting the wall around to the south side. About two hundred yards east of the corner Ben could see a larger gate, this one attended by watchmen on the wall, but also closed.

The entrance measured about twelve feet wide and maybe ten feet tall. The wooden gate hinged on both sides with doors meeting in the middle. Everything about the gate communicated sturdiness and security, especially for those inside of it.

Al-alif looked toward the top of the gate, to a small window. "Mercy for weary travelers?" he called.

In a moment a man's face appeared in the shadow of the window. None of his features could be clearly seen, but he answered in a friendly tone.

"Al-alif! Welcome! We have expected you these last three days. Yes, there is mercy. But you must pass through the eye of the needle, for I cannot open the gate for anyone. The sun has already set."

"Very well. We have been expecting this. We could hope for no more. We are at your service." Ben thought he could detect a tone of weariness in the ramrod's voice.

In about half a minute a man appeared about twenty feet to the right of the gate. Al-alif led the caravan toward him, and stopped near the wall.

He turned to Ben and Sethur and asked, "Will you help us through the needle's eye? It will deliver us from sleeping in the open tonight."

Sethur nodded, so Ben also nodded, though he had no clue as to what might be involved.

Immediately, all of Al-alif's men began coaxing the camels to kneel, and proceeded to relieve them of all burdens—passengers, shipping containers, saddles, blankets, rope. Everything, it seemed, but leads. All unloading took place as near as possible to where they'd first seen their wall friend at ground level. Ben could discern a small opening in the wall, about forty-two inches high, he thought, and nearly three feet wide. This would be their way into the city after hours, but it appeared that it would be very inconvenient.

When cargoes and all other burdens lay in a pile beside the wall, Al-alif lamented, "Alas, we are somewhat heavy laden. No matter. Cargo first, men." A low, four-wheeled cart had been pushed out through the needle's eye. Al-alif picked up a bundle that UPS would someday have to reject due to weight restrictions and began loading the cart. Sethur picked up a bundle and followed suit, motioning Ben to do the same.

A single camel can carry up to five hundred pounds, and though seven men worked on the project, it still proved difficult and time consuming. By the third trip through the tunnel, Ben wondered whether sleeping outside the city might not have been a bad idea. Inside the wall, the opening became both narrower and shorter, so that a man had to bend over nearly double as he passed under the lowest point. In the middle, Ben could see in the tunnel's dim light, a space where a door about six inches thick could slide down from above, effectively blocking the passage.

With all saddles and personal gear finally needleized, Al-alif sent Lydia and Patricia through. Then he handed the men lead ropes and said "Follow me. The girls will know what to do. Do not crowd, but let your charge set the pace. It will be slow."

Taking the first camel, he entered the needle's eye. His ship of the desert approached the opening and knelt before it, then began to slowly work her way through on her knees. As soon as she was completely inside, Sethur took his place at the door, and slowly started through. When he was out of sight, Ben followed, marveling at how intense security in this neighborhood had to be. He began to think of this process as a primitive precursor to the ATS, and wondered if it caused thoughts of a private gate in anyone's mind. They inched through, and with the help of the gatekeeper, each man had to make only one trip with a camel.

At the far end of the tunnel, frenetic activity resumed as the beasts accepted their burdens once again. Minimal distance would be traversed that night, so the lading was done quickly and efficiently. As this process continued, Al-alif made a final passage to the outside to insure that nothing had been overlooked. When he returned empty-handed, the gatekeeper turned a large crank mounted beside the opening on the inside, and the wooden slab resumed its resting place.

Sethur caught the busy ramrod by the sleeve and stopped him. "These, my traveling companions," (he indicated Ben and the two women) "must come and share my hospitality for this night. Do you have arrangements made for you and your men?"

"That we do, and thank you. You have been both great company and effective caretakers of my stock." He turned to Ben. "My brother, I am now compelled to tell you that a common fare for a camel's ride from Damascus to Jerusalem is but five denarii. I smiled at my good fortune when you agreed for ten, but I have determined I cannot in good conscience keep your money beyond fair businessman's share. Please accept this gift from me. It is yours anyway." He handed Ben five silver coins.

Ben felt at a loss as to what to do. But an idea came to mind, and he asked, "Will you keep them and use them to teach me how to bargain as men do here?"

Al-alif thought for a moment, then answered. "Meet me at this gate at the third hour tomorrow. I can teach you much."

Sethur thanked Al-alif, and assured him that Ben would keep the appointment. Then he turned to Ben and the women. "Please allow me the honor of providing you hospitality this night. I can assure you we have ample space and provision. Other arrangements can be made for you tomorrow should you desire. If you will come with me, my wife and daughters will welcome you with the best cooking in Jerusalem."

The three nodded their thanks, so Sethur said, "This way, then."

CHAPTER XV

The four travelers started up a dark street. Their host murmured, "Be careful lest you dash your foot against a stone." The lack of light had no effect on Sethur. He kept Ben at his left side, and the women fell in behind them. In the space of what would have been a city block in Ekalaka, they turned off to the right and stopped at a narrow gate, which was closed.

Sethur rapped on the gate with a stout rod that hung there on a leather cord. Directly, a voice responded to his knock. "Who seeks entry at the gate of Sethur Ben-Judah?"

"It is none other than Sethur Ben-Judah and his guests!" Sethur proclaimed with a laugh. "Caleb, open to us. I must see my family and be refreshed from my journey."

The gate swung open, and they heard the sound of retreating footsteps. A boisterous announcement that the Master had returned filtered back to them from the house. Immediately Caleb reappeared, carrying a small lamp, illuminating an exuberant smile on a friendly, enthusiastic face.

"We have been awaiting your return with great anticipation. The gatekeepers had expected you for several days. The evening meal has been prepared, and we rejoice at your arrival!"

"Thank you, Caleb. We have three guests—Parker, Lydia, and Patricia. Please tell my wife that they will stay with us at least tonight, and perhaps longer. Prepare water to wash their feet."

"Yes, Master." Caleb briskly preceded them through a small courtyard to the door of the house and entered to do his Master's bidding. He stepped aside as Sethur entered the Ben-Judah household, but he got no further than two feet inside, when three women, one about his age, and two perhaps in their late teens accosted him with exclamations of love, with hugs, and kisses.

After a few seconds of this positive relational pandemonium, Sethur extricated himself from them. "We must not ignore our guests. Friends, this is my wife Hannah—"

Another one, thought Ben,

"—and these are my daughters, Debra and Ruth. Here before you are Parker, who saved my life five days ago, Lydia, a merchant from Thyatira, and Patricia, her attendant. Please be seated, friends." He gestured with a sweep of his hand toward a bench against the wall.

Ben's eyes slowly began to focus, for though the room was well lighted by current standards, the sources of light weren't as industrious as newly energized low wattage CFLs. In the illumination available he could see a square room about sixteen by sixteen feet, with ceilings about seven feet. There were beds along one wall, and a door at the far end. Four small lamps provided the lighting. These had been fashioned from some sort of clay and plastered into their places in the walls like modern-day sconces. But the modern-day sconces existed only as a potential reality in Ben's mind. In the center of the room a large steaming kettle seethed. The place looked simple and inviting, an honest room, a room with nothing to hide and nowhere to hide it.

As they sat on the bench, Caleb returned with water and cloth. Beginning with Ben, he carefully removed his sandals and gently rinsed the dust of the journey from his right foot. He then asked about the bandage, and Ben gave him leave to remove it though Lydia had said it should stay for another day. The wound had completely closed, leaving only a ruddy spot on the skin about the size of a denarius. Caleb carefully massaged and rubbed and cleansed the wounded foot also, then he moved on to the women.

With the task of foot-washing completed for the guests, Caleb approached Sethur. "Master, may I wash your feet now?"

Sethur nodded and sat on the end of the bench next to Ben. Caleb repeated the service, but with an air of awe and reverence, as if the servant received honor in the performance of the washing. With the laving completed, Caleb took the basin and cloth and left the room.

Meanwhile the Ben-Judah women had been deployed to their venue. They prepared to feed the family and guests in style, with not only stew, but fresh bread, roasted grain, fruits and cheeses. When all had been made ready, Hannah nodded to her husband.

"Come, my friends. Join my beloved family, who will all have much to share about happenings in Jerusalem during my absence."

Hannah arranged them at reasonable points around the steaming pot, and began to ladle a savory stew into each one's bowl. She provided flat bread in abundance, and also set wine before them.

This sort of wine presented a new experience for Ben—not that he'd never partaken of such beverages, because he already had in the future, but to this point water only had been provided with meals. He found it to be refreshing. Its taste reminded him of wholesome grapes, of rain and sun and fertile ground, of joyous harvest and a bountiful wine-press. He tried not to think about the feet that had crushed the grapes.

It tasted healthy.

Minimal conversation took place among the travelers as they ate, but the Ben-Judah women revealed a wealth of information—the ancient version of social media. As they finished the meal, Hannah spoke to Ben.

"Parker, how is it that you saved my husband's life?"

197

Ben looked at Sethur, who nodded for him to proceed.

At the inception of his tale, Ben asked his companions to interrupt with any pertinent additions or corrections. Then he began the story with the adder, the lizard and the storm. He gave the whole account, downplaying his own heroics, but was corrected at several points by Patricia, who evidently possessed Holmes--like powers of observation and an excellent memory.

When he had concluded the tale, complete with the invention of black light and the pied piper style ridding a campsite of scorpions and the subsequent reunion with Al-alif, Hannah said, "Parker, my daughters and I will be forever in your debt. We are honored to have you under our roof."

To her husband she said, "Sethur, the hand of God rested upon your trip for your safe return. And it is such a blessing to have you home again. We have been expecting you these past three days. We understand now your delay in coming, and we thank God that we have you home and safe. Did the synagogue work go well?"

"It did. But my dear, I must tell you of it later. Our guests and I are tired from our journey, not to mention a trip through the eye of the needle this night. Beyond that, Parker has planned an exhausting day for himself tomorrow. Al-alif has promised to teach him the ways of the marketplace!"

Hannah laughed in enthusiastic, musical tones. "Al-alif surely knows how to strike a bargain. But now, my friends," she said, "we will show you to your sleeping arrangements."

Debra and Ruth rose from where they had been seated and led Lydia and Patricia through the door at the back of the room. Hannah spoke briefly to Sethur, who nodded to Ben to follow him, and led him outside.

The blackness of the sky amplified the silver light from the stars. Ben thought the new moon should be visible by the next night. He had stopped wondering which day of the week it was. He knew that nearly two thirds of his time,

historically speaking, had already been spent, and he knew
that his task demanded alacrity. He hoped that somehow
instructions in bargaining, although it appeared as a delay,
might assist him in some fashion.

Sethur led him to a narrow stairway attached to the
outside wall of the home to the right of the front door.
Carrying a small lamp, he preceded Ben up the steps. The
stairway terminated next to a wooden door, which Sethur
pushed open. He set the lamp on a small wooden table, and
by its light Ben saw a wooden chair, a table, a crude bed,
and a small basin full of water.

"This water is for your refreshment and for washing,"
Sethur instructed. "I will awaken you tomorrow in plenty of
time for your appointment. May God give you good rest,
my friend." With that he bowed slightly and departed,
leaving the lamp alight beside the basin of water.

In the solitude that engulfed the room after Sethur had
left, Ben began to collect his thoughts. This should not have
been a difficult job, as he should have been so totally
focused on finding one man and asking one question. Could
it be too late to regret the decision to make his start in
Damascus rather than in Jerusalem? But other thoughts
intruded. Sherry's smiling face, Gramps' suspicious nature,
Doc's obsession with palindromes, Adam's faith. He
wondered if Adam would be interested to know the extent
of the impact of Jesus' life. And the scandalous rumors! The
credibility problems!

Then he thought of Lydia and Patricia and Debra and
Ruth. All possessed their own natural beauty. None of them
looked overweight. But then, Dunkin' Donuts had not yet
come on the scene. All had dark complexions, snappy dark
eyes, and long dark hair. Even Hannah—probably his
mother's age—showed no visible gray yet. He thought
about how gratifying it had been to hear Patricia speak, and
wondered if these women liked their lot in this place. *In this
time,* he reminded himself.

At length he began to muse on how difficult it would be
to find one rich man in this city, estimated population fifty

thousand. He imagined the difficulty of knowing how to search, how to inquire without being rude. He realized that he was not as alone as he might be, and trusted that Sethur would give him aid.

These thoughts were still in his mind when heard a knock at the door. "Please come in," he called.

Morning sunlight blazed into the room as Sethur entered.

"I hope you have rested well, my friend," Sethur began. "My beloved bride has prepared a meal for us, and invites you to break your fast with us. Will you join us?"

"Yes, sir," Ben answered. "Evidently, I have rested well, and I feel as though a meal would be a good idea. I shall join you shortly."

Sethur left, and Ben rose to begin preparations for his day. He opened his shepherd's bag and looked at the purple robe, considering whether to wear it on his bargaining tour. He decided against it, because if he wore it people might automatically think he had large amounts of money, and might not bargain in the same way they would with a commoner. Besides, Al-alif knew about it, and had not instructed him to wear it.

He washed his face. The water had become cool from the ambient temperature in the room. He dressed himself in the pedestrian brown robe and descended the stairs. They seemed narrower and steeper now, in the daylight. After a couple of steps down, he returned to the room for the lamp and brought it with him, in case he did not sleep there during the upcoming night. He hoped to save someone a trip.

At breakfast he met the usual crowd, plus the Ben-Judah women. They sat, as they had the previous evening, around a steaming pot. This one contained a dish somewhat similar to oatmeal, with abundant fruit and cinnamon stirred in. The ubiquitous flat bread occupied its place, and as the guests ate, Sethur outlined some plans he had made for their day.

He knew a man who worked for Pontius Pilate, the Roman governor, and offered to introduce Lydia and Patricia to him. Maybe that would lead to an interview with the Governor, and a chance to show him "your wares." He also had connections among the people that could be considered rich by those of lesser means. Ben understood this, because wealth is (or will be) relative. Sethur assured him that he could find out if anyone new to the area fit the profile. By the end of his outline, they had finished eating. It remained only to return to the gate to meet Al-alif.

When they stepped out of the courtyard into the street, Ben looked about in amazement. Up the hill to his left he could see a large white marble building, brilliant in the morning sun. Sethur explained that this was his place of work. On that same side of things, for Sethur's home seemed to mark some sort of unofficial division, dwellings stood spaced generously apart. Rich men's houses: not many were rich. Down the hill to the right, the neighborhood appeared more inner city. No lawns or grass or trees, only houses next to houses. Ben asked about a high point from which he could get a good overview of the city. His host promised such an opportunity sometime after he had learned to bargain.

In due time they arrived at the Fish Gate, where they would have entered the previous evening had they been a bit earlier. Al-alif waited there with his generous picket-fence smile, and that voluminous body concealed beneath that robe.

"Parker, my friend, and Sethur, my friend! What a blessing to have you in my caravan. We must leave tomorrow for Egypt and the south, but today is ours! Let us learn to bargain!"

Sethur told Ben he would be welcome back at the domicile when he finished his lesson.

Al-alif steered Ben toward a narrow street, where temporary shelters housed a great variety of open-air shops, squeezed together like pips in a pomegranate. Some of them

201

connected directly to buildings—shopkeepers had access to permanent places of business, or home, through back doors.

All the stalls displayed useful things. There were no toys or knickknacks, no fad products such as the (future) hula hoop. There were no miniature camel souvenirs, no racks with postcards. Nearly all focused on utility, that which the populace needed in order to live. Jewelry provided an obvious exception to this rule, though opinions vary as to whether or not it is a necessity.

They saw shops with lamps, oils and wicks. Shops with clothing—some of it ornate and beautifully fabricated. Folk sold cooking and serving pots, utensils, and food.

The aroma of the fish shop made Ben a bit queasy. He hoped he smelled today's catch, for sure. Some shops sold bread and other baked goods, and the produce of the land—mostly grapes, figs, and olives. Ben noted a great variety of leather products. He puzzled over his rich target. Might he be somewhere nearby, doing some bargaining of his own? Might he be incognito? Ben decided to be on the alert.

Al-alif made his way to one of the fruit stands and began to examine a basket of dried figs. "How much for these?" he asked the shopkeeper.

Ben attempted to evaluate Al-alif's strategy. His choice of shopkeeper seemed advantageous. This particular man, slight and small, seemed inordinately quiet. He came and stood behind the basket and began to speak. Ben could not understand all the man said, but he seemed to be explaining how unique these particular figs were, how they'd been shipped in only yesterday from one of the finest fig farms in a place called the Negev.

"How much?" Al-alif persisted.

"For the lot?"

"Yes. For these figs."

"Five denarii."

"Five days wages for one basket of figs? The Negev is but a short distance south—not even a day's journey. You must have overpaid your shipper."

"Perhaps I could let them go for four."

"These figs are not among the best I have seen. I could not give you more than two for them."

"Two denarii? I have a wife and four children to support and you want me to give you the food from my table? I can perhaps allow the figs to sell for three. That is all I can do for you."

"You drive a hard bargain. We will take the lot." With that, Al-alif produced the denarii and handed them over, and hoisted the basket of figs onto his shoulder.

"Not the basket! I will wrap them in cloth for you."

Al-alif made pretense of being flummoxed. "But I just bought this lot—figs, basket and all. Three denarii. Do you have such a short memory?"

The shopkeeper looked at Al-alif the way a chicken looks at a fox. There remained only one reasonable way out of this, and he took it.

"Safe journeying, my friend. May the figs be nourishment for your loved ones."

Al-alif nodded to the shopkeeper, signaled to Ben, and weaved his way through the throng to the south. At the end of the alleyway, they turned left toward what smelled like it had to be the stable district.

"Now you see how it is done? You carefully choose your target, you assume that his selling price will be about half what he asks. You try to put yourself in position to profit even if you cannot get the price you desire. The figs are good, worth two denarii, perhaps a bit more. The basket, however, is another matter. I can use it in my business, and it adds value to the purchase for me. Remember mainly that every man with a product and a price (myself included) expects his customer to enter into this competition. If you had a better grasp of the language, I would have considered you a fool. As it was, I assumed rightly that you were merely ignorant."

At one of the stable doors, Al-alif called for Hilkiah, who appeared almost immediately. "Place these figs among our food provisions. You and the men may have some today as well. I have more business in the city, and I will join you later."

Hilkiah disappeared, and as he did, Al-alif handed Ben five denarii. "Now, my lad, I must send you 'into the arena' as we say. Do not worry if you do not do as well your first try as you think I have done. No matter what, we will not throw you under the caravan. But now, can you think of anything I might need in my business?"

Ben had been considering this, and offered the suggestion of a new lead rope.

"You are right, my brother. Now we must be off to the leather goods section of the market." Al-alif led the way and Ben followed, back to the market and up the narrow alley. On both sides, in nearly every shop, small competitions were occurring, verbal wrestling matches, all related to the value of a product in relation to its asking price. Ben wondered if any of these bargainers were rich and young.

Finally, they stopped at a small booth filled with leather products of all descriptions. A few saddles, ropes, bags—even a bag very similar to the one that contained Ben's earthly possessions, or at least what he possessed at the time. Coiled lead ropes hung on the partition to the left. Length varied somewhat. Most were braided strands of animal hide. All looked sturdy. Ben chose one of the most expensive-looking models and cast a questioning glance at Al-alif, who nodded.

He then located the shopkeeper, a shorter version of Al-alif—compact and powerful-looking. The man smiled in a way that reported the same absence of certain teeth, and brought his sturdy frame to bear on the situation.

"How much for this?" Ben enunciated carefully, hoping not to give away too much about his novice status with Aramaic.

"That, my friend, is as fine a quality lead rope as you will find in all Judea. Wisdom from the sharp edge of the sword went into its making. These are shipped here from Tarsus by Saul, and I just received new inventory. They span an additional two cubits beyond anything else you will find in this market, and many of my customers have returned to buy more. That rope is eight denarii."

"Perhaps I could mend the old one," Ben said. He wanted to establish a lower price even before he entered his own offer.

"Beasts of burden are a great asset, and must be protected. A weak or frayed rope can cause no small amount of trouble in the desert."

Ben nodded and waited. He resisted the urge to launch into his account of how much trouble a weak or frayed lead rope could cause.

"Perhaps I can let it go for seven."

"I mean no insult to you, but as you know, denarii are hard to acquire. At this time I can offer you only two."

"Two! Have you not seen the quality of this rope? It is unlike any made in all this region! The leather of Tarsus is thicker, longer lasting and of higher quality. And the workmanship is superb. I must have six at the very least."

Ben paused. He had six denarii. He had plenty besides the five Al-alif had given him. This torture could be over in moments, and he would have what he wanted. And the money did not matter.

But Al-alif stood nearby, watching.

In the arena, Ben reminded himself. "I will give you three."

"I am so sure you would, my friend. You could resell it and gain two days wages in the twinkling of an eye. I cannot sell it for less than five, for the sake of my wife and my little ones, who depend on me."

Those references to family always tugged at Ben's heart strings. He steeled himself, and said, "Four, and we have a bargain."

"Four! For you only I will do this, but you must promise me you will not publish this price, or I will have to close my shop for good at day's end. With your promise, I make the exchange."

Ben counted out the coins and accepted the merchandise. He handed the lead rope and the remaining denarius to Al-alif as they wound back through the brabble and cacophony that made up Jerusalem's market. They walked to the stable district in silence, but presently Ben spoke to Al-alif.

"You know of the other robe I have in my bag?"

"Yes, I do. I remember when Lydia asked you of it that night we were reunited with you. It must be very impressive."

"Would it help," asked Ben, "to wear such an impressive thing when I am trying to bargain? Would it give any advantage?"

"That depends on the kind of person you are. Here we have a system in which a man always asks twice what he knows is a fair price to sell a thing, whether the customer is rich or poor. When the bargaining is finished, the seller is happy. He knows he received fair exchange for his merchandise. The buyer is happy. His pride is stroked by what he perceives to be success in bargaining. Rich men naturally have a reputation for driving a hard bargain. To look rich may even intimidate some sellers. In some cases, that is how they got rich. It is a mystery to me, but poor men seem willing to pay a lot more for the same product.

"Now you ask me. Should a man wanting a good bargain look rich? I say no. It is better to work just outside the watchman's view. Don't dress like a rich man. Bargain like a rich man, and you may become one! But truly, my friend, you did well in the arena today. That is how it is done here. It is a simple process. There is no need to discover the wheel all over again. How do you make purchases in the west of Tarshish?"

Ben's mind went blank, perhaps like a locked-up computer, unable to sort out the data and answer the question. Credit cards came to mind, and debit cards. Coupons flashed by, internet purchases, garage sales and flea markets. The wheel of fortune finally came to rest on used cars.

"Some things are sold as you do it here," he sighed. "Most things are not."

That part of the day that required heat mitigation arrived, and Al-alif invited Ben to share some of the afternoon with the crew. This turned out to be mostly resting in the shade through the warmest part of the afternoon, then some minor preparations for the following day's departure. Al-alif intended to continue south to Egypt. Ben thought about how great it would be to see the sphinx with its nose intact. But with no camera, and such a limited time, he had to let the opportunity slide by. But what a wonderful place the past sometimes turns out to be.

In late afternoon, Al-alif took Ben aside and privately thanked him again for the safe return of the camels, and for Ben's part in the protection of Sethur and the women. Ben took the Jimmie Dean "Aw, shucks" approach, but appreciated the expression of gratitude. He then received a hug, which, if categorized by geologists, would have registered at least 1.5 on the Richter scale. He wished Al-alif well, and retraced his steps through the market and back to Sethur's home, ever on the lookout for a rich young man. In the shadow of an alley Ben's subconscious attempted an alert. There was a thought within a thought, recognition without cognition, the irresistible impression that he'd seen someone he knew, someone he knew from home. It was impossible, so he treated it like the tax code.

Arriving at the gate, he used the primitive knocker to summon Caleb, and received welcome through that same exuberant smile. In the light of day, Ben noticed that the man's right ear had a small hole in it. No adornment or ear ring, just an empty hole.

"Master told me to watch for you. Please come in and sit down. I will make ready for you." So Ben sat and waited on the bench Caleb had indicated.

Caleb soon returned with a basin of water and a towel, and again gently removed Ben's sandals. "Nice workmanship. Were they made locally?" Caleb asked.

No, but they will be, Ben squirmed a bit at the irony. "I'm not sure who made them, but I think they are from around here somewhere."

Caleb massaged and rinsed and cleansed the dirt of the marketplace and the stable from the feet of Benjamin Parker. Ben felt as if his entire life were being cleansed.

When Caleb finished washing and drying feet and replacing sandals, Ben took the opportunity to ask. "Why do you have a hole in your right ear?" It didn't actually qualify as a Ben blurt, because he could have stopped it. Just the same, he did wonder after he'd said it if it were a polite thing to ask. But Caleb reacted with eagerness. Ben could see he welcomed the question and would delight in giving answer to it.

"It is as my Master said. You come from far away, and know little of our customs." He smiled broadly. "I must tell you my story, for it is also the story of my Master.

"My family had fallen on difficult times—my father became ill and could not work, so my older brother began to manage our little farm. There was not room enough for me to live there. In Ephraim's hill country the land is not so fertile. And with my family in need, I came here to Jerusalem to seek a way to earn money.

"I did many things—cleaned out stables, stomped grapes a few days, I even worked briefly on a camel train. But I could earn nothing on those jobs beyond my daily necessities.

"After some thought, I decided to sell myself as a slave, with my family receiving the money for the sale."

Ben's jaw dropped. Not only was Caleb serious about the "sale", this slavery concept seemed perfectly acceptable to him.

"It so happened that on the day of my sale, my Master came to market to buy a young man." (Ben noted that he always said "Master" and never "Sethur").

"When the time arrived to bid for me, no other bidders entered the fray. Naturally, opening bid marked selling price—not nearly enough to put my family on good financial footing. My heart sank.

"As Master brought me home, he spoke to me not as a slave, but as a son. As we walked I told him of the plight of my family, and my hopes to help my mother, my brother, and my two sisters. When Master realized our situation, he sent my family *double* my sale price. Can you imagine? Can you imagine how I felt?

"My brother expanded the farm, and made enough to care very well for himself and the women in our family.

"He will soon be able to marry." Caleb's eyes sparkled. "She is a beautiful girl.

"So, in our land God has given us a law for slaves. A person may sell himself for six years. After the six years he may go free and return to his life as before.

"But if he loves his master, he may stay a slave forever. And if that is his choice," Caleb stopped, and appeared to be composing himself. Tears were forming in his eyes.

"If that is his choice," he continued, "his master takes him to the doorpost of the House of God. He takes a sharp awl and drives it through the slave's right ear. As this is done in the House of God it is a sacred thing. And that is why my ear has a hole in it. I have no more desire for my own freedom. Master says that in two years I may be betrothed to a wife, as my brother has done.

"I have already made my choice. She also is beautiful."

Ben wondered how long a person could kneel on flagstones. "Will you be a slave forever?"

"Ever is a long time. But it is possible you cannot understand. I am not a slave now. I obey my Master because I love him. Even as my own father. I fear not for any future that may come as long as I belong to my Master. I serve his household at least until his death. Perhaps Mistress Hannah will need me then. No matter. What would please my Master will please me."

"But how will you support yourself in fifteen or twenty years when your Master dies?"

"Parker, friend of my Master, I know this certainly. Master has treated me with love from the first day he met me. He has much power, and with his power he has done me much good. I have no fear of what life may bring. My occupation and my joy is to serve my Master. There is nothing else for me."

Ben's mind flashed back to Adam. *"With Him as my God, I have only optimism about the future."*

Slowly, Caleb rose from the stone floor. Even a young man can eventually become stiff. "Now," he said, "You may refresh yourself before the evening meal. Come with me please."

Beside the door stood a pitcher of water. Caleb picked up the pitcher. *That must be heavy*, Ben thought. *Clay pitcher, more density than water. And water—sixty five pounds per cubic foot.* Ben noticed no particular strain in Caleb's manner. They exited into the late afternoon sunlight and ascended the stairs to the apartment above.

Once inside, Caleb took the basin from the table and dumped yesterday's water onto the ground below the stairway landing. He returned to the table, rinsed the basin, and then poured the fresh water from the pitcher into it.

"We here would drink, if need be, before we wash." Caleb said carefully. *Such sensitivity*, Ben mused.

"Thank you, Caleb. Will you please call me at mealtime?" Caleb smiled, nodded, and left the room, pitcher in hand.

Ben drank freely, then disrobed and washed as well as he could. His mind became that freeway interchange of thoughts and questions. He made himself comfortable on the bed.

What if slavery is a good thing? It seems to be working out, at least for Caleb, but would it work as well if Sethur were not such a compassionate master? And it's not like slavery back home. These people volunteer for it. How can one who has totally devoted himself to the service of another for all the foreseeable future be so happy? Does the rest of his family appreciate what he is doing? A wild guess

210

would be that they do. It seems to depend totally on the Master.

He thought again of Al-alif and hoped he'd have a safe journey down to Egypt. He thought about being responsible for "saving" the camels, and hoped everyone involved would soon forget. He wondered if he'd swerved into changing the course of history, which, on the one hand he must not do, and on the other hand may be impossible anyway. He thought about the difference Gloria had made by sending a purple hanky along. Such good fortune to have it. "Fortune", he repeated to himself. Such good fortune to get the crazy idea to use it to make black light, and to somehow remember that scorpions show up in it.

Then a more serious thought merged. *What about the mission?* In the context of being a stranger in a strange land, it was easy to lose track of why he had begun the mission.

His mind went back to his assertion to Lydia that things seemed to be working out. *Time is certainly of the essence,* he thought. *But why would all the events so far line up if in the end I am to fail?*

More practical thoughts kicked in. *Where should I look if I want to find a rich young man? How can I be sure if he's the right one when I find one? Is there any chance I've missed him already? Maybe that was last week.*

Ben considered this. He remembered Sethur's confidence that rescue was eminent as things began to fall into place for them in the desert. Maybe he could also hope along those lines.

He had made it to Jerusalem. The timing seemed to be about right. He had found trustworthy friends who had also accepted him. Reportedly, Jesus was around as well. It was not a big place. There weren't many places to hide, as it were, for the wealthy people.

But the city itself presented a puzzle. It appeared that about ninety-five percent of the people were "commoners" or else somewhere below that. A very few, like Sethur, were in between. Then there was this thin upper crust, this twentieth part, who were really wealthy. His recollection of the Matthew passage was that the young man was "very rich". That should cut it down. But these five percent took up about half the city with their homes. So he had half the city to search, but at least it was the sparsely populated half.

The woman thing bothered him a little bit. Not that they were around, but that they could not be heard in public without permission. He remembered his relief when he finally heard Patricia speak. He knew he'd be glad to get back to a time when both genders could express themselves freely.

He then thought also of Sherry, and her propensity to speak her mind. "Next time, no beard!" *Okay, no problem,* thought Ben. *I might even be able to do that in Ekalaka. Assuming, of course, that the return trip works as advertised.*

Ben didn't realize he'd dozed off until he heard a knock on the door, and Caleb's voice announcing the evening meal. He rose, reclaimed his robe, and passed through the door and onto the top of the stairs. He saw the sun's last rays coming in from the west. *Ninety-three million miles away,* he thought. *It works whether you understand it or not.*

Caleb preceded him through the front door, and he took his seat with the family around the large iron pot.

"It is the new moon, so there is an abundance of meat," Sethur informed him. "We have mutton now, and leeks and onions. Please, share heartily with us."

Some habits die hard, and one of them was the three meals a day thing that Ben had grown up with. *Would grow up with.* He had been sharing heartily, and would have no trouble doing it now. As had been true every day since his arrival, he welcomed daily bread into his life.

The meal was a sort of thick stew mixture of the aforementioned ingredients, which Hannah ladled into bowls for each of them. Ben remembered the other Hannah and her stew. Both tasted delicious, and he struggled a bit, comparing the present dish to one that was definitely in the future, though he'd eaten it in his past. *Time travel's biggest problem will likely turn out to be verb tenses*, he reminded himself. Again

As they shared in the stew they shared also about the day. The daughters questioned Ben about his morning, and after he had given a brief summary, Sethur broke in. "We must now allow Parker to purchase all of our supplies. I saw Al-alif late this afternoon, and he says Parker could talk the Dead Sea out of its odor. But I think he will not have time to shop for us. He must be about his business in the city."

Sethur turned to Ben and said, "Good news, Parker. Tomorrow, if you desire, I will introduce you to one who has many rich friends. That lot of men should know most or all comings and goings among folk of their society. If you are invited to the evening meal, you will find the selection of edibles much broader than what you experienced on the trail, or even here. You will probably find it most advantageous among this group to wear your more extravagant robe."

At this point Lydia said, "Parker, you must allow us to see this in the morning. Such things are our trade, and you must allow it."

Well, thought Ben, *it's not as though they'll be able to admire my masculine physique through it*. But Gloria had done a good job. He smiled. "Tomorrow, you shall see it."

If high fives had been invented at that time, the women would have shared in them.

There are things that never change, thought Ben. *Like women and what they think of clothes*.

213

CHAPTER XVI

Following breakfast that morning—day eleven of the
time event, Ben noted, with a tinge of urgency—he donned
the purple robe. *No, it is imperial indigo*, he reminded
himself. He made sure that he fastened all the ties and that
even his sandal straps were uniformly in place. Then he
descended the stairs to present himself to the judges.

Hannah, Patricia, Lydia, Debra and Ruth had arranged
themselves in a semicircle facing the door as Ben entered. It
pleased him that none of them spoke. They emitted a
collective gasp.

"Do you like it?" How strange to hear these words
coming from his own lips. He usually heard women ask
men that question.

Lydia spoke first. "May I touch the fabric? And yes, we
like it very much!"

Ben nodded, so Lydia approached and took the loose
part of the left sleeve between her thumb and first two
fingers. She rubbed it gently for a couple of seconds, then
carefully examined the stitching on the cuff, and the seam
that ran up toward the elbow.

"May we also touch it?" Hannah asked.

"Certainly you may. Is it that special?"

215

"We have never seen fabric as fine as this. Parker, can you get more of this from west of Tarshish?" Lydia was thinking business. The girls had now encircled Ben and carefully examined the robe, gently caressing the cloth.

"Why do you have the blue tassels of a devout Jew?" Hannah's question sent Ben's mind spinning. He remembered he had tried the robe on and liked it, and that Gloria had kept it because she had said (will say?) she wasn't quite finished. She must have added them...

Now what? I am not a devout Jew. What should I do?

"My seamstress must have put them there without my knowledge. Shall I cut them off?"

Sethur began to speak. He chose his words carefully. "Parker, in our way of worshiping God, there is such a thing as a proselyte. This is one who is not a Jew but accepts our laws and our way of life. He must especially desire to follow the Ten Words."

"What are the Ten Words?" Ben stood near the center of the room, still surrounded by the women, who were not, in any particular sense, distracted from the robe.

Sethur, standing up to full height, said, stentoriously, "These are God's Ten Words.

"You shall have no other Gods before Me.

"You shall make no graven image or likeness of Me from anything you see in heaven above or on earth beneath. You shall not bow down and worship them.

"You shall not take the name of the Lord your God in vain.

"Remember the Sabbath day to keep it holy.

"Honor your father and your mother.

"You shall not murder.

"You shall not commit adultery.

"You shall not steal.

"You shall not lie.

"You shall not covet.

"These are the Ten Words. What do you think of them, Parker?"

Ben stood dumbfounded. In his mind's eye, he saw The Words plastered all over his homeland, sometimes the subject of lawsuits, but they were nevertheless all over—in courthouses, state capitols, federal buildings. He thought it odd that such good moral and societal underpinnings could be so controversial. But he guessed that the real problem had to be that concept of worshiping one God and the assumption that no others were worthy of worship. Or perhaps the premise that God existed.

Ben agreed with the Ten Words, at least with their moral teaching. He had always thought they encapsulated a very good code of ethics.

"I think they are words to live by, and I try to do that. We have heard of the Ten Words west of Tarshish."

Sethur remained thoughtfully silent. Eventually he said, "Were you only circumcised, I could take you to the temple."

"I am. Most all males in my homeland are." This was probably, in all of recorded history, the most classic Ben Blurt. And he did it in Aramaic. Sethur and the Ben-Judah women stared at him, united in their shock.

After a few very long seconds of silence, Sethur asked, in hushed tones, "Do you live in a nation of circumcised Gentiles?"

"Yes. For us its purposes are health and cleanliness."

Sethur pondered silently, cogitating carefully. Then he took a deep breath. "My friend, you never cease to amaze me. I will bring you to the temple at first opportunity. You must leave the tassels in place, though you did not know that they were there, nor what they meant. No doubt you will continue to surprise many even today."

By now the women had ceased to do what, had men been doing it, would have been called slobbering over the fabric. Lydia, though, had sent a question to the table some minutes previous.

"Parker," she repeated, "can you get me fabric such as this from west of Tarshish? White would be acceptable, as we know how to reproduce this color, or any other. Also, I

217

would like someday to meet your seamstress. Her sewing appears to be the most perfect I've ever seen."

In the small, self-righteous courtroom of his mind, Ben accused Gloria of cheating and using a machine. But then he remembered Doc's pronouncement after his own inspection, and decided that she had just done a really great job, which was what he'd paid for. The tassels perhaps required later conversation, but how could she know? Then he remembered. He'd said, "I want to look so totally first century that no one will be able to tell I'm not the real thing."

"Lydia, I am sorry that I cannot acquire more of this fabric for you, and I must be honest. You are not likely ever to meet my seamstress." *You won't live long enough.* As an afterthought, he wondered if he should promise her she could have the robe in a few days, but he somehow prevented this blurt from spewing. He remembered Doc's admonition not to give his clothing away. Instead, he reached into his pocket and found the handkerchief of unusual size. He hoped that it did not qualify as clothing. "Please accept this from me as a reminder of how we were able to cleanse our camp site of scorpions. It is made from a leftover piece of the fabric in the robe." He handed it to her, and she took it, almost reverently.

In a few moments, Sethur announced that he and Ben should begin their quest.

Near the fourth hour of the day they left the courtyard and turned toward the upper side of the city. Spacious and ornate houses had been erected here. They had more marble, more trees, more garden space, more of everything except people.

Shortly they came to a lane that led up and to the southeast. Sethur chose that road, greeting many of the men they met as they walked. Near the street's end, in sight of the city's southern wall, Sethur stopped and knocked on a garden gate.

A solemn male servant, probably about twenty years old, answered Sethur's knock. "Sethur, welcome! Master told me to expect you and a guest this morning. I shall announce you and your friend as soon as I have proper knowledge."

"You may announce us as Sethur Ben-Judah, and Parker from west of Tarshish." Sethur smiled. "Thank you, Gideon."

Gideon escorted them into the courtyard. The humidity registered notably higher, and the reason for that became obvious. A large pond, the size and shape of a generous backyard pool dominated the garden. Ben guessed its depth to be inadequate for swimming. Two large white birds fed on the opposite shore.

Presently Gideon reappeared, and reported that the master would receive them.

Gideon led them up a gently inclined path, as broad as a spacious sidewalk, paved with white flagstones. Slightly above the pond Ben could see the residence, though its ornamentation brought to mind a public building or perhaps a temple. The front door loomed large; wide and tall, constructed of a dense, dark wood that seemed similar to oak. It opened from the center, so that the visual effect was that of entering a city's gate. As Gideon led them inside, Ben noticed that the room's illumination came through window-like openings near the ceiling, and that marble covered the floor. The room had been built square, or very nearly so, and the walls stood taller than those at Sethur's house, giving a sense of wide open space. White plaster surrounded the interior, and two round stone pillars supported the flat roof.

Couches and cushions amply furnished the room and the floor's accents appeared to be Persian rugs. Ben thought he might ask about them.

Standing near the center of the room, its sole occupant seemed to be reading something. He also seemed well dressed, wearing a robe similar in style to Ben's, but colored a bright blue. It also sported blue tassels on the fringe.

He looked up from his scroll and smiled. "Sethur, my friend! And is this the man Parker of whom you spoke yesterday? Come, my friends, sit. We shall talk."

Sethur said, "Mordecai, this is Parker of whom we have spoken, and Parker, this is Mordecai of whom we have spoken."

Mordecai gestured toward two couches set at right angles in a corner. "Gideon, bring us refreshment if you would. Only the best for Sethur and for Parker from west of Tarshish."

As each man took a seat, Mordecai dropped a small verbal grenade in the form of a simple question. "So, then, Parker. You must have passed through Tarshish on your way here. Did you find it pleasant there?"

Mordecai waited for a response. Sethur also looked at Ben expectantly.

At times the truth will not serve. Consider when a wife says to her husband, "Does this robe make me look fat?" What can a man say? There is no right answer to the question. Ben could not speak of the way from Ekalaka to Damascus as though it did not pass through Tarshish. As the silence lingered between uneasy and awkward, Ben rescued himself by asking, "What is it about Tarshish that you enjoy, Mordecai?"

"I find the weather is very pleasant there—neither hot nor cold. The seasons do not severely differ one from the other. Also, the people seem to be at peace with their surroundings and their lot in life."

It sounds like San Diego to me, thought Ben. But he had the advantage of having been to Spain on a couple of occasions. "I agree with you. I also appreciate the weather there."

This seemed to satisfy Mordecai, so he moved on to another topic. "Sethur speaks of you as boundlessly resourceful. How do you come by knowledge of such a broad variety of things?"

Ben thought about libraries, and schools, and the internet, newspapers, and magazines, and The Discovery

Channel. "In my country many men know all that I know and much more. Our children are taught many things as they grow. Some ideas are like tools, and can be used at any time. My mind must be somewhat like a bag of tools."

"Sethur tells me also that you are here in search of someone. Do you know his name or his whereabouts?"

"I do not know him. He is from somewhere nearby, and he is rich, and young, and would be considered by most devout Jews to be a good man. He is curious about how to earn eternal life." Ben could have added the part about has or soon will talk with Jesus, but he was getting better all the time at avoiding the potholes of having to explain how he knew all that.

"And are *you* interested in eternal life?"

Sethur spoke up then. "He knows the Ten Words. He says they are common in his land. He says he agrees with the Ten Words. He says they are written in many prominent locations west of Tarshish. He says that most males in his land are circumcised. He says that he too is circumcised, though I have not seen this.

"He is a proselyte. We must bring him to the temple."

Mordecai looked from Ben to Sethur and back to Ben again. "Parker," he said quietly, "Are there synagogues in your land?"

Ben could not remember seeing one. He knew Woody Allen had a Jewish background, and perhaps Henry Kissinger. And he'd heard the phrase, 'church or synagogue', so he said, "Yes, we have synagogues."

"Are there Jews there?"

"Yes." *Or at least there will be.*

Mordecai and Sethur stared at each other, as if attempting to read each other's thoughts. Then Mordecai appeared to collect himself. He turned to Ben. "Parker, tomorrow is Sabbath. I will be entertaining some friends this afternoon, with all intentions of disbanding our gathering before the celebration of Sabbath begins. Will you join us? Sethur, please, if you could also attend? All manner of folk will be here that will want to speak with

221

Parker. We will conclude before sunset. Could both of you come? But I forget myself. Gideon, the refreshments, please."

Gideon had been waiting in a doorway to Mordecai's left, and upon hearing the order, he entered carrying a small short legged tray, and set it on the marble floor before them. On it Ben saw three flagons of wine, small slices of cheese, and a crisp flat bread similar to crackers. *Cheese, crackers and wine,* he thought. *Some things never change.*

Ben graded the wine excellent. But he detected the aroma of goat in the cheese. Once, as a child, he had been volunteered by his parents to take care of some animals on a small hobby farm near his home while the "farmers" went on vacation. Goats lived there, and they had to be milked. (*Why hadn't those farmers asked me if I were qualified as a goat milker?*) The milk itself smelled rotten, even fresh out of the goat. The goats possessed cantankerous natures, too. But the milk from goats seemed so useless to his family that they dumped it directly into the septic tank. It probably fostered good bacterial action in there.

This cheese brought all that back to his mind. Just as the wine sent pictures of grape vines loaded with grapes through his head, so the cheese brought back a picture of his father dumping goat milk down the sewer.

He ate some of the cheese anyway, and the "crackers" were good, though they could do with a little bit of salt. The world had so much to learn. After this brief time of wine tasting, Mordecai asked again, "Sethur, can you two stay the afternoon, until Sabbath preparation? You are most welcome."

Sethur considered this, as he had not anticipated being invited. After a few seconds he agreed. Mordecai then called to Gideon. "Send messengers immediately, and begin preparation for this evening's meal. All we've invited are welcome, and our door is open."

Gideon immediately left the room. Then Mordecai turned again to Ben. "You must now meet my wives and

222

sons. Sethur, please accompany us. We must leave this room forthwith, as it will be used in the preparations."

He rose and led them to a door on his right, which opened into a room similar in size to the one they had exited, but, if possible, more luxuriously furnished. Cushier cushions, couchier couches, so to speak. More ornate floor coverings. This reminded Ben that he had not yet asked about the rugs.

Four people occupied the room. Two women, and two boys. The boys seemed to be nearly identical in age, twelve or so. The women also shared a similar age bracket.

Mordecai spoke with pride in his voice. "These are my wives and my sons. Parker, this is my wife Elizabeth and our son Boaz, and here we have Naomi and our son Jachin. To you, my family, I present Parker from west of Tarshish."

For a few seconds, no one spoke. The Elizabeth smiled. "You honor us with your presence in our home. You must introduce us to your tailor." Naomi smiled and nodded agreement, then asked, "May we touch your robe?"

Ben offered his right sleeve in answer, and Naomi began examining the fabric. For just a moment Ben thought negatively of Gloria. *She has made me stand out like a freak,* he thought. But again, how could she have known? Then he remembered that she had warned him that such a robe would "stand out like your Bentley." At least he stood out like a well-dressed freak. Naomi's voice brought him back to present reality.

"We would love to have a robe such as this for our husband. He would look so grand, so royal. Wouldn't he, Elizabeth?"

"That he would, though he needs little help to look it now. But could you imagine? And that black sash around his narrow waist, his broad shoulders defining what should be inside of a robe..."

"You women embarrass me. Come, Parker and Sethur. We will await the arrival of our guests on the veranda."

At the far end of the room, a door led to the outside—the north side, which afforded a small amount of

223

shade next to the building. There, against the house, a bench, two chairs, and two small tables took advantage of the shadows.

"Gideon will deliver the early arrivals here, where we can have private conversation. It may help you, Parker, to know at the outset that our nation has been afflicted of late with a teacher who seems to be leading the masses astray. He has many friends among the underclass, and enjoys very broad public approval. He makes his home in Galilee, and many of his close friends come from that area. He had the support of the Baptist while he yet lived." Mordecai paused here in response to Ben's unspoken question. "The Baptist came to us from the wilderness dressed like our prophet Elijah. He claimed to be sent by God as a forerunner to our Messiah. Our prophet Malachi spoke of this forerunner. This Baptist also enjoyed great popularity among the masses, and was called 'the Baptist' because he claimed that God had called him, as part of his ministry, to baptize people and tell them to repent of their sins. Up until he came, people who thought they needed special cleansing baptized themselves. There is some agreement among the priests that he had a legitimate calling. Herod beheaded him last year for speaking against Herod's marriage to his brother Philip's wife. That's all complicated, but the point is that he gave his support to this Jesus of Nazareth, who is a thorn in all of our sides."

Ben remembered parts of this, and needed a bit of fill-in. "Was this the same Herod that slaughtered the babies in Bethlehem?"

"No. This is one of his sons, and definitely the same kind of man. Cursed Idumean. Not one of our own people. He is from Edom. Remember the prophecy of Amos. "For three transgressions of Edom, and for four, I will not revoke her punishment." But back to our informal gathering. All of the people you meet here today share concern for our nation and for our religion. There has been so much tumult lately that we fear losing the little freedom we still have, and this Jesus is adding to our problem."

Gideon joined them at that moment, followed closely by a middle-aged man in a red robe, sporting the mark of the spiritual man, the blue tassels at the fringe. With proper sense of occasion, Gideon announced, "May I present Hezron Ben-Shallah of Judea." Hezron wore, affixed to his forehead, a small wooden box secured with a leather strap.

"Thank you, Gideon. You may assume your other duties. I will make the necessary introductions."

"Yes, Master." Gideon passed through the door into the house.

"Hezron! Welcome! You, of course, know Sethur. His guest, here with us today, is Parker from west of Tarshish. Yes, I know. We can talk about geography later. He is interested in our problem, most particularly in your opinion of Jesus of Nazareth. Do you have anything new to report?"

"Mordecai, if this man is a newcomer to our land, perhaps a bit of background would be helpful?"

Mordecai nodded and signaled Hezron to continue. The generous gesture encompassed whatever must be said.

"As you may know, God Himself created the Jewish nation, and our law was given to us through Moses at Mount Sinai." This Ben did know, because he'd seen Charlton Hesston in *The Ten Commandments* on American Movie Classics, and because Sethur had recently provided detailed review.

"Our lawgiver told us that our law would be the envy of surrounding nations, as it was fair and just. It instituted the simple concept of crime and punishment, and adjusted the punishment to fit the crime." Hezron looked at Ben. "Did you know that nations surrounding this area were ruled by laws of cruel retribution, such as cutting off one's hand for stealing an egg? Through Moses, our God introduced restoration, with a reasonable penalty, so that such arbitrary violence had to stop, at least in Israel. This is the great wisdom of our law.

"There were few capital crimes, and our God drew distinction between a murder with forethought, and accidental slayings. He ordained cities of refuge, so that one

225

who had need could find safe haven there, and retributive punishment would not be enforced as long as one accepted this protection.

"You, of course, see my point. Our law is better. It is kinder, gentler, safer. It treats people as people and brings them to a higher plane. It gives stability to every level of our society. Because of our law, every one of us knows who he is and what God expects of him."

Hezron leaned close to Ben, and hissed, "This Jesus of Nazareth has said that the law is not good enough. God Himself ordained the law and gave it to us in the hands of a mediator. It has in it all we need to show us how to live. It creates the traditions that lend stability to our lives, and has done so for fifteen hundred years. Do you see what this means, Parker? Do you know what this world will be like in another fifteen hundred years?" Before Ben could confess that he did have a good grasp on that, Hezron continued. "None of us know! But our lives will be good if we follow God's law. And this Jesus says the Law of Moses is not good enough! Who does he think he is?

"It is my opinion, and many agree with me, that this man must be stopped." As though the word applied to him as well, Hezron stopped. He reached up to the box on his forehead and removed a small square of parchment with a flourish. It was covered with tiny writing, the manually produced small print version of something. "These are the Ten Words. These are rules to live by. Are they not enough? ARE THEY NOT ENOUGH?"

Ben feared to answer. The man seemed inordinately angry, and Ben could see that his own ignorance might provoke Hezron further.

Suddenly calm, Hezron said, "So you see why he must be stopped."

Mordecai intervened then, and announced the arrival of another guest. "While you two were so occupied, we have been honored by another arrival. Parker, may I present to Eliakim. He is one of the Sadducees."

Ben smiled and nodded in greeting as Eliakim took the seat immediately to his left.

"Our friend Parker comes from the far west of Tarshish. He is here in search of a friend of Jesus of Nazareth. It may be helpful for him if you give him your own perspective. Keep in mind that he is a stranger, and unfamiliar with our customs."

"Well then, my friend. Do you know what a Sadducee is?" Ben shook his head, hoping that this gesture signified a negative. "A Sadducee is one who accepts the Law of Moses, but not all of the traditions that have been grafted on by Hezron and his brothers. We recognize that Abraham's God has been at work in the establishment of our nation. In accepting Moses' Law, we do not see the necessity, or the likelihood that the human spirit manifests itself on this earth. We do not see the necessity of believing in an undying soul inside of man, as the law does not teach it.

"The problem we have now is with the masses. This Jesus of Nazareth is misleading normal, peaceful folk with all this talk about the kingdom of heaven. Moses did not teach us that there is a heaven for us. The Nazarene troubles our nation by building in people a false hope for a life that is not available to them. It appears to me he must be stopped."

At that moment, Gideon again entered, followed by two more men, introduced as Melchi and Abinadab. He also reported to Mordecai that preparations were completed for the meal. The entire gathering, led by Mordecai, passed back into the room where Ben had first met the wives and sons.

The place had been completely transformed.

In the center of the room a low, U-shaped group of tables had been arranged. The open part of the U faced the main entrance into the room from the house proper, and the bottom, so to speak, faced toward the door through which the men had just entered. Ranging out from the sides and bottom of this squared U were low, soft-cushioned couches, four on a side, creating twelve consumer units. (Ben could

227

not shake the habit of thinking in terms of consumer units.) Mordecai arranged the guests around the table in short order. He assigned Ben to the left bottom corner of what he found out much later was called a triclinium. He also later discovered that his place identified him as the guest of honor. From that location all other guests could easily be addressed.

After Mordecai had arranged his guests, (no place sat empty) he invited Melchi to address Ben concerning his perspective on the Jesus situation. Meanwhile Gideon and other young men brought bowls of bread products, fruit, roasted meat, nuts and olives. The men reclined on their respective couches, each man resting his weight on his left elbow and using his right hand to reach for the different delicacies. Ben assimilated quickly, so he initially felt very comfortable with the situation. After a brief respite, Melchi, reclined immediately to Ben's left, began to speak to him.

Other conversations sprouted up all around him, so this presented a new challenge. Ben would be required to listen while shutting other interesting talk out of his mind. At least he'd be required to work at paying attention. The fact that no one spoke English created even more difficulty.

"I realize that you are new to our area, and new to our language. I will speak to you as well as I can in simple terms. Do you understand our present political situation?"

Again Ben shook his head. It had worked well before.

"Our present leader, our so-called king, is not a king at all. He is an appointed despot; that is, he is a wicked ruler, placed over us by the Romans. He is not even a Jew. He is Idumean. From Edom. Even you must know about *them*. He has no love or loyalty to us, and treats us with the same disdain that a foreign conqueror would. That is probably why Rome has appointed him.

"Through these last hundred and fifty years, all of our leaders have been set over us by the Romans. Prior to that, in spite of brief uprisings and periods of freedom, marauding peoples from outside our nation governed the people here in our lands. All of our rulers of late have been sent to us from Rome.

"We could attempt an overthrow, but should we do that, Rome would send her legions and force us back into submission. We are no match for them, and this is obvious to us all.

"They have their eye on our land—not because it is rich in any resource they need. It is merely part of the territory which they've conquered. It is a crossroad of trade, but what is that to them? The parasite is never concerned with the health of the host.

"So they are our conquerors and our rulers. They leave us alone for the most part, though they expect their share of taxes, and their Roman laws override our Jewish laws. They maintain roads and keep order. It is rumored that Greek is spoken throughout their empire. This is an advantage to some.

"Our problem is one of stability. These people here with us today, and myself, our challenge is that we must all be looking at the same area of the parchment. When one like this Jesus comes on the scene, he disrupts the normal. I admit that the normal is not that good, but it is stable. Should he cause an uprising, the Romans would be on our necks in a moment.

"We Herodians see the danger of all of this, and we are trying to prevent the disaster that surely would come to us should the Nazarene cause the people to think they can turn against the Romans. We support Herod not because he is good, but because at this time supporting him is good for our nation. Most of us here agree that Jesus is bad for us politically. Some think we should take some sort of action in order to neutralize him."

Maybe I should try to warn him, thought Ben. Then he remembered Doc's admonition to avoid direct impact upon history. Since Doc had demonstrated insight about wearing his sandals to the tanning booth, Ben decided to ignore that thought, tempting though it was.

229

But he needed to know how to find Jesus so that he could find this rich young guy. So he said, "Where does Jesus spend most of his time?"

In an old western movie, there is always that scene where the wrong thing is said in the saloon. The piano player stops playing, people stop talking, the poker players stop bidding. Everyone looks at the guy who said whatever it was. Whatever it was, Ben had just said it.

All eyes were on Ben. He thought everyone else should be caught up in private talk, but it turned out that no one had been ignoring him.

"I may need to find him in order to solve my problem," Ben continued. "I have no interest in him personally."

Abinadab said quietly, "I hear he spends his nights out on the Mount of Olives with his followers. You may be able to contact him there."

Hezron also seemed to want to speak. It was slow in coming, but at last he said, "Much of his time is spent in and near our Holy Temple This is a great bother to us. For those of us in this room, the less we know of his movements, the better off we are. And the temple is the center of our worship, and no place for the likes of him.

"But you have said that you do not seek him. What is it then that you do seek?"

Grandma's maxim about the truth being the best way out of tight spots had, with the one exception, held up so far. "I seek a young man, about my own age, who is rich, and who seeks wisdom from Jesus." *How crazy is it to even be doing this? How can it seem so impossible?* If he had only foreseen these "little" problems, he might never have considered trying to solve the larger one, the time one.

Mordecai then resumed a master-of-ceremonies role by asking, "Can you, my friends, keep your eyes open and report to me of a rich young man trailing after Jesus? I am sure Parker will be in our debt. But out yonder the sun is sinking low, and tonight is Sabbath. Join me now as we thank God for our meal, then go in peace to your loved ones, and thank you for coming to my house today."

After the prayer (similar in some ways to church, Ben observed) Mordecai blessed those who had shared his table and sent them off, one by one, with personal regards to the loved ones of each. Sethur and Ben left last, but had no need for inordinate haste, with sundown some minutes off, and Sethur's home so nearby.

CHAPTER XVII

The Ben-Judah front door opened onto a flurry of activity. Caleb, the rest of the house servants, and the five women all claimed ownership of some household chore. All tasks appeared to be time-sensitive. No one stood idle, and as the two men entered, Sethur called greetings to his wife with offers to help with any random task. Hannah claimed that Patricia and Lydia had pitched in so enthusiastically that nothing remained to be done. Just the same, Sethur found a pot that needed stirring and directed Ben to keep an eye on some flat bread baking out back.

As the sun set, the home took on an aura of peace with the completion of preparations. They partook of the evening meal quietly, with conversation noncontroversial. Sethur and Ben participated sparingly in the repast, having just eaten.

The evening seemed perfect for quiet contemplation, Ben noted. After some thought, he addressed this question to Sethur.

"What really is Sabbath?"

Sethur sat in silence for some time. Eventually, he said, "Perhaps I fail to understand. You know the Ten Words, and you have synagogues in your land, yet you lack knowledge of the Sabbath?"

Ben nodded, and did not offer further explanation. Sethur continued.

233

"Our sacred writings tell us that our God created our world and all that is in it in six days. On the seventh day He rested from His labors. He tells us through our lawgiver Moses that this is His pattern. Our Fourth Word is that we will keep the Sabbath day, the seventh day, holy by quiet rest, and by using that time solely for Him. Because of this we prepare in advance for it. We cook the meals we plan to eat. We close our shops. We allow no Gentile, or Jew, for that matter, to trade in our cities on Sabbath. At least, this is done by all of us who truly fear God. It is one of His Ten Words from Sinai through Moses. The Sabbath's duration is from sundown the sixth day until sundown the seventh day, as God shows us this concept in the Scroll of Beginnings. "The evening and the morning were the first day." Our day begins at the sun's setting. So we are now in Sabbath, until tomorrow at sunset. I hope you will enjoy it with us."

"So what will the Sabbath be for you?" Ben possessed sensitivity enough not to ask what Sethur would "do", as doing seemed to be the enemy here.

"Tomorrow I will rise at first light. I will eat that which the women have prepared. I will spend time in prayer and contemplation, and I will hear my Rabbi speak. And I will rest, as my God did. If you wish you may join me in all of this. If not, it would be my desire as your host that you refrain from pursuit of any unworthy goal or servile work. It would be well also for you if you rest."

Ben retired to his upstairs apartment soon after the conversation with Sethur. He lay on the bed thinking about having a day set aside for rest. *How beneficial could this be?* He figured Adam would think it was a great idea, but then, Adam was a Jesus freak anyway. He thought of all the people who have to work on Sundays and thought of the people who used their services. Mostly shoppers and eaters, as banks and insurance places closed religiously, it seemed. So if everybody stayed home from stores and restaurants, the wait staff and clerks could have the day off. But what would they do? They couldn't go out and eat somewhere, because those places would be closed. It would only work if everybody wanted the same thing.

So he was marooned nearly two thousand years in the past, paying roughly fifty thousand dollars a day for the privilege. He had lost three days due to the sandstorm. And now the Sabbath just might become an issue.

What is this? Day what of the trip? He counted them, just to be sure: *Damascus, trail, storm, water hole, trip back north, Yarmuk Valley, Alexandrium, Sychar, Jerusalem, the market and tonight. That leaves three more days if Doc had calculated correctly, and he has been dependable up to now. Three more days, plus maybe twelve or fourteen hours.*

Could a man in his position afford a day of rest?

No one woke him next morning, and he wondered if the same rules applied to meals. They were prepared ahead of time, but how could one avail himself of this food? Did serving a meal amount to unworthy pursuit? Did he have refrigerator privileges?

It seemed as if in answer to his question that a quiet knock, barely audible, interrupted his thought.

Ben donned his robe and opened the door.

Caleb stood there, holding a tray laden with bread, cheese, cold meat and fruit.

"Please accept this gift from the household of my Master."

"Please come in. Are you able to share it with me?"

Caleb smiled and entered, setting the tray on the table next to the basin. He arranged the chair, ostensibly for Ben, and stood to the side.

Ben slid the chair to the opposite side of the table and pulled the bed near, indicating the chair for Caleb. They both sat and began to form sandwiches from the meat and loaves.

"Can you tell me," Ben inquired, "more about the limitations of this Sabbath day?"

"Some of them you know." Caleb answered. "No servile work, no business. Travel is very limited. Contemplation of God is encouraged.

"This tray of food I brought you, we assembled last night before sundown, and Master could not send me here to serve you. But I may come as to a hungry man. That is helping one in need, and that is allowed to some degree, especially if I do it of my free will, and not as obedience to an order from Master."

"You said travel is limited. How limited is it? Can I leave this home?" Ben's mind moved in a direction no truly devout Jew would admit to choosing. Knowing the Ten Words will only get you so far.

"We must walk sometimes, and when we do, we must not exceed five stadia, all told."

'How many stadia is it to the temple? Could I go there and back?"

"The temple is very near, not more than two stadia from this house. To go there and return is less than a Sabbath day's journey. Shall I show you it to you? It can be seen from the top of the stairs."

As they had been sharing the food on the tray all during the conversation, little remained of it. The men stepped out onto the small landing at the top of the flight of stairs.

Caleb pointed northwest, between two buildings. His gesture indicated a white marble wall, which appeared to Ben to be about five hundred yards away. Only a part of the building could be seen between the residences, and it looked like a small section of a much larger structure. A bit of parapet had been built along the top of the wall, and since plastic and sheet metal facades lay somewhere far in the future, Ben reasoned that what looked like white marble would be white marble. Ben recognized it as the building Sethur had pointed out: the place where he worked, the temple of his God.

"Follow this street before the house to the west. When you see three identical sets of steps to your left, that is the Temple. If you plan to go there, you must first allow me to prepare you for what you will find. As you are a Gentile, there are things you must be told."

The two men reentered the sleeping quarters and sat down side by side on the bed. Caleb leaned over and began to draw a map on the floor as he spoke. "Here is the street leading to the temple. You will see the stairways here, going up from the gate of the temple to the court of the Gentiles. Jews pass through this area into the court of the Israelites. Further in you will find the court of women, and beyond that the court of prayer. To this court all clean Jewish men may come, and also true proselytes to our faith. Beyond this," (the rectangles were getting smaller) "we see the court of priests, and here" (a very small space indeed) "the Holy of Holies, which only the high priest can enter, and that only on the day of atonement, which will not be upon us for another half of a year. In this area next to the Holy of Holies, the priests do the work of sacrifice. So you see how it is. Anyone could be here, on the far outside. The further in you go, the holier you have to be. It would be very easy for one such as yourself to wander into the wrong area. Though you look like a devout Jew by the way you dress, your ignorance (Not to offend you. It is no insult not to know.) may give you away. No harm will come to you in the court of the Gentiles. If you have truly become a Jew, you may go in here, beyond the court of women to the court of prayer. Here to the southeast of the temple you will find what is called Solomon's porch. It is very beautiful, and sometimes teachers are there, especially on Sabbath."

Ben looked at the map that had not been drawn on the floor and wondered if signs were posted. No matter. He was not reliably literate in Aramaic. But it stunned him that people took this Jew/Gentile thing so seriously. "What happens if I accidentally rove too far into the restricted areas?"

"I do not know. Perhaps someone would kill you. God does that on His own behalf sometimes, and sometimes the priests have done it. Some action would probably be taken were some *Barnyeipheyph* to discover your misconduct."

"If what was to discover my misconduct?"

"It's an old Israeli phrase. It means 'brainless zealot who enforces law to sustain his manhood.'"

What are the odds? Ben thought.

"I think I must go there. Thank you for your help."

Caleb nodded, rose, picked up the tray, and moved the remaining edibles from it onto a plate on the table. "I wish you well, my friend." He gathered the remnants of his ancient room service and returned to his pursuit of Sabbath rest.

In only a few minutes Ben had arranged his robe, his sash, and headgear into what he imagined passed for acceptable first-century fashion. He supposed that with a robe such as he wore he could get on the cover of the Jerusalem equivalent of Gentlemen's Quarterly. He hoped he had not overlooked anything as he descended the stairs and merged onto the street.

More pedestrian traffic than he had anticipated crowded the street, some coming toward him, and some moving toward the temple. *People back home have a tendency to walk toward the right of any given thoroughfare,* he thought. But no such unwritten rule existed in this time slot. People walked where they walked. So he joined the flow as well as he could and headed for the temple

As Caleb had predicted, Ben found the three sets of stairs on his left. He stopped to take stock of the situation and to figure out where he should not be. It looked to him like no one was using the stairs, and that the first of the surrounding rectangles could be accessed by some opening around the corner.

The stone wall rose to a height of about twelve feet. Square pilasters divided the length of it into thirds, and the sets of stairs centered on the divisions the pilasters created. Each stairway had been constructed of finely carved stone, and all consisted of seven steps. To his right Ben saw that the wall took a turn to the northwest, and people seemed to be using a large gate at that end of things. Towering above stood a narrow rectangular structure far to the northeast.

Built of marble, and trimmed in what could probably pass for gold, it appeared both imposing and inviting in the morning sun.

Ben decided to head for the main entrance, and expected that the first level, or whatever you should call it, would be just inside. That should be the court of Gentiles, the safe place for a guy like himself. Even though he agreed with the Ten Words and had been circumcised, he thought it best to take no chances that there might be a Barney Fife around looking for something to do.

Quite a lot of people were coming and going. Ben thought, *It must be a busy occupation, worshiping the true God.* Some of the people had animals with them, though animal traffic moved only one way. People exiting seemed never to have an animal in tow. Ben thought this did not bode well for the animals in question. There were sheep, goats, occasional bulls, and some birds securely incarcerated. Some people carried bags that must have contained grain or flour, and some had skins similar to those that had held water on his camel trip. A short distance down to his right he could see a small group gathered listening to someone teach. *Even here,* he thought, *they must have their version of Jimmy Swaggert.*

He passed through the gate to where he could see the inner wall, separating the next court from the one he presently occupied. He surmised that must be the court of women. Handwriting could be seen on the wall, but of course he could not make sense of it.

Immediately to his right was a short line of people doing some sort of obeisance. After a few moment's observation, Ben noted that there was a box, presumably for contributions, at the outside of a small ornate booth. He thought of how few days remained of his time in Jerusalem, then got in line. After a brief and mobile wait, faster than most fast food lines but slower than subway turnstiles, he fished ten denarii out of a pocket in his sash, and dropped them into a small, artistically carved cask with a hole bored in the top. In his mind, he explained to whoever wanted the money that it contained mostly silver, though counterfeit, so it retained most of its value.

Offering concluded, he turned again toward the temple proper, and noted the colossal columns holding up the south edge of the roof. More marble, more gold leaf. Someone had spared no expense to make this place appear impressive, ornate, unique. At least unique in this city. The Temple of Jupiter had been under construction, but still an architectural wonder in its own right. But that vision belonged to another locale.

He stood in the morning sun and stared at his surroundings. People entered and exited through a large gateway. Ben could smell a fire blazing, creating by virtue of vaporization a stench that he somehow related to New York City. He remembered reading somewhere, with some satisfaction, that the smell of the Big Apple was akin to that of a frying goat.

This was that kind of smell—of burning flesh and bone and hide and hair. The odor was reminiscent of something badly in need of cleansing. Here also, the thought of New York City seemed to fit in.

One who has been transported, as Ben was, to another place and time, is easily transported again. He stood there, lost in thought, in reverie, in wonder of sorts, when he heard a female voice whispering, "Nice robe for a camel driver."

Transportation goes both ways, so in milliseconds Ben snapped back to reality as he presently understood it. Immediately to his left stood a woman in a crimson robe and headgear with a black veil across her face.

Not all cognitive synapses had been shut down, so after a couple of seconds he feebly whispered, "Lydia?"

Then he remembered. "Are we not supposed to speak to each other in public?" Assuming his guess to be correct—proper height, weight, hair color, etc., they both still had to cope with the culture in Jerusalem.

"It may be just a crack in the law, but we are Gentiles, in the court of the Gentiles. I know that we can't in there."

She nodded toward the gate, and still kept her voice to a whisper. It struck Ben then that no one around them could be heard carrying on a conversation.

"All the same, why would you do something like this?"

"I had to," she whispered. "The girls dared me." She made a gesture toward her right. Ben turned and followed her signal, and guessed that the three veiled women, about fifteen feet behind them, shaking with silent laughter, were Patricia, Debra, and Ruth. Right size, right hair color.

Some things don't change, Ben thought.

"Have the girls gone in to the court of women? Are you going?" He still whispered, hardly looking her direction, barely moving his lips.

"No, and no. I am going to look for Jesus. I heard he teaches today, outside the temple, in Solomon's Porch."

Ben remembered noticing someone teaching, and the stray thought about Jimmy Swaggert. He wished he could have that one back, but of course it was too late. He silently apologized, in a general sense.

"May I go with you? I need to find the one who knows the answer to my question."

Lydia nodded, and turned to her right. She and her companions ignored Ben, and he reciprocally ignored them. *Safest in here, anyway*, he thought. They did not speak again in the open, but backtracked through the gate toward the cluster of people surrounding the teacher. A man's voice could be heard over the busy temple noises that created a sonic confluence from the other side of the wall.

They joined the crowd, and tried to catch the drift of the conversation. Someone had just completed a question about proof, about the ability to show signs in the sky—to make lightning, or darkness in the midst of day, or daylight at night, to prove one had spiritual authority.

"You are good at reading the weather signs of the skies."

Ben considered how normal this man looked. If this was Jesus, Ben could see no halo, no incredibly bright colored robe, no terrifically fetching hair style. The speaker looked ordinary in all those respects. Didn't seem all that special. Ben smugly thought *he looks like a good moral teacher*.

Jesus continued. "Red sky tonight means fair weather tomorrow; red sky in the morning means foul weather all day. But you can't read the obvious signs of the times. This evil, unbelieving nation is asking for some strange sign in the heavens. But no further proof will be given except the miracle that happened to Jonah."

Then the teacher, with his entourage of followers, moved a short distance away, as if decreeing that a new topic would be in play soon.

Jonah again, Ben thought. *He must have been more important than I thought. I wish I could listen to that sermon again.* He struggled to remember. *Ninevah, a wicked city. Capital of the worst enemy of Israel. Destruction would be too good for them. They were extremely brutal even by the standards of the day. Some think that they were the fathers of all future terrorism. They used to put the heads of their defeated enemies on pikes and make the conquered people look at them. God sent Jonah to Ninevah. He didn't want to go. Would rather have his enemies destroyed by God than to have them repent and become brothers. Tried to refuse God's call. During his getaway God apprehended him, and he spent three days and three nights in the belly of a fish. So then he still had to go, and he looked like death and he smelled like fish guts—the people repented, and he became the most successful evangelist in history. And he was mad about it but God still tried to teach him. He was a sign. The trip should have killed him, but God preserved him. Pastor Rick had said that the three days and three nights were like Jesus' time in the grave. That was a sign. The fact that the people of Ninevah were Gentiles was a sign, too. A sign of what? That God wants to save Israel's enemies too? What would these Jews think of a God like that?*

As Ben's mind refocused on his surroundings, he recognized some of the men in the circle where the question originated. Fellow guests from yesterday's meal at

Mordecai's house stood among them. Hezron and Abinadab had their heads bowed toward some other men in a circle. It reminded Ben of a football huddle. Someone was calling a play. But none of the guys looked pleased. They must be behind in the score.

Emboldened by the previous day's familiarity, Ben approached the group. As he came near, Hezron noticed him, and said, "Parker! Welcome! Did you hear what was just said?"

"I think so," said Ben. "We were not given a sign in the sky to validate the message. Only the sign of Jonah. What does it mean? And was that Jesus of Nazareth?"

"That it was, my friend. We hear of miracles all over Judea, and some in Samaria and Decapolis, and Galilee. But will he do anything here where we can witness it with our own eyes? Oh, no! And he goes on to insult us all!"

"How does he insult you?" Ben possessed a level of ignorance immediately obvious to those around him, so no one took offense at his question. Abinadab answered.

"He gave us the sign of Jonah. And, he said we're evil because we want validation."

Ben had perfected the slight bend of the head, the simultaneous raising of the eyebrows, and the optional open handed thumbs-out gesture which would signal that more explanation was needed. He employed the first two-thirds of this trio, and held the last part in reserve.

Abinadab understood the unasked question. "Jonah was a prophet of ours, sent to Gentiles, to enemies of our country, so he tried to avoid doing God's bidding by fleeing to Tarshish. Do you know where that is?"

Ben nodded, and he thought he heard Hezron chuckle. Abinadab continued.

"Jonah's flight from God proved ineffective, and eventually a large fish swallowed him. The fish vomited him onto the land, and still he had to go to Ninevah, to our enemies. God promised to destroy the city if they did not repent. But they did repent. So God spared them and they continued to harass our nation for another hundred years. What do you think of a God who would do that?"

Before Ben could answer, Abinadab went on. "The miracle of which he speaks is that Jonah, though swallowed by the fish, and in the fish's belly in the sea, lived three days and three nights. This is supposed to mean something? I don't think so. Besides, these are the spiritual leaders of the people! He does tricks for the riffraff, runs around with fishermen and tax collectors, claims to be a shepherd, of all things, and who can believe anything a shepherd says, no matter how good he claims to be?"

Hezron came in at this point. "It serves no purpose to become emotional like a woman, Abinadab. I am sure we will soon see whether this one is from God."

Ben took a moment to contemplate. *What do you think of a God like that?* The same question posed to him from two entirely opposite perspectives, but he could clearly see the struggle. The teacher had just referred to those asking for a sign—Hezron and his friends, as evil and unbelieving. They saw themselves as the good, the believing.

He began to wonder how long all this had been going on, when he remembered Lydia, Debra, and Ruth. A quick glance revealed them clustered about fifty feet away, no doubt near the teacher. He took his leave and drifted in their direction. He wanted at least the appearance of impartiality.

As he entered the audible orbit of the small crowd, he could hear someone asking about greatness, and who would be the big guys in the upcoming kingdom.

If there is a kingdom, does that not require a king? Is this where people get the idea that he might rule over them, and send the Romans home?

Jesus called a small child over to him and set the little guy down among them, and said, "Unless you turn to God from your sins and become as little children, you will never get into the kingdom of heaven. And any of you who welcomes a little child like this because you are mine, is welcoming me and caring for me. But if any of you cause one of these little ones who trusts in me to lose his faith, it would be better for you to have a rock tied to your neck and be thrown into the sea."

So. Greatness is not bigness or toughness. It's in being like a child. Anyone could say that, Buddha, or Zoroaster, or Ellen G. White. What does it matter? You won't evict the Romans by acting like little children. These thoughts kicked around in Ben's mind as he listened, but they did not last. Because Sherry intruded. In his heart and life none compared to her. She somehow gave flesh and blood to innocence and honesty, and humility, Ben mused. And he wondered if all children possessed that same capability. He theorized that those with healthy loving relationships with their parents probably did.

Then he began to wonder about conflicts: war and other such large international cataclysms. *Could war even exist if all adults were as tender and loving and compassionate as Sherry is? What if society truly saw greatness in this way?*

And what about Jesus protecting little ones, and those who cause them to lose faith, who'd be better off with a rock tied to their necks and being thrown into the sea? Not fair, he thought. *Cannot consider my skepticism in that light. How can I make an honest decision under that kind of pressure?*

"Woe unto the world for all its evils. Temptation to do wrong is inevitable, but woe to the man who does the tempting. So if your hand or foot causes you to sin, cut it off and throw it away."

You can not be serious, Ben fumed. He was again unconscious of the fact that he was giving voice to his inner John McEnroe.

"Better to enter heaven crippled than to be in hell with both of your hands and feet. And if your eye causes you to sin, gouge it out and throw it away. Better to enter heaven with one eye than to be in hell with two."

What are my other options? Ben wondered.

"Beware that you don't look down upon a single one of these little children. For I tell you that in heaven their

angels have constant access to the Father. And I, the
Messiah, came to save the lost."

*Okay. You can't get much clearer than that. He said he
is the one, the messiah that these people have been looking
for. He said children have guardian angels or something
like it, and he said he was trying to save the lost. You can't
get plainer than that. Where are all these Jewish teachers
when you need them? But the part about gouging your eye
out, or cutting your hand off, what is all that? Some of this
stuff is really hard, but if he is who he says he is, what
would I think of a God like that?*

"If a man has a hundred sheep, and one wanders away
and is lost, what will he do?"

Ben noticed that Hezron and Abinadab and their gang
had rejoined the crowd and lurked nearby. He could see
Lydia on the other side of the natural circle that formed
with the self-proclaimed Messiah at the center. He noticed
how quietly they stood, and how Jesus could easily be
heard by anyone in the vicinity. Their surroundings
provided very little by way of background noise, no cars or
boom boxes or buses or aircraft. Thoughts seemed to have a
little better chance around here.

"Won't he leave the ninety-nine others and go out into
the hills and search for the lost one? And if he finds it, he
will rejoice over it more than the ninety-nine others who are
safe at home! Just so, it is not my Father's will that even one
of these little ones should perish."

Adam came to mind then. It seemed to Ben that he had
said something like this after the Jonah sermon. God out
seeking the people of Ninevah, leaving Israel behind, safe
in the fold, looking for the lost. Shepherds in there again,
too. *Why in the world does Jesus never speak of priests or
Levites or spiritual leaders as the heroes in his stories?
Why do the people who are totally lacking in credibility
always get top billing? Why does he hang around
miscreants so much?* Then Ben thought it might well be
the other way around. *Miscreants probably like Jesus better
than the priests do. And Jesus must like them better than the*

CREIGHTON / THAT OTHER TIME ZONE

priests do. And maybe he thinks they're closer to God than all these so-called religious guys. So now we get to find out what it feels like to be left in the pasture while the shepherd goes out and looks for someone we probably wouldn't bother with saving.

So Jesus says <u>that</u> *is God's priority.*

For just a moment Ben's mind wandered to what he'd heard about Jesus. He thought maybe he'd see a miracle a minute but presently, he'd only witnessed talk. Very provocative talk, too, at least from the perspective of these traditionalists.

It struck Ben as odd that the wayward, the wanderer, the one who'd forsaken the fold got the focus. *What about those ninety-nine? What about doing the right thing all of your life, and God leaves you by yourself to go look for some fool who doesn't know a good thing when he sees it?*

"If a brother sins against you, go to him with his fault. If he listens to you and confesses it, you have won your brother."

Now what? Forgiveness? Toward other people? Doesn't God know how to keep us focused on Him? Now we have to run around making up with people that don't even know they've wronged us? Can't all this be between a man and his God, a private thing? Like Adam has—or will have—a relational thing with Jesus that satisfies you and makes you better? Or whole? Ben thought of Laurie and Sherry. How impossible it would be for Adam to truly believe anything "spiritual" without affecting them. The concept of keeping something between a man and his God was more pie in the sky. He thought of his own life. There was a chance, maybe, he could believe in something without having to disclose it to anybody. But he wondered. He realized that he'd been totally distracted. Again. Jesus was responding to a question. Someone had just asked, "Seven times?"

"No!" Jesus replied. "Seventy times seven!" This emphatic language Ben had seldom heard since he'd been in Jerusalem. Seven what? Obviously, the answer is four hundred ninety times. Almost five hundred.

247

Jesus continued, "The kingdom of heaven can be compared to a king who decided to bring his accounts up to date. In the process, one of his debtors was brought in who owed him ten thousand talents. He couldn't pay, so the king ordered him sold for the debt—also his wife and children and everything he had. But the man fell down before the king, his face in the dust, and said, 'Oh, Sir, be patient with me and I will pay it all!'"

Yeah, I bet you will, though Ben. *I bet a talent is way more than a denarius.* Then he found himself wondering about a debt that size. Would the sale of a guy's self and home and family and property make a sizable dent in it? Ben thought of Caleb, and his plan to help his family. A slave probably didn't bring all that much.

"Then the king, filled with pity for him, released him and forgave him the debt."

Cool.

"But when the man left the king, he went to a man who owed him a hundred denarii, and grabbed him by the throat and demanded instant payment. The man fell down before him and begged him to give him a little time. 'Be patient with me and I will pay it,' he pleaded."

Trouble brewing. I am beginning to remember this part, thought Ben.

"But his creditor wouldn't wait. He had the man arrested and jailed until the debt would be paid in full. Then the man's friends went to the king and told him what had happened. And the king called before him the man he had forgiven, and said to him, 'You evil-hearted wretch! Here I forgave you all that tremendous debt just because you asked me to—shouldn't you have mercy on others, just as I had mercy on you?' Then the angry king sent the man to the torture chamber until he paid every last penny due. So shall my heavenly Father do to you if you refuse to truly forgive your brothers."

Man, that sounds serious. Whatever I've thought up to now about Jesus seems to have been wrong, or at least incomplete. It doesn't sound credible. Ben purposefully

248

used the word credible in its proper context, because he was somewhat a literalist, which annoyed many of his friends. They erroneously assumed that such a literalist attitude was incredible.

A voice speaking near his left ear extricated him from the present line of thinking. "Please follow me. We will discuss what we have just heard." Ben turned to see the speaker, and to his relief, recognized Sethur. He had been momentarily apprehensive about last night's dinner, of being drawn toward people with real axes to grind. He saw no reason why Jesus should be "stopped" as he had heard several times already.

Ben could see Jesus and his entourage moving out of the area, toward the southeast, and could see no rich man among the followers or in the crowd being drawn in the wake. He knew his opportunities were very limited, but he didn't bother to regret the sandstorm or the wasted days. He did not think about the three quarters of a million American dollars he had spent on this little excursion, and cared not at the moment how much that would be in denarii. What he did consider was that he might get one, or perhaps two further chances to find the man he sought. He began to entertain the notion that he might not locate him at all. The chance of landing in the right four-day period in a four-year ministry was roughly one in three hundred sixty-five. Not impossible, but long odds by any measure. But then he thought of all the unlikely events that had led up to his present position. *All in all*, he figured, *why not? It's impossible that I'm even here. Besides, good things happen to good people.*

He turned and followed Sethur, and after a few paces, Lydia, Debra, and Ruth joined them. They walked together in silence the short distance to Sethur's home. The sun stood straight above them, and the heat of the day had begun to amass its strength. The whiteness of the temple's wall radiated a warmth that gently massaged them as they passed through it.

They soon arrived at the Ben-Judah domicile, and congregated in the cool of the living room.

"Well, Parker. What do you think of our teacher?" The question seemed safe. Ben thought he could probably give no wrong answer.

"He is not what I expected. In our land, most accounts of Him speak about blind men being made to see, and lepers cleansed, and lame men walking. This morning all he did was talk. And he talked about things that seemed strange to me. He leaves the good people by themselves and looks for bad people. He thinks the mindset of a child is extremely valuable. He thinks people should forgive each other. A lot."

Sethur sighed. "He is not what my brothers have expected, either. They point to the prophet Isaiah when they say that the government shall be upon his shoulders. They say he should be the hub and wheel of a righteous kingdom. From what I see in the sacred writings, they are correct. Lydia, what do you think?"

"I thought some things made a lot of sense. Some of it would be quite a challenge. When that man asked about how many times to forgive, he mentioned seven. I thought your law, or perhaps your tradition, says three times for the same offense." Sethur's nod of agreement signaled her to continue. "My father allows one in our business—that is, if anyone orders dye or cloth, or whatever we sell, and does not pay, that man is not forgiven. Ten thousand talents is a lot of money. Possibly all the silver that a thousand camels can carry. It is an unthinkable debt. But in the teacher's story, a man was forgiven for that. A hundred denarii is more common, but still a large sum—a big portion of a year's wage. Some men carry that much in their money belts. But for one just forgiven of ten thousand talents, a hundred denarii should seem as nothing. It is only a handful of coins. Was he speaking of physical debt, of earthly business? He did say he was referring to some 'kingdom of heaven'."

250

Sethur inhaled deeply, then said, "Herein lies the problem. He speaks of a kingdom, but when it is examined, it is not like the kingdoms we usually see. He seems to have no interest in delivering us from the Roman jack-sandaled thugs. This is what our nation longs for. This, as I said that night in the desert, seems to be a special one, but not the special one we wanted. He can, and sometimes will, do miracles. But I know a lame man who has been carried to the Gate Beautiful every day for over twenty years. Jesus has seen him, and passed by him numerous times. Jesus has directed his followers, or at least one of them, to give this man alms. But the lame man is still lame. There are wild stories about how he can multiply bread for the crowds. Fish as well. When this last happened, we heard that the people wanted to make him king immediately. He would not accept this idea. Instead he ran from it.

"But the political side is only half of our problem. The other half is the spiritual side. All of us charged with spiritual teaching in Israel seem to be constant targets. He speaks of all of us as if we were evil. He calls the scribes and Pharisees hypocrites, and he continually points out places where he thinks we are misguided—we, who have centuries of Scripture and tradition to follow. And these traditions are based on the history of our God dealing with us, His chosen ones.

"And all of this, as I have said before, blends into a third problem. This Jesus is leading the masses astray, and whenever that happens, Rome always steps in with military force. Our nation, as we know it, seems to many of us to be in jeopardy every day that Jesus walks free."

The group sat silent for a time, when Debra cleared her throat. "Father, may I speak?"

"Certainly, my daughter. Your sister also, if she desires." Ben could see that thoughts lurked there as well.

"I love the way he speaks of children. I have seen groups of little ones—they enjoy life so much, being lifted, being held, being loved. He said that no one should ever harm one of these, or lead them astray. I love little ones and

251

look forward to holding my own in my arms someday. I know that young mothers value their little ones like Jesus does. But I have heard no other teacher speak of them that way. I know this does not solve the problem with the Romans and politics. But I love what he says about little ones."

Debra looked at Ruth, as a signal that she had finished. Ruth took a deep breath, much like her father so often did, and began to speak her heart.

"Father, you have said before that long ago Simeon told this man's parents that he was the glory of Israel, and a light to the Gentiles." Here she glanced at Ben, and he suddenly felt more like an outsider than at any moment since he'd left the time shed. (If it could be called leaving.) "Although some of the wise ones of our nation have said not to try to teach women, you have read to us the sacred writings, or at least some of them.

"I remember the passage you mentioned about the government being on His shoulders. And His name shall be called wonderful Counselor, mighty God, everlasting Father, Prince of peace. And of the increase of His administration and of peace shall be endless.

"But later on in that same scroll, it was days later, perhaps even a month. It was just before the feast of tabernacles last year when you read something else from Isaiah. It sounded like a suffering servant, you remember?" She looked at her father who sat in stunned silence, but nodded.

"I don't remember it all, but it began with the prophet's surprise that no one took his prophecy seriously. 'Who has believed what we are saying? To whom has God revealed Himself?' Then it went on about one who suffered. You remember?

"'He was wounded for our transgressions, He was bruised for our iniquity. The chastisement of our peace was upon Him and by His stripes we are healed. All we like sheep have gone astray. We have turned, every one, to his own way, and the Lord has laid on Him the iniquity of us all. He is growing up before us as a tender plant, like a root out of parched ground. He was pierced through for *our* transgressions, He was bruised for *our* iniquity. But we thought God was punishing *Him*.

"There was more, much more in that passage about this that by now I cannot remember. But I've been wondering, what if there are two sides to our deliverance? What if one side of it is that big warrior, the government crusher, the one who sets things right for the nation?"

Then she lowered her voice, almost to a whisper. "And what if there is another side, maybe what we see in this Jesus, who brings people, not just us, but lots of people, maybe even Gentiles, to God? Isaiah says something like that, doesn't he? 'By my righteous servant I will justify many?' And didn't Simeon speak thus as well? This child shall be a light to lighten the Gentiles? These are my thoughts. When he speaks my heart answers inside, not for Israel and Judah, and not for home and family, but for me. When I hear him, I think this one is sent for me."

When she finished, Ben was glad no one seemed to be expecting him to add anything more.

"Beloved, may I speak?" Hannah had joined them. Sethur gave his usual nod, and Hannah took the Ben-Judah deep breath.

"Our leaders fear this man, they say, because he stirs the people to unacceptable action, and the Romans would certainly engage in some brutal reprisal.

"Dear Sethur, please pardon my observations. This one has opened the eyes of the blind. He has made men who were lame to walk. He has touched lepers and cleansed them—some say he has touched dead bodies and brought them back to life.

"Those who officiate at the temple, I daresay, could never do such things. They can teach us the law, and spend all day telling us how we are wrong in the way we live. That is the nature of our law.

"But none of them could do anything for a blind man or a lame man, or a leper, (not to mention a dead man!) except to tell us to give them alms.

"This man has, it is said, healed the lame, and the blind, and lepers, and perhaps raised the dead. Your friends at work are jealous of him, Sethur. They cannot do what he does, and they fight back by claiming that he cannot be from God because he does these things *on the Sabbath!*

"When I hear this, I almost vomit!"

Such passion in this woman. Poor Sethur, Ben thought.

She continued. "Were you, or one of our daughters, lame or blind or leprous, what would we care, what would any thinking person care what day of the week the healing came? None of the miracles this man has done look wrong to me, or to anyone who truly cares about the *people* involved. Your friends at the temple should acknowledge that this Jesus is a good man, doing good things. They should stop fighting the power of God!"

Sethur looked around the room, and seemed to be hoping no one else would appear with a need to share, or spill his guts, or more likely, her guts. After a few seconds, he said, "I agree with you, Hannah. I hope my friends do nothing foolish in all this. Ruth, your grasp of Isaiah's prophecy is excellent. These thoughts I have had for myself, and it stirs my heart to hear you speak this way. Debra, you are correct as well. He does love children and regards them highly, as so few of my colleagues do. And I am also challenged, Lydia, by his teachings on forgiveness.

"Parker, stories coming to your land seem to have exaggerated certain parts of what is happening here, and diminished others. Hopefully, what you seek can still be found." He paused and seemed to stare at nothing in particular. Finally, he said, "Hannah, may we partake of some victuals, just a small meal, before we separate to our Sabbath pursuits?"

Hannah smiled and nodded. She and the daughters rose and left the room, returning almost immediately with a tray of flat bread, fruit and cheese, and a pitcher of water. The tray was set in the center of the room and the extended family sat around it. Small cups were filled with water and passed around.

They consumed the meal in silence. When they had finished, Ben could think of nothing to do but return to his temporary quarters and ponder things.

He supposed it to be the second hour of the afternoon, or the eighth hour of the day. He did not know it, but the clock moved to mark the Jewish hour of prayer. The limit to his time dominated his mind, but then he wondered if he could come to the same moment again. He could be a hero to himself—prevent the minor camel stampede, save the three days, get to Jerusalem more like on time. Then he could have two Bens looking for the same guy and reporting back to each other. The other Ben could stay down at the stable to get broader coverage of the area. Then he thought that maybe he'd gone back to the twenty-first century and sent himself back again already. What if two (or more?) of him were already on the job? How could he be sure he might not do something like that in the future?

He immediately dismissed all of this. He was here. He should assume that no reinforcements were nearby, or even on the way. Besides that, he had promised Doc he wouldn't endeavor to change history, and all that sounded like an attempt to modify events in the continuum. He should dedicate himself to the task at hand. With those thoughts in mind, he stepped outside and down the stairs into the street. He retraced his steps to the temple, and began to execute a rendezvous with the cluster of people that seemed to perpetually surround the teacher, when he again heard his name spoken, this time from behind.

He turned to see Mordecai, his wealthy and gracious host from yesterday.

"Parker, my friend! How is your quest going?"

"Perhaps you can help me, Mordecai. Were you able to gather news of any 'rich young man' who has been known to spend time with or near Jesus?'

"I've been thinking about that. I've heard of no one in Jerusalem that fits that description. Most wealthy men tend to be older. Therefore, it must be a relative newcomer to the city. Rich, and new to the city, and young. There is no one. But Sabbath ends at sundown. Perhaps you could return to my home this evening and partake of another meal with us. We have much more to discuss, much which we did not know even yesterday. And it may be that your insight will help. And also, who knows? Maybe we can still be of help to you."

"Can you give me any clue as to what the new stuff is?" Ben wondered how he'd done with this question. It would have sounded passable in English.

"I would prefer the privacy of our home for that. Will you join me? At sunset."

"I will." Ben wondered what the big deal about privacy was, and theorized that it could not be all that intense. But then he remembered that Jesus did die, and that jolted his brain. Maybe the situation required much more serious thought.

He spent the remainder of the afternoon wandering the outskirts of the temple's south end in Solomon's Porch. The architecture, usually quite an interesting distraction, lay by the wayside like road kill. He kept his mind focused on his situation. Whenever he saw a robed man, mental discipline forced him to check for age and clothing style. No wealthy young men in evidence.

After continued lack of success, his mind wandered to his native century. Long in the future Gramps probably fumbled with his cell phone. Adam and Laurie would be loving their daughter, and Doc and Hannah would be awaiting his return. *No, they said I'd be gone less than two seconds.* He remembered having thought of his native century as some kind of a pretend fantasy thing. *What a world. Life can get pretty confusing.*

The brief hummingbird hover over the thought of Sherry started the older-brother/protector syndrome in motion, slowly at first. It built like an avalanche, until he could think of little else but getting home, shaving, and flying to DFW. Then he thought of the wound below his left ankle and Lydia washing it in that tender, loving way. If Sherry knew, could she be jealous? Ben thought not. But then there was that flirting earlier today. At least Ben thought of it as flirting. He could imagine that happening in the twenty-first century, and words about it and pictures of it being posted on someone's Facebook page. He thought that a world without computers would not be a loss at all.

Around the Portico he walked, with no other aim but to observe people. It crossed his mind that maybe a day of commerce would be better for finding a rich young man, but then he remembered the guy was religious, too, or at least claimed to be. He would just as likely be around on the Sabbath. Or, maybe resting.

Activity in the temple area increased a bit as the afternoon waned. As the sun crept lower, more people seemed to be willing to use up their "Sabbath day's journey". *Three eighths of a mile,* thought Ben. He feared he'd already exceeded that, but he defended his action by not claiming to be a Jew.

As sunset neared, he drifted off toward Mordecai's neighborhood, with a brief stop at his home base. As invitation had also been extended to Sethur, Ben waited in his quarters. With the expiration of the day, Sethur and Ben walked the short distance to Mordecai's manse; Gideon met them at the gate. "Master is expecting you. Please follow me."

He led the way to the room that had formerly contained the triclinium, but now seemed somewhat less formal. A large table sat in the center of the room, laden with bowls of raisins, olives, figs, breads, cheeses, and roast beast of some sort. Servants constantly bustled in and out, renewing supplies as guests celebrated the end of the Sabbath and the resumption of business as usual.

For about an hour, Ben and Sethur mingled with perhaps a dozen or so other men, Mordecai almost omnipresent in their midst. They enjoyed the table's fare—the meat succulent, the wine gentle but strong, the atmosphere positive in general.

Ben had Sethur inquire about any rich men who had been hanging around asking Jesus questions. No credible leads could be uncovered.

Eventually Mordecai had the table of food removed, and arranged his guests in a quadrangle of couches facing inward. He expressed gratitude that all could be there on such short notice, and then introduced his "business".

"Many of you have heard of this Nazarene, Jesus, who seems to be some sort of teacher among the commoners. He does miracles for them sometimes, but so far has refused to validate his power (if indeed he possesses any) to the religious leaders of our beloved city. An event of some import has occurred which requires our attention."

While he listened, Ben studied faces in the lamplight. Most of these men had been with him at dinner the previous afternoon, and in some instances he could provide himself names for faces. A large percentage of them had the phylacteries, the memory verse boxes on the forehead, or more frequently, on the right forearm.

Mordecai continued. "Our temple, today has been witness to an event that must be evaluated. I will now ask Hezron to supply details for us."

"Thank you, honorable Mordecai. And I speak for all of us when I again express gratitude for your generous provision this evening." A murmur of agreement worked its way through the group like a tiny wave. Ben inserted his thanks as well.

"At Bethesda Pool lie many sick and infirm. They wait there for an agitation of the water, for when the water is moved, (some say an angel stirs it up) the one who enters the water first will be healed of his infirmity.

"Beside the pool, for many years, has been a lame man. Who knows why, because as you know, lame men are not good at races." This struck some of the gathered guests as humorous, and nervous laughter tittered around the room.

"The man's name is Manoah, and until today, he awaited his turn to be healed in the pool.

"At approximately the second hour, a stranger approached him and asked him if he would like to be healed. He said he would like that very much, but he could never get into the pool fast enough. So the stranger told him, just this morning, to arise, and take up his pallet, and go to his home.

"This he did, but did not get far before one of the priests, Zadok, I believe, saw him and reminded him that carrying his pallet could be considered work, and should not be done on the Sabbath. He then told Zadok his story—that a man had healed him and instructed him to take up his pallet and go home. We all wondered who this could be, so we asked him, and at the time he did not know. (I am sure you all know where this is going.) But Manoah, being grateful for his healing, walked to the temple, which he has longed to do for many years, in order to offer thanks. There he met the same man who had healed him. The man then said to Manoah, "Now you are well. Don't sin as you did before, or something even worse may happen to you."

"Manoah returned and found Zadok, and reported the identity of the so-called 'healer'. With Manoah's information, Zadok realized that the one doing the healing could be none other than Jesus the Nazarene."

Several men audibly sucked in their breath at this point. Some looked shocked. All seemed troubled, or so it appeared to Ben.

"A group of the priests, Zadok among them, went to speak to the Nazarene. It is one thing to break the Sabbath yourself. Some of you here have perhaps had to do some servile task from time to time. But to foist such deplorable behavior upon another is unacceptable in Israel. Our blessed God does not even allow the gathering of sticks on the holy Sabbath. How much worse is it to carry your pallet?

"So the priests approached the Nazarene and asked him about this breaking of the Sabbath. His reply was (any of you who know better must correct me if I am wrong) 'My Father constantly does good, and I am following His example.'"

At this point the corporate attitude seemed to have a life of its own. Ben could read the thoughts behind the expressions on the lamp-lit faces. And it appeared that most of these men thought that something diabolical had occurred.

"You all see the import. When one calls God his father, he makes himself equal with God. No truly good teacher would say that." *That's what Adam said*, Ben thought. "Now it appears obvious to me, to many of us, that something must be done about this Nazarene. Do any of you have anything to offer?"

"Why do you keep referring to him as the Nazarene?" Ben's words had escaped him involuntarily. Up to this point he had been resolute in his silence. It must have been a blurt.

Sethur came to his rescue. "Hezron, will you allow me to answer? Parker is very new to the ways of our city and our religion. May I answer him?"

Hezron nodded, so Sethur began.

"As you know, Parker, many mysteries and difficult events surround the birth and life of this one called Jesus. Somehow he managed to escape the massacre that Herod perpetrated on Ramah and the Bethlehem area. The next time we could pinpoint his whereabouts, his family dwelt in Nazareth.

"There are some areas well-known for certain things. Thyatira for its purple dye, Damascus for its cloth, Lebanon for its cedars, the Negev for quality figs. In Nazareth, it is the loose lifestyle. Some have accused the mother of this Jesus of being a bit too familiar with a Roman soldier. She lived in Nazareth before the census was announced, so the timing works out. The child could have had a father other than Joseph. It happens a lot in that area, because, as it is a Roman outpost, many heathen Romans reside there. And when they are in Judea, they still do as the Romans do. So being from Nazareth is not a compliment. It is somewhat of a problem, particularly if one is presenting himself as a man of God. All appearances at present seem to indicate that Jesus the Nazarene is the illegitimate child of a loose-living mother. You must have cities in your own land that are that way. Do you understand?"

Ben nodded. There was Las Vegas. *Will be,* he corrected himself. But Sethur's explanation had gently revealed that these people were purposefully insulting Jesus with every reference to Nazareth.

Hezron also nodded. Then he put the meeting back on track when he said again, "What do you have to offer?"

Sethur spoke carefully when he said, "Can anyone here answer for the priests? What have they said?"

A man unfamiliar to Ben began to speak. "I talked earlier today with Joshua. He thinks that the priesthood is united in the conviction that this man must somehow be stopped. Joshua thinks that no one should ever be allowed to claim God as his own father."

Ben's brain became that freeway interchange again. These people had surely gone to a lot of work on the Sabbath to make sure no one carried his pallet around. But merging with that thought, the memory of Adam and Laurie's wedding barged in, where the Pastor had said Jesus taught people to pray saying "our Father which art in heaven." Everyone had joined with him in that prayer. But no one should be able to claim God as his father. *What if God is your father?* But the two thoughts did not fit together like yin and yang. They were like freight trains on a collision course, or Romulus and Remus fighting for control of Rome, or gladiators locked in mortal combat. It appeared that in this conflict, something would have to give.

What will it be?

"Joshua is alarmed by all of this, as you might imagine. Some of the priests desire that we enforce the death penalty. Others are worried, but unsure we should respond in such a way. As I see the scriptures, our God is very intolerant of such behavior."

Hezron turned to Sethur. "Can you speak for the Levite community?"

"No, my friend, I cannot." He took the family-style deep breath Ben had come to expect. "I can only speak for myself, as I have spent the last several weeks in Damascus. We have not recently conversed about this."

"Well?" Hezron looked expectantly at Sethur.

"Well, what?"

"Well, you said you could speak for yourself. What do you say?"

"For myself I will say that I do not judge the man. He seems to have power we do not have. How many of us would have healed Manoah, and many others long ago if we could? And should Manoah leave his pallet lying around, cluttering up Bethesda? Someone would be likely to trip over it, especially by that pool with all the cripples around it.

"But leave that aside. What about our promise for a Messiah? Will God be his father? This Nazarene. His parents claim that Joseph is not his father. Do they lie? Many of us say that such a claim is impossible. If such is the case, could we ever acknowledge *any* man as messiah? Do we want a Messiah who is just another man?

"You asked me to speak for myself, and so I do. I have followed God from my youth. Simeon told me that he waited for the consolation of Israel. He said that God told him he would not die until he had seen the Messiah. And when he saw this man as a baby all those years ago, God said, "This is the One." It appears to me to be very dangerous for any of us to say we know certainly the answer to this.

"For me, I cannot condemn the man."

The room radiated the stillness of mystery. Hezron stared at Sethur, and appeared to be in deep thought. At last he said, "Have others of you somewhat to say?"

A man Ben had seen the previous night, Melchi, he thought, eventually asked leave to speak.

"As you know, many of us, my brothers, have concern for the political picture here in Israel. We walk a narrow knife-edge, with any misstep in any direction likely to adversely affect our freedom and our ability to worship.

"You also know that the Romans have no love for our way of life, for God has chosen us. He has not chosen them. This, among other things, causes them to consider us to be hateful and bigoted.

"The Romans have no reason to love us or our way of life, and plenty of reason to desire to crush us. For them, any excuse is a good one, and the Nazarene may become the excuse they desire.

"I know mobs. I have been at the fore of many of them. Sometimes a small spark will start a towering inferno.

"Many of the people of this city are ready for the spark. You must believe me, for I know this. Should this man be allowed to continue, he will surely supply the spark that flames into an unruly crowd. When that happens, much harm will come to us. We must not allow it, for from it there is no return.

"From our perspective, the Nazarene must be stopped as soon as is reasonably possible."

Hezron scratched his beard. "The Pharisees are in agreement, quite complete agreement. Our faith and way of life are at stake. And that heritage is from God. Abinadab, have you wisdom to shed on the situation?"

Abinadab also looked familiar to Ben from the previous day. It seemed that perhaps this meeting contained a foregone conclusion, meant only to be some rubber stamp on a fateful decision long ago taken.

"Of wise words I have little to add. The scribes are all fearful, but we fear all. That is, to act in some rash way may destroy our life as it is. To remain on the edge of the field while others enter the conflict may also result in the fruition of our fears. We are united in our fear."

Sense at last, thought Ben. He could feel the tension in the air, and it appeared that some of this evening's participants anticipated the warpath. Ahead lay the Little Big Horn. Ben found it difficult to be aware of the future and still remain silent. To steer history was neither right nor safe, and if Doc knew what he was talking about, impossible. It appeared that the murder of Jesus remained inevitable, also that some of these men would be a part of that lynching.

Sethur sat, exemplifying internal struggle, the struggle to speak or not to speak. Several times he seemed ready to rejoin the conversation, but each time his face once again relaxed into silence. Finally he could no longer stay himself.

"You who know the Scriptures, tell me this. Was Moses welcomed when he came to lead Israel out of Egypt? You know he was not.

"Was he welcomed when he led the people through the wilderness? He was resisted at every turn.

"Did *any* of God's prophets enjoy popularity with the leaders of God's people? As I read it, none did save Samuel. Even he felt the rejection of the people in the matter of choosing a king. Throughout our history men who spoke for God have had difficulty plowing a rock-free furrow. And even those immediately before, during, and after our exile experienced resistance to their message from God's own people. From *us.* Even when we knew we were in the midst of God's judgment.

"Moses said there would arise a prophet someday, and this prophet would be 'like unto him'. Can you see a likeness? This man from Nazareth is hated and feared by most in this room. Like Moses was. Can you see a likeness?

"And the miracles! It has not been so in our land since the days of Elisha. Or Moses! Can you see a likeness?

"If there is a doubt that this Jesus is, as Simeon said, the Messiah, then I must still give him the benefit of that doubt. He could be our Messiah."

Then he stood up. He thanked Mordecai and bowed to the men in the room. He took his leave, and Mordecai signaled Gideon to escort him to the gate at the street.

CHAPTER XVIII

Ben remained seated. He wondered if he should have accompanied Sethur. He hoped that no cultural rule demanded his exit. He was the recipient of a man's generous hospitality, and his host had just left. He intended no insult to his friend.

He waited.

After a long silence, someone Ben had not seen before that night spoke. His voice carried force and conviction.

"I have spoken to this Jesus some time ago—over two years past. I met him in secret, after dark, out on the Mount of Olives. That night was completely black, just before new moon, and some of us wanted to get a better idea of who he was and what he was trying to do. Some of us thought maybe we should be available to help him. May I give my report of that meeting for those of you who may not have heard it?"

"Of course, Nicodemus. Please bless us with whatever you can add. We seek wisdom." Thus said Mordecai, still hosting, administrating, facilitating.

"As I say, the meeting took place on yonder hill, and I found the teacher alone. That day he had healed a man by spitting on the ground, making mud from the spittle, and applying it to the eyes of one born blind, a man named Josiah. He then told Josiah to go and wash in Siloam's pool.

This Josiah did, and as a result, (all of you must remember this) he received his sight.

"This naturally caused quite a stir among us, as many of you can recall. The crux of the problem, we said, was that this happened on the Sabbath, in which, of course, no work should be done.

"The more astute among us knew then, as we know now, that if such things continue, religious chaos will be the result. We will eventually be teaching no one." (*And Jesus will be teaching everyone*, Ben thought.) Nicodemus continued. "This is true not only because of his breaking the Sabbath, but also because compassion and power made up part of the mixture. All of us, in our private moments, would concede, wouldn't we, that all healings of compassion could be done on Sabbath, even as an act of worship?

"Most of us would have to admit to at least a small bit of jealousy. We can spit on the ground and make mud all day and none of it will make a blind man to see.

"This created a credibility problem for us—we teach what we believe is the truth of God, but with no power. He exhibits power, but seems to us to lack truth.

"So what was to be done? We talked all that day about strategic measures. In the end, I took matters into my own hands and went across the bridge at Kidron in the dark in search of him. I am convinced that our law fairly condemns no one unless he is given an opportunity to state his case.

"For that reason I sought him out. I did this at night, first because I wanted him to have freedom to say what he wanted to say apart from the crowds. Second, I wanted no pressure applied by any of us, either. We had already accosted him in public so many times that he may have felt threatened, even then.

"My memory of it now is, I think, still accurate though all this time has passed. Besides, he has not changed. And we have not changed.

"Initially, I acknowledged that we could see that he must have been sent from God, primarily because of the miracles he could perform. His reply startled me, as his words often do.

"He told me that a man must be born again in order to see the kingdom of God. I took this to mean some miraculous physical rebirth process, the impossible hope of beginning again, because of his impressive power to do amazing things.

"He said no, but that it was a spiritual rebirth, and that it had nothing to do with physical life. I have since thought of God's promise of a new heart that our prophet Jeremiah speaks of. Ezekiel as well. But that night I was at a loss.

"He told me then that flesh is flesh, and spirit is spirit, and they don't intermingle. And it was then that he told me that he was surprised that as a teacher of Israel, I did not know this. Then he mentioned Nehushtan, the serpent. You will remember the account of our fathers in rebellion in the wilderness, and as punishment for their complaining, God sent fiery serpents among them, and whoever experienced the puncture of those poisonous fangs would die. Our God, in his mercy, commanded that Moses make a likeness of one of the serpents out of brass, and put it up on a pole for all to see. Any who were bitten would then only need to look at the brass likeness of the serpent, and he would be healed of the poison. Jesus claimed that the Son of Man must be lifted up the same as Nehushtan, and people who look at him will live also.

"Much of this is still a mystery to me, even with two years to think of it. He claimed that God loves this world and sent his son, so whoever believes can have eternal life."

Eternal life. Maybe this is a clue to what that rich young guy is after. Ben began to wish Lydia were with him to hear this part.

"What he meant by eternal life I do not know. He claimed that God's plan was to redeem, not to condemn.

"This left me with many questions. Eternal life, for a start, is one of them. The idea that looking at this "son of man" raised up like Nehushtan would have any beneficent power is another mystery to me. The largest problem I see,

269

and I have thought a lot about this, is the idea that God does not condemn. What is our way of life but to teach our fellow man that which pleases God, that which God allows, and that which He does not allow, which does not please Him? This is condemnation. Do not the Ten Words deal mainly with what should not be done?

"But in all of this I saw no threat. The story of the existence of our people from the Scroll of Beginnings to the present day is the story of God showing Himself. He did so with Abraham, Isaac and Jacob, and with the twelve patriarchs. Most notably with Moses. All of the prophets add to what God has shown us. Perhaps this Jesus shows one more step. As it is, I wish it were a cleaner sweep, and by that I mean that I wish he had not such a checkered past. But Hoseah was commanded to marry the prostitute, was he not?

"He does not look like we do or act like we do or talk like we do. But he seems to be a reasonable man, and does have power to use for good. He seems never to do an evil thing, but he chooses what seem to us to be evil times to do good things.

"I cannot prove to myself that he is not from God."

All around the dimly lit room, Ben heard only the sound of men breathing. No one spoke and no one moved.

Eventually Ben stood. He thanked Mordecai for his hospitality, and attempted to duplicate Sethur's bow to the enclave of men in the room. Gideon stepped from a darkened alcove to escort him to the gate, and so for him the meeting adjourned.

He thought on all that he had heard as he walked slowly to Sethur's home. His host awaited him in the darkness by the gate.

"How did the meeting go, my brother? How did the lots fall?"

"It's not over yet. Some there share your view, some do not. Not all would hope to rid themselves of the Nazarene. Some probably would. They are still there, as far as I know. Nicodemus thinks Jesus may be from God."

"That is such a hard mystery. Perhaps tomorrow, in the light of day, things will become more clear."

"I hope so." Ben wished his host a good rest, then mounted the stairs to the upper room.

Contrary to established pattern. Caleb brought water and a small tray of bread and fruit for the start of Ben's day. He informed Ben that Master had gone out early, and that Ben should choose to do whatever pleased him.

It would please me greatly, Ben mused, *to find this rich guy and discover why he would be able to walk away from an opportunity to follow Jesus. Did he know Jesus to be a fraud? Or are material riches that much more important than what people call salvation? Does it boil down to a choice between the material and the spiritual? Is there a spiritual world? How would you know?*

He ate the food provided, and drank a bit of the water. He then cleaned up as best he could, and reapplied his vestments.

With no mirror available, he took it on faith that all was well on the clothing front. If he had not been embarrassed to do so, he might have gone to the main floor and asked the girls to give their approval. He feared this might appear flirtatious in that culture, so he accepted whatever he had as presentable.

He walked to Solomon's Portico, and observed as he proceeded that it was about the third hour of the morning. He was struck by the smug realization that "third hour" popped into his mind before the future standard nine am.

By now he harbored no doubt about his destination, and he considered how small the city measured on a worldwide scale. *How could the events of this time in this place have such a lasting impact on the world?* But then he thought of Salamis and Sparta and the Battle of Hastings, and Gettysburg, and even the Bulge. The insignificant faithful actions of a few people often provided the hinges on which larger gates of history would swing.

He looked around the Portico that Sunday morning. He thought of Adam and Laurie, probably going to church,

271

except no time should be passing there. Besides, church had not yet been discovered.

He scanned the area for clusters or crowds or gatherings. Eventually he noted a small group of men knotted together at the far northern end of the courtyard, so he surreptitiously allowed himself to be drawn into their orbit.

Some of them he'd seen before, at Mordecai's house, and some he'd seen hanging around the temple. He thought they were Pharisees, and they appeared to be on a mission. A few moments of quiet eavesdropping confirmed that they had a goal; find Jesus and ask him a question.

The group had a recognized leader. His name was Ezra. Hezron also mingled among them, but did not say much. They hung together, and kept a lookout posted. Their desire came to fruition with a sharp cry of "Here he comes!" from one of the men.

Jesus and his followers approached them, and the group launched itself onto a collision course with the Nazarene and company. They walked purposefully toward each other until one or the other would have to give way. Neither gave way. Both stopped.

"You intend to question me, do you not?" The Nazarene had spoken.

Ezra dispensed with formality. "Do you allow divorce?"

Of all the things to ask. Is there a trap in here somewhere? Ben could not afford to waste opportunity. His time was short.

"Don't you read the scriptures?" he replied. "In them it is written that in the beginning God created man and woman, and that a man should leave his father and mother and be forever united with his wife. The two shall become one—no longer two, but one! And no man may divorce what God has joined together."

Good answer. Ben had begun to root for Jesus to overcome this bunch of bigots. But the marriage issue looked like a tall order. Two becoming one, and never getting divorced? All through his life he'd seen the family carnage created by the failed marriages of school buddies. *How do two become all that inseparable?*

But Ezra's team had not yet given up. He came back with this. "Then why did Moses say a man may divorce his wife by merely writing her a letter of dismissal?"

Okay. So there's the trap. Get this guy in an argument with Moses. We know who would win that one.

"Moses did that in recognition of your hard and evil hearts, but it was not what God had originally intended. All I will tell you is this—that anyone who divorces his wife, except for fornication, and marries another, commits adultery."

Wow. That's sticking it to a lot of people, not just these guys here. Lots of celebrities and politicians and such might be offended. No points for positive public relations.

The next question came from the other way. This confused Ben, because of the seeming nature of the 'trap'. "If that is how it is, isn't it better not to marry?" This came from one of the Nazarene's own followers.

Well, it makes sense. If there's only one legitimate way out, a guy might be better off not going down that road.

"Not every one can accept this statement. Only those whom God helps. Some are born without the ability to marry, and some are disabled by men, and some refuse to marry for the sake of the kingdom of heaven. Let anyone who can, accept my statement."

It would be fair to say that at this point, everyone but Jesus had been stunned. Ben heard murmurs from all around, some from Pharisees claiming that no one knew better than Moses, and some from the disciples, more along the lines that they were worried that they might not make the cut. Ben had one of those little flashbacks to the previous night, and to Sethur's speech and the overall feel of the group. But the idea that a person preferred no divorce over divorce, (a higher standard even than Moses?) should be welcome in any culture, he reasoned. At least anywhere that family stability carried value. He wondered if Moses

273

would like to cut down on divorces. He stepped back a pace and surveyed his surroundings.

A young mother approached the group, child in tow. She accosted the disciples and asked if Jesus would bless her son. "The Master is very busy with divorce right now. Can you come back some other time?" Another added the necessity of getting all this straightened out soon, so there would be stable marriages from which children could come who could grow up and get divorced. This got a hearty laugh from the disciples, but as the woman turned to leave, Jesus spoke to the disciples, not to her.

"Let little children come to me, and don't forbid them, because this is how it is in the kingdom of heaven."

The woman, interrupted in the process of leaving, turned about and brought her son to him. He gently took the boy and held him, praying quietly, so that the mother and those nearby were the only ones who heard. This only consumed about a minute, but before Jesus had finished a line was forming.

One by one the teacher touched the children, prayed for them. Sometimes he spoke briefly to the parents, asking, it seemed, concerning the welfare of the child, or some special need. But as long as they were there, Jesus had time for them.

Ben watched this as carefully as he'd watched anything up to this point. *If there is a Jesus, a real one, a Messiah,* he thought, *this is how I'd like Him to be. Sharp as a razor with stupid, stubborn adults begging for permission to abandon their mates, but soft as a down pillow with innocent children. This man keeps saying that the kingdom of heaven is formed around the hearts of children.*

He found his mind again wandering to Sherry. He had seen pictures she had colored and brought home from Sunday school—pictures of Jesus. He'd seen her eyes sparkle when she spoke of her Lord. Admiration and love and adoration radiated from her at the thought of Him, the one standing before Ben now.

At that moment he began to cogitate, to calculate, to compute, perhaps even to connive. He would come back again, to this moment, and he would bring Sherry, and she could be blessed and prayed over by the Lord Himself. That would be among the most precious memories she would ever have. Doc's obsession with leaving the past in this pristine, unchanged state would *have* to be laid aside, and there was no better reason, no higher justification than this. But then his mind took that extra step. *If I decide now to do it, might I not be in line right now with that little brown-eyed girl? Would I try to hide from me? Wouldn't it be great to get a look at Sherry? Maybe take her to meet Lydia? What will my other self think?* He knew if Doc could do this once, he could do it twice, and he knew he was able to pay whatever price Doc demanded. But he doubted that Doc would have allowed it. He wondered about other possibilities.

During Ben's tangential mental foray, the line of parents, mostly young mothers with their children, had run out. They had all gone. The Pharisees retreated, probably to make a new plan, and the Portico had become quiet.

And the entire group of disciples, following their master, had moved off toward a small gate to Ben's right. Haste would be required in order to maintain surveillance level proximity. He scooped up his robe in his hands and sprinted awkwardly to his "reasonable boundary". As he stopped, he realized that all of the men in Jesus' entourage were staring at him.

CHAPTER XIX

Ben returned the disciples' stare. He tried to quiet his breathing after the exertion. No one else was in the picture, and he wondered why he had their attention.

Jesus also stared at him. And the look in his eye reminded Ben of a man who would leave ninety-nine sheep in the fold and go out looking for the one. The lost one. This one.

When the earth moves under your feet, the sensation is unmistakable.

In his mind's eye he could see himself reading that Gideon New Testament, and wondering about the possibility of coming face to face with someone like Jesus and just walk away. It sounded at the time like someone had made it up. Either there are no saviors like that, or there are no men like that.

In his mind's eye he could see the magazine open to the classifieds.

In his mind's eye he could see himself making preparations with Doc for the trip to the past—getting clothes, money, suntan, beard, F-ben gas. It had taken a lot of work.

He could remember his final conversation with Adam and the promise to give a fair shot to the man in front of him should he turn out to be real.

He could see his own skepticism laid out before him like a Texas road. It went on and on and on. He couldn't see the end of it. But he could also remember his own words. "I will be given an answer."

He could see what should have been obvious from the beginning. The bait had been switched. He had to come to this century, he had to be here, he had to fulfill this quest, because he was the man. He remembered his former confidence. *I will be given an answer.*

So very rich, and so very young, and with a question on his mind.

He thought of all that it had taken to get him to this point. *How much of it was me, and how much of it was arranged by that so-called omnipotent Father in heaven? The One I claimed not to believe in? Can there be more of a manipulation than this? Can there be such a thing as an all-powerful God who has to use legerdemain and sleight of hand to prove a point?*

He wondered who had a choice, because it seemed to him that he did not. Then he remembered the response of the young man in Matthew's Gospel. That man had a choice. And so did he, even though the picture in his mind revealed a chess piece moved on a board by an invisible and omnipotent hand. How could he hope to win the game?

He ultimately submitted to losing hope. He knew that he would never find the man he sought. There remained no need to persist in the search. Because he was *the man.*

He knew that he would never in the future wonder if it that rich young guy ever found what he sought. He knew that none would know better than he. He knew that the real encounter began now (whatever now is) and the question hung in the air like the sun above.

He knew that no matter how intensely he wished it were not so, he would have to explain it to himself. *Do I obey the command? Is it worth it? Are there any treasures in heaven? What would it be like to follow him? Or to turn away? Is he a savior like that? Am I a man like that?*

All that practice to be able to hear the question. Did God put him up to that as well? The memory of Lydia's patient coaching flashed through his mind. The abstract concept of fairness, or a lack of it, lurked in the wings. Deep inside, in the dark and private part of his mind, a voice said, "You don't have to do this."

He understood that. He did not have to do this. He did not have to be here. He did not have to leave his own time at all. He could have refused at any of a hundred different junctures along the way. And he could refuse now.

"You don't have to do this." The thought galvanized his will. He opened his mouth and began to speak very familiar, carefully rehearsed words.

"Good master, what must I do to have eternal life?"

"When you call me 'good' you are calling me God," Jesus replied, "for God alone is good. But to answer your question, you can get to heaven if you keep the commandments."

"Which ones?" Ben remembered this from Adam's New Testament, but he could feel the question flowing from his own heart.

"Don't kill, don't commit adultery, don't steal, don't lie, honor your father and your mother, and love your neighbor as yourself."

Despite the temptation to see himself as a game piece in the hand of a capricious God, Ben forged ahead. He thought he had to be right in there, or at least close on most of them. He hadn't thought much about the last one, but comforted himself with the observation that back home no one seemed to be mad at him. Maybe he could hire someone to keep track of that.

"I've always obeyed every one of them. What else must I do?" *Even though you do pretty good, why do you feel like it's never quite enough?*

Not good enough. How could that be? In the end nothing seems to be good enough for God. Why? What is it about us that makes it so hard to get it right?

279

Ben's admixture of thought distracted him for a moment. He recovered his sense of the occasion, and he looked at Jesus. "If you want to be perfect, go and sell everything you have, and give the money to the poor. And you will have treasure in heaven; and come and follow me." The words came from someone Ben knew would never hurt him. He could tell that this man loved him. He could tell that nothing else mattered more to Jesus at that moment than Ben Parker. He understood what the children must have felt—love and acceptance and mercy and compassion.

And still he had his answer. There are times when the well-known, even the anticipated is nonetheless unsettling. Ben had read his own story and knew what the teacher would say. He thought of the parameters of "all that you have." In his case, it was quite a bit. Comfort, security, independence. He had heard of Mother Theresa and the sisters of mercy and had lauded them in his mind. He wondered what it might be like to have to work somewhere for twelve bucks an hour, and drive around in an old Chevy. To have no trust fund, no options financially. To rely on others for food, or medical needs. To be unable to choose where his time was spent, or how. To be unable to be deliberately generous with loved ones.

Unbidden to his mind came the first Word. "Thou shalt have no other gods before me." *What is this? Money is not my god. Yes, but how do I feel about parting with all of it?*

This revelation of Ben's own soul sent a wave of sorrow through him. All through his ordeal he had, he now realized, thought of himself as better than the young man he'd read about in Adam's little New Testament. He'd secretly hoped for the chance to show everyone that he knew the question demanded an immediate response. He sadly thought that there was probably no answer to his question that he would like less than the one he'd received. *Not only am I no better. I am him.*

Jesus and his entourage had moved on. Jesus expounded on what had just transpired.

"It is almost impossible for a rich man to get into the kingdom of heaven. I say it again—it is easier for a camel to go through the eye of the needle than for a rich man to enter the kingdom of God."

Ben had seen that. They had to be totally unloaded, and had to crawl through on their knees, basically naked. So a guy could maybe do it if he were totally stripped of anything that might take the place of God. But evidently not otherwise.

The disciples were, for the second time in mere moments, completely baffled. "We thought riches were among God's greatest blessings. Who then can be saved?"

Jesus had reached a distance that put him almost out of earshot now, and Ben felt no need to follow. But he heard this. "Humanly speaking, no one. But with God, everything is possible."

Ben wondered what Sir Edmund Hilary thought after Everest. The quest arrived at a terminus in the most obvious and painful way. He now understood. He knew it all, better than anyone who had ever read Matthew's Gospel. He could see the answer better than anyone. To seek further at this time would be ludicrous. Had he found useful knowledge?

He attempted to console himself with the idea that maybe all of this could contribute to science—he could redeem the trip on the basis that time had now been conquered. What would it be like to return to time shed central and report that he'd spent the entire two weeks in the ancient Mideast, albeit mostly on the back of a camel? He wondered about the Today Show. *Is there a tomorrow show? Maybe they'll make one just for me.*

This thought opened up a lot more merging on the interchange. *If people begin to move freely to the past and back, what will happen to history? Will it become flexible and meaningless? Was Doc right? Or could you change what you did not prefer? Would there be any longer a Waterloo, or a Little Big Horn? Would Lincoln still be assassinated? Would Hitler live until 1945?*

Ben imagined all that. He had just come looking for some random rich guy, and he'd wound up changing the way people would think of the non-present for all of the foreseeable future.

This, too, was ridiculous. He was still where he was, not home and dry. Not even close. And he knew that such thoughts were asinine. His mind had attempted its own bait and switch.

To say that he still had a lot to consider understated the truth by a great deal. How would he respond to all of this? What would he decide?

Concede, then, he thought, *that Jesus really existed. If that were true, and it evidently is, then should a person do what he says to do? And what about the physical limitations? Come and follow me. Here? Now? Time is very short. He should know that. I cannot follow him for long because I have less than forty-eight hours in this century. He must mean the rich people that are here, not me. I'm out of here in less than two days. Besides, all I have here are a few denarii that are left over after that offering thing. They could be useful when I bring Sherry back.*

The sun blazed upon his head with full power. Ben decided to spend the afternoon, or at least the warmer part of it, back at Sethur's. He looked for shady places along the quiet streets. Few people were out. On arriving at his first-century home, he stole quietly up the stairs to the second floor and let himself in. The darkness and solitude greeted him as a friend. Caleb had delivered more fruit and clean water. Ben snacked on figs for a few minutes, had a drink of water and lay down on the bed. He could not think of these last twelve days as a job well done.

Whether he intended it or not, he slept. He awoke to a gentle knock on the door. Caleb entered at his permit, and announced the evening meal, and requested Ben's presence there.

Seated at meat were Sethur and Hannah, Debra and Ruth, Lydia and Patricia. Ben joined them in a meal of roasted grain, mutton, leeks, onions and flat bread.

The conversation swam in the shallow end of things until Ben asked Lydia about the success of her quest. "Did you get the contract for purple sashes for the retired soldiers?"

Lydia smiled. "It may be that I have. I spoke this morning with the official appointed by Rome named Pontius Pilate. He remembered my father, and also assured me of a need for our product. He appreciated the quality of our fabric. Of course he has not yet seen *your* robe with which, I think, none can compete in this region. But he will inform me within two days of his decision.

"I also saw a religious man named Caiaphas this afternoon. He too liked our product, and much purple fabric is used in the garments of the priesthood. He also has requested two days for deliberation.

"And did you find the man you sought? The girls told me that you spoke with the teacher."

Some things do not change, thought Ben. *Social media, first-century style.*

"I found the man."

"And did you find your answer?"

"Insofar as an answer could be found, I have been successful."

"And are you satisfied?"

Now what? Are all conversations with this woman like this? "I have gained all the knowledge I could possibly gain about my question. Your aid with the wording of it helped greatly. But there is still much I do not know. Both of your proposals may come to naught. Would you be satisfied?"

Lydia thought about this for a few seconds. "Yes. I had my chance. Both of those men seemed nervous in speaking to a woman about business. I hope each can set aside previous ideas about limits of women in the marketplace and make a wise decision. Yes, I had my chance."

It seemed then as if they both suddenly remembered that they were not alone in the room.

"Perhaps others would like to tell about their days," Lydia sighed.

For what seemed like a very long time, no one spoke. But in the end Sethur took a deep breath. *Some things never change*, thought Ben. "Last night's meeting proved to be divisive, and that is positive. I spent much of the afternoon with Hezron, and it seems that some of our leaders may be beginning to make progress. Perhaps all of them are. The most crucial aspect of all is that people must make an informed decision. It seems that the more people see of this man, the more strongly they hold their opinions. And he is a controversial figure. People love him or they hate him. No one seems to be neutral."

"What kind of progress do you speak of?" It was a rare foray into dinner-time conversation by Hannah.

"We pull in two directions," Sethur sighed. "Against each other. But I call it progress because the longer we pull against each other, the more time is given to Jesus and to the masses." Ben observed that Sethur had not referred to Jesus as 'the Nazarene'. "This will eventually result in some culmination. We see so many times in our history the buildup to a crisis and then the sudden activity of God. We saw it at the Red Sea, at Jericho, at the Jordan, at Mount Carmel, at coronations and assassinations, and all sorts of other emergencies. This will most likely be similar to many of those events.

"So that is my encouragement. I hope we can compete among ourselves until the critical moment arrives. When it does, I hope we will be able to recognize it."

"What do you think of him?" Ben had, heretofore, not heard Caleb enter into the evening talk. He stood nearby, ready to serve, and suddenly realized he had no platform from which to participate in the family's conversation. He immediately attempted to retract his question. "Master, I am so sorry. I forgot myself and my post. Please forgive me."

Sethur's gaze seemed piercing, but he spoke gently. "Caleb," he said quietly, "You are a son to me. And I answer you now as if you were born to me and Hannah.

"He is strange, and he has strange ways. As did Moses. As did Elijah. What from God would not seem strange to me?

"He seems good. Someone who is evil would not be doing what he does. He never harms anyone, he only does them good. He has power over demons, and liberates people from that bondage. He asks for nothing from people and has built no monument to himself. In all things he raises our eyes to God, and lifts us *above* the standard of what we thought was good."

Ben remembered from earlier that very day. *"When you are calling me good you are calling me God."* The phrase 'good moral teacher' flashed through his mind. And Sethur continued.

"Caleb, I would like to give you a very short answer to your question. But I am afraid there is no short answer. But I can tell you that on the rope of the religious leaders, I am pulling to keep out of his way and to give him more time."

There must have been something in Sethur's tone that signaled the end of the evening's activities. Hannah and the girls rose and began to clear the meal's detritus from the room. Ben also rose, bid his friends good night, and retreated to the upstairs apartment.

Caleb had preceded him. The room was "straightened up" as his mother would have said, and there was fresh water in the basin. The lamp on the stand had been lit.

Ben felt totally exhausted. He extinguished the lamp, went to bed and immediately fell into a dreamless sleep.

CHAPTER XX

Ben awoke to the sound of a rooster crowing. He could hear no evidence of activity beneath him. He lay in the early morning quiet, thinking.

By his own calculation, this should be his last full day in this century and this place. The second hour of the next day should be the terminus of the mission, and the time of his retrieval to the twenty-first century.

Doubts, he thought, *must be a part of life. Doc got me here right on target, but will the other half work?*

Ben began to consider first-century life. He understood that he had no income, but assumed that he could get a job working for someone. His brain then raced ahead. He could invent things! Then he remembered that patents did not yet exist, and everyone could legally copy anything he came up with. But what about business, commerce. Maybe he could do some kind of import/export thing up in Damascus. *And,* he thought smugly, *I am also good with camels.*

He thought of Doc's admonition to leave nothing behind, and that Doc had seemed to exempt his denarii, which were meant to "fit in". He spent some time wondering whether it made sense to attempt to arrive home with any of them left over. Through a few minutes of contemplation, he worked out a reasonable plan.

Unbidden, a chronology formed itself in his mind. The trip from Damascus, the snake, the storm, the waterhole in

287

the canyon, the reunion with Al-alif, the arrival in Jerusalem, the time spent in Sethur's home, (a very unlikely and fortuitous acquaintance) the eventual meeting with Jesus and finding out that the wealthy young man was he. Or he was him.

This brought him around to wondering how things happen. Did the hand of God, if there was a God, guide his trip? Sethur obviously believed this. Doc had also assumed this to be the case. If it were true, was he, as he thought yesterday, merely a pawn? Jesus needed someone to play the part of a rich young guy, so he called Ben Parker of the twenty-first century to journey two millennia into the past. (This when everyone knows that time travel is not possible.)

Ben realized that his thoughts were of no consequence. He was the man who asked the question, and he was the man who, so far, was unwilling to face the response.

What would it be like to follow?

What would it be like to sell everything and give the money away?

These were difficult questions and required more than the slack time of the previous day to answer. How could God, if there was a God, expect that? If He were there and in charge of everything, He had moved all the other pieces into place—Gramps to his friends, Ben's patience with them, the original idea, the implementation of it, Apple, Dell. *Would He now demand it all back? What would I think of a God like that?*

As he mused on these questions, Caleb's gentle knock preceded his entrance. He brought fresh water, a smile, and a request. "The women of the house have big plans for this day. It may involve both of us. If you are willing to lend your aid, could you present yourself downstairs soon?"

"Yes, I will, Caleb. I will be down soon."

Caleb left and Ben began what had become somewhat of a morning ritual. He looked at his fingernails and toenails, he ran his fingers through his hair and beard, he drank deeply. He washed. He then began to dress. His royal robe felt foreign and unfamiliar, almost useless. He made the decision then to wear the more pedestrian robe, which he pulled from his shepherd's bag.

He shook the dust off the imperial indigo garment and carefully folded it, along with the snappy black sash, and stowed them away. He examined the brown robe carefully, and mentally affirmed the style and color. It still fit very nicely, and in his mind he complimented his seamstress again.

Looking about the room, he saw nothing that needed attention in the immediate future, so he made his way to the ground floor and entered the residence of Sethur Ben-Judah. The Ben-Judah family awaited him there, along with Lydia and Patricia.

Sethur welcomed him, and motioned him to be seated. As if awaiting his arrival, they then broke their fast on fresh bread, figs, dates, and cheese.

While they ate, Sethur explained that his wife had a "project" under way, and could he provide some manual labor? Ben understood this part of the female psyche, and immediately volunteered. Some things do not change, and Ben recognized this opportunity as practical as well as social. He knew it would require little or no skill. If it did, he would not have been asked to participate.

Upon hearing of Ben's willingness to lend aid, Sethur said, "No doubt you are familiar with the process of spinning flax. Hannah is among the city's most accomplished spinners, and we have redded flax, which must be broken, skutched, combed, twisted, and spun. If you and Caleb would aid in the process, much could be accomplished today. Did you have other plans or expectations?"

Ben had to admit that he had none. He thought of his impending departure, which should occur within twenty-four hours. He'd mentioned it to no one as yet.

With breakfast out of the way, Caleb led Ben to the back of the room and through a door that opened onto a veranda. He showed Ben a huge stack of what appeared to be straw, arranged in small bundles.

"This is Master's crop of flax," Caleb began. "It must, as you probably know, be processed into useable fabric. Our part will be out here, the breaking and skutching. I will show you."

He selected a fist-sized bundle from the top of the stack and took it to a small, narrow bench. The flax had been pulled, with its roots intact, he explained, then soaked in water and dried on the roof, just as Rahab had done in Jericho. Ben knew nothing of Rahab, but did not interrupt, though he wondered if this Rahab was still living in Jericho.

"Our mission, if we choose to accept it, will be to separate the flax's inner fiber from the chaff. That process begins here, with the break."

The narrow bench turned out to be a tool. It resembled a long jaw with three wooden "teeth" sticking up from the bottom, each tooth the entire length of the bench, about a cubit. Two more teeth in the top of the jaw slid between the bottom teeth when the jaw was closed.

A handle protruded opposite the hinged end of the jaw, which when lifted, separated tooth from tooth. Caleb opened the jaw, and inserted the flax bundle about half way into it. He closed the jaw, then opened it again and pulled the flax toward him. He repeated the process all along the bundle, separating the flax fiber from the chaff. After a robust few seconds, he reversed the flax in his hand to break the other end. *Noisy and labor-intensive,* Ben thought. But any work these days was bound to be labor intensive.

In a very short period of time, Caleb had produced a hank of flax; he motioned Ben to follow and watch. He stretched the flax over the end of a nearly vertical board, and took a long dull knife and beat the flax as more chaff flew from it. He repeated the process on both ends of the bundle, and continued until all he had was a fine silvery handful of fabric. Ben realized that up to now (whatever *now* was) he'd never fully appreciated the descriptive

290

phrase, 'flaxen hair'. Caleb laid the silvery hank in the bottom of a large woven basket.

"Our part will be to keep this basket full of broken and skutched flax. The women will take over from this point."

The stack loomed large. There would be blisters and dreams of automation.

"I will skutch if you will break."

"Wait. Which was which?" Ben's confusion was excusable at this point.

"The flax break is yonder tool. It seems to me to be the easier job, so I hope you will allow me the honor of skutching."

Ben could see no reason to discuss it. He did not doubt that skutching would probably be harder, and he didn't mind giving up that honor. In answer he picked a bundle of flax from the stack and manned the break. As he took up his position, Caleb said, "We will be alone here and out of view. The morning is pleasant. If we are careful, we may strip." So saying, he removed his robe, revealing the muslin-colored tunic beneath. Ben followed suit, hanging his robe on a peg which protruded from the back wall of the house.

The skutching and breaking proceeded at an industrious pace, a pace as industrious as Ben could manage. He found that fatigue and blisters could be minimized by switching sides occasionally on the break, thus using the rested hand to supply the jaw muscle.

Caleb worked with abandon, skutching like what Ben perceived to be a madman. Ben himself, inspired just a bit, enthusiastically broke flax through the morning and into early afternoon, interrupted only occasionally by pauses for water. In the end, the flax stack did not loom as large as Ben had first imagined. By late afternoon all of it had been broken and skutched, and delivered to wherever it was needed for whomever needed it.

Just at the time one might wonder, "Now what?" the answer presented itself. "Mistress Lydia requests now that you provide her with company as she combs. She is in the dining room." Caleb offered this bit of information along with a cake of figs and a wedge of cheese.

Okay, then there's no problem. I'll just go there, Ben decided all on his own. He donned his robe.

Some things do not change.

Piles of flax dominated the dining room. Lydia sat between two small mountains of it, or between two large mounds of it. Ben merely suffered a very small blister on the palm of each hand, but could not yet feel sorry for himself. Lydia worked on this 'combing' with a great degree of intensity and alacrity.

When flax is combed, the hanks are pulled through a large, coarse device made of iron nails driven in close pattern through a heavy wooden block. The shorter fibers, thus separated from the longer, are set aside for use in pillows and pads. This, indeed, seemed to be most of the flax. The uncombed flax accounted for one mound; the combings comprised another mound. A smaller stack made up of much thinner hanks twisted together seemed to be the finished product, at least for this phase.

Lydia spoke without ceasing her work. "Parker, will you please sit with me while I work?" Ben sensed that he could answer negatively without consequence. He silently repented of his recent sarcastic thoughts.

"Yes. May I sit here?" He indicated a stool nearby. She nodded, and he sat.

"My time in Jerusalem is near an end. By tomorrow my questions of these officials should be answered and Patricia and I will be journeying back to Thyatira. Al-alif must soon return from Egypt to provide us passage to the north."

"I, too, will be leaving tomorrow." He then thought he should perhaps unsay that, but words cannot be unsaid.

"How do you plan to leave? I know of no caravan leaving tomorrow." He could read nothing in her face. She cast a momentary glance in his direction.

"I think I must begin by walking."

"Tarshish is far, and you live beyond that. Walking will take a long time." Then she brightened up. "Perhaps your young woman will be of age by the time you arrive?"

Ben wished he could laugh. "My journey should not take that long. In any case, I must make my start tomorrow. Time is somewhat of a mystery to me anyway. But I must begin before the second hour of the day."

Lydia continued combing, separating, staging the flax for spinning. "I see you wear your less impressive robe today. I knew that would be what we would see before you joined us."

"How did you know?"

"I also have such a question for you. But I heard you shaking, snapping a garment, and that could only mean you were clearing dust from your aristocratic robe in order to store it. Most men would not do such a thing merely to enhance a robe about to be worn."

Ben made no reply.

"Now. How did you know certainly that Patricia and I agreed that you would choose to take us north to find Al-alif?"

"Does it bother you that I would know?" *Miss Marple,* Ben almost added.

"In some ways, yes. We had not spoken, yet you knew. How could you be so certain?"

"Words are not the only way people speak," Ben began. "Your eyes and your face, and Patricia's eyes and her face, reveal things at times (not always) which you do not speak. In the desert that day I could see your thoughts without hearing your words." Ben resisted a temptation to embark on a lecture on James Borg and body language and the theory that ninety three percent of communication is outside of the syllables we utter, contained in gesture, posture, tone of voice, facial expression. But he stifled himself.

"How are women treated in your land?"

Somehow this question seemed alarming to Ben. It was straightforward, answerable, even objective. He wondered

293

what about this particular woman required such vigilance. He saw almost immediately that it wasn't she. It was he.

"In my land," he said slowly, hoping to be accurate and unbiased, "we attempt to treat women as equals to men. They may help us choose leaders, they may do as you have done and have their own businesses and livelihoods. They may travel, and they may choose not to depend on men or on any man for anything. They have the right to do, or try to do, nearly anything that men can do. Many of them become great in business; some of them have become leaders in our government. It has taken them much time and effort, but they seem to be able to do as they please. In my homeland women would have been expected to express their opinions when a choice needed to be made. That is why I attempted to include you in the decision-making process. At home women can speak to any man they wish to at nearly any time. They can travel as they wish; they can stay at home and raise their children as they wish. But few of them seem to have such a wish any more. They seem to want all that men have." *Lack of sleep, ulcers, heart disease, and alimony payments,* Ben thought he might add.

Lydia continued combing flax. "May I come there?"

"It probably would not be wise. The journey would be long." *Very long.*

"Does your land need my cloth or my dye? Do they have royalty and military?"

"We do not have there what you have here. We have important people, but they do not necessarily wear such fabric as you provide. We select our leaders differently than you do."

"How are they selected?"

Where to start with that one? Local politics, county commissioners, sheriffs, representatives, senators, the procedure of primary elections, the two-party system, the never-ending emotional toll of a campaign, the agony of an election? "When a post for a leader becomes vacant, usually two or three people will want the opportunity to lead. Each man or woman tries to speak to the common

294

people about what kind of leader would be the best to have. Then the common people involved are allowed, both men and women, to say which person is best, or which person they want to have the job of leading. The one who gets more people to agree with him, or her, and gets these people to say that they want that person for the job will be awarded that position. That person is then the leader."

Lydia still continued her work. "Must you return to west of Tarshish? Perhaps you would like to stay and work for my father."

A job offer. That solves that problem. "I do not totally understand my method of travel. It may be impossible for me to leave, and it may be impossible to stay. But I hope to be on my way tomorrow. But I thank you for offering me work. If I cannot return to West of Tarshish, I will need to do something here."

During this time the combings had grown and the uncombed pile had shrunk. Lydia neared the completion of this step. She looked seriously and directly at Ben. "Parker, you are a good man and a good friend. I thank Sethur's God that our paths have crossed. I hope that you will come back. I hope to see you again."

"It seems unlikely. May Sethur's God guide and protect you."

"Thank you, Parker." Lydia's face glowed with enthusiasm. "Sethur's God proves to be very good indeed."

Lydia finished combing out the last hank of flax, and carefully gathered the fruits of her labor into her arms. "I shall take these to Patricia and the girls. They are spinning the flax from the distaff to the spool. Perhaps we will see you as we sup."

Ben took the hint, and made the circuit back to his upstairs quarters. He found a small square of cloth, perhaps a doily, and counted out his remaining denarii. They numbered seventeen. He wrapped them in the cloth and left them on the table. He took a careful inventory of the few items he must take with him the following day. The rich man's robe, the sash, the shepherd's bag, the sandals. Not much to pack for a voyage of nearly two thousand years.

He wondered what it would be like to go home. It might be a different world. He had to force himself to think in terms of the era he had left. He hadn't missed his cell phone so far, with the possible exception of the GPS app, but of course that would have been useless now anyway. Besides, there was always the K'mal on a clear night.

He thought more about what he hadn't missed. Chemtrails, the roar of motor vehicles, the cacophonous ring of an alarm clock. He found it difficult to miss things like that when no one else did.

The food would be different. Sleeping would be different. A shower would be different in a nice kind of way.

Which of his friends from college might like to come back and help the world get an earlier start on central plumbing? That would have its advantages.

He wondered, would Jesus like to take a shower? He could have come to the twenty-first century as well, or a person would at least think he could have. Would that have been better? If a person could make the entire universe out of nothing, could he make a shower?

Caleb's knock pulled him away from all these hypothetical questions. He entered as Ben gave permission, carrying a pitcher of water and wearing a smile. "Our evening meal is soon ready. Will you join us?" Caleb set the pitcher down.

Ben stood. "Caleb," he began, "I am hoping to leave tomorrow. I would like you to have this. I know it isn't much, but perhaps it can be of help to you."

He picked up the cloth bundle and handed it to Caleb, who accepted it without a word. He opened the cloth and looked inside. He carefully counted the coins, then said with a gasp, "Seventeen denarii! This is riches!"

"Please accept this as a gift. You have represented the house of Sethur well, and I am grateful."

296

"But will you not need silver for your journey? How can you travel with no silver?"

"Be assured I will not need it. Please accept it, and keep it as our secret until after I am gone. Reassure Master that my passage home will incur no further expense to me."

Caleb re-twisted the cloth and put the bundle in the pocket of his robe. "Let it be as you wish, my friend. You bring me ever closer to my own wedding."

Ben nodded, then poured some water into the basin. Seeing this, Caleb left the room. Ben drank deeply from the pitcher, washed as well as he could, then he, too, exited the room.

The diners partook of their meal in silence except for Hannah and Patricia. Evidently, much more flax had been processed than Hannah had hoped for. She basked in the glow of a job well done and surpassing quota. Patricia pantomimed all the work she had been able to observe, including what Ben and Caleb had done, with no reference to the fact that they had been working in their underwear.

Following supper, the women left the room, and Caleb went about his duties. Sethur turned to Ben. "I am told you must leave us tomorrow. I hoped to persuade you to stay with us. Debra would make a fine wife for you."

Ben laughed. *So would a lot of women, I guess,* he thought. "I am sure she would. But I cannot stay. I must be on my way tomorrow. You have been a most gracious host."

"I will say my final goodbye tonight then, for I must be at Temple at first light. Thank you, my friend. You saved my life. I am ever indebted to you."

"You are welcome. I did only what I was able to do, and it was for me as well as for you," Ben replied.

"And the women, too. They also are indebted to you."

"Then let them count it as a blessing from your God."

Sethur's look was intense. "Parker, do you trust my God?"

Breathe in slowly, then answer. "I don't know."

297

"Then may God deliver you from your doubt, my son."
Sethur embraced Ben, and the friends parted.

Ben returned to the apartment, and sat on the bed in the
dark. He remained there for a long while. After he heard no
more movement beneath him, he arose, disrobed, and
prepared to sleep. As his consciousness balanced on the
brink of slumber, he thought of friends his age, already
married and divorced. The guys he talked to reluctantly
described how crazy their lives had become. All that
concern over money and possessions, and unfortunately,
children. He recalled one friend who fought with his wife
in court over custody of their dog. Up to now, that had
been a high water mark. His own life may be crazy, but at
least he had no court battles over custody of a dog. But the
final prop holding his sanity in place had been removed.
He was living *la vida loca*. And it didn't matter whether
you translated it into Aramaic or English or Slovakian. It
did not compute, because in his heart he cradled the
impossible hope that tomorrow he would be two thousand
years away.

CHAPTER XXI

Ben could not remember a torturous attempt to fall
asleep, so morning's arrival shocked his consciousness. He
could tell that it couldn't have been even the second hour,
when Caleb knocked and brought in fresh water. As he
entered, Ben saw that he also carried a large towel and an
extra basin.

"In preparation for your journey, I must wash your
feet." He smiled as he said it, and Ben imagined people
only smile that way when they are ready to embrace pure
joy. *He must think he needs to do this. Okay.*

Ben sat as Caleb examined each foot, and carefully
brought water to bear on all places, especially those visibly
unclean. The water was warm, not cool, and impregnated
with some sort of surfactant as well. Caleb carefully washed
and dried each foot, then produced another cloth and
meticulously removed the dirt from his sandals. After that
thorough purging, he gently placed them on Ben's feet and
tied them securely in place.

"Master has very high regard for you. He says you are a
true man in all that he can see. He does not yet know how
right he is. He is already serving at Temple, but bid me ask
you—would you like your morning meal in privacy? And
he bid me to wish you Godspeed."

It had not occurred to Ben, but now he thought the
option of a private breakfast might be beneficial. He nodded

agreement, and Caleb responded with a slight bow and an immediate retreat from the room.

Within a few moments Ben had donned his traveling robe, checked his shepherd's bag one last time and reseated himself in the room's only chair. Caleb returned, knocked and entered without waiting for a response. He carried a tray laden with flat bread, cheese, figs, dates and raisins. "My mistress may have gone past the top of the camel's hump with our provision this morning. She is still thrilled to have all that flax spun into thread."

He placed the tray on the table. He bowed and said, "Have safe and pleasant journeys, my friend. And may the God of Abraham bless you and keep you."

Ben rose and embraced him. He did not trust himself to speak, and Caleb seemed to understand this. He turned and left the room, gently closing the door.

The breakfast provided more than adequate fare, and Hannah had included a small dish of honey, which went well with the flat bread. Ben savored the entire meal, eating heartily in preparation for his upcoming journey.

As he finished, he heard an unfamiliar knock at the door. "Please enter," he responded.

Debra carefully entered. Ben wondered about the acceptability of having a woman in the room.

"How may I serve you?" he asked.

"My mother does not know that I have come to you. We discovered from Caleb that you would not join us in breaking fast.

"You are a good and brave man, Parker. Father says there is no doubt that you saved his life. We, my sister and mother and I will live forever in your debt. You cannot guess the gratitude we all have for you. Your departure is a great loss to us all." With that, she quickly embraced him and exited without closing the door. Ben stepped forward and pushed it closed.

He had scarcely reoriented his mind to the task of preparing to leave when he heard another gentle, unfamiliar knock. "Please enter," he said.

Patricia carefully stepped into the room. "Lydia does not know that I have come to you. You are a fine and gentle man, Parker. You have showed us much, and mean much to us. We would surely not have our freedom were it not for you. I came to wish you God's speed and to say that we are grateful to you. I think my Mistress will not come here, as you desire privacy. Well, I also desire things, and one thing I desire is to express my thanks."

She embraced him and kissed him on the cheek. "Fare well, Parker. We will not forget you." Then she turned and left, closing the door behind her.

Okay, thought Ben. *That's a long speech for Patricia. At least it's out of the way.*

He began to take a final inventory. He possessed no currency. The remainder of his possessions he had carefully stowed in the leather bag. He had drunk deeply of the water, and planned to carry none with him. At that moment the door opened again without knock, and Hannah stood on the landing.

"Forgive me for not knocking. I was afraid you might have already left, or would not answer. I must tell you of my gratitude, for my husband has told me all concerning your heroism at the watering hole. How I wish you would stay and marry Debra or Ruth," at this point she embraced him and kissed him on the cheek, and whispered in his ear, "or Lydia." With that, she was gone.

Full daylight fell on the street as Ben passed quietly down the stairs. On guard for Lydia or Ruth, he furtively dodged through the gate. He figured it must be about seven as he began the journey back to Solomon's porch. He had to skirt the temple complex on the north, and then work his way back south through the throng entering Susa Gate. He realized that this was contra traffic, going out when so many came in. He progressed slowly, but eventually he gained the gate and passed through onto the steep road that led him to the Kidron Valley floor. He hoisted his shepherd's bag higher onto his left shoulder and climbed the trail that led, had he known it, to the Mount of Olives exit.

He passed that access without knowing what kind of a tourist attraction he had missed, and retraced the route the caravan had traversed into the city scant days before. He sensed a need for privacy, so he worked his way further afield, away from the city's crowded streets.

For about three quarters of an hour he walked in a northwesterly direction, and finally found a small grove of trees, which would afford seclusion. He entered their cool shade and sat down to wait for whatever might or might not happen.

He did not know what to hope for. He'd come to accept, even to like this time, and the people seemed to be honest and forthright. He could come to love them, just as he loved the ones in that other place. His change of mind came when he thought of Sherry. He could not imagine a future without her as part of it.

During his thought of Sherry things changed—not like scenery outside a car window, but with a speed that assaulted the senses, and challenged your view of the universe. In a moment, Ben passed from solid reality to solid reality. The trees disappeared instantly, and in their place the time cylinder materialized.

So Doc was right again. Two weeks. And now I'm back.

Sitting in the leather seat, Ben peered through the plastic window. He could see no yellow vapor. Across the room hung the digital clock. After a long moment in which his mind reoriented itself to reading Arabic numbers, Ben deciphered the time as 2:15 a.m.

Without question, Hannah had enthusiastically secured him. The shed lacked any occupant or welcoming committee, so he began the rigors of liberating himself. The cloth wrist straps released when he flexed against them, freeing his hands for the rest of the process. The vital sign sensors had already been removed. He released the lap belt, shoulder harness, and forehead strap. Even his ankles had been secured, an event of which he had no memory. He removed the oxygen mask last of all, and held his breath as he opened the transparent door. He stepped onto the concrete pad that supported the cylinders.

I wonder if I'm glad to be back, thought Ben. His clothing and the items from his pockets lay on the bench, along with his cell phone. The sports bag with the two hundred fifty thousand dollars in it had disappeared. He remembered the text message from Gramps and decided to begin his re-entry into the present with that, whatever it turned out to be.

"Call me. Urgent."

Next to his cell phone, Ben saw Doc's inventory: Fifty denarii— counterfeit, two robes, one sash, two tunics, one shepherd's bag, one pair sandals, one square purple fabric. He hoped that one missing item would not alter the course of history.

True to her word, Hannah had left food. It bothered Ben that Doc and Hannah were not in the time shed, as he supposed they would be. The readout on the digital clock also troubled him. Much more than two seconds had transpired.

Although Ben had eaten a reasonable breakfast just two thousand years ago, he found his attention drawn to the ham and cheese sandwich on the table. Next to it he saw a small cooler in which a large bottle of Diet Pepsi rested in the remains of mostly melted crushed ice. It seemed he had no time lag or any other discomfort, so he attacked the food and drink the way any hungry man would. In short order he'd eaten the sandwich and washed it down with what he thought must be the drink of the gods, though he would surely use a lower case "g" on it.

Jeans caught his attention. Real, comfortable jeans. He decided to change into modern clothes.

That turned out to be a lot of work. Shorts, pants, undershirt, shirt, socks, shoes. Still, it felt all right, he thought. Wearing twenty-first century attire would come back to him, maybe like riding a bike. Or a camel.

Arming himself with the contents of his pockets seemed strange somehow. The simple life of no watch, no cell phone, no car keys, no wallet he had left in the past, and he now needed all that stuff. And more. He stepped toward the door.

Attached to the door at eye level was a note stuck to the rough wood with a pushpin. It read, "To Mr. Parker, the world's first human time traveler: We are sorry we cannot personally greet you upon your return. Urgent matters have called us away. Make use of any of the facilities in the farmhouse as suits your need. Do not bother to lock up when you leave. The county is very sparsely populated, and all the residents are honest folk. Thank you for aiding us in our research. We shall be in touch to obtain your promised debriefing. Yours in a timely way, Doc Resser."

Ben took the note from the door, folded it neatly and put it in his shirt pocket. He then walked into the dark clarity of the Montana night. Out in front of the farmhouse the rented Tahoe waited. *Probably not cooled off from the drive out here,* Ben thought.

He opened the car and found what he'd been missing. No reasonable man should get too far from his electric razor.

He found the rest of it as well-soap, toothbrush, toothpaste. He could not have anticipated his excitement at the sight of a comb.

Confidently, he barged into the house. Even before Ben turned on the lights, he could see that something wasn't right.

He remembered being impressed by all that computer equipment. It had all been removed. The diplomas and pictures on the wall had disappeared. The dents in the carpet from the legs of the desks could still be seen.

He passed through the front room into the kitchen.

No surprises here. Hannah had not left much behind. He began to sense the growth of a suspicion that he would not see them again.

The dinette set remained, for the moment, in the kitchen. He sat in an arrow backed chair to think.

Otto chose that moment to scratch on the door, and Ben let him in. He found the dog food and poured some out, and filled the water dish.

Now what? This thought had become a familiar one.

Then he realized he still had his shaving kit in his left hand. His second random choice of a door revealed a three piece farm bathroom. He'd not seen a working commode for thousands of years. It was an emotional experience.

He made full use of the facilities, as he'd been given written permission to do. After a long shower, he found a towel and dried himself. Then he stared at his face in the mirror. He looked dark and healthy, and his beard thick and robust. After only a few seconds, he wearied of his narcissism and began to think about getting rid of the whiskers.

He found an old Wahl multi-cut clipper in the top drawer of the vanity, so he adjusted it to its closest setting and mowed the main growth off and let it fall into the sink. With this done, he put his electric razor on the job. He had to pass over several times, but eventually achieved a smooth shave, one he hoped Sherry would approve of. But his razor could do no more on its remaining charge.

His face, protected by his beard, had received none of the desert tan that the exposed parts had achieved. He thought he might look unhealthy. He guessed he'd also lost a few pounds.

He plugged his razor in to charge and went to work on his teeth. This job also used a lot of time, since each tooth seemed to need special attention.

Eventually his mouth felt clean.

They hadn't yet removed their couch. He stretched out on it, intending to think until daybreak. Otto came and curled up on the floor next to him. Predictably, Ben fell asleep.

CHAPTER XXII

At about seven, Ben's phone interrupted the morning silence. He'd set the ring tone to some hip jazz music twenty centuries ago, and had forgotten what it should sound like. He'd also forgotten that cell phones ring and that he now resided in his own time. So he wasted a few seconds on twenty-first century reorientation, while looking around for some kind of clock radio. In due time he figured out the source of the noise and answered his phone.

It was Gramps.

"You all right?"

"Yes."

"Coming home soon?"

"Today."

"Good. We have a lot to talk about."

Ben briefly considered his options. His inner decision arrow wavered between Gramps in Green Bay and Sherry in Dallas. "Uh, Okay. I'll call you when I get in. I need to get to Dallas real soon, though."

"Okay. Call me the minute you get here."

"Right. I will. I love you, Gramps. I'll see you soon."

Otto looked hungry, so Ben made sure he had food and water, and let him out to do his business. He remembered his razor, so he retrieved his toiletries and loaded them back into the kit.

It took very little time to gather his belongings into the Tahoe. As he started the engine, he caught a glimpse of Otto on the porch. By all the evidence he could see, the dog had been abandoned.

Ben returned to the kitchen, grabbed the bag of dog food and the Otto dishes and put them in the back of the car. He called Otto and opened the door, and the dog jumped in.

"For now we'll have to leave you at the shelter. If Doc doesn't come back for you, and if no one else adopts you, I'll come and get you."

Some people say that it's stupid to talk to dogs because they can't understand English. *Doesn't matter,* Ben decided. He had even made a Mideastern camel understand English. It was all in the tone of voice. Otto seemed comforted.

First stop, Wagon Wheel in Ekalaka.

"Doc told me yesterday you'd probably be coming in this morning. You all right? You look pale. Oh, it's the beard. What can I get for ya?"

Ben had taken a seat at the counter. Otto lay waiting in the car. Ben ordered an omelet and considered how to proceed. Other patrons were conspicuous by their absence, so the waitress had time to focus.

"Was Doc in here recently? The last day or two?"

"Yeah, Darlin', he was. Yesterday." *Some things never change,* thought Ben. *If there had been diners like this in Jerusalem, some waitress back there would have called me Darlin' in Aramaic. But they call all the guys that.*

"He had his truck and trailer with him. He and Hannah were headed somewhere. He didn't say where, though."

"They left their dog behind."

The waitress stopped and stared. "Otto?"

"Yep."

"Can I keep him? He's been in here, and I love that dog!"

Solves problem number one, thought Ben. "Yeah, he's in the car. Shall I invite him in?"

"You get him in here this minute!"
You forgot to call me Darlin', but I'll overlook it this time. Ben brought the dog, the food, and the dishes, and delivered them to the waitress. In a place like Ekalaka, name tags seem extraneous, so the girl introduced herself as Suzie, with a z-i-e, not a z-y or an s-i-e. Otto was excited about spending time with Suzie, and that delayed the omelet by a couple of minutes. After its delivery, Suzie again became distracted with Otto, so Ben ate in silence and planned his next move.

Because of his earlier conversation with Gramps, he had to go home to Wisconsin first. He'd rather have headed straight for Dallas, but maybe he could still get there late tonight.

As he chewed, a thought struck him. "Suzie, what day is it?"

"It's Tuesday, all day."

"Thanks." *Should I be wondering where the missing twenty-seven hours and fifteen minutes went? Was Doc wrong and I came back a day later? Or, more likely, if he planned for it to be this way? Why did Monday disappear? All in all, though, if I were going to be robbed of a day, it's best to get rid of a Monday.*

Suzie agreed to trade the dog for the omelet. So he left a tip, said goodbye to Otto and climbed into the Tahoe. Suzie and Otto waved to him as he pulled away, and Ben waved back. He drove the mostly desolate miles to Billings, turned the car in and boarded a flight to Minneapolis.

Due to the Bakken oil boom, a lot of Tuesday travelers crowded the plane, but Ben, luckily, secured a seat in first class. He hoped the flight would give him time to ponder.

Doc had known he'd lost a day. That explained Doc's prescience concerning the stop at the Wagon Wheel. It would also explain the computers all being absent. It would account for the kitchen being all cleaned out. It explained the time-frame of Doc and Hannah's premature departure. The mystery was *why.* Doc had sent him off, and he had returned. He could see the seven hundred fifty k as a bargain-not that he had the answer to his question, but he'd gotten there. Ben had paid an agreed-upon fee for an agreed-upon service. No harm and no foul. The Resser evacuation made no sense at all, unless Doc did not *know* his plan would work.

He had, he thought, been to *the past*. Jesus had existed, had walked this earth. He didn't yet know for sure about the savior part, but the history could not be denied. There had been real people healed of real sickness in real time-usually on Saturday, and in violation of the code, Sethur's friends' blue laws. Real political and religious ramifications had showed themselves all over. And Jesus had real followers, despite his lack of credibility.

If he had real followers, should everyone be following? Having followers did not guarantee goodness. Jim Jones had followers. So did Hitler. Now that he'd been there, or rather then, Ben realized he may have been in search of the wrong answer; that is, he would now have to figure out if he had been asking the right question.

And that proved to be a problem as well. There he was, minding his own business, reading the nineteenth chapter of Matthew's Gospel, when he came across a story with no closure. Then he became obsessed with the closure, and bam! He entered the scene himself, discovering that the reason for the lack of closure sprouted from the fact that the rich young man currently resided nowhere near Jesus. He sat on a plane between Billings and Minneapolis.

And why? It seemed pretty stupid, Ben had to admit. He thought he needed a simple answer, and the God he didn't believe in or trust manipulated him into the story. He did not want to be *in* it. He wanted to find out if the man continued business as usual, or if he left it all to follow. And either way, he simply wanted to know the answer to this: Was it worth it? *Now I have to face the question of whether I will pursue business as usual.*

That's still the problem, he thought. *Knowing if it's worth it before you start. How can you know?*

310

The nature of knowing makes its own problem. (It seemed to Ben like everything was a problem.) He knew he skated on thin ice, but he had no name for his dilemma. How do you know you know what you know? He had no idea that Descartes and Hume and Locke and Voltaire and scores of others had preceded him onto the pond, nor could he know that their conclusions would not now be of help to him.

How would you know? If you knew, how would you know you have known? In some ways, he anticipated his next conversation with Adam as the most important in his near future.

He felt the MD 111 begin its descent, and tried to recall the layout of the Minneapolis airport. He figured he should be able to get some kind of flight to Green Bay that afternoon. He began to look forward to being in his own apartment, looking out over the water.

Sometimes a plan comes together. He could book a flight that got him into GBIA at about seven, and contacted Gramps about a ride home. He spent that entire time rehashing the events of the last two days, which in Ben-days equaled sixteen. He considered briefly the idea of a book and the fun of promoting it from place to place all over America, but then he realized no one was going to believe this. *Especially not Gramps,* he thought. *But what if I make it a novel?*

The grandfather of all skeptics met him at baggage claim. *I hate it when I'm right,* he silently complained.

He had no luggage, just his overnight case and his shepherd's bag, so they had no wait at the baggage claim. When Gramps first saw Ben, he expressed concern about Ben's health-he looked so pale. Ben assured him that he felt great. He just needed some actual food.

So Gramps phoned Grams, who insisted he be brought straight to their house and she slaughtered the fatted calf, so to speak. And that gave Gramps his opening, his opportunity for "sharing".

"When we first went to Resser's," Gramps shared, "I have to admit I harbored suspicion, curiosity, and mistrust. I stayed on my guard the whole time and when we were in that farmhouse, I turned on my camera on my phone and left it in my pocket. I recorded every word, and as I went around the room I got pictures of all those diplomas and such. There were eight of them, and they made up a very impressive dossier of accomplishment. They're not still up, are they? Thought not.

"When I went out to take a leak, you remember? When I went out, I found a spot where I had cell service, and I emailed (with your help, of course) all the audio and pictures to my home email address. And naturally, I forgot I had done it. So when Doc erased my phone stuff, he didn't realize the cat was out of the bag, so to speak.

"Well, a few days ago someone called me (a car friend) and told me he'd emailed me a picture of a car he wanted to buy and would I have a look at it and tell him what I thought. So when I went in to look at the picture, I found this stuff from me to me. So I started looking at that.

"I knew Doc wanted money from you, and I didn't trust him, so I started to look into things. I checked into every diploma and every award from every college. Some of the colleges did not even exist, so this shortened up the job a little bit. The four college diplomas on his wall from legitimate places weren't as easy. All of them posted lists of their graduates, year by year, on the internet. Doc Resser's name did not appear on any of them. Then I checked on whether he had ever enrolled as a student at any of them. That came up negative as well. I could find nothing to indicate that this man knows anything about anything except maybe flimflam!"

It appeared to Ben that Gramps had run out of steam, and that it might be his turn to say something. He remembered the Ben-Judah family method-breathe deeply, wait, answer. "You may be right."

"May be? MAY BE!?"

"George," Grams interposed, "There is no need to raise your voice like that."

"Yes, dear, you are correct as usual. Ben, our visit to the Resser's bothered me a lot. Remember all the fuss about that rat and how he ended up on the floor? I am willing now to bet your entire fortune that during those few seconds, while we chased Bob, Doc Resser switched the surveillance disc."

"What about the red tape around his leg with my initials?"

"Ha! He knew you were coming. You were his mark. You had money, and he wanted some of it, and he arranged this whole thing so that you would trust him. And, he diffused your suspicion by doing the opposite of what a normal con man does. When he saw you were interested, he *lowered* his price.

"When I put all this together, I sent you a text message right away-that was very late last Sunday night, maybe even after midnight. I have been on pins and needles these last two days, because I didn't know if maybe you were in danger."

"Ben's supper is ready now, George. Can you give him a break?"

Two weeks on two meals a day tends to starve a body. Besides the stress of all this discovering uncomfortable facts, and having survived all day on an omelet gotten in trade for a dog, he had done all that flying and landing. On top of that, Grandma's cooking remained incomparable, in any century. Neither Hannah even came close. Ben enjoyed his meal, mostly in silence, listening to two lovers heavily invested in each other talk about their day.

When Gramps could see the meal winding down for Ben, he asked the question. "So what happened out there?"

Ben looked at his watch. He remembered some news blurb about a presidential debate turning on a candidate doing that. *But that was different,* he thought. *That guy looked like he was bored. I just have a lot to tell. Too much for tonight.*

"No harm has come to me," he began. "What did happen is a story too long for tonight. And I have to go to Dallas as soon as possible. We will talk soon, and I'll tell you all I can."

"Are there things you can't tell? Are you implying that?" Gramps sounded worried.

"No, but it's a long story. For tonight could you just drop me by my place? I had a good time, and want to tell you all about it. Just not tonight."

"George, Ben must be tired after all whatever happened. Maybe you could give him another break. He woke up this morning in that other time zone."

So Gramps took Ben home. The clock read ten p.m. when he was finally ensconced in the privacy of his own apartment. Would it be too late to call Adam? Ten. Nine in Texas? Ben opted to call.

What transpired in the phone call seemed to Ben to be the worst news-at least not good news. Laurie had family visiting until Friday, and could Ben wait until Saturday?

CHAPTER XXIII

Can one week last forever? Wednesday and Thursday dragged by. Friday dragged by too, even though the office demanded so much from him. By early Saturday morning, Ben felt antsy, like a high school kid before the prom. But not like that, either. He just anticipated being near one of his favorite people, and after so long. Two weeks longer than it had been. Admittedly, one of the intervening days seemed somehow to have disappeared, but that did not ease his need for a Sherry fix. So in preparation, he made sure that he shaved off everything he could. He hoped Sherry could love the finished product.

He had booked the earliest flight he could get out of Green Bay. The only flight available provided a leg to Memphis with an hour layover, then on to Dallas, arriving at 4 pm. He'd never been to the Memphis airport, and always liked seeing how different cities handled the problem of transporting people.

The layover in Memphis turned out to be longer than expected. The maintenance crew discovered a mechanical problem during a routine inspection, and decided that a hydraulic line needed to be replaced. Though Ben agreed with these kinds of decisions, he rued the time it took. As the flight had merely been delayed, not canceled, the airline made little effort to reassign any passenger who showed DFW as final destination. The airline's normal practice of

315

overbooking prevented Ben from just buying another ticket. So he sat through nearly five hours of waiting while maintenance procured the part, installed, tested, retested, and inspected it, and completed the paperwork. Though he worried that he might not get to see Sherry that day, he had no desire to be sitting around at thirty thousand feet in a vehicle less than airworthy. It made for a fall more dangerous than from the hump of a dromedary.

Thankfully, *lost time* became the only major result of the delay. He arrived at the DFW terminal at about nine pm. Adam collected him, and explained that the girls had turned in early due to entertainment exhaustion.

Adam and Ben made small talk on the ride back to Adam's house. Neither one seemed to want to break the time barrier, so those questions hung there, unasked and unanswered. There is some code of manliness that allows for this, the ignoring of the elephant in the room. Ben reflected that women seem to be unable to comfortably participate in this code.

Ben bunked up in the guest room and waited patiently for the morning. He slept fitfully, but awoke and arose with enough time to cut the stubble.

The family tradition included an early breakfast in preparation for first service at church. Ben spent the "spare" time that morning reading Sherry a story about two hippopotami, George and Martha, who spent their days learning lessons about friendship. Those kinds of moments Ben treasured as pure gold. Sherry enjoyed them with no thought to their future value.

The family tradition stretched even to the breakfast menu-waffles and scrambled eggs. Ben partook gratefully-effusively so. Laurie thought he was joking.

Church blindsided Ben and presented him with a whole set of new and different challenges. And the differences showed up in unpredictable ways.

The first difference revealed itself in how Ben listened to the sermon. Pastor Rick talked about Jesus as if he were related, as if he knew all about him, as if Jesus were some sort of famous person that the pastor knew and you should know too. This offended Ben. As probably the only living person to speak to Jesus face to face, he figured maybe the pastor should call on him for some eyewitness input.

And then the man started talking about the road from Jerusalem to Jericho-narrow and dangerous, with travelers vulnerable to villains who could easily hide along the way. *He doesn't know the half of it,* Ben fumed.

But the *piece de resistance* came during the parable of the Good Samaritan, with a seriously wounded Jew passed up by a priest <u>and</u> a Levite. This agitated Ben even more, because Sethur was a Levite and he would never leave a fellow traveler in need.

Suffice it to say that the sermon frustrated him. Historical inequities all over it. And this name-dropping syndrome. Just a bother.

The second difference sneaked in like a scorpion after dark, presenting a problem less obvious, but in some ways more inconvenient. Sherry had gone to children's church, in which she'd been taught about Jesus blessing the little children in Solomon's Porch outside the Temple. She had been given a picture of the scene to color. Jesus wore a non-exceptional robe, and little children surrounded him. Sherry took pride in her coloring job, and displayed her masterpiece to Ben.

The caption at the bottom read, "Jesus blesses the children in Solomon's Porch." The porch had been drawn with small columns and a shed roof extending from the wall of the temple. And the temple looked all wrong too-wider than it should have been, and not nearly tall enough. Not enough marble on the front, no matching steps up to the court of the Gentiles like there should be. And the children's parents were not even in the picture.

Some things do not change, and Ben-blurts are on the list. Before he could stop himself, Ben shared these observations, albeit with a compliment to Sherry's coloring, which thrilled him immensely.

Both Adam and Laurie stared at him.

317

Eventually, Adam broke the silence. "How do you know all that?" The question came out flat, even, and sharp.

Sethur method. Deep breath, then speak. "I was there." The answer was equally flat, equally sharp.

Adam overcame his initial lack of vocal control.

"Are you telling me that Resser was on the level? That it worked?"

"No. I don't know. Resser was probably a con man. But it worked. I was there."

"Can we just pick up a couple of pizzas for lunch? I can see I won't be able to cook today." Laurie could sometimes predict the future.

"Laurie, that's a great idea! Let's get Hawaiian and pepperoni." Adam seconded.

With that they left church, not really talking to anyone else. Following the stop at Little Caesar's, they wound up back at the house for lunch.

Adam initiated conversation tentatively, and after a few false starts, finally asked, "Did you get the answer to your question?"

"Yes."

"And can you tell me about it?"

"Yes."

So in between pizzas Ben tackled the whole story from the beginning because Laurie had not heard some of the initial information about the classified ad and the original contact with Doc. He covered the demonstration with Bob, the basic agreement, the preparation for the trip, the launch, the time in Damascus and Israel, and the return. The whole thing took about three and a half hours, much of it spent with Sherry peacefully asleep on his lap. When Ben reached the end of his tale, Adam said, "Can you be sure it was real?" Somehow this question seemed familiar to Ben.

This started the second avalanche, which involved about an hour and a half of Doc's strange activity, his sudden evacuation, and his total lack of credentials, topped off with Gramps' theory about how the initial demonstration had been a fake. In the end, Ben's concluded that it *seemed* real. But he had no proof. He hoped that the fact that he'd personally experienced it would count for something. Somehow, that thought also seemed familiar to him.

Laurie called a halt at about six pm, and reheated pizza for supper. Ben again thanked her effusively, and Laurie again thought he was joking.

After supper Ben pursued a different course. He attempted to tactfully address the credibility problem Jesus had with being from Nazareth and looking so illegitimate and always coming out on the wrong side of the law. Besides that the shepherd problem had to be addressed, them not being reliable witnesses to anything, but they were the ones out announcing that Jesus came from God. And add to that the purposeful offense Jesus gave to the religious leaders by always doing his miracles on the Sabbath, and calling the spiritual leaders hypocrites and speaking so mysteriously, and always taking Jonah's side in things. Adam said he knew all that, and that none of it made any difference. Some of it enhanced his resume a bit, Adam thought.

Then they started talking about the culture. Laurie and Adam, but Laurie especially, wanted to know about particular details of life in the first century. How did people live, what did they eat, what did they wear, what were the social customs? She expressed shock when Ben explained how people handled their shopping, and wondered how she would do with the shopkeepers. The concept of women not being allowed to speak to men in public intrigued her the most. She wondered how people ever got together romantically. But Ben assured her that a good man didn't need a date. Fathers of young women kept a sharp lookout for good prospects, and commonly offered their daughters to men that would make good sons-in-law. He told her Sethur's suggestion, and also Hannah's observation about Lydia. Ben had not, to that point, mentioned her name.

"Do you mean Lydia from Thyatira?" Adam cross-examined.

"Well, yes, she said that. But how did *you* know that?"

"Did she sell purple cloth for a living?"

"Well, yes. How do you know this stuff?"

Adam got his Bible and showed Ben the passage in Acts where Paul came to Philippi and met Lydia and she became the first convert to Christianity in Europe.

"So you *knew* her."

"I *know* her."

"Can you tell us more names? Who else did you meet?"

Ben went through the list-Al-alif, Sethur, Lydia, Patricia, Hilkiah, Tullus, Mordecai, Hezron, Gideon, Caleb, Debra, Ruth, Elizabeth, Melchi, Nicodemus-

Here they stopped him with a united chorus. "What?"

So he said the last few names again. Ruth, Elizabeth, Melchi, Nicodemus-

"Okay, stop right there. You met a man named Nicodemus?" This was Adam demanding an answer.

"Yes, and he said he asked Jesus about how to be born again, and-"

"Look here," Adam interrupted. He flipped his Bible open to the third chapter of John's Gospel. "Was this what he said?"

Ben read the account and confirmed it. "Yes, that's just about what he said. Except the snake had a name. It was Nehushtan."

Adam said quietly, "You have never read John's Gospel, have you?"

Ben shook his head. "I inched my way through Mark and most of Luke before I left, but in so many ways, there was no John."

"You've never read Acts either?' Ben persisted in his denial.

Adam looked at Laurie. "What do you think, Hon?"

"Something happened for sure. I'm not sure just what it was, but something credible has happened to Ben."

Adam turned back to Ben. "Do you think Dr. Resser is a fraud?"

"This has taken about half of my attention since Tuesday when I got back. Why would he leave like that? Why would he have faked all those academic achievements if he weren't a fraud? And then there's Gramps' theory about how Bob's time trip could have been faked. That's logical, too. And then there's his dog, not that abandoning a dog has any reference to his science credentials, but it reflects on him as a person. And where is my missing day, and why would he tell Suzie on Monday I'd be coming in on Tuesday?

"By now it's pretty clear that the man was in need of a lot of money, and he got some. But the real question in my mind is, did he know what he was doing? And did he do it?"

Adam didn't answer right away. He stared in the direction of the refrigerator, deep in thought. When he did speak, he seemed to be changing the subject.

"Do you remember Scott Hermon, who lived across the hall from us our junior year?"

Ben nodded.

"Scott is now with the CIA and he works here in Dallas. We run into each other once in a while. He's a Christian now, too. He would probably be able to tell us more about Doc Resser. And I think I could get a day or two off from work. What say we look him up tomorrow?"

CHAPTER XXIV

The CIA office in Dallas is a scary place to visit. The building is not unique-it's like a hundred other office buildings in the area. What makes it scary is the fact that anyone can tell by looking at it that somewhere in the back some guy in a three piece suit is certain to be waterboarding some drug lord from Central America and enjoying it very much.

The place looks normal, Ben thought. *The people, though. Dark suits, dark ties, dark glasses. Must be black ops.*

A receptionist greeted them as they entered. She seemed already aware of who they were and what they would want. She gave them both little badges to wear, stamped, MINIMUM CLEARANCE: TEMPORARY, and directed them to Scott's office.

Scott hadn't changed much, except for the suit. Hadn't put on much weight, still clean-shaven, hairline still pretty much intact. After renewal of acquaintances and handshakes all around, he wasted no time, but brought them right to the point.

"About Doctor Resser," he began. "Strange dude. He definitely has a criminal record. He has spent about fifteen years in jail, and that's a shame for he truly is a brilliant man."

He picked up a file from the top of his desk. "He is about as creative as any criminal I've investigated. His jail time has mostly been for fraud, for misusing scientific data in order to obtain money. Has no history of involvement with, trade of, or usage of any controlled substance. Has been married to the same woman, one Hannah Zerimar-Ramirez for over thirty years. So almost half of their marriage he's spent behind bars, but she seems to stick with him. Con men are that way. They can keep a woman interested even when it seems hopeless. Even Charles Manson had a girlfriend on the outside.

"Hannah, the wife-she has no criminal record. She is an anesthesiologist, and was involved in a malpractice suit eight years ago. It seems something went wrong, and the patient could not be brought out of an induced coma. Though Hannah was not found criminally negligent, the board of anesthesiologists in her jurisdiction pulled her license for a period of ten years. She is eligible to reapply in two years. Meanwhile, her continuing education is current. She is, of course, unable at this time to acquire malpractice insurance.

"She has a brother. His name is Siris. Siris Zerimar-Ramirez. He works for the Department of Defense as a civil servant in the Specialized Minerals Management Service. The SMMS. His job with the DOD/SMMS is in procurement of materials deemed necessary for the manufacture of weapons we do not currently manufacture. He, therefore, must have had some slow days, or else the DOD is less than forthcoming about the currency of the project.

"He has a squeaky clean record.

"That brings us to the substance called Femio Bosic Enriched Neutrinic Gas. This substance is the natural by-product of nearly any usage of nuclear power. It is easily collected and contained. It is colorless, odorless, and non-toxic when properly refined. This is why we had no problem with your purchase, storage and transfer of those four canisters. What we could not figure out is why you gave the guy five hundred thousand dollars for it."

"How did you know that?" Ben demanded.

Scott dismissed him with a wave of his hand and a smile. "What's the CIA for if we can't know things? And since FBEN gas is not a controlled substance, and useful in no known commercial application, you must have wanted it for something important, a process of which we here possess no practical knowledge."

"What about the treaty with the Ukraine? They had to get rid of their supply of FBEN!" Ben blurted.

"They did recently sign a treaty. You may have seen that in the news reports. But it had nothing to do with FBEN. Since the disintegration of the Soviet Union, they wound up with quite a stockpile of nuclear weapons. An attempt to get their cooperation in disarming some of their arsenal required the negotiation of the treaty. But it made good cover for your overpriced acquisition.

"That's about the extent of my research. Would you like the file?"

"Wouldn't that be illegal for us to have?" Adam looked worried.

Scott laughed. "It all came off of Google anyway. Help yourselves!"

Adam grabbed the file, expressed deep gratitude, told Scott to come by for dinner sometime, and then they left the office.

They got out of the building just before their temporary badges expired.

"Now what?" Ben thought it looked like a dead end.

"We should verify the FBEN question," Adam sighed. "Maybe we should try to talk to Prof Hickston."

Prof Hickston headed the physics department at Texas A&M. Since they desired to ask only one question of him, Adam thought perhaps a phone conversation could accomplish the goal.

Thankfully, they caught Prof Hickston in his office, able to take a call. Adam had been one of his favorite students, a star pupil.

"Adam, my man. What can I do for you?" Prof was always jovial, always accommodating, except when he wasn't.

"Prof, we don't want to take up a lot of your time. We just want to be sure of one thing." Adam began.

"And what is that thing, my man?"

"We were wondering if FBEN gas has any possibility of affecting the dimension of time."

"Do you mean, Adam, that you want to know whether FBEN would be useful in effecting time travel?"

"Yes. We need to know that. We've heard from sources less reliable than you are, that it has no commercial application. Could it be useful in regard to time travel?"

"I would be curious my good man, as to why you also want to know about this.

"But if you took physics 101 from me, and you did, you should remember that early research with FBEN gas in a particle accelerator showed promise of bending time, but by twenty-five years ago research demonstrated that such a hope was unfounded. FBEN turned out to be useless in affecting the time continuum. Is there anything else you'd like me to remind you of?"

"Thank you, Doctor Hickston. That's all. But we'll drop by if we get on campus."

"You're welcome, my man. I'll expect your visit. Good day!"

Adam put the phone down slowly, thoughtfully. "Do you think we could get to Billings today?"

Laurie readily awarded her stamp of approval, and getting plane tickets did not present any problem: DFW to MSP, MSP to Billings in time to rent a motel for the night. The Bakken fracking field demanded all but the executive suite, so Ben and Adam had to rough it with king size beds and a huge flat screen TV.

But they didn't turn on the TV. They talked about the next morning, about renting a pickup and getting to the ranch. They talked about Doc and Hannah and about what had happened to Ben, and why, and whether it was illusory, divine revelation, an extended and very detailed dream, or an actual trip back in time. Doc had made Ben promise, so he'd brought nothing back. Only memories-and a scar on his left foot. Ben bitterly ruminated on the words, "content with the subjective nature of the results of your research."

They turned in early, setting their wake-up call to come at 6:15. After that pre-dawn reveille, they grabbed muffins and bananas at the continental breakfast while dodging between oil riggers, then rented a Ford pickup from Hertz.

They drove directly to the time farm and found the place completely empty. All the furnishings had been evacuated-appliances, every bit of everything. The horse, the pig, and the chickens no longer inhabited the barn,

The time shed also had nothing left in it except the Steiger tractor and the empty concrete pad.

"I had hoped," Adam sighed, "to get the canister that fed your oxygen mask to find out if anything in it contained traces of anesthetic. That was Hannah's forte. Now I guess we'll never know. I thought we might at least theorize about your missing day."

Ben nodded. It looked as if a really thorough person or agency had swept the place clean. None of Doc's equipment remained in evidence. You couldn't tell that anything had recently been in the building. He thought about the three quarters of a million dollars he'd paid Doc, and where it might be right now. He knew it didn't matter. Doc had delivered exactly what he'd been paid for. And he began to wonder if Doc's credibility presented a relevant issue.

They drove back to Ekalaka in silence. When they passed the Wagon Wheel, Ben wanted to stop and see if he could say hi to Otto.

Suzie said Otto had stayed at home. Ben went across the street to a small grocery store and bought dog treats and gave them to Suzie. "For Otto," he said. He thanked her for taking the dog, and gave her his phone number. "Call me if Doc stops back, or if Otto needs anything." he said.

Adam and Ben made the trip back to Dallas mostly without meaningful conversation. Laurie picked them up at the airport. Ben stayed that night and the next morning, spending as much time with Sherry as he could.

"What do you think, overall?" Adam hauled Ben back to DFW, as Ben rethought the private jet.

"Overall about what?"

"Well, what's happened to you. It looks like you've been back in time. Jesus was there. What do you think of Him?"

"I haven't told you that when I met him, he looked at me with such powerful love. It's hard to describe, but it was real. And he kept talking to his followers after they'd started to move on. He told them that people like me are pretty much hopeless as far as getting into heaven. He said it's easier for a camel to go through the eye of a needle than for a rich man to get into heaven. He said that with God all things are possible.

"When you put a camel through the eye of the needle, (That's a sort of security tunnel they use after the gate is closed at night. Did I tell you about that? No?) You have to completely unload all her burdens. She is stripped of everything. She basically crawls through naked except for the lead rope. It all comes off. So I never really got my answer. I hoped that this rich young guy would tell me, "Hey, go for it. I gave it all up for Him, and it's worth it. "Or else he would say, "No, I kept it all. And I'm glad I did." But I couldn't find that answer. It was just me. So I don't know. I felt sort of cheated, thinking all that time that I could find someone who had either made the decision, or not, and that I could just ask him if it was worth it. But there is no him. There is only me and the question is for me. And I think that at the bottom of things I've wasted a lot of time thinking I was better than this guy. But now I see that's not true. I have to make the decision and pay for

it, and both sides of the coin look pretty pricey." Adam
waited, and when he perceived Ben had finished, he
breathed deeply, then he spoke.

"I don't have what you have. Never did, except back in
college. But I would tell you now that I wouldn't trade
what I have in Christ for double the money you've got, or
for all the money in the world. What you have to figure out
is if you would trade with me."

They were at ATS then, and Ben hugged his comrade,
and went through the airport humiliation ritual that gets
everyone thinking about private jets.

He had a mind full of divergent thoughts on that mental
interchange throughout his trip home. It became even more
complex, now that he knew that Doc looked more crooked
than Otto's hind leg.

As he finally entered the building that housed his
apartment, he realized that it had been some time since he'd
checked his mailbox. Most of his business took place
online, and printed mail rarely arrived at his home.
Nonetheless, he had a look just for fun, and found a
magazine in the box. He could not immediately recall
having subscribed to any magazine. He hurriedly folded it
in half and stuck it in his back pocket, then headed for his
apartment.

The next morning found Ben sitting at his dining room
table eating raisin bran, which he much preferred to leftover
goat cheese and flat bread. He had taken time earlier to
completely unpack from his trip, and he'd hung all his
Mideast gear carefully in the closet. He did not know why
he would do this, except perhaps for that coveted feeling of
closure. He had discovered, in the pocket of the
plainclothes robe, the copper coin he'd received as change
when he had bought the life-saving fruit and meat in
Damascus. The coin in itself proved nothing. He wondered
if Doc could have taken all the silver coins and left him that
one as a sort of tease. But how would he know? And there
it lay, on the table in front of him. He stared at it. He
reasoned that in a way, he and Adam were in the same boat

with the subjective side of things. He mused that everyone has doubts. Then he remembered Sethur's last words to him not so very long ago. "May God deliver you from your doubt, my son."

I wish, thought Ben

He saw the magazine on the table, folded the long way to fit into the back pocket of his real jeans. He opened it up and began to look through it as he ate his cereal. The International Antiquities Society issued their newsletter monthly. They had given him permission to copy some denarii as long as he inserted five percent antimony into the silver. It still bothered him a little that all of his bill-paying, and his personal largesse had been done with counterfeit money. But it consisted mostly of silver, and the silver preserved the value. He began to flip through the magazine like guys flip channels, when something familiar caught his eye. In an article about the temple of Jupiter in Damascus, he noticed a picture of the remains of the temple. It seemed to him as if he were looking at the face of an old friend after thirty years. The visage appeared familiar, but a lot of aging had taken its toll in the interim.

In bold print opposite the picture he perused an article with the headline:

BLOCKBUSTER FIND AT EAST GATE!

It described the layout of the city of Damascus in the first century. Eventually, the article came around to the information contained in the headline. A leather page from a gatekeeper's tablet had been discovered, apparently from the spring of the year thirty, CE. Archaeologists calculated that the date of the tablet page would correspond to March 11 of that year. The log had been used by several different quaternions of Roman soldiers, and it seemed to be a record of incoming traffic through the Gate of the Sun. Nearly all entries were mundane and predictable, except for one entry made by a gatekeeper named Tullus. The direct translation to English of the entry in question read that Tullus had, at approximately nine a.m. on March eleventh, logged the arrival of one "Parker from West of Tarshish".

Okay, Ben concurred. He picked up his phone to call Adam.

The End